About the Author

John Bennett has had a successful career in the construction industry before becoming a professor at the University of Reading. His research team published many influential reports including 'Investing in Building' endorsed by Prime Minister, Margaret Thatcher. He has undertaken research at universities in the USA, Japan, Australia and the EU. He was founding editor of the academic journal 'Construction Management and Economics'. He is married, has a son and daughter and five lively grandchildren who keep him in touch with today's young adults. Since he retired, he has turned to writing novels; 'Design for Life' is the latest.

Design for Life

John Bennett

Design for Life

Olympia Publishers
London

www.olympiapublishers.com
OLYMPIA PAPERBACK EDITION

A CIP catalogue record for this title is
available from the British Library.

ISBN: 978-1-80439-184-6

This is a work of fiction.
Names, characters, places and incidents originate from the writer's
imagination. Any resemblance to actual persons, living or dead, is
purely coincidental.

First Published in 2023

Olympia Publishers
Tallis House
2 Tallis Street
London
EC4Y 0AB

Printed in Great Britain

Chapter 1

Jake Brown qualified as an architect just over a year ago and was now working for an architectural practice in Swindon. The firm had well-established business relationships with nearly all the major local companies, and this helped ensure a steady stream of work which kept the firm's eighteen employees busy. The architectural practice had three partners who were all much older than Jake. The partner who Jake worked with, John Brentford, clearly recognised Jake's undoubted talent as a creative designer. This was the main reason for him asking Jake to design the science faculty building for the new Swindon University even though it was the biggest project the practice was currently working on.

Jake had been working on the university building for over a week and knew he was close to creating a design he could show to John Brentford. He decided to make a subtle change to the shape of the roof and then he sat back and stared at the new image on his computer screen. Then he slowly rotated the image of his design to check that the roof really integrated the separate elements of the building. Jake looked at the building from every angle and became increasingly certain that this was the best design he had ever produced.

Jake continued looking at his design with an increasingly broad smile on his face until he noticed that it was gone five thirty and as it was Friday, he was meeting Jane at six o'clock. So, he hurriedly transferred the current design onto his laptop, so he could work on it over the weekend, and then rushed out of the office and drove into the centre of town. Luckily, he found a place to park straight away, and almost ran to the town's central library where Jane was waiting outside the front entrance.

She looked amazingly attractive as she smiled and waved to him. Before Jake could apologise for being late, she pulled him into a long kiss. Then with her arms still around his neck she looked at him and said, 'I know you have had a busy week and I'm looking forward to hearing all about it. So, let's go to the restaurant and you can tell me all about your design while we have a drink before dinner.'

Jake's sense of excitement was evident as he and Jane walked to their favourite restaurant. They asked the head waiter for a table in the corner, and both ordered a glass of wine. Jane then smiled broadly and said, 'I know you want to tell me all about your design for the university's science block.'

Jake laughed and nodded his agreement as he said, 'I began, as I usually do, by thinking about the internal spaces the university's science departments need in their new building. These include laboratories, lecture theatres and a variety of seminar rooms, offices for the academic staff and areas where the students can relax. Anyway, as I worked at understanding exactly how big each space should be, what they should look like and how they needed to relate to each other, they gradually began to fit quite naturally into five distinct blocks, and I decided to reflect this in my design.'

Jane was clearly listening carefully to Jake's description and to ensure that she understood what he was telling her, she asked, 'Do you mean the science department will be housed in five separate blocks?'

'Yes, but I realised that I had to tie them together visually because it is one building. I think I have achieved this by adopting a classical style of architecture and using the same facing bricks and hardwood windows and doors on all the blocks. So, although there are five separate blocks, the classical style brings the design together and gives it a coherent look. But, as I expect you know by now, I always want to add a distinctive element to my designs; and, as I have mentioned several times before, Sydney Opera House is my favourite building in the whole world. So, I based the design of roof that links the five blocks on the opera house's roof; and my intension is that when anyone looks at the whole building from any direction, the roof makes it merge into a single image that should remind them of Sydney Opera House.'

Jane was listening very carefully as Jake described his design ideas and as he paused, she said, 'That all sounds amazing. I 'd love to see a picture of the building.'

Jake took out his phone and found what he thought was the most interesting image of his design. Jane looked at it carefully and then with a big smile, said, 'This is very impressive. It really will put Swindon on the tourist map. You are in danger of becoming a great architect. When your design gets built, I think you will start to be recognised as one of this country's best architects.'

Jake looked hard at her and then laughed as he said, 'I'm just doing what I enjoy. I must admit, I don't know what the partners in the firm will think and I'm a bit nervous about showing it to them in case they don't like it. I keep working on it to make sure it's as good as I can get it before letting other people see it. The real test will be when we show it to the client. That is the Vice-Chancellor, and my hope is that he will decide that the building will add to his university's reputation.'

Jane put her hand on Jake's arm and said, 'Thank you for

letting me see your work. It is a beautiful building, and I do think it will attract visitors to Swindon and help establish the new Swindon University's reputation. I happen to know, because he is a customer at our bank, that the Vice-Chancellor is working hard to make sure that the decision to create a separate university here is seen as a success. I think he will want to go ahead with your design because it is great architecture. Also, it will establish your own reputation and almost certainly give you many more interesting opportunities.'

Jake was obviously delighted by Jane's reaction, and he leant forward and kissed her before saying, 'I am so pleased to hear what you think of my design. It means a lot to me. Now, what have you been up to this week?'

'I don't think I can match your achievements, but this week may be the start of the next stage of my career. The bank has a scheme for training staff who have the potential to become managers. It involves a mixture of training and working as an assistant manager and then after a few years of successful practice in that role, you are eligible to apply for any branch manager's role that becomes vacant. Anyway, my manager told me this week that, if I want, I can go on the next selection course.'

'That sounds great. What does the selection course involve?'

'It's a two-day event where the participants are tested in various ways. There are interviews, short written tests and practical exercises that test an individual's ability to lead a team. Then those who pass are given a two-week training course and offered a choice of branches where they can work as a trainee assistant manager.'

Jake smiled broadly as he said, 'That is great news. From many of the things you tell me about your work, I know you have a real understanding of banking. Do you know when the selection course will take place?'

'The next one is in two weeks' time. My manager gave me quite a lot of material to read that describes the selection process and other things about best banking practice which he thinks will help me. So, I have work to do over the next couple of weeks because I want to pass the course. We have two assistant managers in the branch, and I have often thought that they have interesting jobs. So, maybe we have both had an important week.'

Several more couples had come into the restaurant as Jake and Jane talked which made Jake suggest it was time to order dinner. Jane agreed and Jake called the waiter over and they each ordered their favourite starters and main courses and asked for another glass of wine. Jake then asked, 'Would you be an assistant manager here in the Swindon branch?'

Jane shook her head. 'That is unlikely. People almost always move to a new branch when they are promoted to assistant manager because there usually isn't a vacancy in their own branch. Also, it's probably easier in many ways to make a fresh start in a different branch when you are promoted. Your relationship with all your colleagues would need to change if you were promoted above them and I can see that would be tricky. I think it would be easier to fit into the role of assistant manager in a different branch. Obviously, I will have to spend some time learning about the new branch's customers and so on, but I think it is probably easier to make a fresh start in a different branch when you are promoted.'

Jake hesitated before responding to Jane's news. He didn't want to lose touch with her. He wasn't sure if he was falling in love with her, but he certainly wanted her as his girlfriend. So, rather casually, he said, 'That's interesting because I hope that as the partners in my firm come to recognise my talent, they will offer me a partnership. Indeed, I hope my design for the university science block will make a big contribution to that. The point is that I will probably be working in Swindon for the foreseeable future.'

Jane smiled as she replied, 'I know you work in Swindon and that you live in Cirencester and thinking about it, those two towns are within a reasonable distance of quite a range of interesting towns and cities. So, when we know what you are likely to be doing over the next few years and, assuming I am offered the chance to become an assistant manager, I can work out where there is a vacancy that works for both of us.'

At this moment, the waiter brought their starters and their wine. Jake and Jane concentrated on their food, which as usual was very tasty. When they finished their starters, they talked about where Jane might work when she became an assistant manager. Jane laughed as she said that there is a large branch of her bank in Cirencester where she would enjoy working and that would be very convenient as she could come and live with Jake and his parents. Their meal continued in much the same way until Jake looked at his watch and said, 'I have a big cricket match tomorrow. We are playing Cheltenham away which is one of the toughest matches we have. As you know, because I keep mentioning it, we have won every match since I became captain of Cirencester's first eleven; and I want to do everything I can to keep up this winning run and Cheltenham are always tough opponents. They often include at least one of the Gloucester County team who happens not to be playing for the county that weekend. Last year, one of the county's best batsmen came in at number three and scored a very fast fifty which changed the whole outcome of the game. The point is I will need to be at my very best; so, I would like to get to bed reasonably early tonight.'

Jane said she was ready to go, and Jake paid the bill and then drove Jane home. She lived some ten miles out of Swindon in a small village on the edge of the Wiltshire Downs. Jane still lived with her parents but recently had been looking for somewhere to live in Swindon. Now, the possibility of becoming an assistant manager somewhere else meant she had put that search on hold. When they reached Jane's parent's cottage, she said, 'I know you want to get home; so, thank you for a lovely evening and good luck in the match tomorrow. I will see you at your match on Sunday.'

They kissed good-night and Jake watched as Jane went into the cottage and then he drove home. He could not help thinking that Jane was very attractive and was obviously good at her work. She was the most exciting and interesting woman he had ever had as a girlfriend. It was time they had sex. They often kissed and fondled the interesting parts of each other's bodies, but Jane seemed to set distinct limits on how far she was willing to let him go. They had never discussed having sexual intercourse, but Jake somehow felt that things Jane had said, and her general behaviour meant that this was not something that Jane was willing to do.

When Jake arrived home, his parents were still up and his mother said, 'You are back early. Did you have a good evening?'

Jake told her that he and Jane had a very good dinner in Swindon and then he reminded his mother that he had an important match on Saturday and needed to get a good night's sleep. His mother said, 'You are spending a lot of time with Jane, so are you serious about her?'

Jake smiled, 'That's a good question. I'm not looking for another girlfriend so, that may be a clue as to what I really think. She is beautiful and intelligent and she always sems to be happy when we are together. So, maybe it's serious but it is early days yet.'

Jake's mother nodded as she said, 'That is all good. I must say you seem more settled and happier with life since you met her. For what it's worth, your father and I both think she is good for you.'

Jake kissed his mother and said, 'Good-night Mum and thank you for asking about Jane. I will tell you when I work out what my feelings for her are.'

On Saturday Jake travelled with the first eleven on the team bus to Cheltenham. He had been captain of the team for just over a month following an acrimonious selection meeting. Selection meetings always took place on Thursday evenings after practice and brought together the first eleven team captain and vice-captain, the second eleven team captain and vice-captain, and the club chairman. The significant meeting was during the fourth week of the season. The first eleven had lost all the six matches they had played, while the second team had won all their matches very convincingly. At that time Jake was vice-captain of the second eleven. The captain was an older, very experienced cricketer, called Alan Morris. He began the meeting by saying, 'We cannot go on as we are. The present first eleven is way past its best and we now have the best second eleven this club has ever had. I suggest that Jake should be made captain of the first team. He is ready for this because I have trained him in captaincy over the last two seasons; and we have seven or eight players in the second eleven who are better players than any of those in the present first eleven.'

The captain and vice-captain of the first eleven both said this was nonsense and the captain continued. 'Okay, we have made a poor start to the season, but we have the experience to get through this. It would be madness to throw all that away. We must stick to our established first eleven.'

Alan Morris shook his head as he said, 'Look at last season's results. They were the worst I can remember. What did the first eleven do? I think you won just three matches while the second eleven lost only one match all season and that was because we were caught out on a rain affected pitch by Bath. It is time to pick our best eleven, beginning by making Jake the captain. He is ready, and most of the second team are more than ready, to be playing first team cricket.'

A very angry debate followed which eventually was stopped by the club chairman, Henry Roberts. He held up his hand and said, 'Enough; we will vote on Alan's proposal. All those in favour.'

Alan, Jake and Henry all indicated that they supported the idea of changing the first eleven. At this point the first eleven captain and vice-captain walked out of the meeting. Henry Roberts said, 'That settles the matter. We can appoint Jake as captain and pick the best first eleven we can.'

As a result, only four of the established first eleven kept their place in the team, one of whom, Bill Stones, agreed to be vice-captain. The club recovered from this shock surprisingly quickly and this was reflected in their results. The excitement of being in the first eleven helped all the newly promoted players perform at the top of their game; and the four established first eleven players who kept their place in the team all accepted that what had been done was sensible and they worked with Jake to help the new members of the team adjust to the new level of cricket.

Most of the old first eleven who had been dropped from the team decided to leave the club. Two said they were happy to play in the second eleven and Alan Morris was glad to have their help in developing the group of promising young players he had been working with, on practice evenings, into a new second eleven.

The most important outcome of these events was that the new first eleven had won eight matches in row and Jake had shown that he knew how to get the best out of his team. Now they had their biggest challenge yet. Cheltenham away was a match that Cirencester first eleven had lost for the last five seasons. Jake managed to push all this to the back of his mind as walked out to the pitch with the Cheltenham captain for the coin toss. Jake won the toss and decided to ask Cheltenham to bat first because, although the pitch looked good, it had rained during the week and Jake thought it would take spin. Jake decided to open the bowling himself. He was an off-spin bowler who normally bowled at almost medium pace, but he decided to bowl slightly slower than normal to give the ball every chance of turning. His first three balls all turned off the pitch back towards the stumps. The batsman played them carefully. Jake then bowled the fourth ball at his normal pace. It did not turn, and the batsman tried to play it the same way as he had the first three and edged it towards the slip fielder who easily took the catch. This was exactly the start Jake had hoped for and when he finished the first over, he asked the team's young leg-spin bowler to bowl the second over. The pitch suited his bowling even more than it did Jake's. As a result, the two spinners bowled Cheltenham's first seven batsmen out for sixty-five runs in the first hour and a half. As Jake had hoped, the pitch was drying and taking less spin, so he asked the normal opening bowlers to finish the innings. They both felt somewhat frustrated about not being involved until the innings was almost over and as a result, they both bowled very fast and were much too good for Cheltenham's tail-end batsmen. When the last wicket fell, Cheltenham had scored a ninety-two which was their lowest total for more than six years.

Cirencester scored the runs needed for the win for the loss of just four wickets. At the end of the match, the Cheltenham captain came into the Cirencester dressing room and said, 'I came to congratulate you on winning. It was a strange but very interesting match and I'm looking forward to the return match when we will obviously need to be at our best.'

Jake thanked him, agreed it had been a good match and said that he too was looking forward to the return match in Cirencester in four weeks' time. The whole team were happy as they knew that Cheltenham were probably the best team they played. This mood was evident during the team's traditional stop on the way back to Cirencester. Jake had phoned the club secretary to tell him the result and asked if he could arrange for the pub, where the team bus normally stopped on the way back to Cirencester, to prepare some food for the team. When they arrived at the pub, they were met by the landlord and his wife who took them by a side door into a private room where an excellent looking buffet dinner was set out on a long table and a hatch into the bar was open so the players could order whatever drinks they wanted. To start the celebration of a famous win, Jake ordered himself a beer and bought the team's umpire and scorer and their bus driver their first drinks.

Soon everyone was eating, drinking and chattering happily. Jake knew he had a team here that was going to have an outstanding season. As he thought about this, the club chairman, Henry Roberts, walked into the room. He went round the room shaking everyone's hand and telling them how pleased he was at the way they were developing into the best first eleven he could ever remember Cirencester having. Once he had got a drink, he indicated that he wanted to say something and the room fell silent as he began. 'I want to congratulate all of you. This team has the potential to beat everyone we play against and when this becomes widely known in the cricketing world, I am sure that some of the very best clubs, who have been unwilling to play against us for the last few years, will want to arrange fixtures with us. Also, I am certain that some very good players will want to join the club but in my mind you, all of you, have every right to be in the Cirencester first eleven. When I heard how you had beaten Cheltenham on their own ground so convincingly, I had to come here to congratulate you.'

Jake stood up and thanked Henry Roberts for his encouraging words and added, 'I know that Henry is largely responsible for creating this new first eleven and I also know that we are all determined to make him even more proud of what we can do this season and on into the future. So, lets drink a toast to Henry Roberts, chairman of the best cricket club in Gloucestershire.'

Everyone laughed and stood up to drink the toast to Henry Roberts. It was a very happy team that completed the journey back to Cirencester when the pub closed. Jake went straight to bed when he got home and slept until gone ten o'clock the next morning. Over his late breakfast, he began to think about this afternoon's match. It was against one of the weaker teams they played against, and he recognised that after yesterday's success and long celebration, there was a risk that the team approached the game in too casual a mood. He spent much of the morning thinking about how he would make sure the team was well motivated. He did however manage to also get in an hour's work on his design for the university science building.

Jake was happy with the arrangement of the internal spaces and the external appearance of the building, but he had decided that since the building would house people working at the leading edge of modern science, it should be as sustainable as possible and add as little as possible to global warming. He identified several reports on the internet describing new sustainable technologies being developed in the UK. He was attracted by a description of a new and highly effective solar panel and wondered if they could be made to imitate the tiles which cover the roof of Sydney Opera House. He also found a description of small wind turbines which looked as if they could be incorporated in the vertical elements of the roof to provide yet more electricity. Then he read about an attempt that was being made to make a building in Europe self-sufficient in water by surrounding it with a man-made lake equipped with highly efficient water-treatment and sewage-treatment equipment. The water used in the building was continually recycled through the lake and treated to remove any impurities as it entered the building's water distribution system.

Jake decided it was sensible to discuss these ideas with the heads of the relevant science departments who would be occupying the university's new building. Then if they were interested in them, the Vice-Chancellor might well be willing to incorporate at least some of these ideas in the building. It would certainly add to the publicity the building attracted if it was self-sufficient in energy and water. As Jake began to make a note of his ideas, his mother called up the stairs to him to say that it was lunchtime. This reminded Jake that Jane was coming to watch at least some of the match that afternoon and then they would spend the evening together.

What exactly were his feelings for Jane? She was an attractive and intelligent woman; and it was obvious that she was making a success of her career. She certainly seemed to like spending time with Jake, but she had not ever said what her feelings for him were. Was he falling in love with her? Maybe it was sensible to carry on as they were, enjoy spending time together and just see how things developed.

Jake felt happy that he would be seeing Jane that afternoon but recognised that he needed to concentrate on captaining the team. That afternoon's match was one that Cirencester should win, and Jake decided to use it to give the batsmen who most needed it some match practice and challenge his bowlers to develop their most challenging deliveries. Jake won the toss and decided to bat first. He explained to his most experienced opening batsman that he was going to move him down the batting order, just for this match, as he wanted several of the less experienced players to practice specific improvements to their batting technique. He involved the experienced opening batsman in his briefing of each of the batsmen before they went into bat. Jake had decided to suggest one specific change to their batting to each player and ask them to practice it once they had played themselves in.

The team they were playing seemed particularly weak that afternoon and all the batsmen did well. As a result, Jake declared the innings closed at tea-time with the score at two hundred and twenty-six for five. As they were going in for tea, Jane arrived, and Jake brought some sandwiches and cakes and two cups of tea out onto the pavilion balcony where they could sit together. Jane said that her journey had been straight-forward and both the bus from her village into Swindon and then the one from Swindon to Cirencester had run exactly on time. She then asked Jake how the match was going, and he was happy to explain that he was using it to get some of his younger players to improve their technique. He added, 'This is working well so far; so, I plan to do the same with our bowlers. I want to win the match to keep our winning run going but I also want to make sure the team keeps improving.'

Jane smiled, 'That seems to be a very sensible approach. I look forward to seeing how it works out for you. What do you think we should do this evening?'

Jake was about to say that he they should get something to eat, when he wondered if Jane had a different idea. So, he asked her what she would like to do. She looked thoughtful and then said, 'Since we are in Cirencester, it would be nice to meet your parents. Can we do that?'

Jake phoned home and explained to his mother that Jane had come to the match, and they wondered if it was okay to call in home before they went out for the evening. His mother said, 'I have been thinking that you have been seeing her for some time and that we should meet. Why don't you stay for dinner? It's only ham, salad and potatoes and I may be able to find something for dessert. What do you think?'

'I'll have to check with Jane but let us assume that is fine and thank you for suggesting we have dinner together. I will let you know if there is any problem with that idea.'

This was agreed and Jane seemed happy to have dinner with Jake's family. He wondered if this was a good idea and felt somewhat distracted from the match as the Cirencester first eleven walked out to continue the match. He started with his usual two opening fast bowlers and set very attacking fields for them. This went well and after they had both bowled five overs, their opponents were twenty-two for four. Both bowlers had taken two wickets and Jake told them they had just the start he wanted and now they should rest and be ready to finish off their opponent's innings later in the afternoon. Jake asked his steady medium paced bowler to bowl the next over and suggested he try varying the pace at which he bowled and to consistently attack the stumps. The batsmen were clearly struggling but survived the first medium paced over. Jake then asked the team's young leg-spin bowler to bowl the next over. He deceived the batsman with his fourth ball which was an almost perfectly bowled googly. Clearly the batsman had been playing for a leg-break and was clean bowled .

It took less than an hour for these two bowlers to reduce their opponents to ninety-two for nine. At this point, Jake asked his opening fast bowlers to finish off the innings. Somewhat surprisingly, it took another four overs for them to get the last wicket which came from an acrobatic catch by the wicketkeeper. It was just after seven o'clock and it was obvious that the team were very happy with the weekend's results. Their mood was improved even further by the visiting team's captain; he came into the dressing room and shook Jake's hand as he said, 'I must congratulate you on this afternoon's performance. That was the best I have seen Cirencester play for over ten years. I think if you keep playing like that, maybe next season we should play your second eleven. I will have a talk with our club chairman and see what he thinks but your team have clearly gone up to a whole new level of performance. So, congratulations and very well done!'

Jake thanked him and said, 'That is very generous of you, I have to say the team is right on top form. I don't know about next season but no-doubt the club chairmen will need to discuss next season's fixtures at some time. I'm not involved in that; and thank you again for your kind words.'

As the visiting captain left the dressing room, the team broke into spontaneous applause and the vice-captain said, 'Jake, we know we are good team and an important reason for that is the way you captain us. We all know what you want us to do and that makes it easy for us to concentrate on playing as well as we can. So, three cheers for the captain of Cirencester's best ever team.'

There was a fair amount of laughter as the team cheered Jake. He laughed and then said, 'I now have a difficult challenge, my girlfriend and I are having dinner with my parents so they can meet her for the first time. So, I will see you all at practice on Tuesday.'

Jake then left the dressing room and found Jane waiting outside the pavilion. She looked very beautiful and immediately kissed him and said, 'That was an impressive win this afternoon. Now, I hope I am ready to meet your parents.'

Chapter 2

Jake's mother and father were both looking forward to meeting Jake's girlfriend. As his mother said while they were getting dinner ready, 'He's been going out with Jane for several months and it is time he got serious about his future.'

Jake's father smiled, 'Let's not try to rush him. He's his own man and he has just started an important stage of his career. After all, he is only just twenty-five and people nowadays don't seem to settle down until they are in their thirties. Anyway, it will be nice to meet another of his girlfriends; as far as I can remember, we have only ever met two of the many girls he has been out with. There was one called Sam and the other was Amanda as far as I can remember. Neither of them lasted long even though they were both attractive young women. So, let's not make any assumptions about Jane.'

As they finished setting the dining table for four, they heard Jake come into the house. He brought Jane into the dining room and introduced her to his parents. His father then asked Jane what she would like to drink and said they had red and white wine or apple juice or water. Jane decided on a glass of white wine and Jake said he would get the drinks. When he came back into the dining room, carrying a tray with two glasses of white wine and two of red wine, Jane was explaining that she worked in a bank and was hoping to be promoted to being an assistant manager very soon. She added, 'That means that I will almost certainly be working somewhere else, but I don't know where yet. Most assistant manager posts that become vacant are in and around London or Birmingham but there may be something more local.'

Jake's father said, 'As far as we know Jake plans to keep working in Swindon for the immediate future. I guess if you moved to London or Birmingham, you would want to find somewhere to live near the branch you were working in. Of course, that would be very expensive in London.'

Jane smiled as she said, 'My bank like their staff to live close to the branch where they are working and, you are right London is very expensive, but they own some apartments that are available for staff working in the main London branches. That means they can live close to work at a very affordable rent.'

Jake's father nodded as he said, 'That sounds like an attractive arrangement. I worked in London for about three years as a project manager on a development close to Broadgate and my company provided me with an apartment close to the construction site. We enjoyed discovering London's great theatres, bars and restaurants. It really is a world class city.'

Jake's mother added, 'I also enjoyed the big-name shops. It was a good time and I have to say that I enjoyed our time in London. In fact, Jake was born in London, and it was soon after we had him that we moved back to Cirencester. I think it's better than London when you have a family.'

Jake laughed as he said, 'I think Jane's favourite possibility is that she joins the Cirencester branch and comes to live with us.'

Jane smiled as she said, 'I did say that as a joke because I want to stay local so Jake and I can carry on seeing each other. We are good together; don't you think, Jake?'

'I feel very happy with you, Jane. So, we must wait and see where you decide to be an assistant manager. I hope it's local because as Dad said, I expect to keep working in Swindon but that may depend on the partners recognising that I should be offered a partnership fairly soon.'

Jake's father asked, 'You were saying that the design you are working on at the moment may help convince the partners that you are the right person to take over the firm when they retire. How is that going?'

'I'm pleased with it so far. I am sure it's the best design I have ever produced, and I am thinking about making the building totally sustainable, so it generates its own power and maintains its own water supply. I think that would make sure it gets good publicity; as well as being the right thing to do. There are some new technologies which I think will fit in with my design. That's what I'm working on at the moment. I haven't discussed this with the client yet, but I know the Vice-Chancellor wants the building to make a real contribution to Swindon University's reputation.'

Jake's father interrupted to say, 'I thought the building was for Oxford Brooks University. There isn't a Swindon University is there?'

Jake nodded. 'The man I call the Vice-Chancellor is the senior member of the staff at the Oxford Brooks campus in Swindon. In fact, there are several universities with various departments in Swindon, but I know that he has serious plans to bring them all together to form Swindon University. I also know that he hopes the new science building will become a big step towards achieving his aim. That is why I think he will like my design. It is distinctive and it should arouse a lot of interest in the media, particularly if I can use the latest technology to make it self-sustainable. I am pretty confident that my design is good, but global warming and all that means for human survival is a major issue, so a beautiful building which is fully sustainable should attract a lot of publicity.'

Jake's father said, 'That sounds like a good plan. I have worked on a couple of buildings that included a lot of energy generation and some that included major water treatment equipment. It would be interesting to see your design for the science building when it reaches a stage where you are ready to talk about it.'

Jake thanked his father and said that sometime during the next week would be a good time to look at his ideas for the science building. They were all just finishing their dessert, so Jake suggested it was time to take Jane home as he had a busy day on Monday. Jane seemed happy with this and thanked Jake's mother for a very enjoyable dinner and Jake's father for his wise words about London. They both said it was good to have met Jane and that they would see Jake in the morning.

As Jake and Jane drove to her parent's home they chatted about life in Cirencester and in London. Jane seemed to be impressed by Jake's father's description of the world-class attractions in London and said, 'Maybe we should get to know London. Working here in Swindon, we know about local companies and the issues that are important for them, but London would take us into a global community. We should think about it.'

Jake looked very thoughtful and then said, 'There are world-class architects in London. I spend quite a lot of time looking at their designs in magazines and on the internet. The practice in Swindon is all I know really, and I have to say they have been good to me. I can see myself as a partner, just continuing my present way of working. Maybe I should be more ambitious. I need to see how my design for the university science building is treated by the media and indeed by other architects. That may help me to think differently about my future.'

Jane smiled broadly as she said, 'Let's not get too far ahead of ourselves; but I will tell you when I know what the options are for me, assuming I get through the assistant manager selection process.'

Jake took Jane straight home. They agreed to meet on Wednesday evening and Jake drove back to Cirencester. During this journey, he thought about the design of the internal spaces in the university science building. He was confident he had managed to create an overall classical design with a roof which owed much to the distinctive style of Sydney Opera House. The question churning around his mind was how to reflect this marriage of styles in the lecture theatres, laboratories and seminar rooms. He wanted the lecture theatres to look like modern theatres. He envisaged the seats being arranged on two levels with the front of the balcony being a great sweeping curve that reflected the style of the roof. The lecturer's platform would look like a stage framed by a three-dimensional arch again mirroring the appearance of Sydney Opera House.

Once he reached home, he went straight up to his bedroom and began sketching his ideas for the interior of the lecture theatres on the drawing pad he used for his preliminary ideas. He looked on the internet at images of the interiors of some of the world's great theatres and this helped him settle on a design he felt very happy about. Then he began sketching designs for seminar rooms which looked like small, very intimate theatres with some of the students sitting on the stage around the teacher. Once he had a sketch that look right, he began thinking about the laboratories but quickly decided that he did not know enough about the furniture and equipment they had to accommodate. He began making a note of the kind of questions he needed to discuss with the university Vice-Chancellor or maybe with the heads of the various science departments; but Jake suddenly felt very tired and just lay on his bed and fell asleep without changing into his pyjamas.

This was how his mother found him next morning when she brought him a cup of coffee as he was late getting up. She put the cup down and gently shook Jake's shoulder. He woke up slowly and seemed confused about finding himself fully dressed on his bed and his mother bringing him a cup of coffee. She asked, 'What on Earth are you doing? Have you been asleep all night in your clothes?'

This seemed to help Jake focus and he suddenly laughed and explained that he had been working late and just fallen asleep. His mother noticed the drawing pad on Jake's desk and said, 'I can see you have been working on designs for something. Is it a theatre? It looks very modern. I like the look of it, but I didn't know you were working on a theatre.'

Jake was now sat up and was drinking his coffee. He joined his mother in looking at his designs and he explained that these were his initial ideas for the lecture theatres and seminar rooms in the university science building. He added, 'I was working on these until late last night and I must have just fallen asleep. I need a shower and a change of clothes as I should be in the office this morning and I am going to be late.'

Jake got to the office almost an hour late to be met by the partner he worked with, John Brentford, who was clearly irritated by Jake's late arrival. Jake explained that he had been working late on the design for the university science building and not woken up at his usual time. Once he showed John Brentford his design ideas, the mood changed. John looked at the overall design in which Jake had arranged the internal spaces in five separate blocks which combined to form the whole building, and then Jake showed him his initial design ideas for the lecture theatres and seminar rooms. After nearly thirty minutes spent studying Jake's design, making various comments and asking questions, John Brentford said, 'This is outstanding. It is a remarkable design. We should do a formal set of floor plans and the main elevations and check that the images of the overall design and the main internal spaces are accurate and then we can get a preliminary estimate of the likely cost . Then we can show the Vice-Chancellor your design and see what he thinks of it. When do you think that will all be ready?'

Jake said, 'I can get the drawings and the three-dimensional images done over the next two days, but I don't know about the cost estimate.'

John Brentford nodded and said that he would organize the estimate when Jake had finished the drawings. He then asked Jake how far he had got with his idea of making the building self-sufficient in energy and water? Jake explained that he had found descriptions of some leading-edge technology that he hoped would allow him to imitate the tiles on the roof Sydney Opera House with solar panels. He continued, 'I hope the solar panels don't alter the look of the building. The information I found on the internet suggests this is possible, but I need to check with the company that manufactures them. Then in the vertical areas of the roof design, I am thinking of incorporating small but highly efficient wind turbines. I see them forming a pattern which mimics the appearance of the rest of the building. Then there is the water. There are water treatment plants that are small enough to be incorporated in the building, but they would need a fairly large volume of water to keep the whole building supplied with clean water.'

John Brentford interrupted to say, 'It occurred to me that your building would look even better than it does if it was surrounded by a small lake. You would get reflections of the building in the water just as you do, from some angles, with Sydney Opera House.'

'I like that idea. It would add to the initial cost but having a sustainable building would reduce the running costs.'

Jake paused as they both thought about the idea of positioning the building in a man-made lake. Jake then continued, 'I will try a few sketches to see what it could look like; but I can see that it might well add to the design. I will bring you my ideas when I have got some good images.'

John Brentford asked, 'How will that affect when we can talk with the Vice-Chancellor?'

Jake thought for a few seconds and then said, 'I don't know how long it will take to get a good estimate of the cost. Using leading edge technology is always a bit risky and will add to the cost. Also creating an artificial lake is likely to be expensive and we will need some expert advice on exactly what is needed. I can get all my work done over the next two days but it's best if you talk with the quantity surveyors about the likely costs and how long they need to get a good estimate. Also, we probably should talk to some engineers about the lake and to the companies that make the solar panels and the wind turbines. Can I leave that with you to organize?'

John Brentford looked very thoughtful and then said, 'Okay, you concentrate on the design, and I will talk to the quantity surveyors, some engineers and the companies who make the sustainable technology you want to include in your design. I think this is all going well, and you are making decisions that should appeal to the Vice-Chancellor. He wants the building to attract publicity because he thinks that will increase the pressure on the university in Oxford to allow an independent Swindon University to be established. I may want to involve you in the discussions with the engineers and the sustainable companies but give me a note of the various technologies you will need to make your building sustainable.'

At this point John Brentford left Jake to get on with his work. Jake concentrated on designing the lake which surrounded the science building. He knew that he needed expert advice on how deep it would need to be, and the technology needed to keep the water in a suitable condition for fish to live in the lake and for the water to be used in the building. So, Jake played with various designs for the edge of the lake. He envisaged a paved area where people would need to walk to get in and out of the building. This was connected to the footpaths and car park that served the building. Then he designed a natural looking bank for the rest of the lake. He added trees and shrubs to his design and tried several different overall shapes for the lake. He worked on these ideas right through lunch time and it was gone three o'clock in the afternoon when Jake felt sure he had the design right. He suddenly realised that he was very hungry and decided to give his design to John Brentford and then go out and get something to eat.

The discussion with John Brentford took longer than Jake had expected mainly because John had contacted the companies that made the solar panels and the wind turbines and arranged a meeting with them for the next day. He wanted to check with Jake exactly what his ideas were for using these leading-edge technologies. He also wanted to understand Jake's ideas for using the lake to provide the water supply for the science building. As a result, it was gone four o'clock before Jake could leave the office; so, he agreed with John Brentford the time for the next day's meetings to discuss the various technologies and then drove home.

Next day, Jake and John Brentford met a senior engineer and a researcher from the company that manufactured small solar panels. This meeting went much better than Jake had expected. The company's representatives were clearly excited by the chance to see the leading-edge technology they had developed used in an important building. They were sure that they could make their small panels imitate the tiles on the roof of Sydney Opera House. They also described how they had developed very efficient energy storage devices which they described as super-efficient batteries. The engineer added, 'I am certain that the roof area on your building can accommodate enough batteries to supply all the building's needs for electricity for about a week. Given that our panels work well in daylight at any temperature above freezing, I think the university would very rarely need to use mains electricity.'

Jake explained that he planned to incorporate small wind turbines in the building to provide an alternative sustainable source of power. The researcher nodded and then asked who would be providing the wind turbines. John Brentford told him the name of the company they were meeting that afternoon. The solar panel company's engineer said, 'That is very interesting because we are in discussions with that company about the possibility of linking our two businesses in some way. In my view they are the best sustainable energy company in the UK and there is a real possibility that we form some kind of joint enterprise. I suggest you mention to them that you are considering working with us and maybe your building is just the right opportunity to bring us closer together. I will be very interested to know how the meeting with them works out.'

Jake made sure he had all the technical information he needed to design the roof of the science building so it would provide an ideal site for the small solar panels; and John Brentford handed over copies of Jake's design and asked the company's representatives to send him an indication of the likely cost of providing and installing the solar panels and a sufficient number of their super-efficient batteries to supply the building with electricity for a week. The senior manager asked when they were meeting the wind turbine company. John Brentford said, 'I don't see any reason why you should not know; and as it happens, we are meeting them this afternoon.'

The senior manager looked thoughtful and then said, 'I think it is very possible that we could work together on your building. Can I suggest that you ask the wind turbine company if we can have a joint meeting? Thinking about it, I suggest you meet them as you have arranged and explain your ideas for the science building. Then tell them that you are talking with us and suggest that we are invited to join in this afternoon's meeting. We will wait for your phone call and join you if the wind turbine people are happy with that. I do think that by working together on this building we can make real progress in devising genuinely sustainable energy generation and storage.'

This was all agreed and the meeting ended with the senior manager reminding John Brentford that he would be waiting for his phone call that afternoon and be ready to join the meeting with the wind turbine company. When the solar panel company's people had left, John Brentford was more excited than Jake had ever seen him. He patted Jake's back and said, 'This is really exciting. Not only do we have some outstanding architecture, but we could well be making a major contribution to making buildings genuinely sustainable. I must congratulate you on bringing all this together. What are you doing for lunch?'

Jake said that he had no plans and some thirty minutes later found himself sat in Swindon's best restaurant with the firm's three partners. John Brentford explained to his partners what was happening on the university's science building and finished by saying that Jake had produced an outstanding piece of architecture which incorporated ideas which could well make a major contribution towards developing genuinely sustainable buildings.

The most senior partner, Henry Masterton, nodded towards Jake and said, 'I agree that your design for the university building is one of the finest that this firm has ever produced; and linking that to its use of some very advanced sustainable technologies means that it will arouse a lot of interest in the media. So, it is important that we all understand your thinking. For instance, what led you to divide the building into five blocks, why did you choose to combine elements of classical architecture with the very modern looking roof which has very obviously been influenced by Sydney Opera House, and why do you need the lake? There may well be other issues, but we felt it best to have a discussion amongst ourselves before the press start asking questions. Then we will all be on the same page, as they say.'

The food in the restaurant was beautifully prepared and presented but Jake hardly noticed it as he concentrated on explaining his design decisions. The partners all seemed happy with his thinking until they started to discuss the lake and the possibility that it might be part of a self-sufficient water supply for the building. Henry Masterton asked, 'Are you really thinking of incorporating a sewage treatment plant in the building?'

Jake felt uncomfortable about this and was obviously

struggling to know how to reply. John Brentford, the partner that Jake usually worked with tried to help, 'We haven't really made any firm decisions about that yet. We are still looking for the right company to discuss this with. We are confident about the solar panels and small wind turbines, but we haven't yet found any technology that would allow the water to circulate safely through the building and the lake.'

The third partner, Bill Connelly, said, 'I will be very surprised if it makes sense to duplicate the public sewage treatment system and indeed the water supply system that serves the whole town. Particularly in a science building where unusual chemicals are likely to be used in the laboratories. I have never heard of any technology that would make economic sense in that context. It must be cheaper and probably more sustainable to use the well-established public systems.'

Henry Masterton added, 'The real issue here is whether the lake is necessary if it proves impossible to find a practical approach to recycling the water? We all recognise that the lake adds to the overall appearance of the design, but my feeling is that it will be fairly expensive to construct and then there are the running costs of maintaining the quality of the water. The issue is whether or not the university will be happy with these extra costs?'

Jake had no idea what to say and John Brentford came to his rescue, 'It seems to me that if we can find the right technology to allow the lake to make the building self-sufficient in water, then that is worth doing. The decision to include a lake in the design will only be questioned if that technology cannot be found. Then the lake has a purely aesthetic role, and it will be for the university to decide if they want it.'

Jake decided that he should add, 'When I first developed the design, I assumed the building would just stand on the ground. It looked good when I developed the design on that basis but then when I started to think about making the building totally sustainable, it made sense to include the lake to provide a large store of water. As I designed it, I realised that having the building sitting above a lake improved its appearance quite dramatically. So, I am keen to keep the lake even if we cannot find the sewage and water treatment technology needed to make the building self-sufficient in water.'

The discussion continued in this way with Jake gradually feeling more confident about being involved in this discussion of his design ideas. As they reached the end of their lunch, Henry Masterton, the most senior of the partners, said, 'This has been a very useful discussion. I think we all have a good understanding of the issues raised by Jake's design. It is one of the very best designs ever produced by this practice and Jake should know that we are all very pleased with his work. It is obviously important to have an open discussion with the university about the lake and indeed the whole issue of making the building sustainable. I am happy to leave this with Jake and John, but I would like to be kept in the picture as the discussion progresses.'

John Brentford realised that he and Jake needed to get back to the office for their meeting with the company that manufactured the small wind turbines that Jake hoped to incorporate in his design. The company's representatives had arrived early and were waiting for them when they reached the office. As with the mornings meeting with the solar panel company, Jake showed the representatives his design and explained that he hoped the company's small wind turbines could be incorporated in the vertical sections of the roof.

The engineer representing the company asked how many

turbines Jake planned to incorporate in his design. Jake explained that his idea was for the turbines to be arranged in three columns which mirrored the pattern of the windows in the walls below the vertical sections of the roof. As the columns of windows were all two metres wide, Jake guessed that each block could include five wind turbines.

The company's engineer asked several questions about the appearance of the windows and then said, 'I think we can produce turbines that will match the shape, colour and style of your windows and you are right, each of those gable ends will accommodate five turbines. It's good that they will all be facing in different directions. They will not all get the benefit of any wind at the same time but most days there is some movement of the air, and our turbines are very sensitive; so, I think that on most days you will have more than enough electricity being generated to run the five blocks. We will need to do some detailed calculations and talk with the university to check their needs but given that the solar panels will generate electricity and there will be effective storage batteries, I am almost certain that most days the university will be giving electricity to the national grid, or they may prefer to provide it to other university buildings. Thinking about it, that is almost certainly a better idea.'

At this point John Brentford remembered that the solar panel company had asked if they could join this meeting. He explained this to the wind turbine company's representatives who quickly agreed that this made good sense. Less than fifteen minutes later, the solar panel company's engineer and researcher who had attended that morning's meeting joined them. It was obvious that the companies had worked together on other projects and that the university building was the biggest and most important opportunity they had ever had. John Brentford and Jake mostly sat and listened as the representatives of the two companies worked out exactly what they each needed to supply, how they could use the same battery storage system and exactly how their products could fit in with and indeed compliment Jake's design.

John Brentford listened carefully to detailed conversation and then asked, 'Is there any way your two companies could work together so the university has a single organization to deal with in making sure this all works well?'

It was agreed that the two companies would discuss this and, hopefully, come back to John Brentford with a joint proposal. In any case they could within a couple of days provide sufficient information for Jake to complete his design and give John Brentford an indication of the likely cost. This seemed to finish the meeting, but John Brentford asked the representatives if any of them knew of technology that would enable the water in the lake to be recycled through the building, so it was self-sufficient in water. This was met by silence. After an embarrassingly long pause, the engineer representing the wind turbine company asked, 'Do you mean repeatedly using the same water over and over again by having something like a sewage treatment plant in the building and presumably a water treatment plant as well?'

Jake said, 'I guess that is what would be needed. It just seemed to me that for the building to be really sustainable, it should have its own water supply. I have to admit I have not been able to find any company that advertises this in their publicity material. Is it something you could work on together so that buildings really are fully sustainable?'

The company representatives all agreed that in the long-term that might be a possibility but for the moment it was probably most sensible to use the main drainage system and normal water supply. The solar panel engineer added, 'The public systems for dealing with drainage and providing water are very efficient so there is not any real incentive to develop alternatives.'

John Brentford thanked all the representatives and closed the meeting. Once they had gone, he said to Jake, 'That meeting went well. We should be ready to talk to the Vice-Chancellor next week. Make sure you have clear and attractive images of your design. These need to include the main internal spaces as well as the exterior. Also, I need to get a robust estimate of the likely cost including the lake and an alternative cost without the lake.'

Chapter 3

Jake felt the meetings with the solar panel and wind turbine companies had gone well and he could now complete his design. He began by thinking about the design of the laboratories. He was increasingly impressed by an image he had found showing a laboratory in which each bench was supported at one end by the external wall and at the other end by a wooden structure spanning from the floor to the ceiling. These wooden structures housed a sink and the gas and electricity supply needed by students working in the laboratory. The wooden columns gave the room a clear and elegant appearance which Jake thought would provide a good basis for his own design.

Jake did several preliminary sketches of laboratories before he noticed it was nearly six o'clock, and as it was Tuesday, there was net practice at the cricket club that evening. He rushed home, told his mother about his excellent lunch and said he only needed a cup of tea. As a result, he was one of the first to arrive at the nets where he joined the club chairman and the captain of the second team. Henry Roberts, the chairman, said to Jake, 'It's good that you are here early. Alan has been telling me about the opening batsman who joined the club two weeks ago. We put him in the second team to find out how good he is, and in Alan's view he is the best opening batsman in the club.'

Jake was clearly surprised and just said, 'We have two good openers in the first eleven. Still there is no harm in a bit of competition for places, so I will have a look at him assuming he comes to net practice. What is his name?'

Alan Morris said, 'He is called Ben Stanley and he has just moved to Cirencester. He moved here from Nottingham and apparently, he played top class club cricket up there; and I promise you, you will want him in the first eleven. He has played three matches for us and scored over fifty in all of them.'

At that moment Ben Stanley arrived at the nets and Alan introduced him to Jake and then said, 'I suggest you bat first so Jake can have a look at you.'

It was obvious that Ben Stanley was a very accomplished batsman. Jake got all the first team bowlers to bowl at him and he looked confident against the fast bowlers and played the spin bowlers equally comfortably. Jake bowled his full repertoire at Ben and was impressed by how well he played even his best balls. After some twenty minutes, Henry Morris suggested it was time for another batsman to get some practice and Jake joined Ben as he was removing his pads. Ben looked at the first eleven captain and said, 'I enjoyed batting against you. I had to concentrate, and I couldn't always pick which balls would come straight through after they pitched, and which were going to turn. Added to that you were varying the length of your bowling, so, I had to watch each delivery carefully. That made it difficult to attack your bowling; but I guess you know that.'

Jake laughed, 'Thank you for that; I will take it as a compliment. I did think I may have got you caught in the slips once, but it would have been a hard chance. Anyway, when did you move to Cirencester?'

Ben explained that he was a project manager in the construction industry, and he had come to work for a local builder. 'The company has just won a large contract to build a block of new classrooms at The Royal Agricultural College. They have a lot of work on just now and needed a new project manager to take charge of the classrooms project. This is a promotion for me, but I know I can manage the work. I have been working as an assistant project manager on bigger contracts in Nottingham. Obviously, I will need to get to know the local sub-contractors and material suppliers, but the company is well organized, and I have experienced people to ask when I need help.'

Jake smiled and said, 'You never know but we might well be working together sometime. I am an architect. I work for a firm in Swindon, and we design projects around here as well as across most of Wiltshire.'

Ben looked surprised as he said, 'It would be good to work together as well as play cricket together. As I guess you know, I expect to get into the first eleven very soon. That is the level I am used to playing at. I know the present first eleven is having a good season, but I hope I could make the team even stronger. What do you think?'

Jake was not sure what to say so he just replied, 'The selection committee meets on Thursday evenings to pick the teams and I don't know what view we will take. I suggest you come to practice on Thursday so we can all see you in action. The team is on a winning run and one of the main reasons is the very positive team-spirit we have built up. We all support and encourage each other. and we have had a settled team ever since I took over as captain. On the other hand, you are clearly an exceptionally good batsman; so, we will have to think about what is right for the club.'

'That all makes good sense to me, and I can already see this is a club that is in good shape and has the potential to become even better. I am keen to be part of that development, and I do understand the importance of team-spirit. I hope we work together sometime and play cricket together very soon.'

Jake shook Ben's hand and said, 'I can see that you have a lot to offer the club and I will think about the team selection between now and Thursday.'

Practice continued until it started to get dark, when Jake decided to go home. Several of the first eleven asked him if he was going to the pub, but he said he had some work to do and needed to get home. Jake's mother had put some supper together for him and his father asked how the net practice had gone. Jake smiled and said, 'It threw up a problem in a good kind of way. An experienced opening batsman has joined the club. He has played a few games in the second eleven but is clearly very good and should be in the first eleven. However, as you know, we are doing very well since I became the captain and I think that has been helped by us keeping the same team together. We get on well and support each other so, there is no reason to make changes, but Ben Stanley is almost certainly the best opening batsman in the club. He has moved to Cirencester recently from Nottingham and is used to playing top level club cricket.'

Jake's father smiled as he said, 'That sounds like a good problem to have. For what it's worth, I think you should pick your best team; but would that be a problem?'

'The present first eleven works well as a team. We all support each other, and no-one deserves to be dropped. However, Ben Stanley is good and should be in the first eleven. Anyway, I need to do some work on the design for the laboratories in the new building for the university in Swindon.'

Jake found it difficult to concentrate on his design and kept going through the members of the first eleven trying to work out who should be dropped to make way for Ben Stanley. The obvious answer was to drop one of the opening batsmen but which one? The experienced opener was better than the younger player they had promoted from the second eleven; but the younger man was learning fast and probably had more potential in the long run.

Jake decided to concentrate on his design. He had sketches of three possible designs for the laboratories in the university building, but he was not entirely happy with any of them. As he stared at each of the three sketches, he began to wonder if the younger opening batsman might have the potential to become an outstanding number three batsman. Then the question was which of the remaining batsmen should be dropped to make way for the new opening batsman? Did they need all five of the team's bowlers? They provided a very balanced attack that had enabled Jake to keep the opposition batsmen under pressure in all the matches they had played since he had taken over as captain.

Jake decided to go to bed and somewhat surprisingly fell asleep almost straight away. He woke up early next morning and could not get back to sleep as his mind was churning round with questions about his designs for the university laboratory and who he should leave out of the first eleven to make way for Ben Stanley. This continued throughout the day and as a result he made little progress with the design of the laboratories as he explained to Jane when they met that evening. She smiled as she said, 'That is the job of leaders; to make the tough decisions and then make sure everyone understands your thinking, but you need to get things straight in your own mind before you take any action. Can you show me your ideas for the university laboratories?'

Jake had his latest design ideas on his mobile phone and showed Jane the three possibilities for the laboratories. She looked at each of them for some time and then said, 'They are all good. You could use any one of them and the students would have really interesting and distinctive laboratories. I think any one of them would make a positive contribution towards helping the students to enjoy science. However, the one I like best is the second one where you have included arches spanning between the tops of the wooden columns that support the laboratory benches. It brings the whole room together and it looks very stylish. I really like the look of that. Which design do you like best?'

'I like them all, but I can see what you are saying. It is the most integrated design; but is it a bit over the top for a student's laboratory?'

Jane shook her head and said, 'I think it suggests the university takes science and the students very seriously and that has to be a good thing. Especially when you think of the very high fees students pay to go to university these days.'

Jake laughed, 'That is a good point; and thank you for your help. I will probably take your advice. I guess I also think that is the best design. Now tell me how your promotion to assistant manager is going.'

Jane looked very serious as she said, 'I am going on the training course next week. The bank rushed through my application to be promoted as they have several vacancies at the moment, and my bank manager was very enthusiastic about my potential. So, I will be in London for the next two weeks and then, assuming the course goes well, I am not sure where I will be working. I think that most of the present vacancies are in London. As I explained before, the bank like their staff to live reasonably close to the branch where they are working. This is particularly true of senior staff so that they understand their customers better.'

Jake asked if Jane would be staying in London for the two

weeks. She said, 'The course takes place at a hotel, and I think the idea is that we stay there for the full two weeks including the middle weekend.'

'So, I won't see you for the next two weeks?'

'I think that is inevitable. I finish work here in Swindon on Thursday evening and I have to be in London in time for dinner on Friday evening and stay until mid-day on the Saturday two weeks later. It would be nice if we could meet during that time in London, but the course is pretty intensive, so, I don't think that is really possible.'

Jake laughed. 'Well that gives me time to sort out the cricket team and finish my design. So, we won't be able to meet until the Saturday evening after your course has finished. I'm looking forward to that already.' Jake looked at the cricket club's fixture list and said, 'We are playing Swindon in Swindon on that Saturday so I could easily drive out to your parent's home after the match. Then we can decide what to do. Will that be okay?'

They agreed this was a good idea and chatted happily for the rest of the evening. It was still early when Jake suggested that he should take Jane home and she was happy to agree as she wanted to re-read some of the material describing how the bank functioned ready for the start of her training course. As they said good-night, Jake wished Jane good-luck with the course and said he was already looking forward to seeing her in two weeks' time. Jane kissed Jake good-night and told him he now had time to concentrate on completing his design for the university science building.

In fact, as Jake drove home his mind was preoccupied with trying to decide who should be dropped from Cirencester's first eleven to make way for Ben Stanley. Jake had little doubt that he was the best opening batsman at the club and should be in the first eleven. The problem was the team was well balanced and the present opening batsmen were an important part of that. Next day at work, the only way Jake could get these concerns out of his mind was to very deliberately concentrate on finishing the design of the university science building. John Brentford was clearly delighted when Jake showed him the finished design. He said, 'This is outstanding. It will establish your reputation as an outstanding architect; and the good news is that the preliminary estimate is just within the money the university has available for this project. That includes the cost of the lake and the sustainable technologies you want to include. The main reason is that your design uses very traditional technologies for constructing the five individual blocks. So, although the building looks complicated, it will be straight-forward to construct. So, we are ready to talk with the Vice-Chancellor. I will arrange a meeting as soon as possible.'

In fact, the Vice-Chancellor could not meet Jake and John Brentford until Tuesday the next week. As John Brentford was telling Jake when the meeting would take place, he obviously had a sudden thought and said, 'I suggest you take tomorrow off. You have put in a lot of extra work in your own time on this design and Monday is soon enough to prepare for the meeting with the Vice-Chancellor.'

Jake thanked John Brentford and drove home slowly thinking about that evening's selection meeting. In fact, the meeting developed in a way that Jake had never anticipated. As the five members of the selection committee met in the pavilion, the Chairman, Henry Roberts, began by saying, 'We all know that it is good news that Ben Stanley has joined the club and I believe there is general agreement that he is by some measure our best opening batsman. Given that, he obviously must be selected for the first team. The question is: who do we leave out to make room for Ben?'

The other four members of the committee all looked at Jake. He felt embarrassed as he said, 'We have got a very effective first eleven. Our record since we made the big changes earlier in the season speaks for itself. We now have ten wins in a row and my understanding is that the club last achieved that in the 1960's. I agree that Ben is now our best opening batsman, but we have a very balanced team that works together and supports each other in a way that I am reluctant to change. So, I have not been able to work out who should be dropped.'

This produced an awkward silence that was broken by the chairman. 'We all agree that you have built an outstanding team and we could not be happier with the way you have captained the team and the way it has responded to your clear leadership. However, this is a cricket club not just a first eleven. By keeping a rigidly consistent first team, we are denying some very promising players the opportunity to develop by getting experience in the first eleven. They should be included in the team when you are playing against some of the weaker teams the first eleven plays. The point I am trying to make is that we have a responsibility to develop the whole club not just the first eleven. So, we need a pool of players who form the first team. You have done an outstanding job of building a first-class team, but we have a responsibility to the whole club.'

Jake understood what Henry Roberts was suggesting but was not sure what he thought about this idea, nor what it would mean for him as captain. Henry Roberts continued, 'I have talked this over with Alan Morris and he feels there are at least two young players in the second team who would develop significantly faster if they had a few games, against our weaker opponents, in the first eleven. At the same time, it would benefit the second team players if one or two of the first eleven dropped into the second team for one or two matches. They would be able to see what standard is needed to get into the first team. So, just to be absolutely clear, we allowed the previous first eleven to grow old together and we didn't change it even though they had several poor seasons. We kept them together too long, and we now risk repeating that mistake if we keep picking the same first eleven. We need to take a more modern approach and develop the whole club. Ben Stanley's arrival has made us all think about these matters. So, unless anyone disagrees, we want you to act as captain of the whole club not just the first team; and I suggest we select Ben Stanley and Richard Bradley, the medium paced bowler who has been doing so well for the second team, for this weekend's first eleven. My thought is that it is sensible for them to replace the players who play those roles in current first eleven.'

Jake said, 'We have two opening batsmen. Which of them are you suggesting we leave out?'

Henry Roberts smiled as he replied, 'I think we are happy for you to decide. Think of this as your first decision as captain of the club not just the first team.'

Jake looked round at the other members of the selection committee and then said, 'Okay, we will drop Peter Henderson into the second team for this weekend. Let's see how the two younger players get on opening together. I have been very impressed with the way young Tom Stones has played in the last few matches. I think he is developing into a very impressive opener. If you look at his scores over the last month, he is probably one of our two or three best batsmen. Thinking about the bowlers, I guess we leave our established medium paced bowler out.'

This seemed to settle matters until Jake asked, 'How are we going to tell all the players about our new approach to running the club and team selection?'

Henry Roberts nodded and then said, 'I have been thinking about that, and my suggestion is that we hold a club dinner on Monday evening. I am pretty sure that my golf club will be able to accommodate us, and I may be able to arrange a bit of entertainment. Give me half an hour and I will check that I can get it all set up. Then we can announce the dinner and email everyone in the club to explain what is happening and why. At the dinner I will make a short speech explaining our future plans, and I suggest that Jake says a few words to tell everyone that he is on board with our new idea of developing a first team squad that links both elevens and gives us a more secure basis for the club to move forward.'

This ended the meeting and less than half an hour later Henry Roberts came out to the nets to tell everyone that they would be getting an email telling them about the Monday evening dinner at his club. He added, 'I hope to see everyone there and I can promise you a good meal, and some entertainment that you should really enjoy. I have booked *The Good Time Girls* to entertain us with one of their sexy performances.'

Chapter 4

Jake woke early on Friday morning but as he did not have to go into work, he stayed in bed thinking about the changes the selection committee had made to the first eleven. He could see the sense in treating the cricket club as a whole, rather than as separate teams but how would it affect the way he captained the first eleven? Then Jake suddenly remembered that Jane also had the day off, at least, until she needed to go to London. He picked up his mobile phone and called her. After a minute or so, she answered and explained that she was still in bed. Jake laughed and said that he also was in bed and that he had the day off and was wondering if they could meet before Jane set off for London.

They discussed various possibilities before deciding that it might be fun if they met earlier, and both went up to London. Jane said that she could probably leave her luggage at the hotel where the assistant manager training course was being held; and that way they would have most of the day together in London . As she said, 'The people on the course all meet just before dinner, and I assume that is when we meet the people running the course. Anyway, the point is I don't need to be back at the hotel until about six o'clock, so we will have all afternoon to explore the greatest city in the world!'

Jake and Jane took the train to London and found the hotel where the course for assistant managers was being run. When Jane had booked in and put her suitcase in her room, they decided to take a walk in St. James's Park and get lunch in the café overlooking the lake.

As they sat next to the café window enjoying the sandwiches and coffee they had chosen, Jane said, 'There are a lot of people taking advantage of the sunshine. Some of the girls out there lying on the grass have very little on. Look there is a couple really exploring each other's bodies. I don't think they are actually having sex, but they seem to be getting quite close to it.'

Jake laughed as he said, 'They certainly seem to be enjoying themselves. Is that what you want to do after lunch?'

Jane looked serious as she said, 'I need to keep my clothes neat for the course. I must look like a manager. In any case I don't think of sex as a public activity.'

'What do you think of sex? I was just thinking we have been going out for some time and we kiss and cuddle but so far you have not suggested that we have sex.'

Jane put her coffee down and said, 'Full on sex is for people who are married. At least that is how I see it. I like kissing and exploring each other's bodies, but full-on sex should be special. In my view it should be for married couples not an everyday activity for boyfriends and girlfriends. I have just assumed that you agree with that.'

'That is a pretty old-fashioned idea. I don't think I know anyone else who takes that view.'

Jane looked seriously surprised; and then said, 'Sorry, I just assumed you took the same view as me. Are you saying you think we should be having sex?'

Jake was clearly struggling to know how to reply. The last thing he wanted was to upset this beautiful woman, but he did want to be honest with her. Jane continued, 'You look as if you don't agree with me. So, to repeat my question, are you saying you want to go back to the hotel and have sex?'

Jake said, 'I assume that is a rhetorical question, not an offer. But to answer your question, of course I would love to have sex with you. The opportunity just hasn't come up before. You are beautiful and intelligent, and, in my view, anyone would feel very privileged to have sex with you.'

'I guess that is a compliment but just to be clear, sex is designed to produce babies and they have every right to have two parents who are married to each other to look after them. That is what both of us have and our parents have been important in helping us have a good start to our grown-up lives. Given that, I think it would just be wrong to risk putting a new baby in an inferior position just to give ourselves an exciting experience.'

Jake looked hard at Jane and then said, 'There are reliable ways of ensuring that we don't create a baby; but I can see that this is an academic discussion, and we are not discussing a real possibility for us this afternoon. So, what shall we do?'

'We could walk into Parliament Square and across Westminster Bridge to The London Eye. Then when we have looked at London from The London Eye, we could come back across Westminster Bridge and then walk along Whitehall to Trafalgar Square and maybe go to The National Gallery. They have several of my favourite paintings, and they do a good afternoon tea.'

Jake half heard what Jane had suggested because he was thinking about her clear view that sex was for married couples. He was sure that no one else he knew had ever expressed that view so clearly and seriously. He now knew that if he wanted Jane as his girlfriend, it would be on different terms from all his other girlfriends. It was true that he had only had sex with two previous girlfriends but none of the many girls he had been out with had ever expressed the view that sex was something just for married couples. What did he think? Somehow this question reminded him that Jane had just suggested what they should do that afternoon; so, he replied, 'That is a good plan. Let's go.'

As they crossed Westminster Bridge, they could see the modern architecture which now dominated the central City of London. Jane asked Jake what he thought of it and was it a step forward from, for example, the architecture of the Houses of Parliament and Westminster Abbey which they had just passed? Jake looked thoughtful as he said, 'It's certainly different; and I guess that is the aim. All those buildings are designed to stand out. The architects wanted people to notice their designs and discuss them. I don't think they are as good as the Houses of Parliament or Westminster Abbey, and I don't think most of them will last anything like as long. People will come to see just how superficial they are, and in my view, they will be replaced by more mature designs over say the next fifty years.'

Jane seemed surprised by Jake's response to her question and asked him what he aimed for in his own designs. Jake thought for a moment before he replied, 'My design for the Swindon University science building shows what I want to achieve. It is based on traditional style and so has much in common with the Houses of Parliament and Westminster Abbey, but I have tried to take that forward. I used a great building, which is my favourite modern design, Sydney Opera House, to add to the traditional style. I think it works but if it gets some publicity, I will be interested to see what reaction it gets from architectural journalists and indeed from other architects.'

'When do you expect your design be seen by that wider audience?'

'We are meeting the university Vice-Chancellor on Tuesday and, if he likes it, I think he will want to get publicity for his new building. He still needs to raise more money to fund the construction. For all these kinds of reasons, I think he may well ask us to make sure that the design gets the maximum possible publicity.'

Jane had listened carefully to what Jake had just said. She looked thoughtful as she asked Jake if he was happy for his work to be used in that way. Jake nodded and said, 'I will be happy if my work gets publicity. That could start to establish my reputation as a good architect; and maybe give me some interesting opportunities. I don't know what these might be but, for instance, it might attract more clients who want me to design new buildings for them. That would be great.'

Jane asked, 'Would you think of leaving the firm in Swindon if a better architectural practice approached you?'

'I can't see that happening. There are plenty of good architects about and I am sure the best practices have no shortage of talented people wanting to join them.'

They continued talking about possible futures as they queued to go on The London Eye. Once aboard, they were both fascinated by the views of London it gave them. This was initially dominated by the Thames where a surprising number of cruise boats made it look very busy. As they got higher, Jake particularly enjoyed seeing the Houses of Parliament, Big Ben and Westminster Bridge from a new angle. Jane then pointed towards Tower Bridge and the City and then said, 'Look you can see St. Paul's Cathedral. I think that is my favourite building in London. What do you think Jake?'

Jake had been looking at Embankment station and the Golden Jubilee bridges but looked to where Jane was pointing. He nodded. 'St. Paul's Cathedral does stand out in that scene. I have to say when I look at the city, there are so many missed opportunities. Obviously, those high-rise buildings needed a lot of money to design and construct and yet most of them are really quite ordinary. I do like the Shard but most of the high-rise buildings which dominate that part of London are just ordinary or downright silly.'

Jane smiled as she said, 'It's really interesting to hear your views. I know some of them have been given ridiculous names to describe their appearance. I've heard of "The Walkie-Talkie" and "The Razor" and I think there are others with funny names. I guess you wouldn't like one of your buildings to get called something like that.'

Jake laughed and said, 'At least I would be famous; but you are right, I would struggle to regard that as a compliment.'

When they had finished their ride on The London Eye, they continued to talk about London's architecture as they walked to The National Gallery in Trafalgar Square. Jake explained at some length that he was not keen on high rise buildings and used Whitehall as a beautiful example of an area where the architects who designed it had respected the human scale. Jane agreed and said, 'What you are saying reminds me of a visit to Paris where I was told a joke about the Montparnasse Tower. It is said that the observation deck in the tower enjoys the most beautiful view of Paris because it is the only place from which you don't see the tower.'

Jake laughed and said that he agreed with that thinking. As they crossed Trafalgar Square walking towards The National Gallery, they agreed that this must be one of the most attractive squares in the world. As they entered The National Gallery Jake asked Jane what she wanted to look at. She said, 'I have been here before because they have some of my favourite paintings. I love the *Child with Dove* by Picasso and Van Gogh's *Sunflowers* and Claude Monet's *Water Lilies*. What do you like here?'

Jake said, 'I like the paintings you mentioned. They are all really great, but I do enjoy looking at the older paintings by people like Turner, Constable, Rembrandt, Michelangelo and Gainsborough. They look so complete. I find myself thinking about them when I am designing a new building. That helps me make sure my buildings will form an integrated whole when people look at them. I know that's odd, and I can't really explain it but thinking about Constable's *Hay Wain*, for example, helps me make sure that all the parts of the building I happen to be working on fit together to form a beautiful whole design. Does that make any sense?'

Jane smiled broadly and then slowly said, 'That is very impressive. There is nothing in my work that compares to your way of working. I am beginning to understand why you are at risk of becoming a great architect. I am so pleased we are together but now we should go and look at some of the paintings that inspire you. It may help me to understand you even better.'

As they walked round the gallery, Jake stopped several times in front of pictures which he said were the kind of image that came into his mind as he reached key stages of his design process. Jane could see that each of them was very beautiful. They included a lot of detail but managed to form a completely integrated whole. She said, 'I am beginning to understand why you find these pictures so inspiring. It's something I will think about over the next few days. You have a adopted a really creative way of thinking and I must say it's really interesting; perhaps we can discuss it more over afternoon tea.'

Jake smiled and agreed it was time for tea. They found a table overlooking Trafalgar Square and enjoyed watching the people playing with the fountains, pointing up at Nelson's

Column and generally enjoying the sunshine. When they had finished their tea and cake, Jane said she should get back to the hotel to make sure she was ready for the start of her training course. They walked to the hotel and Jake came into the reception area where Jane said, 'I should go now. Thank you for coming up to London with me. It has been a lovely day.' Then she kissed him and added, 'I will see you in two weeks' time.'

Jake watched her get into the lift and then wandered out of the hotel and decided to look round Soho. He passed several interesting looking nightclubs and thought it would great to take Jane to one of these. Several had attractive young women outside who invited Jake to come in and see the show. He laughed and told them he needed to go home. Quite quickly he decided this was a good idea as he had his changed first eleven to captain over the weekend. As Jake travelled back to Cirencester, he thought about the changes to his team and how he should deal with them.

This thoughtful preparation probably contributed to the team having an exceptionally successful weekend. Ben Stanley, the new opening batsman, was clearly a very accomplished cricketer. He not only had a good innings in both the Saturday and Sunday matches, but he helped his opening partner, the younger Ton Stones, by telling him what to watch for in the opposing bowlers. As a result, the two openers gave Cirencester an excellent start to their innings in both matches. Ben Stanley also helped Jake by quietly suggesting a few changes to the field placings when any of the opposing batsman seemed to be settling down.

The Sunday match was away and during the journey back in the team bus, they stopped at a one of Jake's favourite pubs. As they all got drinks and settled down to chat, Ben Stanley said to Jake, 'I've been looking at your fixture list for the season and it seems to me that this team could get fixtures with one or two better teams. I have also looked at the fixture lists of some of the best teams in Gloucestershire and I think the results you have achieved this season would persuade them to give you a fixture for next season.'

Jake said he would discuss this with the Chairman at the dinner on Monday evening. Ben smiled and said, 'If I can help with that discussion, let me know. It should be a good evening. Have you got your speech sorted out?'

Jake laughed, 'I will think of something to say. My understanding is that Henry Roberts, who is organizing the dinner has got some very attractive young women to perform for our entertainment. They are called something like *The Good Time Girls,* and I won't want to delay us from watching them by talking too much.'

Ben agreed but added, 'We do want to hear your plans, as captain, for taking the club forward.'

This conversation kept coming into Jake's mind throughout the day on Monday even though he was busy helping make sure that he and John Brentford had everything they needed for their meeting with the university Vice-Chancellor. This was scheduled for Tuesday morning and they both knew it was an important stage in ensuring that Jake's design was accepted by the university.

Thanks to all the careful preparation that John Brentford had insisted on, Jake felt very confident that the meeting with the Vice-Chancellor would go well. He was not so certain about his speech at the dinner that the club chairman had arranged for that evening. It was held at Henry Roberts' golf club which provided a very comfortable venue even though almost every member of the cricket club had come to the dinner. Once everyone was sat down and decided what they wanted to eat and drink, Henry

Roberts stood up and said, 'I think I should start the evening by explaining why we are meeting here tonight. First, it is to celebrate the excellent form of both our teams over the last few months. Cirencester has not had such a long run of wins for over forty years. Secondly, I want us to think about how we maintain that excellent form and indeed build on it over the rest of the season and on into the future. I know that in recent years we have stuck for too long with the old first eleven even though we had better players in the second eleven. Well, as you all know, we have put that right, but now we need to make sure we don't fall into the same trap of sticking to a fixed first eleven. Indeed, the teams we fielded this weekend show that the change has started. Our aim is to create a first eleven squad that includes both teams and deliberately works at developing everyone's talent. That means selecting first elevens to win all our matches and at the same time giving valuable experience to our most promising younger players. In other words, our aim is to ensure that Cirencester is a cricket club that keeps getting better and better. On that note, I will hand over to Jake Brown.'

There was a round of applause as Henry Roberts sat down. Jake waited until the room was reasonably quiet before he stood up and said, 'I must first thank the Chairman for his clear explanation of his important new ideas about how we should think about the club. I know from my own experience the importance of both our teams. The first team has a real responsibility to do everything it can to win all our matches and the second eleven provides important support. It is an exciting training ground for young players as well as a place where first team players can practice specific improvements to their game. So, my understanding is that in future, as Henry Roberts said, we will think in terms of a first eleven squad which overlaps with the second eleven. We made a start this weekend and as we all know, it worked well. Both teams won and the players brought into the first team played a big part in our success; and those who moved to the second eleven clearly provided important role models for the younger players hoping to break into the first team. In future, we will think about the two elevens as one joint club in which everyone contributes to our success. I find this a really exciting idea and look forward to working with you all as we make Cirencester the best place to cricket in Gloucestershire.'

Jake then sat down, and everyone again applauded. This seemed to set the tone for a very enjoyable dinner during which each table discussed the ideas that Henry Roberts and Jake Brown had described. Jake could sense a real feeling of excitement around the room which grew noisier as the evening wore on. Once the deserts were cleared away, Henry Roberts again stood up and said, 'Now that we have all finished our dinner and I think we all have a drink, I want to introduce this evening's entertainment. Gentlemen, I am pleased to tell you that we have with us this evening a very exciting group that is starting to be recognised as one of the UK's leading pop groups. I give you *The Good Time Girls!*'

The curtains at one end of the room opened to reveal three musicians sat at the back of a small stage. As they started playing a lively tune, four attractive young women wearing very revealing costumes walked onto the stage and began singing. They immediately had the full attention of their audience. Jake decided that the young women were good singers and he settled back to enjoy the songs. Some were popular tunes that he knew but several of the numbers they performed were new to Jake. He began to wonder why he had not heard of this group as they had real talent. Gradually his attention began to concentrate on the taller of the two blondes in the group. She had a very attractive figure, big and shapely breasts, a beautiful face and long blonde hair. He thought that she fully embodied his ideas about a classic sex symbol. As he concentrated on her, he decided that she was a good singer and was performing a series of very sexy dance moves as well as looking beautiful.

Each number *The Good Time Girls* performed was warmly applauded by everyone. After just over half an hour, the man who played the guitar in the trio that provided the backing music for the group stood up and announced that the group would now do one more number and then take a break. He then added, 'We will be back in about twenty minutes to do another performance for you all.'

This was greeted with enthusiastic applause; and the group then performed a particularly sexy number which was greeted with sustained applause. The group's guitar player thanked the audience and promised they would be back in about twenty minutes. He added, 'I suggest you stay to see our second performance as it is much sexier than what you have seen so far.'

With that the guitarist laughed and the curtains closed to enthusiastic applause. As everyone at the dinner began to talk about the group, Henry Roberts turned to Jake and said, 'I am going back-stage to congratulate the group on giving us such an excellent show. Would you like to come with me?'

Without any hesitation Jake said he would love to meet the group. When the two of them reached the room where the group was resting between their two performances, Henry Roberts congratulated the group on their excellent performance which had been enjoyed by all the members of the cricket club. He then began talking to the group's guitarist about the arrangements for them to perform again on Wednesday at a golf club dinner. Jake walked over to the young blonde he had been admiring and said, 'Hi, I'm Jake; I must say I was very impressed by your performance. What is your name?'

The woman looked at him and then smiled as she replied, 'I'm called Linda; and thank you for those kind words. I hope you enjoy the rest of our performance just as much.'

Linda hesitated and then continued, 'You are the cricket club captain, aren't you? I watched your speech at the start of the dinner. It was very impressive. Do you live in Cirencester?'

Jake confirmed that he did, and Linda said, 'Well we are due to perform here at this golf club again on Wednesday. So, I have decided to stay here in Cirencester. The rest of the group are going home and coming back on Wednesday, but I don't have anything to go home for and I thought it would be nice to look round the town tomorrow. Maybe you can join me at some time.'

Jake explained that he was an architect, and he had a crucial meeting with an important client tomorrow morning. Then thinking quickly, he said, 'I think the client will want some time to decide what we do next on his new building, so, I may well be free tomorrow afternoon. I could phone you at lunch time and let you know if we can get together. I must say I would enjoy showing you what Cirencester and the surrounding villages have to offer.'

Linda took Jake's hand, leant forward and kissed him on the cheek. She then said, 'I am already looking froward to an exciting afternoon. I will give you my phone number and be expecting your call round about lunch time.'

Linda gave Jake a card which told him that her name was Linda James and gave him her mobile phone number and email address. Jake took out one of his own cards and gave it to Linda. The guitarist then told Henry Roberts and Jake that the group needed to get ready for their second performance and it would help if the two of them returned to dining room. As they left, Linda said to Jake, 'I will see you tomorrow. We have had a busy day today and so once we finish tonight, I need to get to the hotel and catch up on my sleep.'

As they walked back to the dining room, Henry Roberts said to Jake, 'That is one of the most beautiful women I have ever seen. You are very lucky to be seeing her tomorrow; but you deserve it. Make the most of your time with her.'

Chapter 5

Jake woke early on Tuesday morning and lay in bed thinking about the day ahead. The meeting with the university Vice-Chancellor was important and he hoped it would be straight-forward. That would mean there was a good chance that he could leave the office early and spend some more time with Linda. She was beautiful, a good singer and she danced in a very sexy way. As he thought about her, the question of why he was meeting her filled his head. Jane was his girlfriend and he had started to think he was in love with her. Now, the first time she had been away, he was seeing another woman. Jake laughed and decided to get up and concentrate on being ready for the meeting with the Vice-Chancellor.

When Jake and John Brentford arrived at the Vice-Chancellor's office, he was obviously waiting for them together with the university's Buildings Officer. He welcomed them and asked them to sit around the table in his office. The Vice-Chancellor began the meeting by asking John Brentford to show them the proposed design for the new science building.

John Brentford began by giving the Vice-Chancellor and the Buildings Officer copies of the best images of the design that Jake had produced. They were both clearly impressed; and the Vice-Chancellor said, 'This looks magnificent. It provides everything I could have wished for in terms of its initial impact. The roof is particularly impressive.'

The Buildings Officer agreed and then asked how it was

proposed to construct the roof. John Brentford asked Jake to explain. He smiled and then said, 'You can probably guess that the roof design is an important part of my design. As I developed my idea, I found myself looking at images of Sydney Opera House. That is a wonderful building and I have tried to make the classical style of the external walls provide a clear progression from the lake up to the magnificent roof. It is not a copy of Sydney Opera House's roof, which as you may know is formed of reinforced concrete covered with glazed tiles but my idea for the science building roof is different. The basic structure is timber. In many ways this is a traditional form of construction except the roof trusses support a curved surface. The actual surface of the roof is formed from a fairly new material which consists of three layers of strong plastic with two layers of stainless-steel wire netting between them. The whole material is formed rather like plywood but, as I said, it comprises strong plastic sheets and steel netting. This is then covered with a copper roof, which, as it weathers, will turn green. Then, rather than the glazed tiles that form the roof covering on Sydney Opera House, my idea is to use small solar panels coloured various shades of green and white. They will create a look that is similar to Sydney Opera House's roof which uses tiles coloured various shades of blue and white; and, of course, they will provide electricity for the building. I should have mentioned that the copper roof will incorporate small clips which support the solar panels. Then, finally, the vertical sections of the roof are a straight-forward extension of the external walls, and so form gable ends which incorporate small wind turbines. The wind-turbines continue the visual pattern of the windows up into the gable ends and, most importantly, provide a second source of electricity. My design includes batteries in the roof that will be capable of storing about a week's supply of electricity. I have discussed all this with companies that manufacture the plastic ply sheeting, the solar panels, the wind turbines and the storage batteries. The costs of all this leading-edge technology are included in the cost estimates that we will show you in a few minutes.'

The Vice-Chancellor was clearly impressed by the idea of using solar panels, wind turbines and state-of-the-art storage batteries. He looked very thoughtful as he said, 'These are exciting ideas. The Building Officer will need to discuss the implications with the companies you have been talking to about the roof and the solar panels, the wind turbines and the storage batteries but I like the idea of the science building being self-sufficient in electricity. It will save us some money and it will generate good publicity for the university. I hope these ideas all work out. Now, can we see the floor plans to see how this exciting design accommodates all the spaces we need?'

John Brentford produced copies of each of the floorplans for the Vice-Chancellor and the Buildings Officer. They studied these for some ten minutes and as they did so they asked various questions which Jake answered confidently. Once they were clear that the design included all the internal spaces they needed, the Buildings Officer asked what the cost of the construction was likely to be. John Brentford gave him and the Vice-Chancellor a summary of the estimate their quantity surveyors had produced.

The Buildings Officer almost immediately said, 'This is a bit higher than I had hoped but the benefit of generating its own electricity probably goes a long way towards compensating for the extra cost. I notice the lake you have added to the design is quite expensive. You haven't mentioned that. What is the point of including a lake around the science building?'

John Brentford looked at Jake who smiled as he replied, 'I

have to admit that the lake is something that I have struggled with. Initially my idea was to make the building self-sufficient in water by collecting rainwater, storing it in the lake and including a water treatment plant in the building. Then the water would simply be re-cycled round and round the building. I couldn't find any technology that made economic sense of this idea but by the time I had reached that conclusion, it had become clear to me that the lake was an important element of my design. Quite simply, it adds to the look of the whole building, so I decided to retain it. I have included a small water-treatment plant so the water will be safe if any students fall in but for the various functions of the building, I have decided that mains water and the public drainage systems provide the most appropriate answer. I do have a couple of images of the building without the lake on my computer, if you want to see them.'

The Vice-Chancellor asked to see the images without a lake and quickly decided that he agreed with Jake about its visual impact. The meeting continued for about another quarter of an hour and then the Vice-Chancellor said, 'This all looks very good. The Buildings Officer and I need to discuss several things, but I am now ready to make a public announcement about the design. This is a key stage in the process of getting the publicity needed to ensure we have the finance needed to construct the building and set up the new and bigger science departments. So, thank you both for your excellent work and I will be in touch towards the end of the week.'

John Brentford decided they should walk back to the office. They both felt pleased with the Vice-Chancellor's very positive reaction to the design, so, Jake found it relatively easy to ask if he could take the afternoon off. John Brentford just said, 'That's the least you deserve as a reward for your outstanding design. I must talk to the other partners about how we recognise your obvious talent. Do you have any views on how you want your career to progress over the next few years?'

Jake was clearly surprised by this question and somewhat hesitantly said, 'I'm happy working in the firm for now and I haven't really given much thought to my long-term future. Obviously, I would like to become a partner in due course but as long as there are interesting projects for me to work on, I am happy to concentrate on my designs. As you know, I am captain of the first team at Cirencester Cricket Club and we are having a very good season; so, I feel happy with life just now.'

John Brentford said, 'That is all good, but the partners need to discuss your future. The design you have produced for the university science building is exceptional and I would not be at all surprised if you get some interesting offers from other practices.'

Jake looked surprised and just said that this had not occurred to him. He then added, 'If I do get any interesting offers, I will let you know, and I will be happy for us to discuss what I should do.'

John Brentford nodded and said it would be interesting to see what publicity the Vice-Chancellor is able to get. Then looking hard at Jake, he said, 'It's clear that you have been working hard on this project over the last few weeks, if you want to take tomorrow off as well as this afternoon, that will be fine. I don't expect the Vice-Chancellor to get back to us until Thursday at the earliest. You might think about how we organize the production of the working drawings assuming he wants to go ahead. Obviously, you need to be involved in that to make sure your design ideas are properly embedded in all the details of the building.'

Jake agreed that was important and thanked John Brentford for letting him have the afternoon and all day on Wednesday. He finished by saying, 'I do have things I want to do, and I will be in on Thursday with a plan for the working drawings.'

Once they were back in the office, Jake phoned Linda and arranged to meet at the hotel where she was staying. She sounded excited and said, 'You will be just in time for lunch. I had a walk around the town this morning and there is a restaurant that looked really good.'

They met in the hotel reception area and Jake was totally captivated by how attractive Linda looked. She was wearing a summer dress with a very short skirt and a low top. She had used a minimal amount of make-up which made her look even more beautiful than Jake remembered. She smiled broadly when Jake came into the hotel and took his hand and moved very close to him as she asked, 'Have you had a good morning? You can tell me about it while we walk to the restaurant where I thought we could have lunch.'

Jake said, 'You look even more beautiful than I remembered from yesterday.'

Linda laughed and said, 'This is the real me. When we are performing, it's my stage personality that you see. I like being on stage but that is me being an actress. I'm pleased you like the real me. Now shall we eat?'

Linda was clearly listening carefully as Jake described that morning's meeting. She asked if she could see his design. He explained that he had his design on his computer which he had left in his car. She said, 'Maybe I could see it after lunch and then we could take a drive to see some of the Cotswold scenery.'

The restaurant Linda had picked was one that Jake had never used before. He was surprised when they got inside by how attractive it was. Linda had reserved a table and they were soon enjoying their starters and the glasses of wine they had selected. Jake asked if being one of *The Good Time Girls* was Linda's full-time work or if she had another job. She explained that the group had only been together for a few months, and she wanted it to be a success and so she had not tried to get another job when she finished at university. Jake asked how the group had come together and she explained that the four singers had been at university together and had formed a group that did a few performances in the student's union during their final year. 'At first, we just met and enjoyed singing together. Then as more people heard us, we were asked to sing at various events that were held in the union building. We used recorded music as the backing to our performances. Then we were invited to perform at a club near the university and it was after one of our performances there that Harry Masters approached us and suggested we talk about forming a joint group. Harry is the guitarist in our backing group, and they had been playing together for some time. Anyway, we all met and tried playing together and agreed that when we four left university, it was worth trying to see if we could turn professional. So, it's very early days for us but I'm enjoying life. We get bookings two or three times a week which brings in some money but, for the moment at least, my parents are happy to finance me.' Linda paused and then smiling at Jake added, 'Another advantage is that I meet interesting people!'

Jake laughed and asked Linda what she had studied at university. She said that her degree was in psychology, and she was finding that it helped her in writing the words for some of the numbers the group had composed. Jake smiled and said, 'I did think some of your numbers had interesting words. It would be good to hear them again as I guess they have interesting messages. How do you see your future developing?'

'Well, we have a performance at the Cirencester Golf Club tomorrow. Maybe you could come. You could ask Henry Roberts if he can arrange that for you. I would like to see you there.'

Jake agreed that sounded like a good idea; and then added, 'I'll phone him now to see if that is possible.'

Jake phoned Henry Roberts and explained that he was having lunch with one of *The Good Time Girls* and she had suggested he should come to see their performance at the golf club on Wednesday evening. Henry Roberts laughed and then said, 'I think that is a good idea. The dinner starts at seven thirty and it's formal. That means wearing your dinner jacket. I will let the club secretary know that you are coming as my guest. So, see you tomorrow evening.'

Linda looked really pleased when Jake told her that he was coming to the golf club. As they had more or less finished their lunch, she said, 'You were going to show me your design for the university building. You said you had it on your computer which is in your car. Maybe we can go for a drive as well. I really would like to see some of the beauty spots in the Cotswolds with you.'

Linda was clearly impressed by Jake's design. As he showed her the three-dimensional sketches of the proposed building, she said, 'This is amazing. It's a remarkable building. It reminds me a bit of Sydney Opera House; can you see why?'

Jake nodded and said, 'You obviously know about architecture. I did have Sydney Opera House in my mind as I was designing the general shape of the roof. There are differences of course. The Opera House roof is much bigger. Also, I have imitated the tiles on its roof with small solar panels. I also included some wind-turbines, so the building will be self-sufficient in electricity.'

Linda nodded as she said, 'That is very important these days. We have got to stop heating the planet by burning fossil fuels to make electricity. So that is good; but your design really is exceptional. This building could make you famous. Have you thought about that?'

'I enjoy working on my designs and I just hope that I continue to have interesting buildings to work on. Anyway, for the moment I like the idea of walking round one or two of the Cotswold villages.'

They spent the afternoon looking round some of Jake's favourite villages before reaching Cheltenham just before six o'clock. It was too early for dinner, but Jake knew a stylish pub where they found a table and ordered their pre-dinner drinks. There was a television in the corner of the bar which was showing the evening news. It switched to the local news which was not very interesting until Jake's attention was grabbed by the television showing an image of his design for the university science building. The news reader was saying, 'This remarkable building will provide a new science block for Swindon University. It has been designed by a young architect from Cirencester, called Jake Brown. The university's Vice-Chancellor announced this afternoon that they are going ahead with the construction of this remarkable building. Our architectural correspondent feels it is quite exceptional.'

The screen changed to show a distinguished looking woman. A note along the bottom of the screen explained that she was the Architectural Correspondent. She said, 'I saw this amazing design for a new building in Swindon just this afternoon; and I have to say that in my opinion, it is one of the best designs I have ever seen. We are in the process of contacting the young architect,

Jake Brown, who is clearly outstanding. We hope to bring you his description of his exceptional design tomorrow evening.'

Then a series of images of Jake's design appeared on the screen and then the news reader switched to a different subject. Linda stared at Jake as she said, 'Did you know that was going to be on the news? Your building looked more amazing on TV than it did in the images you showed me.'

Jake still looking totally surprised managed to say, 'I didn't know anything about that report. I must contact my firm to see if they knew about it.'

He then phoned John Brentford, the partner he worked with, who, as soon as he realised it was Jake phoning, immediately asked, 'Jake, did you see your building on the TV news? They want to do an interview with you for tomorrow's news. Where are you? I have been trying to contact you, but your phone seemed to be switched off.'

Jake explained where he was, and John Brentford told him that this was an important opportunity for the firm to get good publicity and certainly a real opportunity for Jake himself. He then added that the television company want Jake to contact them, and Jake should do that as soon as possible. Jake agreed and John Brentford asked to be kept in the picture about any arrangements that Jake made with the television people. As he put his phone down, Jake told Linda that the television company wanted to interview him for the news programme tomorrow evening. She said, 'That is great news. As I mentioned we have been trying to get just that kind of publicity for *The Good Time Girls*. Maybe you could mention us when you talk to the television people. You could invent some link between your design and our group.'

Jake looked startled by this thought but he phoned the

number that John Brentford had given him and found himself talking to the television architectural correspondent. She explained that they would like to interview Jake tomorrow. She added that their computer experts were producing a computer based three-dimensional model of the design and she hoped to use it in her interview with Jake. She then asked several questions about the design and Jake found himself explaining that he thought the lake represented the natural world, the classical design of the main structure of the five blocks represented humanity emerging from nature and the free-flowing roof represented art and creativity as the highest achievement of humans. The architectural correspondent sounded excited as she said, 'That is exactly the kind of comment that I would like you to make tomorrow.'

At this moment Linda put her hand on Jake's arm and said, 'Don't forget *The Good Time Girls.*'

Jake thanked the architectural correspondent and then continued, 'I don't know if this helps but I have recently watched a new singing group perform and the words of many of their songs embody similar thoughts. They have a very masculine trio of musicians and four very attractive young women singers; and listening to them and watching them perform helped me understand how my design reflects the sequence of nature, humanity and creativity. The group is called *The Good Time Girls* and they are performing in Cirencester at the golf club tomorrow evening. I think they could make a real contribution to your programme especially if we get them to perform one of their songs that reflects the thinking behind my design.'

The architectural correspondent said, 'That is an interesting idea. I would need to see the group in action before we agree to that kind of link, but we do often have a musical conclusion to the programme. We could get a camera team to the golf club at five o'clock tomorrow evening, do your interview and film the group and then decide what to include in tomorrow's programme.'

Jake agreed to check these arrangements with the golf club and let the architectural correspondent know when it was all sorted out. Linda was delighted and immediately kissed Jake. Then she said, 'That is great news. I must tell the rest of the group to be at the golf club early. I will suggest they get there at say four thirty and we can get all set up. As you were talking on the phone, I decided that the song that best fits in with what you were saying is the one we call *Creative Imaginations.*'

Jake nodded and then said, 'I remember that song. It is certainly one of your best and you are right, it has echoes of the way I think when I am designing. This could be great for both of us. I must check with Henry Roberts that it is okay for the television people to use the golf club. I will phone him now.'

Henry Roberts was obviously delighted that his golf club would get some publicity and said it was great news that Jake's work was being recognised and *The Good Time Girls* might get to perform on television. He finished by telling Jake that he would speak to the club secretary and give him Jake's phone number in case he needed more information about what is happening.

Linda then phoned Harry Masters, the guitarist in her group, who was also effectively the manager of the group, and explained what was happening. He was obviously very pleased and agreed to make sure the group was at the golf club well before five o'clock. He also agreed that *Creative Imaginations* would be a good number for them to perform.

Jake and Linda settled back to have dinner feeling that this was an important day; and life was good. As they finished their starters, Linda took Jake's hand and said, 'I'm so pleased we have met. I feel really good about life right now. I just have the feeling that we are both about to start a really significant time in our lives and it's great that we are together.'

Jake kissed Linda's hand and said, 'Tomorrow could be a very day important for both of us. I think when we have finished dinner, we should get back to Cirencester so we can both have a good night's sleep, ready for a big day.'

Linda looked hard at Jake as very carefully she said, 'I assume you are not suggesting we sleep together?'

'Is that an offer?'

'Not yet; we need to get to know each other much more before we make love; but it's a lovely idea.'

'You're right, we need to get ready for tomorrow. It's a big day. Shall we have lunch together to check we are both ready to appear on television.'

Linda laughed, 'That is a very mature idea. The hotel I am staying in has a good restaurant. I will book a table for say twelve-thirty. Now let's concentrate on the rest of our dinner; and we can continue the process of getting to know each other better. Now we know where it might lead!'

Jake smiled broadly and agreed that was a great plan. His mind was now swirling with thoughts about Linda, who was without doubt the most beautiful woman he had ever spent any time with. This was all mixed up with thoughts about Jane, his girlfriend, who he had thought he was falling in love with, and tomorrow's television interview at the golf club.

As they ate the main course of their dinner, Linda said, 'You look very thoughtful. Have I upset you?'

Jake looked at her carefully as he replied, 'You are beautiful, and I want us to get to know each other much better; and I want to be honest with you. I have a girlfriend. She is away doing a training course for two weeks. She works in a bank and is about to be promoted to be an assistant manager. Now, that we have met, I have to admit that I am confused about my feelings.'

'Thank you for being honest. I guess I am not surprised that you already have a girlfriend. You are a very attractive man. So, it would be odd if you didn't have a girlfriend; but we are here together, so, let's enjoy ourselves and see where we are in a couple of weeks.'

Jake took her hand and said, 'Thank you. Now I think we should make sure we get ready for our big day tomorrow.'

They finished their dinner and Linda said she should get back to her hotel and make sure she was ready for the group's performance on television. Jake drove them back to Cirencester and took Linda to her hotel. She kissed him and said, 'I need to check the words of the number we are doing for television; and get a good night's sleep. So, I will see you at lunchtime tomorrow.'

Chapter 6

Jake was still dozing off in bed on Wednesday morning when his phone rang. He looked at the time and it was just gone nine o'clock. When he answered, it was someone from the BBC saying that it turned out to be too complicated to film his interview at the golf-club; and it had been decided to do the interview at their studio in Cheltenham at two o'clock that afternoon. The woman also told him that *The Good Time Girls* were going to be recorded in Cheltenham at much the same time. Jake checked the address of the studio in Cheltenham and promised to be there in good time.

As he put his phone down, it rang again. This time it was Linda to tell him that she would not be able to join him for lunch as *The Good Time Girls* had to go to Cheltenham to record their performance. He laughed as he said, 'I may see you there because the BBC have decided to do my interview at their Cheltenham studio at two o'clock.'

When Jake got downstairs and explained what was happening to his mother, she said, 'I suggest you have a good breakfast at about ten thirty. Then you can get ready to be on television. What are you going to wear?'

Jake agreed that it was a good idea to have a breakfast late and then admitted that he hadn't thought about what he would wear. His mother suggested that he wore the suit he had bought a few weeks earlier. She added that she would make sure his best shirt was well ironed and suggested he should wear the green tie she had given him for his birthday earlier that year. Jake looked at her carefully and then said, 'You are right. I will look like a stylish professional in my new suit; and I do like that tie. I think it came from South Africa. Your sister sent it to me last Christmas. I think she said it was the tie of the local golf club.'

When Jake arrived at the television studios, he was taken to a small studio set out to resemble an office. The Architectural Correspondent was already sat at a table, and she invited Jake to take the other chair. She introduced herself as Lizzy Johnson and explained that she would ask Jake questions and the team on the far side of the room would film their conversation. Then a striking three-dimensional image of Jake's design for the university science building appeared on a small screen set up on the table in front of Jake. The image changed to suggest someone walking around the building and looking at it from all sides. Lizzy Johnson explained that viewers would be shown these images at various points in the interview, but Jake should keep looking at the camera. She added that this would allow them, when they came to edit the interview, to include images of him at appropriate points in the discussion.

Jake said this all sounded straight-forward and so Lizzy Johnson said she would begin. 'First, I must congratulate you on producing such an outstanding design. Could I ask you how you set about designing the university science building?'

'I began by studying the list of internal spaces the university told me they needed. I played with the shape and design of the main spaces. These included the lecture theatres, the science laboratories, space for the teaching staff and the students. I looked at the most highly regarded designs for theatres, laboratories, offices, restaurants and cafes and so on. As I worked at this, I found the spaces fell naturally into five related groups.

So, I decided that the building should comprise five separate blocks. I made them all more or less the same size on plan and they worked out to be somewhat different heights. As I tried various arrangements of the blocks, I began to sketch a number of designs for the roof which I needed to hold the whole design together. That is how I came to develop the highly curved shapes, which some kind people have said reminds them of Sydney Opera House.'

Lizzy Johnson smiled as she said, 'That is very interesting. Can I ask why you added a lake to the design?'

'During the discussions with the university about the building, the possibility of making it self-sufficient in terms of energy and so on was mentioned. That is why the roof is covered with small solar panels; and the areas where the external walls of the blocks continue into the roof area to form gable ends include small wind turbines. These technologies all generate electricity which is stored in highly efficient batteries housed in the roof area. I have been able to find established technologies that work well to provide all of that. However, I also wanted the building to be self-sufficient in water. So, I added the lake. Unfortunately, the technology needed to allow the water to be re-circulated through the building, treated and stored in the lake turned out to be far too expensive. So, the building is connected to the water mains and the main drainage system. However, as I worked on the design, it became clear that the lake added to the appearance of the whole building. So, I have kept it in my design.'

Lizzy Johnson said, 'That is fascinating. When we spoke previously, you mentioned an interesting new pop-group whose songs have helped you think clearly about your design and indeed to realise that it was complete.'

Jake smiled as he replied, 'Yes, the group is called *The Good*

Time Girls and some of their numbers seem to me to have a very deep meaning. One of their songs in particular, which is called *Creative Imaginations,* made me recognise that my design begins with nature, represented by the lake. Then emerging from nature is humanity, represented by the human scale of the classical design of the external walls of the five blocks. Finally, humanity rises to great artistic and creative levels which I hope is represented by the design of the roof. I feel that the three elements fit together and will cause people to think about the world we all inhabit and work and play in.'

Lizzy Johnson said, 'That is a strong note on which to end; and it provides a wonderful introduction to our final item which is a performance of *Creative Imaginations* by *The Good Time Girls.*'

Lizzy Johnson stood up and shook Jake's hand as she said, 'That went extremely well. I am sure we have everything we need for this evening broadcast but let me just check with our producer. I will get someone to bring you a cup of tea and be back in about twenty minutes.'

When Lizzy Johnson returned, she looked very pleased and told Jake that they had everything they needed, and he could go. Jake asked if *The Good Time Girls* were in the studio. Lizzy Johnson said that as far as she knew they were coming in later.

Jake left the studio feeling pleased with how he had explained his design but disappointed that he did not know where Linda was. He decided that she would probably be busy, and, in any case, he would see her at the golf club that evening; so, he decided to go home. That evening he sat with his parents to watch the six o'clock news on television. As the programme neared its conclusion, Lizzy Johnson appeared on the screen to say, 'One of the most exciting buildings in Europe is planned to be built in

Swindon.'

Then a three-dimensional image of Jake's design for the university science building appeared as Lizzy Johnson continued, 'This remarkable design is the work of a young architect, Jake Brown, who I interviewed about his work this afternoon.'

Then Jake appeared on the screen and Lizzy Johnson began the interview. As Jake watched himself, he felt happy with his answers to the Architectural Correspondent's questions. As she asked each one, different images of his design appeared and then as he answered, he reappeared on the television. As he finished his final answer in which he mentioned *The Good Time Girls,* Lizzy Johnson reappeared and said, 'We are very pleased to be able to finish tonight's programme with the group that Jake mentioned, *The Good Time Girls.* They are a new group who look likely to become highly successful in the near future.'

Then the group appeared and performed *Creative Imaginations,* the song that Jake had mentioned. They had clearly given a lot of attention to their appearance and to the performance of the number. As the programme finished, Jake's father said, 'We are so proud of you Jake. You looked completely at home on television and your design is amazing. I think it will come to be seen as one of Britain's greatest buildings. You also have surprisingly good taste in popular music. How did you come to know *The Good Time Girls*?'

Jake laughed and his mother gave him a hug and said she agreed with everything Jake's father had just said. She then repeated his question, 'How do you know *The Good Time Girls*?'

Jake explained that the group had performed at the dinner the cricket club had on Monday evening. He added, 'I talked to one of girls afterwards and I hope to see her again at the golf-club dinner this evening. In fact, that is the main reason I am going; and I should get ready because it's a dinner jacket affair.'

As Jake was getting ready for the golf-club dinner, his phone rang. It was John Brentford, the partner he worked with. John Brentford said, 'Jake, I have just watched the news report about your design. It went very well. You are to be congratulated.'

Jake thanked him and John Brentford continued, 'You are very likely to get attractive offers from other architectural practices as a result of them seeing your design and the publicity it has attracted. Please, let me know before you make any decision about any offer you get. The partners have a meeting on Friday, and I feel sure they will want to discuss your future with the firm.'

Jake again thanked him and promised to let him know if any other practice contacted him. As he finished the call from John Brentford, Jake's phone rang again. It was Jane. She said, 'Jake, I have just seen you on television. You looked really good, and your design for the university building looked amazing. I felt so proud of you and can't wait to see you again as soon as the bank's training course finishes.'

Jake asked how the course was working out; and Jane said that it was interesting, and she was learning a lot about all the various activities the bank was involved in and it was teaching her how to deal with major customers which she had not really done during her normal work at the bank in Swindon. She paused at this point but then continued, 'The people running the training course make dealing with major customers seem very interesting. They started by giving me a file describing a customer who has various financial problems. They give me fifteen minutes to study the file and then one of the training people acts the part of the customer coming into the bank to discuss their situation. I play the part of the bank manager and deal with their requests for help. Then when I have finished the discussion with the customer, the trainer comments on how well I did and suggests any changes to my approach that he thinks I should make. I have already done three of these sessions and I have learnt a lot.'

Jake said that all sounded interesting and then he told Jane about the phone call with John Brentford. She sounded interested and said, 'I think the partner is right, you are very likely to get a number of interesting offers. Some of things I am learning on this course may well be relevant to any decisions you make about your future. I will be happy to discuss all this with you when we meet on Saturday week.'

Jake said, 'We did talk about me coming out to your home after our cricket match in Swindon. Is that still okay?'

'The course ends at lunch time on the Saturday, and I will need to get home and sort out my clothes and things. So, if you come out to my home at about eight, that will be fine.'

Jane then added that she was already looking forward to seeing Jake again. As Jake finished the call, his phone rang again. When he answered, a woman said, 'I am Sir Andrew Zain's personal assistant, and he has asked me to contact you as he saw your design for the university building on television and would like to discuss it with you.'

Jake knew that Sir Andrew Zain was probably the most famous architect currently working in London. It would be great to talk with him; and so, with very little thought, Jake agreed to meet Sir Andrew on Saturday morning in London. Sir Andrew Zain's personal assistant said that she would send Jake an email with full details of where they would meet. Jake asked if the meeting could be early enough for him to get back to Cirencester in time to play cricket on Saturday afternoon. The personal assistant agreed that the meeting could be at nine thirty and would take no more than an hour.

Jake turned his phone off and concentrated on getting ready to go to the golf-club. When he arrived, he was surprised by the number of cars in the car park. When he got inside the club house, he was surprised at how big the dining room was and he had to ask several people where Henry Roberts' table was. Eventually he found it right in front of what was obviously the stage. Henry Roberts was already there, and he introduced Jake to his wife and the other people around the table. Jake recognised two of the men as directors of local companies.

Jake found that he was sat between Henry Robert's wife and a man who introduced himself as Stanley James and explained that he was a director of the firm that owned the hotel where Linda and the rest of *The Good Time Girls* had been staying. Jake said that he knew the hotel and thought it was the best hotel in Cirencester. Stanley James thanked him and said that he has seen the news programme that featured Jake that evening. He added, 'That was why I asked Henry if I could sit next to you because for some time now, I have been thinking that we need to increase the hotel's capacity. So, it would be very helpful if you could look at what might be possible . We need to expand but I need a professional view on the best way of creating more rooms. Would you be interested in looking round the hotel with me?'

Jake said, 'That is very flattering of you. I can probably manage sometime next week. What is the best way of getting in touch with you?'

Stanley James gave Jake his card and suggested that he should phone and arrange when he could look round the hotel. He added, 'We have the car parking areas at the back of the hotel, and we own the building next to the hotel. Currently it is a successful clothes shop, but the current lease does not have long to run, and, in any case, there is quite a lot of under-used space on both the upper floors.'

Jake said it would be interesting to think about the possibilities. They chatted about various ideas for some time which helped Jake to understand what Stanley James wanted. As he sat thinking about hotels, Henry Robert's wife interrupted his thoughts by saying that she had been listening to their conversation and added that she thought it is a very stylish hotel and she felt it was important for Cirencester to keep the essential character of the hotel. Jake turned towards Henry Robert's wife and was immediately surprised by how attractive and how young she looked. He was surprised because he was sure that Henry Roberts was well into his fifties. She smiled at Jake and asked him what other buildings he was working on at present. He had now turned so he was looking straight at her as he explained that he had more work to do on the university science building. He then added that he was supervising the construction of a factory and an office block on the industrial estate in Swindon. As they chatted, Jake remembered that a few years ago, when he was in the Cirencester second eleven, there had been talk about Henry Robert having an affair with his secretary and then getting a divorce. Jake thought that if this was his secretary, he could understand any man falling for her. He was certainly enjoying talking to her. It suddenly occurred to him that he didn't know her name. So, he asked her what he should call her.

She smiled at the obvious effect she was having on Jake and said, 'You can call me Goldie. That is what my friends call me; I'm not sure why, but the name has just stuck.'

'That certainly reflects your beautiful hair; but I guess that is not your actual name.'

Goldie laughed and said, 'No, my actual name is Jennifer Roberts; but I like being called Goldie.'

She then changed the subject, 'When Henry was telling me about tonight, he said that you were interested in one of *The Good Time Girls*. I can understand that; they are all attractive. I have seen them perform at several dinners that Henry has taken me to. Which one do you know?'

Jake said, 'She's called Linda James. I have only just met her, but she is interesting. She told me how she helps write some of the songs they perform.'

'Yes, you mentioned *Creative Imaginations* during your television interview. Was she involved in writing that?'

Jake nodded, 'She has a degree in psychology and that obviously helps her add real meaning to the songs she writes. That particular song did seem to reflect similar ideas to those I used in describing my design for the university building during the television interview.'

Jake and Goldie continued to chat through the dinner until a man appeared on the stage to announce that it was time for the first performance by *The Good Time Girls*. The room fell silent, the curtains in front of the stage opened and the group began playing a lively number. Linda was dancing and singing just a few metres in front of Jake wearing a costume that was more revealing than any of those he had seen her in before. She looked amazing and seemed to be singing and dancing just for him.

The group performed for some twenty minutes and then the man who had introduced them came back onto the stage to thank the group for a remarkable performance and explain that it was now time to finish dinner and the group would be back for their main performance later. Goldie turned to Jake and said, 'They are very good. Which of the girls is the one you know?'

Jake told her and she nodded as she said, 'Linda is beautiful. I can understand why you are interested in her.'

Stanley James had obviously over-heard their conversation and joined in to say that the group were staying at his hotel, and they had asked him to arrange a late supper for them when they returned to the hotel. He added that he would be happy for Jake to join them if he wanted to. He explained that he had arranged for the group to be taken from the golf club to the hotel in a small bus after their second performance. Jake thanked him and said, 'I will certainly call in and congratulate Linda and the rest of the group on their exciting performance.'

As a result, Jake arrived at the hotel just after the group had started the informal supper that the hotel had arranged for them. Linda saw him as soon as he walked in and came to meet him. 'Hello, Jake. I'm pleased to see you. Did you enjoy our performances at the golf club?'

Jake smiled and replied, 'I think everyone there enjoyed your performances. You looked amazing and the group's singing and dancing is really good. Now you have been on television, I think you have an exciting future.'

Linda asked if he wanted anything to eat but Jake said that the dinner at the golf club had been very good, but he would like something to drink. She asked a waiter to get Jake a glass of the red wine and brought her supper and glass of white wine over to an empty table. She said, 'The whole group is very grateful to you for mentioning us on television and getting us included in the item about your great design. Apparently, we have already been approached by a smart nightclub in London who want to discuss the possibility of us performing there. This is exactly the kind of thing we need to build our reputation.'

Jake nodded as he said, 'The television broadcast may have

worked for me as well. I have a meeting with one of the UK's best architects on Saturday morning; and his practice is based in London which is where we are meeting.'

They both had another drink of their wine and then Linda said that she needed to check something. She went over to the guitarist who Jake understood was the group's leader, spoke to him and then returned. 'We don't have anything booked for Friday evening. So, we could both go to London and stay the night. That way you will be sure to get to your meeting on time.'

'Where would we stay in London?'

'You said that your meeting is in Mayfair and I know a comfortable hotel in Soho. That would leave you with an interesting ten-minute walk after breakfast. I will need to get back to Birmingham and you said that you have a cricket match to get back to; but we could have a good time in London on Friday evening. What do you think?'

Jake smiled broadly and said, 'Go ahead and book the hotel. I am already looking forward to Friday evening.'

'That's great, I'll send you details of the hotel and see you there as early as you can get up to London after work. Now, I need to sleep, it has been a busy day and the rest of the group want us all to get back to Birmingham early tomorrow. So, I will see you on Friday.'

Linda then kissed Jake and said, 'Good-night my lovely man. I'm already looking forward to Friday evening.'

Jake wandered back to his car with his mind full of just how beautiful Linda was; and wondering if she would book one room or two at the hotel. These thoughts were probably responsible for Jake waking early next morning. As a result, he was in the office early to make a start on the working drawings for the university science building. He began by discussing his design with the firm's senior draughtsman, Joe Davis, so they could develop a plan for producing all the working drawings. Joe was happy to work with the drawings that Jake had already produced for the overall design but explained that he needed Jake to concentrate on designing all the details of the building. He emphasised this by saying, 'The detail at the edge of the roof needs thinking about carefully. I will also need your ideas for the details around the windows and external doors. Internally, the laboratories and lecture theatres look impressive, but I need your ideas on all the internal details. Anyway, I am ready to make a start based on your sketch plans of the design and I suggest we meet again tomorrow and check that we are getting it right.'

Jake had an unusually relaxed Thursday and Friday. He enjoyed sketching the details of his design to guide the draughtsmen as they produced the working drawings for the university science building. He thought Thursday's net practice and the selection meeting had gone well. As a result, he felt very happy as he and Linda met in London on Friday evening at the hotel that Linda had booked. Jake immediately noticed that they had adjacent rooms and they both had double beds. Linda let Jake choose which room he wanted and said that they should go to a nightclub in Mayfair where a group was performing that was similar to *The Good Time Girls*. She explained, 'I may learn something useful that helps us when we perform in a London club.'

Jake was very impressed with the nightclub. It was stylish, comfortable and strangely sexy. They had a table which gave them a good view of the stage where a group were playing straight-forward dance music. They ordered drinks and told the waiter that they wanted dinner but first, they would have a couple of dances. Not surprisingly, Linda was an accomplished dancer, but Jake felt he was moving well as they danced together. The evening continued happily, dinner was good, and the group played tunes that were ideal to dance to. As they finished their dinner, the group that Linda had wanted to see came onto the stage. There were four musicians and three tall, attractive women who moved suggestively as they sang. Jake decided that they were good, but *The Good Time Girls* were better. Their songs had more interesting words and he thought most of their tunes were better than the group at the nightclub. So, when Linda asked him what he thought of the group, he said, 'They are good; but I really do think that your group is better. Your songs are more interesting, you dance more energetically, and you are more beautiful.'

Linda laughed, 'I won't argue with that judgement. I do think we are good enough to appear at clubs like this one. I wonder if we could find the manager and discuss that possibility.'

'Let's try. I'll ask the waiter.'

Jake called the waiter over and explained that Linda was a member of *The Good Time Girls* who had been featured on television that week and she would like to talk to the manager about the possibility of the group performing at this excellent nightclub. The waiter said he would tell the manager. Some ten minutes later, a woman in a stylish evening dress came over to their table, pulled a chair from the next table and sat down. She smiled at Linda and Jake as she said, 'Thank you for coming to our club. I hope you are having an enjoyable evening. Your waiter tells me that you want to discuss something.'

Linda said, 'I'm Linda James, and this is my friend Jake Brown who is an architect. I am a member of a group that we call *The Good Time Girls*. I think we have reached a level of performance where you would be happy to have us appear here at your club. We were featured on a television news item that was mainly about Jake's design for a new building in Swindon which apparently is already being seen as great architecture. He was interviewed for the television news item and mentioned us, as he has seen us perform several times. Anyway, the news item finished with a recording of one of our best songs. It's called *Creative Imaginations* and I have a copy of the news item on my phone if you would like to see it.'

Linda found the item on her phone and handed it to the manager. She watched it carefully and then scrolled back to watch *The Good Time Girls* again. Then she handed Linda's phone back to her and said, 'I would like to see the group perform but you are good; and I like the idea of having you perform here. You may be interested to know that this club is part of a chain of nightclubs. We have seven clubs, four in London, one in Birmingham, one in Manchester and one in Bristol.'

Linda said, 'I didn't know this was part of a chain. Our group is based in Birmingham. Which is your club in Birmingham?'

The manager told her, and Linda said, 'We haven't performed there but we do perform at several clubs in the city fairly regularly.'

The manager said, 'I have to be in Birmingham on Wednesday next week. Why don't you come with the rest of your group to our club on Wednesday afternoon? I could watch you perform live and if you are as good as you looked on that television programme, we could talk about working together.'

Linda had a quick look at her diary on her phone and said, 'That should be fine. We could arrive at say two thirty, do a performance and then talk about where we go from there.'

The manager was about to go but she hesitated and then looked at Jake and asked, 'Did the television programme say that you were the architect responsible for that university building in Swindon?'

Jake confirmed that it was indeed his design and the manager said, 'That is interesting. The club in Birmingham needs to be up-dated. Would that be of interest to you?'

'You mean you might like me to do a new design for your nightclub?'

'Yes.'

'I will try to come to your club in Birmingham at the same time as *The Good Time Girls* next Wednesday; if that is helpful.'

This was agreed and the manager stood up but then paused and said, 'By the way my name is Ruby James. This is my business card in case you need to get in touch with me before Wednesday. I look forward to seeing you both again.'

Linda leaned towards Jake and kissed him. 'Thank you for helping arrange a meeting with Ruby James. I must tell the others what is happening.'

Linda then sent a message to all the other members of *The Good Time Girls* and suggested to Jake that they have one more dance before they walked back to their hotel. She added, 'You have an important meeting in the morning. So, you should get a good night's sleep.'

Jake had not been thinking about his meeting with Sir Andrew Zain, but he could see the sense in what Linda was suggesting. When they reached the hotel and walked up to their adjacent rooms, Jake wondered what might happen now. Linda answered his unspoken question by saying, 'Jake, thank you for a lovely evening. Now, you need a good night's sleep to make sure you are ready for tomorrow's meeting. So, I will see you at breakfast. Let's say at about eight o'clock.'

With that she kissed Jake and went into her room. Jake felt

somewhat disappointed but as he went into his room, he decided that Linda was being very sensible. Next morning, they spent very little time over breakfast, mainly because Jake was thinking about his meeting with Sir Andrew Zain. As soon as he finished his coffee and toast, Jake said he needed to check out and make sure he got to his meeting on time, Linda agreed and added, 'I'll see you in Birmingham on Wednesday. I am already looking forward to that. You are a lovely man.'

Jake gave her a quick kiss and then hurried up to his room. As he packed his bag and checked out, his mind was filled with thoughts about his design for the university science building and how he should describe it to the man who was without any doubt one of the world's greatest living architects.

Chapter 7

Jake arrived at Sir Andrew Zain's office on the Saturday morning a few minutes early to find Sir Andrew waiting for him. Sir Andrew was a tall, impressive man who looked as if he was in his early sixties. He had built an international reputation as one of Britain's greatest architects by producing stylish designs for important buildings that were widely admired by other architects and the media.

He welcomed Jake and suggested they sit in his design studio. Sir Andrew began, 'Jake Brown, I'm very pleased to meet you. I watched the news item on television earlier this week in which you described your design for the university science building in Swindon. I was very impressed by your design and also by the way you described it. So, would you like to begin by describing your thinking as you created the design.'

Jake explained that he had the key information about the building on his computer which he opened and began by showing Sir Andrew the list of internal accommodation the university had provided. He then described how he decided the spaces formed five distinct groups and that his design should reflect this by arranging the building in five blocks. Then he showed Sir Andrew his drawings of the overall design.

They discussed these for some time and then Sir Andrew asked what stage the project had reached. Jake said, 'The university has decided to go ahead with the project. They made this decision just this week and I have started work on the detailed information needed by our firm's draughtsmen to produce the working drawings. I can show you my drawings of the key details that I produced on Thursday and Friday.'

Sir Andrew studied his drawings of the main details of Jake's design carefully and then said, 'I am really impressed with the way the details reflect the modern appearance of the roof but at the same time are consistent with the classical design of the main body of the five blocks. You could well be developing a truly original style of architecture.'

Sir Andrew then turned away for Jake's computer and looking very thoughtful, he asked, 'What is your relationship with the firm where you work?'

'I am employed by them as an architect. Following my appearance on television, the partner I work with did say that the partners were planning to discuss my future at their next meeting; but I don't know what they might have in mind.'

'Let me explain why I wanted to talk with you. My firm has three partners, including myself. We are all getting older, and we realise that we need to think about what happens to the firm when we retire. We have talented architects in the firm but at the moment, there is no-one who is likely to maintain the reputation that I have enjoyed. That is why I was excited when I saw your design on television. Now that we have met and discussed your ideas, I am even more convinced that you have the creativity and skills needed to create the outstanding architecture needed to maintain the firm's reputation. So, I would like to discuss how we might work together.'

Jake was clearly delighted by this compliment from a man, who he regarded as one of the greatest living architects. This was evident as he replied, 'Obviously I am flattered by that thought. Most of the projects the firm works on are fairly ordinary and don't really provide many opportunities for me to be really creative. The university building is by far the most significant project I have worked on, and it has been, by far, the most satisfying. I assume that your practice mainly works on really significant buildings, so the chance to work with you on some basis sounds like a wonderful opportunity.'

'Good, my thinking is that you may be right person to take the firm forward when I retire. I am impressed with your design; and also, by the way you describe your thinking. Given all of that, I would like to work with you for say six months and then decide if you are indeed the right person to bring into the partnership to ensure its long-term future.'

Jake took a deep breath and said, 'I assume that I would be employed by you for the six months? Also, I was thinking that I don't know London very well, but I know it is likely to be expensive to live here and the journey from Cirencester, which is where I live, takes quite a long time each way. I guess the point is that working with you would mean a fairly big change of lifestyle for me; and so, I need to understand how it would work.'

Sir Andrew smiled, 'Of course. I should have said that we can provide accommodation for you. We own several apartments here in Mayfair and one of these is empty at the moment and we will be very happy for you to use it. It is a stylish, two-bedroom apartment which is fully furnished. Living there for the six months would allow you to really get to know London; and we can afford to pay you a salary that will enable you to fully explore all that London has to offer. I will get the firm's administrator to send you a formal offer, but the point is that I want you to have every opportunity to do your best work; and I really hope this all works out and that you are indeed the new partner we are looking for.'

Jake looked at Sir Andrew and then said, 'This is obviously an amazing opportunity, and my instinct is to just say yes; but I realise that I need to see your formal offer and think about all the implications of what will be a major change in my life. I do want to thank you for everything you have said about me and my work. I don't think I have ever felt happier; and I really do hope this all works out as you described.'

Jake gave Sir Andrew his contact details and was getting ready to leave when Sir Andrew asked, 'One thing I wanted to discuss with you was your reasons for including the solar panels and wind turbines in your design for the university building.'

Jake explained, 'I think it was because the building will house the university science departments that made me think it should be a sustainable building. As it happens this is something that I think should be considered for all new buildings. I enjoyed working with the companies that make the sustainable technology that we plan to use in the building. They were very helpful in working out innovations that helped me incorporate the solar panels and turbines in a way that was consistent with my design. I did want to make the building self-sufficient in water. That is why I included the lake, but all the currently available technology needed to treat the water as it circulates through the building and the lake is too big and too expensive to include in the project. This may be something that I can work on in future designs.'

Sir Andrew listened very carefully to Jake's explanation and then said, 'All of the issues you mentioned are really important. I have a very important project under discussion at the moment, which amongst other things explores the whole issue of human sustainability.'

Sir Andrew paused and looked hard at Jake. Then he

continued, 'What I am about to tell you is highly confidential, and you must not mention anything about it to anyone else. My great secret is that I am working with the government and a group of companies to plan the building of a new town which provides as close to an ideal life as we can envisage. As you might guess, sustainability is a key feature of what is required. Your interest in this vital issue has helped convince me that you may well be the right person to ensure this practice's future. But that is getting ahead of ourselves. I will leave you to think about our formal offer, which I will make sure you get early next week. Meanwhile, Jake, I look forward to working with you just as soon as everything can be arranged.'

As he travelled back to Cirencester, Jake's mind was churning with thoughts about living in London, working with Sir Andrew Zain, and being involved in designing an ideal new town. As the train passed through Reading, Jake's phone rang. It was Jane who said she had been trying to contact him earlier, but she had not been able to make contact with his phone. Jake explained what he had been doing and why he had turned his phone off. Jane was excited as she said, 'That is amazing. It's great that you will be working in London. I am enjoying the training course, and this has made me look at where there are opportunities for assistant manager jobs. Most of the really interesting ones are in London and I have been wondering how that would affect our relationship but if you are also working in London, that is ideal.'

Jake described his meeting with Sir Andrew Zain which made Jane even more excited. As Jake finished his description she said, 'So you will have a two-bedroom apartment in the heart of London. I will be very happy to use the other bedroom and we can live together. This is fate working for us. Jake, I can't wait to see you again. The course is pretty full on; so, I will be busy until next Saturday when we have arranged to meet after your cricket match against Swindon. I am really looking forward to seeing you, we have so much to talk about.'

Jake agreed and as they ended the call, he said, 'Our match on Sunday is one that we should win easily. I could let Bill Stones, the vice-captain, have a go at captaining the team on the Sunday and we can spend the day together if you like?'

Jane agreed and added, 'We can talk about what we do on Sunday when we meet Saturday evening. Now, I must go, there is so much to do on this course. I am looking forward to seeing you on Saturday. Let me know what you decide to do about Sir Andrew Zain's offer. Now, I must get back to work.'

Jake's head was now filled with thoughts about his relationships with Jane and Linda. He had plans to meet both of them over the next week, but which did he want as his girlfriend? Was it so wrong to have two girlfriends? Did he want to share his London apartment, assuming he accepted Sir Andrew's offer, with Jane? Linda had said that she hoped *The Good Time Girls* would get more work in London, now they had been on television, and Jake guessed that she would be pleased to use the spare bedroom.

When he got back to Cirencester, it was almost lunchtime. His mother had prepared a salad and some cold meat as she knew this was his favourite meal before an afternoon cricket match. Jake thanked her and told his parents about his discussion with Sir Andrew Zain. His mother said, 'So, you may well be leaving home. I guess it is about time. We did get used to you not being here when you were at university, and it will be nice to have somewhere to stay in London.'

His father added, 'I agree. London is a great city to visit.

There are several shows on at London theatres just now that we would like to see. It could be good for all of us. I must say it sounds as if you have a great opportunity to work with one of this country's best architects. We are very proud of you.'

As Jake got ready to go to the cricket ground, he decided that he must put all thoughts about Sir Andrew Zain, London and Linda and Jane out of his mind and concentrate on captaining the team in what he expected to be a tough match. They were playing Bath, one of the very best teams on their fixture list. The match did not start well for Cirencester. Jake lost the toss and the Bath captain decided to bat first. Their opening batsmen were both very accomplished players and they dealt fairly comfortable with everything Jake tried. After an hour, in which Jake tried all his bowlers, Bath had scored fifty-eight runs and not lost any wickets. Jake realised that he was thinking about other things too much and he needed to concentrate. He asked the fastest of his two opening bowlers to bowl again. Specifically, he asked him to bowl as fast as he could outside the off stump and to vary the way he held the seam of the ball. Jake then set a field with only two fielders on the leg side and both of them were behind the stumps. He had three slip fielders and two more fielders some five metres in from the boundary behind them. The rest of the fielders were in front of the batsman on the off-side.

The Bath batsman looked puzzled by the field placings and just allowed the first four balls of the fast bowler's over to pass through to the wicket-keeper. He tried to do the same with the fifth ball but it pitched on the seam in such a way that it came back towards the stumps and hit the off stump. The whole team were delighted, and they all congratulated the bowler. Jake altered the field for the new batsman and included two fielders right in front of him. Then he asked the bowler to bowl at the stumps. While all this was going on Bath's two batsmen were deep in conversation. When the game restarted, the bowler bowled what was probably the best ball of the match so far and the new batsman edged it into the slips where it was caught.

This one over changed the whole feel of the match and Jake kept the pressure on Bath by setting various attacking fields and getting all his bowlers to bowl in slightly unusual ways. The result was that at tea-time, Bath were one hundred and twenty-six for eight. The Cirencester team enjoyed their tea and were not surprised when Bath's captain decided to bat on after tea. It took three more overs to get the last two wickets and Bath scored just four more runs. So, with a target of one hundred and thirty-one runs, Cirencester went in to bat with only an hour and fifty minutes to get the runs. Ben Stanley, the new opening batsman clearly recognised the opportunity to show that it was the right decision to bring him into the team. He encouraged his fellow opening batsman, Ton Stevens, to bat defensively but to score singles whenever he could. That way Ben Stanley faced most of the bowling and demonstrated what an excellent batsman he was. Without taking any obvious risks, he hit the ball again and again into gaps between the fielders, regularly scoring twos and fours. Jake had decided that he would bat at number six, and he did not have to go in to bat until, with just fifteen minutes to go to the end of play, Cirencester were a hundred and eight for four.

Jake decided to settle the match by attacking the bowling. He advanced down the wicket to play the first ball he faced and hit it straight back past the bowler for four. He guessed the bowler would drop the next ball short, so, he played back in his crease and pulled the ball over the leg-side boundary for six. That was the last ball of the over and he and Ben Stanley comfortable scored the last thirteen runs to win the match by six wickets. Ben

Stanley had scored seventy-six runs and Jake insisted that he walked into the pavilion first to enthusiastic applause from the rest of the team and the hundred or so spectators who regularly came to watch Cirencester's cricket team.

As they got changed in the dressing room, Ben Stanley said to Jake, 'I saw you on television earlier in the week. That is an exciting building you have designed for the university. I would love to be involved in building it. Do you think there is any chance that the university would invite my firm to bid for the work?'

Jake nodded and thanked Ben for his kind words about the design and then said, 'I don't get involved in selecting contractors, but I can give you the contact details for the Vice-Chancellor and the Buildings Officer.'

Ben looked thoughtful and then smiled at Jake as he responded, 'I will talk about this with my firm's manager. I know he is keen for the firm to grow. That is one of the reasons the firm decided to employ me; and I want to show them that they made a good decision. Perhaps you could let me look at the drawings and I can see what will be involved in the construction. Is that possible?'

Jake wanted to make sure that he kept Ben Stanley in the cricket team, so, he said, 'I've got the drawings on my computer and I'm pretty sure it's in my car. So, you could have a look before we go to the pub to celebrate a great win.'

'I walked here this afternoon, so, if you like you could give me a lift to pub, and I can look at the drawings. If that's okay?'

Jake agreed and once they were both dressed, Jake thanked the rest of the team for a great win and hoped to see them all in the pub. Then he told Ben Stanley that he was ready to go and once they were in his car, Jake opened his computer and found the drawings. Ben Stanley then explained that the feature of Jake's design that caught his attention was the lake. He explained, 'I worked on a project for a new building just on the outskirts of Birmingham some three years ago that included a lake. The building was an office block and only a small part of it had foundations under the lake; but I learnt a lot about the kind of materials needed to provide foundations which are permanently in water. Also, I was surprised at how careful we had to be to ensure the lake didn't leak. This all made me think that I could well be the right person to project manage the university building that you have designed.'

'That's interesting. Is your company big enough to take on what is a fairly large project?'

'Yes, we are working on several big developments at the moment. All I'm saying is that I would be pleased if the company I work for is invited to bid for the contract to build your design. Could you put in a good word for us?'

Jake was not usually involved in discussing with clients who should be invited to bid for the construction work, but he wanted to keep Ben Stanley happy, so, he said, 'I will talk to the partner in our firm who will be advising the client on the arrangements needed to get the building constructed. Can you send me some information about your firm? Details of its financial situation, similar projects it has undertaken and a note of your comments about constructing the lake and the building foundations under water. This will all help me convince the partner to mention you to the client.'

Ben Stanley looked pleased as he thanked Jake and promised to bring the information Jake needed to the match on Sunday. The evening in the pub, celebrating an impressive win against one of the very best teams that Cirencester played was highly enjoyable.

This mood continued next day as Cirencester comfortably beat the village team they always played against on the Sunday after their tough match with Bath. As Jake went to bed that evening, he was thinking about his meeting with Sir Andrew Zain and trying to decide what he should tell John Brentford, the partner in his firm that he worked with. He knew the possibility that Sir Andrew might offer him a partnership in six-month's time was almost certainly the biggest opportunity he would ever have. Every young architect in the country would leap as such an honour. However, John Brentford and the rest of the firm had treated him well throughout his years of training and university; and they were giving him real opportunities including particularly designing the university science block. Also, there was a real chance that they would invite him to become a partner in the firm where he could build his own reputation rather than work in Sir Andrew's shadow.

Gradually Jake fell asleep but when he woke in the morning and drove in to work, he was no clearer about the best way forward for his career. As he went into his office, he was met by John Brentford who was clearly excited as he said, 'Jake, the Vice-Chancellor phoned first thing this morning and told me that he has been given the money by a large international company to develop a complete university campus. More than that the company want you to design all the buildings on the campus and create the most beautiful university in the country. What do you think? This is a great opportunity.'

John Brentford was obviously puzzled by Jake's immediate reaction. Jake looked at John Brentford and was clearly struggling to decide what to say. Eventually he said, 'You are right, it is a great opportunity. I seem to be drowning in opportunities. The man who owns the best hotel in Cirencester wants me to advise him on the best way of expanding his hotel, and a nightclub chain want to me to re-design their nightclub in Birmingham and I have agreed to look at it on Wednesday. But more importantly than any of that, I met Sir Andrew Zain over the weekend, and he wants to employ me to work with him over the next six months on the design of a new town up north. He also said that if that goes well, he intends making me a partner in his practice. He is going to send me the formal offer which, in addition to all the usual things in an employment contract, will include me having the use of an apartment in central London.'

John Brentford sat down. Then very slowly he said, 'I was not sure what to tell you, but the partners met over the weekend to discuss making you a partner in the practice. We plan to have a formal discussion about this and if we are all agreed, we will be offering you a partnership later this week.'

Jake smiled and shook his head. 'This is all too much to take in. Sir Andrew is a great architect, and it would be ridiculous not to take the opportunity of working with him. But this practice has treated me well and I know how much you helped me make a success of my training and university education. Then there is the fact that I like living in Cirencester. I am captain of the cricket team's first eleven and we are having a great season. I don't know London very well, but it is a world-class city and who knows what opportunities it might provide. I have too much to think about and I do want to make sure the working drawings for the university science building are right. What should I do?'

'You have the potential to be a great architect and the practice want to give you every opportunity to develop your talent and ability. You need time to think what is best for you. I suggest you look at the opportunities to work on the hotel in Cirencester and the nightclub in Birmingham and think carefully about the formal offer from Sir Andrew Zain. At the same time make sure the working drawings for the science block are right. That is a very important project and the building, when it's finished, it will have a big influence on your reputation. Obviously, the chance to design a whole university campus is extraordinary; and I have to admit the chance to help design a whole new town is a great opportunity. So, you need to think; and the partners would like to talk with you, let's say on Thursday afternoon. In the meantime, you have important things to do this week, so, I suggest you get on with them and let me know where you plan to be each day.'

Jake nodded and thanked John Brentford and then added, 'You are being very helpful and that is important to me. I will not make any firm decisions about Sir Andrew's offer until I have discussed them with you.'

Jake began working on the final design details of the university science building and checking the working drawings that the draftsmen had completed. He then remembered to phone Stanley James and arrange to look round the hotel in Cirencester that afternoon. In fact, he arranged to have lunch at the hotel and then look at the hotel with Stanley James. As he finished that call, he noticed an email from Sir Andrew Zain's practice. It set out the terms and conditions that Sir Andrew was offering him for the six months trial period they had talked about on Saturday. Jake was delighted with the salary he was being offered which was almost fifty percent higher than he got at present and in addition he had the use of the apartment without there being any rent or other costs for him to pay. Jake knew that London was a far more expensive place to live than Cirencester but by any standards this was a remarkably generous offer.

Jake sat looking at his computer screen, but his thoughts

were dominated by the realisation that his life was about to change. He could not help mentioning this to Stanley James as they had lunch together at the hotel. Stanley smiled at Jake's obvious excitement and then explained how he approached difficult decisions. He concluded by saying, 'In summary, my view is that you should set a deadline by which you will make a decision, and that should be in one- or two-days' time. Then once you have made your decision, concentrate all your thoughts and effort on making a success of whatever it is you have decided on.'

Jake thanked him and said that this sounded like very good advice. He then added that it probably made good sense to decide about his future career on Thursday evening as he was having a discussion about his future with the firm's partners that afternoon. Stanley James smiled and said, 'That sounds like a good plan. I hope you manage to stick to your deadline.'

They then concentrated on discussing Stanley James' ideas for the hotel. Stanley explained that he had been involved with this hotel for less than two years and it was now clear that it needed more bedrooms to make the finances work out. He also said that he had decided that the main public spaces needed to be up-graded and re-decorated to a higher standard than they were at present. Stanley had detailed drawings of the existing hotel and the building next door that was currently used as a clothes shop. He used the floor plans to explain to Jake that at some time in the past, the hotel had converted every third bedroom into two bathrooms which were then joined to the two adjacent bedrooms. He concluded, 'The resulting bathrooms are ridiculously large and waste a lot of space. Many modern hotels have bedrooms that include a small shower room. By using the best modern sanitary fittings, these could be fitted into all the original bedrooms. That way the hotel would have almost fifty percent more rooms within the existing building. The same approach could be continued into the floors over the existing shop, providing another dozen bedrooms. At the moment, I think we should keep the ground floor as a shop. It's a good quality part of the Cirencester High Street, but any different ideas you have will be welcome.'

Then Stanley James used the drawings to outline an area of the current car parking area that could be developed to provide about twenty bedrooms with separate bathrooms. He explained that he saw this as a luxury annex where the hotel could charge higher prices or reward loyal customers. He finished by saying, 'We can use this space and still provide all the car parking we need by installing a mechanised multi-story car park in the remaining part of the existing car park. I have had these constructed at two other hotels and they work well. They have what is really a small car lift linked to a moving floor that takes the customers' cars to where-ever there is a vacant space in the multi-storey car park.'

Jake could see that Stanley James' plans were well thought out and said he would like to look round the hotel and then come back to him with a design. Jake felt he would have all the information he needed once he had looked round the hotel. Stanley James showed him round all the public rooms, the rooms used by the staff and several of the bedrooms. Then Jake spent some time outside looking at the front of the hotel. It was exceptionally attractive, Cotswold style, classical architecture. Jake had been aware of this fine building for as long as he could remember but this was the first time that he had really looked at all the details and really thought about the elegant proportions of the windows and the main front entrance. It was all exceptional and the interior spaces did not really match this quality.

As Jake walked home, he was thinking about the interior of the hotel and how he could make it match the quality of the front elevation. When he got home, he used the internet to look at images of great classical interiors. He was fascinated by all the wonderful detail and decoration in some of the world's great buildings but realised that it depended on a level of craftsmanship, and indeed artistry, that probably no longer existed or if it did would be incredibly time consuming and expensive. Could modern construction methods re-create the same quality of detail?

Jake thought about the details he had been working on for the university science building in Swindon. Could he develop these to reflect the quality and style of the hotel's front elevation? He began sketching as he tried to work out how modern architecture could include complex details and art. Jake could see he was developing bold ideas for the hotel's internal spaces; but what would his ideas cost? Was he going too far? Jake decided to sketch out his ideas in enough detail to enable the quantity surveyors to give him some idea of the likely costs. Then he could show his ideas to Stanley James.

Jake was getting excited by his design when his mother called to say it was dinner time. He had told her about his lunch at the hotel with Stanley James, so she had prepared a simple salad with some cold meat and new potatoes. As they all helped themselves, Jake's father asked him if he had made a decision about working with Sir Andrew Zain. Jake smiled as he said, 'It would be silly not to take the opportunity of working closely with one of the greatest architects. However, John Brentford hinted that the partners are thinking about offering me a partnership in the firm. The university have decided to make the science building I have designed for them the first stage of creating a whole new campus in Swindon; and they want me to design it. That seems to me to be too good an opportunity to turn down. If I get it right, the campus could come to be seen as a major example of modern architecture.'

Jake's father said, 'Presumably the university don't mind who you are working with. They want you to design the whole campus. So, you could work with Sir Andrew and design the university campus.'

Jake was clearly surprised by this thought, so, his father continued, 'Obviously there would be financial implications for your present practice if you joined Sir Andrew and took the work on the university campus with you. The firm have treated you well, giving you practical experience and money during the university vacations and now you are qualified, recognising your talent by giving you major design projects to work on. Maybe there is some way you could accept both opportunities by linking the two practices in some way. Why don't you talk to John Brentford and maybe the other partners about all of this?'

'I have no idea what is possible, and I don't know how Sir Andrew's practice is organized. But my understanding is that the partners in both the practices are close to the stage of their careers when they want to retire, and they see me as someone who could take over and keep their practice in business.'

Jake's father smiled as he continued, 'Assuming that is the case, you are in a strong position. You need to think what you would like to happen and then talk to both practices about what is possible; but the key is to make up your mind what you want.'

Jake laughed. 'You are right; and I have set myself the target of making up my mind by Thursday evening.'

'That is a good idea; but keep in mind the possibility that you may be able to work with both firms on some basis. If they both want you, maybe they can be brought together in some way. Many of the projects that I have worked on involved firms working in partnership with each other. You are in a strong position to get what you decide is the best arrangement for your future. Let me know when you have made a decision as I may be able to help work out the best way of getting what you want.'

This thought dominated Jake's mind as he did more work on his ideas for the hotel that evening and next day in the office. By mid-afternoon his ideas for improving the hotel had reached a point that he thought provided a reasonable basis for a preliminary cost estimate. He decided it was time to tell John Brentford about his progress and as he made sure he had all the relevant information to explain his ideas, he decided that it might also be a good time to mention his father's idea that he could somehow stay involved in the firm and, if things worked out well with Sir Andrew Zain, maybe the two firms could find some way to cooperate.

Chapter 8

Jake explained his design ideas for extending and improving the hotel in Cirencester to John Brentford, the partner in the Swindon practice he usually worked with, who asked a few routine questions to make sure he understood Jake's thinking. Then he said, 'You have made a good start. I can see that having the owner's detailed drawings of the existing building was a big help and your ideas all look good. I must say that I really like your ideas for the internal details. They really are an attractive take on classical Cotswold architecture. I will get the quantity surveyors to do a preliminary estimate and then we can discuss your design with the hotel owner.'

Jake thanked him and then said, 'I have been thinking about the meeting with the partners on Thursday. Designing a whole university campus is a very exciting opportunity and I enjoy working here; but working with Sir Andrew Zain maybe a once in a life-time opportunity to become a better architect. I was wondering if there is some-way that I can do both.'

'Do you mean have six months leave to work with Sir Andrew and then return here?'

Jake said, 'That would be the simplest arrangement.'

He then hesitated and then continued, 'I have the impression that the partners want me to be ready to take over the firm when they reach retirement age. Sir Andrew Zain hinted at the same thought as he and his partners are a similar age to you. I don't know which, if any of these opportunities, will actually happen, but the thought has occurred to me that maybe the two practices could be linked in some way so that I could do what all of you want. I know it's too early to be discussing any such idea, but can we at least keep all the possibilities on the table?'

John Brentford was clearly surprised as he said, 'Wow, that is quite a thought. There would be many advantages for us but what would Sir Andrew's practice get out of any such arrangement?'

Jake smiled as he replied, 'This is a strong, well organized local practice and it is growing. Being asked to design a whole new university campus is a major step forward. I am sure the university would be delighted if we could link that to Sir Andrew Zain. It would give them international publicity which would no doubt help attract international students. I don't know what strengths and weaknesses Sir Andrew's practice has but it is him that approached me, so he obviously has seen something in me that his practice needs for the future. I would be happy to spend the six months that Sir Andrew has offered me working with him in his practice. That will give me time to see how the two practices might work together for their joint benefit. Maybe the idea won't work, in which case I will need to make a choice, but I feel very reluctant to leave this practice. Maybe the partners' meeting on Thursday could discuss the various possibilities and then we can see where we are.'

John Brentford sat staring at Jake. Then he slowly nodded and said, 'I will think about this and discuss the various options with my partners on Thursday. You are going to Birmingham tomorrow but let's talk on Thursday morning so that I have your latest thoughts before the partners' meeting.'

'Thank you. That is very helpful, and it will certainly help focus my mind to talk with you on Thursday morning.'

John Brentford said he would get a cost estimate for the hotel alterations and give some more thought to the firm's future, so he was ready to talk with Jake on Thursday morning. He then smiled and said, 'It might be more appropriate to talk over lunch on Thursday. I'll book somewhere for say twelve-thirty if that suits you?'

As Jake drove home to Cirencester after work, he felt that he knew what he would be doing over the next six months or so. That evening he enjoyed the cricket club's net practice much more than he expected and felt he was batting and bowling well. Next morning, he had a careful look at Stanley James' hotel, took several photographs and made a series of notes about ways he could improve his initial design ideas. Then he drove up to Birmingham and checked into the hotel where Linda had suggested he should stay. He had just reached his room, when the phone rang. It was Linda who explained that she had asked the hotel receptionist to let her know when he arrived. They decided to have lunch together and plan the rest of the day.

Jake was waiting outside the hotel when Linda arrived. She was wearing a summer dress that Jake thought was delightfully revealing. It certainly helped make her look even more beautiful and sexy than Jake remembered. As they met, she gave Jake a long kiss and then said, 'It's lovely to see you again. One of my favourite restaurants for lunch is just across the road, down the street that has the clothes shop on the corner.'

The restaurant was small but very comfortable and Jake was surprised at the variety of food on the menu. He decided to have a meat pie with a salad and Linda choose a crab salad. They both started with a glass of wine that came with an interesting selection of nibbles. They were sat next to each other on a high-backed bench and Jake was very aware of Linda's leg resting against his own leg and just how much of her breasts he could see. Linda asked how his meeting with Sir Andrew Zain had worked out. Jake described his present dilemma and his current thoughts about the next six months. Linda listened carefully and then said, 'So, you are most likely to be working in London for at least the next six months?'

Jake agreed and she continued, 'Our group are talking about moving to London. Since you helped us get on television, we have had a number of interesting offers from nightclubs in London and also from a recording company that want to publish some of our songs. The recording studios are also in London. We know it is expensive to live in London but there are lots of advantages of being close to the nightclubs and the recording studio. Where will you live if you are working in London?'

Jake explained that the offer from Sir Andrew Zain included an apartment in the centre of London. Linda looked surprised as she asked, 'Do you mean you would get that for free? How many bedrooms does it have?'

Jake laughed, 'I am pretty sure Sir Andrew described it as a two-bedroom apartment. Why do you ask?'

Linda looked very hard at Jake as she said, 'I think you can work out my thinking. I need somewhere to live in London, and you will have a two-bedroom apartment.'

'So, you are suggesting we should live together?'

Linda leant closer to Jake, revealing even more of her breasts and said, 'That could make it a very interesting six months for both of us. Presumably at the end of that six months, if you decide to work with Sir Andrew Zain in London, you would still have the apartment?'

Jake mumbled, 'I don't know what will happen if I decide to move to London on a long-term basis.'

Linda looked very beautiful and was pressing her leg hard against his and leaning very close to him in a very revealing way. He could not resist the impulse to kiss her. She held Jake in the kiss for what seemed like several minutes; then as she released her hold on him, she smiled and said, 'We must discuss this further tonight after we finish at the nightclub. I understand that your hotel is very comfortable.'

At that moment, the waiter brought their lunch and Jake moved away from Linda with his mind racing with thoughts about this beautiful woman who was offering to live with him in London and seemed to be suggesting that she came to his hotel that evening. They both concentrated on their lunch for several minutes and then Linda asked, 'What are your immediate thoughts on my sharing your apartment in London?'

Jake stopped eating and looked at Linda. Then he replied, 'Assuming I decide to work in London, I will have an apartment with a spare bedroom. It makes sense to use it. Yes, I would be happy to share my apartment with you. I think you know that I have a girlfriend, but you are amazingly attractive, and I really like being with you. So, let's see how our lives develop from here. Is that okay with you?'

'Yes, let's see how things develop. You are a very attractive man, and I don't have a boyfriend at the moment; so, I am happy to spend time with you and see how things work out.'

Jake was not at all sure what he was agreeing to but as he concentrated on finishing his lunch, he began to feel very comfortable with life. Linda then said, 'The group have arranged to get to the club just before five o'clock. I think you are meeting the manager at that time. So, unless you have other things to do, we could take a walk round the Botanical Gardens. It's a nice day and who knows, they may give you some ideas for the university campus you have been asked to design.'

Jake agreed as he had no other plans. They drove to the gardens and Linda's suggestion that it might give him some ideas for the university campus meant that Jake concentrated on the layout of the gardens and the appearance of the most dramatic looking plants. Linda pointed out the features of the gardens that she thought were most attractive which helped Jake think about various design ideas. They both clearly were enjoying talking about the gardens and were surprised when they realised that it was almost four o'clock. They decided to get a quick drink at the tearooms and then go to the nightclub to meet the manager.

Linda was the last member of *The Good Time Girls* group to arrive, and the club manager was obviously waiting to talk with Jake. She took him into a small office and gave him a small pile of drawings. She said, 'These are the drawings used the last time the club was brought up to date and as you can see from the date on them, that was twelve years ago. They will give you a basis to work from if you decide you want to do a new design.'

She then used her computer to call up three images of nightclubs which she said were the kind of thing she hoped would be possible. Jake made a note of images and asked Ruby James what she particularly liked about each of them. They discussed her thinking and Jake then said he would look around the club this evening when there would be patrons in and think about what would be needed to create something which matched the quality of the clubs in the three images. Ruby suggested that he watched *The Good Time Girls* performance as she was going to use all the lighting and in her view that was an important part of the club's atmosphere. She explained, 'This will give you a good chance to look at the club without the distraction of all our patrons.'

Jake decided to sit near the back of the club so he could

watch the group's performance and see the whole of the nightclub. Ruby joined him and said, 'What we have at present is okay but the images I showed you are much better. They are all very modern clubs and I want to bring all my clubs up to that international standard over the next few years. This one is the most dated which is why I asked you to look at it first. The main reason I asked you to look at the club is that the understanding of modern style you explained when you were on television, is exactly what I have in mind for my clubs. I think you will design something extraordinary for us. I want you to let your imagination rip.'

At that moment *The Good Time Girls* came onto the stage. Harry Masters said, 'We'll do two of our most recent numbers and then finish with *Creative Imaginations*. As you probably remember, that is the song we did on television.'

It was obvious that the group were concentrating on putting on their very best performance for Ruby James. Jake was surprised at just how sexy and attractive Linda looked. The costume she was wearing showed off her body beautifully and she danced and sang with real style. Indeed, the whole group looked outstanding and as they finished there was a ripple of applause from the club staff who were getting the club ready to open that evening but had stopped to watch the group perform. Jake and Ruby joined in the applause, and she immediately said, 'I must have this group performing at my clubs. They are going to be a great success. Now, I will leave you to think about the best possible design for the club. Right now, I must talk to *The Good Time Girls*. I should have said that I can't really afford to spend a great deal of money on the changes but please let me see your best ideas for creating a really exciting, modern nightclub.'

Jake found the images that Ruby had shown him on his

computer and used them to help him think about how the club could be made to look more exciting. He was busy looking at the drawings and making notes when Linda joined him. She looked happy as she told him that Harry Masters was discussing an agreement with Ruby James that would see the group performing in Ruby's chain of nightclubs four or five times every week. She added, 'This is really great news for us, and it almost certainly means that it makes sense for us to live in London rather than Birmingham. So, we should talk about the apartment you will have when you go to work with Sir Andrew Zain in London.'

Jake laughed, 'That is something I do need to think about; but, for the moment, I need to think about how the nightclub could be improved. What is it like behind the stage? Presumably there are dressing rooms and so on. What are they like?'

'Come and have a look. They are pretty good for a nightclub. We have certainly been given worse at other places where we were performing.'

Linda led Jake up onto the stage where he paused and looked at the club from a new angle. It looked different from the stage, and he made several notes before he let Linda lead him back-stage. She took him first into one of the dressing rooms. This seemed quite small to Jake, but Linda said that there were more dressing rooms on the floor above, and that was where the men had changed. This made Jake think about an image of a stage he had found when he was thinking about the lecture theatres for the university science building. The image was of a theatre in which the stage included two curved staircases that actors could walk down to make a really stylish entrance. Maybe he could design something similar so that performers could come down a curved staircase from the first-floor dressing rooms. He asked Linda if she could show him the upstairs dressing rooms.

She took him up a narrow flight of stairs to a surprisingly big first-floor. It provided two dressing rooms and an office where Jake could see that Ruby James was still talking with Harry Masters about the group performing at her clubs. Jake looked at the drawings that Ruby James had given him and decided that the curved staircase would work but it would probably mean losing part of one of the dressing rooms. He needed to think about this idea before he discussed it with Ruby James. However, being on the first floor gave him another different view of the main area of the nightclub. He made several more notes and then asked Linda what she was doing this evening.

She was explaining that she didn't have any firm plans when Ruby James and Harry Masters came out of the office. They both looked happy, and Ruby said to Linda, 'I look forward to you performing at all my nightclubs over the next few years. In my view, you are going to have a great career.'

She then turned to Jake and asked him when he expected to be able to show her his ideas for improving the club. He said, 'I have a number of ideas already, but I want to stay for at least part of this evening to see the club full of people. I expect it will look and feel different. Also, I need to talk with some technical experts before I really know what is possible; but I am starting to get a few ideas. So, I would expect to be able to come back to you towards the end of next week with some firm ideas that we can discuss. Would that be all right for you?'

Ruby said that was fine and suggested that Jake should have dinner in a near-by restaurant and come back at about eight o'clock. She explained, 'That way you will see the club filling up and by ten o'clock it will be pretty full. I think it's important for you to see it at various times throughout the evening.'

Linda offered to come with him and said that she knew a

good restaurant that they could walk to. Jake agreed and Linda took him to the restaurant which was large, and Jake decided that it had a fairly ordinary menu. When they were seated, Linda said the food is good and at least, it's near the nightclub. Jake asked her what she thought of the nightclub and how it compared to other venues the group had played in. She said, 'To be honest, I haven't really given much thought to the design, which is what, I guess, you are interested in. However, it's pretty typical of nightclubs that were set up about ten years ago. I think the newer ones we play in are more interesting; they use modern technology much more to create a variety of decoration and styles. You probably know what I am talking about, but the walls and ceilings can be changed to be a different pattern and colour from night to night. Also, the furniture in Ruby James' club is pretty old-fashioned. The tables and chairs and the bar-areas were all made of dark wood, which is rather dated. Modern clubs have very sleek furniture that is constructed from some kind of plastic material. The counter in this restaurant is the kind of thing I am thinking about.'

Jake showed her the images of nightclubs that he had found on the internet and Linda said, 'They are very much what I was trying to describe. My guess is that Ruby James wants something like them for her club here in Birmingham.'

Jake agreed and began to feel confident about the kind of design he should produce. The meal was enjoyable, and Jake and Linda returned to the club almost exactly at eight o'clock. Ruby James saw them arrive and made sure they had everything they needed. The club looked to be about a third full, several couples were dancing on the small dancefloor but most of the people were drinking and talking in small groups. Jake felt that it all looked relaxed and comfortable. He noticed that the patrons were mostly older than he would have expected. He asked Linda if she agreed. She nodded and said, 'We do find that different clubs seem to attract people of different ages. This club feels a bit old-fashioned to me and that may explain why it attracts older patrons. I don't know if that is true, but it would make sense. Also, it's the middle of the week and thinking about it, there is usually a younger audience at weekends. So, in a way, clubs need to be able to change their general style and feel to deal with the different days of the week.'

Jake was using his phone to look through the internet and found several firms that advertised nightclub technology. He showed Linda the images of nightclubs that the firms incorporated into their web-sites, and she said, 'As far as I can see, the different effects are being created by the lighting technology. That's not happening at this club. The lighting is pretty ordinary but in some of the most impressive clubs we have played at, the lighting changes throughout the evening and gives the whole club a different feel as we get closer to mid-night and beyond.'

Jake found the web-site of a company that produced a LED lighting system in which the lighting was automatically synchronised to the music. It also produced LED panels on which the lights could be changed to form a great variety of distinctive patterns. He showed several images of this technology to Linda, and she said, 'That is the kind of thing I was trying to describe. In some of the most impressive clubs that I have seen, the walls and ceilings are all painted the same one colour, it's usually grey or blue, but the lights completely change how they look throughout the evening.'

Jake nodded and then thinking aloud said, 'That is what Ruby James should install in this club. She should be talking to some of these technology companies to see what they suggest. The only architectural idea I have had is to build a curved staircase from the first floor down onto the stage so that performers can do a grand entrance.'

Linda said, 'Why don't you go and discuss that with her. She is sat over by the bar and doesn't look busy at the moment.'

Jake did as Linda had suggested. Once he had shown Ruby the images of the nightclub technology he had found on the internet and explained how it could be varied to suit the music being played on any given evening, she looked excited. 'That is exactly the kind of thing we need here. My plan is to up-date this club and if it works to do a similar thing in each of our other clubs. So, are you saying that I should be talking with this company and one or two others who make similar technology? What role is there in this for you?'

Jake smiled, 'The only architectural idea I have has is to build a curved staircase from the first floor down onto the stage. This would provide a visually exciting entrance for the lead singers in the groups you have performing here.'

Ruby said that she could see the point of Jake's suggestion. However, she added, 'Your curved staircase would mean losing quite a bit of dressing room space on the first floor and, to be honest, we cannot afford to do that. The dressing rooms are often too small for some of the groups who play here. So, I don't think that is practical. However, your advice on how I should take the design forward is very professional and I appreciate it. I will of course cover your expenses for coming to Birmingham and I understand you are staying over-night at a hotel. Also, if there is a fee for the time you have spent working out what I should be doing, then let me know; but for the moment, I think your work is done, and thank you very much for your very professional advice.'

Jake felt this was exactly the right response. He stood, shook Ruby's hand and said, 'Thank you. I have enjoyed thinking about the design of your club and if you need any further advice from me, please just ask. I will get my firm to send you an account for my expenses and in my view, my work does not justify a fee, but I will check with the firm's partners.'

Jake returned to where Linda was sitting and said, 'Well, my work here is done. So, when you want to leave, that's fine with me.'

She smiled and said, 'You look happy with the outcome. Which is good. I would like to go now if that is okay with you. It would be good if you could drive me back to my apartment, please.'

They walked back to the hotel where Jake was staying, found his car and Linda directed Jake to her apartment. When they arrived, she said, 'I won't invite you in as I know you have a lot to think about. Let me know what you decide to do and, assuming you do decide to work in London, let me know whether I can use the second bedroom in your apartment in London. That really would be a great help over the next few months.'

Linda then kissed Jake good-night and said that she looked forward to hearing his plans for the future. Jake watched her go into her apartment and the slowly drove back to the hotel. He wondered if he would see Linda again. She was very attractive and was obviously at the start of what promised to be a successful career. But there was Jane who would be finishing her training course that weekend and would almost certainly starting a new job away from Swindon. What if she was working in London? Jake laughed to himself and decided that all these questions would no doubt sort themselves out, one way or another.

Chapter 9

Jake had a surprisingly relaxed lunch with John Brentford during which they agreed that Jake should work with Sir Andrew Zain for six months and if, during this time it seemed sensible, he would discuss with Sir Andrew the possibility of linking the two practices in some way. Jake also agreed it was right that the work of designing a new university campus in Swindon belonged to the practice; and if the university wanted Jake to do some work on this during the six months, he would try to get Sir Andrew to give him the time to do whatever the university needed. Jake also suggested that if he could get Sir Andrew to help him with that work, that would be a good thing. John Brentford smiled broadly and said, 'I am already looking forward to our discussion in six months' time. It could well be a major step forward for you, the practice and the three partners. Having a whole new university campus to design and doing so in collaboration with Sir Andrew Zain would be amazing. I am certain that if you can set that up, the partners will be delighted to bring you into the practice as a full and equal partner.'

Later that afternoon John Brentford told Jake that he had discussed their ideas for Jake's future relationship with the practice and Sir Andrew Zain and they were happy to go ahead on the basis they had discussed over lunch. Jake immediately phoned Sir Andrew to tell him that he could start working in his practice as soon as this could be arranged. He also told Sir Andrew about the new university campus, and he was clearly pleased and told Jake that he could start work in London and have use of the apartment as soon as he wanted. Jake then described the relationship with his current practice that he had discussed that lunchtime with John Brentford.

Sir Andrew's tone became more thoughtful as he said, 'These are all issues that need a great deal of thought. We need to see how we work together on the new town design and the university campus design. I suggest that we work through the next six months and then is the time to think about what new arrangements will suit everyone.'

Jake agreed and said he would like to start working with Sir Andrew on the Monday of the week after next. This was agreed and Sir Andrew suggested that Jake came to the office early on the Monday and the Office Manager would take him to the apartment and make sure he had everything he needed. Jake asked if it was okay if he had someone to live with him in the apartment. Sir Andrew said, 'That's fine. Think of it as your home. Obviously, we need you to look after the apartment properly but what you do there is your business not mine.'

Jake drove to Cirencester that evening feeling very happy that he knew what he would be doing, as far as work was concerned, for the next six months. All he now needed to sort out was his relationships with Jane and Linda. His parents could sense that Jake was more relaxed than he had been for several days and over dinner, he told them that he had decided to work in London for at least the next six months. His father said this was a good decision and they looked forward to visiting him in his apartment. His mother agreed and added, 'I will be able to check that you are eating properly and have everything you need to look after yourself properly.'

Jake thanked them both and then said, 'I know how

important your support and love has been in getting me to this key point in my career. I could not have better parents and I am already looking forward to seeing you in London.'

Jake's mother and father both smiled and his father reminded him that there was cricket practice that evening and asked what he intended doing about his cricket when he went to London. Jake admitted that he had not given that any thought but said that he would need to discuss all of this with Henry Roberts, the club chairman. Then he added, 'I should phone Henry and check that he will be at tonight's selection meeting.'

Jake had just finished his batting practice in the nets when Henry Roberts arrived and suggested that Jake should join him in the pavilion for a chat. Henry first congratulated Jake on being asked to work with Britain's greatest living architect and then said that they needed to decide what to do about the first eleven for the last few matches of the season. They discussed several possibilities before they noticed it was time for the weekly selection committee meeting.

Henry began the meeting by explaining that Jake's career as an architect had reached an important stage and as a result he was going to work in London. He continued, 'I have discussed the implications for the first eleven with Jake and we have agreed that he should captain the team for this Saturday's match against Swindon and then stand down.'

At this point Henry looked at Bill Stones, the first eleven vice-captain, before he continued, 'The normal consequence would be that Bill takes over as captain but in my view, there is a better answer. That is because Ben Stanley has joined the club and, as I'm sure you all recognise, he has an outstanding understanding of the game. Jake tells me that he increasingly relies on Ben's advice during games, and this has often been crucial in winning the match. So, my view is that Ben Stanley should be invited to take over as the first eleven captain.'

This was followed by an awkward silence as the rest of the selection committee looked at Ben Stones. He smiled and nodded as he said, 'I know you are right, and I would consider it a privilege to be vice-captain to Ben Stanley who in my view is the best cricketer in the club.'

Henry Roberts then said that he would go and ask Ben if he was willing to accept this new role in the club. Five minutes later, Henry and Ben Stanley joined the selection committee. It was agreed that Jake would captain the team on Saturday and then Ben would take over for Sunday's match which was one they should comfortably win. Ben asked if Jake would be available to play in any matches. Jake said, 'To be honest I am not sure. I am going to work in London with a very famous architect and this is a great opportunity for me. I am sorry to be standing down as captain in the middle of this highly successful season, but I know the team is in good hands. Once I know when and if I can play for the club, I will tell Henry and you can decide if you want me in the team.'

The committee then selected the teams for the weekend's matches and Jake took Ben Stanley aside and said, 'Thank you for handling the change in captaincy so smoothly. We need to concentrate on beating Swindon on Saturday and then not celebrating too much so you have a fit and sober team on Sunday.'

Ben laughed and said how much he had enjoyed playing with Jake and it was privilege to take over from such a successful captain. Ben then asked if Jake had managed to discuss the possibility of his construction company being invited to bid for the university science block. Jake said they had not reached that stage yet, but he would make sure that the suggestion was put to the Vice-Chancellor at the right time. Ben thanked him and then repeated that it was a privilege to take over the team from such a successful captain.

The planned change to the captaincy seemed to invigorate the first eleven during their match against Swindon. As a result, they beat one of the best teams they played against by six wickets. Ben Stanley batted beautifully and scored an unbeaten eighty-seven as Cirencester passed the Swindon total with ten minutes and six wickets to spare. The team bus took the team back to Cirencester and dropped them off outside Jake's favourite pub. Henry Roberts was waiting inside and had arranged for food and drinks to be available for what he had got into the habit of describing as Cirencester's best first eleven. He explained that the team had won more matches this season than the first eleven had ever managed before. He continued by saying, 'We all know how much this owes to Jake Brown's outstanding captaincy, but he now has a great opportunity to take his architectural career forward by moving to London. So, Jake thank you for giving us such an outstanding season and you will always be welcome to play in the team whenever you are back in Cirencester.'

Jake had just got himself a pint of beer and was thinking about what he would get to eat when his phone rang. He could see it was Jane and he remembered that he had arranged to pick her up that evening. All the decisions about going to London and the captaincy of the cricket team had made him forget. He answered Jane's call and immediately apologised saying, 'Jane, I'm so sorry. There is so much going on in my life just now that I forgot to come and pick you up.'

Jane laughed and said, 'Okay, I am tired after what was a very intensive course and I have also been making decisions about where I should work in future. When can we meet and discuss everything that's happening?'

Jake told her that they had managed to beat Swindon in what was his last game as captain and that he was not playing on Sunday so, he could come over to her home whenever was best for her. She asked if he had any ideas about what they might do, and Jake admitted that he had not thought about it. Jane then suggested that Jake should pick her up at about three o'clock and they could drive up onto the Downs and take a walk. She added that would give them both a chance to talk about their immediate future and what that might mean for them. Jake immediately agreed and said that he was already looking forward to three o'clock on Sunday.

Henry Roberts made sure that no-one drank too much as he reminded them, 'You have another match tomorrow under your new captain; and I know you will all want to keep your winning run going.'

After a couple of hours, the team members began to leave, and Jake decided to go home. He thanked Henry Roberts for a very enjoyable evening and for organizing the change of captain so well. He also confirmed that he would let Henry know when he was able to play for the club in the future. Jake then wished Ben Stanley every success as the new captain, promised he would ask the Vice-Chancellor to include his firm on the list of contractors for the new university building, and left the party to walk home. He felt that his new life was now really starting. He was not playing cricket on Sunday; instead, he was going to discuss the future with Jane. What kind of relationship did he want with her? Then there was Linda; was he happy for her to use the second bedroom in his London apartment?

These questions were still whirling around Jake's mind as he got home, and told his parents that Cirencester had won the match, but he needed to go to bed and then he began trying to get to sleep. He woke up late next morning and realised that he still had no idea how to deal with his relationships with Jane and Linda. This dilemma still dominated his thinking as he drove to Jane's home that afternoon. She came to the door as soon as he knocked and clearly had taken a great deal of trouble to look her very best. Jake smiled as he said, 'Wow, you look amazing. Obviously being a qualified bank manager really suits you.'

Jane came out of the house and immediately kissed Jake and said that it was great to see him. It was a bright, sunny day and they decided to drive to Marlborough, have afternoon tea and then take a walk around the town. As they drove across the Downs, Jane told Jake about the training course and that she had accepted a new job in one of the bank's branches in London. She explained that it was an important branch right in the City of London. She continued, 'One of the main reasons I choose it was because the bank owns three apartments over the branch, and one is vacant at the moment and the bank manager is very keen that I should use it. My salary has gone up by just over fifty percent and the rent is reasonable so I will be comfortably off. I don't know if I have ever mentioned but living at home has allowed me to save a good proportion of my salary so I am reasonably secure financially and working in this branch will allow me to continue to save. Also, it should give me some very valuable experience as we deal with some of the biggest financial companies in the world.'

Jake was obviously impressed. Jane was a very attractive and well-organized woman who clearly liked him. Marlborough looked particularly attractive in the summer sunshine and Jane took Jake to her favourite tea-room where they shared a large pot of tea, and both chose a delicious looking slice of cake. Jake was enjoying watching all the activity on Marlborough High Street, which is very wide, and he decided that this is an important part of making it look very attractive. His thoughts were interrupted by Jane asking, 'Have you seen that girl from *The Good Time Girls* recently?'

Jake was clearly surprised and just said, 'Why do you ask?'

'As your girlfriend, I'm interested in your other friends; and you did seem to be attracted by her.'

Jake tried to smile as he replied, 'Yes, I like her, and I did see her when I was In Birmingham this week. I went there to look at a nightclub where the owner wanted my advice on how it should be redesigned internally, and her group was appearing at the club that evening. I see her as a friend; and as it happens, she asked if she could use the second bedroom in the apartment that Sir Andrew Zain is providing for me when she is in London. I don't see any problems with that.'

'You mean she will be living with you?'

'No, she will just be staying over-night when the group is performing in London.'

'How often does that happen?'

'I don't know. My understanding is that most of their performances are in and around Birmingham. It will save her quite a bit of money if she stays with me when she is in London and, at the moment, the group is not really making enough money for her to live anywhere away from her parents. So, I am just helping a friend. Is that a problem?'

Jane took a long slow drink of her tea and then said, 'So, if I had an attractive young man to stay at the apartment the bank is providing for me in London, you would be happy with that?'

'Do you have someone in mind?'

'Don't be silly. I'm asking a hypothetical question; but in your case it relates to a real situation. You are planning to have an attractive woman staying with you fairly often. Don't you think I should at least try to understand exactly what your relationship is with Linda James? I think I should meet her when we are all in London.'

Jake was clearly unsettled by the way their conversation had developed. He manged to say, 'I don't see any problems with that, if it makes you feel happier. I will let you know when that is possible.'

Jane was obviously not happy, and they finished their afternoon tea almost in silence and then decided to take a walk in the Marlborough College grounds. Jake was thinking about the privileged start to life the college gave its pupils when Jane said, 'I've been thinking about the next few months. They will be significant for both of us. You have an amazing opportunity and will undoubtedly learn a lot from working with a great architect; and I will be starting work as an assistant bank manager and learning to live in London. My only real concern is that I think of you as my boyfriend; but you seem fascinated with Linda James. So maybe we should use our moves to London to take a break from seeing each other for a few weeks while we sort out our new lives. What do you think?'

Jake stared hard at Jane and then without thinking said, 'No, that's not what I want. I want to marry you and I want us to explore London together. It will be amazing. We should concentrate on that.'

Jane stopped and stared at Jake. Then with a big smile on her face, she asked, 'Are you actually saying that you want to marry me?'

'Yes, that is what I want. Linda is just a friend but if she is a problem, I'm sure we can work out something you are happy with.'

Jane put her arms around Jake and kissed him. Then she took a long look straight into his eyes and said, 'Jake, I accept. How soon do you want get married?'

Jake's face broke into a broad smile as he replied, 'Let's get used to being engaged for a few weeks and then when we are both reasonably settled in London, we can think about wedding plans.'

Jane kissed him again and agreed that they both needed to work out the best way for them to live in London before they began planning their wedding. Then she asked, 'When shall we get our engagement ring?'

Jake thought for a moment and then smiled as he replied, 'We both have a busy week getting our apartments in London sorted out but there is an area of London that has a world-famous reputation for its top-quality jewellers. I think it's called Hatton Garden. We could find a time in the next week or so when we can go there and choose your engagement ring.'

Jane kissed Jake again and said, 'That sounds great. I will be busy getting settled in my apartment and my new job, but I will phone you when I know when we could go to Hatton Garden. Is that okay for you?'

Jake agreed and they decided it made sense for them both to go home as they needed to concentrate on moving to London. Jake took Jane home and as they drove across the Downs, Jane said, 'I have never felt so happy. I feel that I will come to see this as the most significant time of my life. I am going to marry the man I love, my career in the bank has moved a very significant step forward, and I am going to live in the greatest city in the world. Life could not be any better.'

Jake smiled broadly and said that he completely understood what she was saying and he felt the same. When they arrived outside her parent's cottage, she said, 'You should come in for a moment while we tell my parents that we are engaged.'

Jane's parents were watching television when Jane and Jake walked into the sitting room. They seemed surprised to see Jake and turned the television off. Jane's mother said, 'It's good to see you, Jake. I understand that you are going to London to work, so, I guess you will still be able to see Jane.'

Jane smiled, took Jake's hand and then turned towards her parents as she said, 'Jake and I have just got engaged. We don't have any plans for our wedding yet, but we are engaged, and we plan to get the ring in London sometime in the next few weeks.'

Both of Jane's parents stood up and were clearly surprised. Her father pulled her into a firm hug and said, 'That's wonderful news. Congratulations to both of you. We are sure you will be very happy together. Do you have any idea when the wedding will take place?'

Jane looked at Jake and then explained that they both needed to sort out their new careers. She added, 'We will get my engagement ring and settle into our new jobs and our new apartments. Then in a few months' time we can think about when we want to get married.'

Jane's father then shook Jake's hand and said, 'Welcome to our family. We are already looking forward to you becoming our son-in-law.'

They all laughed, and Jane's mother suggested they have a glass of wine to celebrate. She hugged her daughter and then said, 'I must hug my new son-in-law.'

She pulled Jake into a long hug and then said she would get the wine. Jane went to help her mother, which left Jake with her father. He asked Jake what he expected to be doing with Sir Andrew Zain. Jake said, 'Well the main thing is that I hope he will help me become a better architect; but the most local project that I expect to be working on is the university campus in Swindon. The Vice-Chancellor wants me to work on an overall design for the campus and the project belongs to my current firm, but Sir Andrew has said that he will be very interested in working on it with me. So, that is a very exciting prospect that raises a number of interesting possibilities for my future career.'

Jane's father smiled and then asked which of the two practices Jake expected to be working for in the future. Jake nodded as he replied, 'That is something I have been thinking about. The partner I work with in Swindon, who is called John Brentford, said that he expects the firm to offer me a partnership when I return from working with Sir Andrew. I don't know if that is what I will do, or if Sir Andrew will ask me to work with him. I have suggested the possibility of linking the two practices in some way but for the moment I need to concentrate on learning as much as I can from working with a great architect.'

Jane's father nodded and agreed that sounded sensible. At this moment Jane came back into the sitting room carrying four glasses of wine on a tray. She was followed by her mother carrying two plates of interesting looking snacks. Jane's father proposed a toast to Jane and Jake and then added, 'I feel you are right for each other, and we are very much looking forward to your wedding.'

Jake stayed for about an hour and then said he should go, as both he and Jane had a lot to do during the next week. Jane came with him to his car, and they agreed to speak on the phone sometime during the next week when they both might have a better understanding of their new life.

Chapter 10

Jake arrived at Sir Andrew Zain's office exactly on time on Monday morning and was met by the Office Manager who explained that Sir Andrew was in a meeting so he would show him where he would be working and then take him to the apartment the practice was providing for him while he was working with the practice. Jake was impressed with the size and quality of the office that the Office Manager showed him. Just to be sure that he understood, Jake asked if he would have exclusive use of the office during his time with the practice. The Office Manager assured him that this would be his office to use as he wished; then he said that he would now show Jake the apartment they were providing for him.

The apartment was just a five-minute walk from the office and Jake was delighted to find it was large and well-appointed. There was an attractive entrance hall with a cloakroom, a large kitchen-dining room, a very comfortable lounge and two large double bedrooms with en-suite bathrooms. The Office Manager took him into each room and made sure that everything was working properly, and that Jake understood how to use it. Jake was obviously delighted with the apartment and told the Office Manager that he was sure he would enjoy living there. The Office Manager then suggested that Jake should unpack and settle into the apartment; and then added, 'We will expect you back in the office at about eleven-thirty when Sir Andrew will be free to talk with you.'

It took Jake less than five minutes to walk to the office, so he arrived well before eleven-thirty. Nevertheless, the Office Manager took him straight to Sir Andrew's office where Sir Andrew was clearly very pleased to welcome him. Once they were sat down, Sir Andrew told him that the man who will become Vice-Chancellor of the newly formed Swindon University had contacted him. Sir Andrew explained, 'I have known the Vice-Chancellor for several years, and he is delighted that we will be working together on the design of the new campus. He was able to tell me that the local authority has agreed that the campus can be sited between Coate Water and the main road that provides access to the M4 motorway east of Swindon. You may know that part of this area is a nature reserve and the local authority hope that our design will maintain this important local feature. Indeed, the Vice-Chancellor would like to go further and make the whole campus totally self-sufficient in energy and not add any pollution to the atmosphere. Anyway, there are many detailed decisions to make, and I would like us to make a start this afternoon. I have a list of the various buildings which will form the campus and I suggest you look through it as you settle into your new office, and we can start work at say one-thirty.'

Over the next few days, Jake was amazed at how much time Sir Andrew Zain was spending with him working on design ideas for the new university campus in Swindon. They had begun by discussing how they could ensure the campus continued as a nature reserve and was, as far as possible carbon neutral. Jake realised that Sir Andrew was excited by these challenges, so he suggested that they might use the contacts he had made while he was designing the science building to identify the right technologies for the whole campus. Sir Andrew immediately

141

agreed and suggested that Jake should spend the rest of the afternoon arranging meetings with the right people as soon as possible.

Next morning, they began making decisions about the overall design for the campus by deciding that the science building Jake had designed should be sited at the edge of the lake. This meant that the lake which formed part of Jake's design, merged into the natural lake. They then tried several possible layouts for the rest of the campus and quickly decided that the best way of maintaining the nature reserve was to site all the university buildings along the edges of the site where it faced the M4 motorway and main road that led from Junction-15 on the motorway into the eastern side of Swindon. This created two long rows of buildings. One began at the edge of the lake with Jake's design for the science building and ran along to the site's south-east corner. The second row ran from this south-east corner, parallel to the main road into Swindon. As they worked on this plan, Jake and Sir Andrew decided to visually define the site by including two more outstanding buildings, one in the south-east corner and the other in the north-east corner of the campus.

They spent most of the morning discussing their favourite buildings before deciding that the one in the south-east corner would be a tribute to Salisbury Cathedral and house the university's departments of architecture, construction engineering and construction management; and the significant building in the north-east corner would house the university administration and its design would be based on the Westminster Houses of Parliament. Sir Andrew was very keen to ensure that the design included a tower that was inspired by Big Ben. The rest of the buildings needed by the university were then arranged in fairly straight rows between these three dramatically significant buildings. The rows of buildings were all kept to just two stories high, so they were significantly smaller than the three signature buildings, as Sir Andrew began to call them. These smaller buildings were designed in a variety of styles, loosely based on buildings which form the most beautiful of the Cotswold's towns and villages.

The result was that people driving eastwards on the motorway towards Junction-15 and then turning off the motorway towards Swindon would have an uninterrupted view of an amazing example of great modern architecture. They would first see Jake's science building which was likely to remind them of Sydney Opera House. Next, they would be delighted by a series of buildings inspired by the best architecture in the Cotswolds. Then, very dramatically, as they turned off the motorway, they would see a remarkable spire rising from an elegant building which should remind them of Salisbury Cathedral. As they drove along the main road, they would see more Cotswold style buildings leading to a dramatic climax, clearly inspired by Big Ben and the Houses of Parliament.

This arrangement meant that a large area between the campus buildings and the lake in Coate Water could remain as a nature reserve. They also felt that the large trees in the nature reserve would provide an ideal background for the buildings viewed from the motorway and main road. As they developed their design over the rest of Jake's first week, Sir Andrew became more and more enthusiastic about it. This was very evident as he said, 'Jake, this is one of the most important designs I have ever worked on. Your creative ideas together with your attention to all the details of the buildings is truly inspiring. I have never worked with anyone who had such creative genius. This is a real privilege for me.'

Jake looked and felt totally surprised by this extraordinary compliment from such a great architect. Sir Andrew could see that Jake was struggling to know how to respond, so he added, 'We have made a great start to our six months of working together. I want to give you every opportunity to make full use of your great talents; and I do seriously hope that we decide to continue working together on some basis in the long-term; but that is getting ahead of ourselves. Now I would like you now to develop our design ideas to the stage where we can show them to the Vice-Chancellor.'

Jake smiled but then remembered that the design of the campus was a project that belonged to the Swindon practice, and they should be involved in any discussions. So, rather hesitantly he said, 'I am very happy to keep working on the design, but I should tell the practice in Swindon what is happening. I guess they will be pleased that the Vice-Chancellor has worked out how to take the project forward and that you are involved, but we should keep them in the picture.'

Sir Andrew nodded, 'Of course, that goes without saying. Can I leave you to keep the partners in your firm informed about what we are doing? I will fit in with whatever suits everyone involved. My interest is in helping create a great design.'

Jake asked if Sir Andrew was in effect putting him in charge of the design. Sir Andrew agreed that was indeed what he had in mind; and he wanted to remain involved in whatever way Jake felt would help produce the best possible campus for the new university. As a result, Jake spent the rest of the week concentrating for almost every waking minute on his design ideas. Friday evening arrived surprisingly quickly, and Jake began his first weekend in London feeling very happy with life. He was being treated by one of the world's great architects as an equal. His design ideas were taken totally seriously, and he was now in charge of the design for the university campus which clearly had the potential to become an important example of modern architecture.

During the week, Jake had only briefly spoken to Jane on the phone on just two occasions as they were both very busy with their new jobs. They had agreed to meet on Friday evening at Jake's apartment. He had only just got back to the apartment and changed into more casual clothes when Jane arrived. She looked excited and very attractive as she pulled Jake into a long kiss. Then she said, 'It's great to see you. I guess we have both had an exciting week exploring our new careers. Let's go somewhere and talk about what we have been doing.'

Jake agreed and suggested they went to one of Ruby James' nightclubs. It was just getting busy when they arrived and were given a secluded table that gave them a good view of the trio that were playing popular tunes on a small stage in one corner of the club. As they decided what they wanted to drink and eat, Ruby James came over to their table and said, 'Hello Jake, I'm delighted to see you here. I'm making good progress on up-dating my clubs based on your good advice. Can I be introduced to this attractive young lady?'

Jake smiled and introduced Jane to Ruby James. Ruby asked Jane what she did and was clearly impressed when Jane explained that she was just starting as an assistant manager in a bank in the City of London. Ruby then pulled a chair from the next table and sat down. She looked hard at Jane and then asked, 'You may be able to help me. I am bringing all my nightclubs up to date with new technology as Jake may have mentioned. I have asked my bank for advice on the best way of funding this and I am not convinced that they have offered me a good deal. I don't have all the figures with me this evening but maybe if you came to another of my nightclubs tomorrow evening, I could give you a copy of the financial statement the bank asked me to prepare; and maybe sometime next week you could let me know what it would cost me if your bank leant me the money. Is that possible?'

Jane looked pleased and promised to look at Ruby's financial statement and get back to her early next week with her bank's terms and conditions. Ruby then looked at Jake and said, 'I suggest you come to my club in Soho, Jake knows where it is, and I will make sure you have a good table. I think you will enjoy it, as *The Good time Girls* are performing there tomorrow evening.'

Jane looked hard at Jake and then said, 'We will see you at your Soho club tomorrow evening; and thank-you for asking for my advice. I am enjoying dealing with the bigger companies and international organizations that my new branch has as customers. So, I am learning fast, and I may well be able to give an immediate indication of the deal our bank is likely to offer you.'

Ruby thanked Jane and returned the chair she had been using to its proper place. Jane looked at Jake with a broad smile on her face and asked, 'Is Linda James staying with you tomorrow evening?'

Jake shook his head, 'I've been too busy this week to have spoken to Linda and she hasn't contacted me. Anyway, you are my fiancé, and we should look at some engagement rings this weekend. What do you think?'

Jane laughed, 'That is a lovely idea. Let's do that tomorrow morning. Now, tell me about your design for the university campus. How is that coming on?'

Jake had copies of his latest ideas on his mobile phone, and he used these to describe his design to Jane. She was obviously very impressed as she said, 'This is remarkable. It will really put Swindon on the map. People will want to visit the town to see this amazing architecture; and it will establish you as a great architect. I knew Sydney Opera House and Salisbury Cathedral were amongst your most favourite buildings, but the Houses of Parliament is a bit of a surprise. It looks good and fits in well with your whole design, but I didn't know it was one of your favourite buildings.'

'You're right. The Houses of Parliament are impressive, but it was the Big Ben tower that seemed to fit into the rest of the design; and, actually, this was Sir Andrew's suggestion.'

Jane then suggested they should go and look at the Houses of Parliament, including Big Ben, tomorrow morning after they had found their engagement ring. Jake agreed and said, 'That might well help me get the design exactly right. I've been relying on images on the internet but seeing the actual building is bound to create a different image. Maybe I should go and walk round Salisbury Cathedral sometime next week. Yes, that is a good idea. It often helps to take a break from detailed designing and think about the bigger picture.'

They continued chatting until they had finished their meal when Jane said that it had been a busy week learning how the bank worked in the city and she needed an early night. She added that it was an easy journey back to her apartment on the tube train, so she would see Jake in the morning. Jake walked with her to the underground station where they kissed good-night and she was gone.

Jake walked slowly back to his apartment thinking about his design. He had just got into his apartment, when his phone rang. It was Linda, who said, 'Jake, I have been waiting in the bar across the road for you to come home. My group is performing in London tomorrow and we have an early rehearsal, so it would be really helpful if I could stay the night. Would that be okay?'

Without thinking, Jake said he would come down to the main front-door and let her in. When he got back to the main front-door, Linda was already there holding a small suitcase. Jake invited her in and led her up to his apartment. Once inside, Linda kissed Jake and said, 'This really is kind of you. The rest of the group are staying with various people they know in London, but you are the only person here that I know well enough to stay with. We are performing at one of Ruby James' clubs tomorrow and on Sunday. That is in the evenings but we have a rehearsal tomorrow morning so we can work out how to make best use of the club's stage and so on.'

Jake grinned as he said, 'I know where you are performing because Ruby James has invited me and my fiancé to the club tomorrow evening. She wants some financial advice from Jane because she works in a bank, and Ruby plans to give her some information about the cost of refurbishing her various nightclubs so she can check that the deal she has been offered is reasonable. When we were arranging this, Ruby mentioned that *The Good Time Girls* will be performing at her club.'

'Sorry, did you say your fiancé?'

'Yes, we got engaged a week or so ago, and we plan to look for our engagement ring tomorrow morning.'

'So, is it okay for me to stay with you? What will your fiancé think?'

Jake smiled thinly before saying, 'Jane does know that I have said you can use the spare bedroom when you are in London. She thinks that she should meet you, so maybe I can at least introduce you to each other tomorrow evening.'

Linda was struggling to hide her disappointment at Jake's

news that he was engaged to another woman, and just about managed to say that she needed to get some sleep and she would see Jake in the morning. Jake showed her to her room and checked that the bed was made up and that Linda had everything she needed. Once she was on her own, Linda changed into her nighty, got into bed and cried herself to sleep.

Next morning Jake was up and dressed before Linda appeared. When she came into the kitchen, she was wearing just a dressing-gown and quickly decided that all she wanted for breakfast was a cup of coffee and slice of toast and marmalade. As she finished this she asked Jake if she could possibly have a key for the apartment as she might well get back after that morning's rehearsal before Jake had finished shopping for his fiancé's engagement ring.

Jake found his spare key and gave it to Linda saying, 'I will need you to leave it in the flat when you leave on Monday morning. I may well be up and out earlier than you because I have a lot to do working out the details of the design for a new university campus in Swindon that I have been working on with Sir Andrew Zain.'

It was obvious to Linda that something about her relationship with Jake had changed. Presumably him getting engaged to Jane meant he had made a big decision about his life and relationships in the future. She was starting to wonder if she should try to find somewhere else to stay in London, when Jake left saying that he had arranged to meet Jane at a café in Hatton Garden.

Jake had just found a table in the café when Jane appeared. She looked very beautiful in a rather revealing summer dress. Jake decided that he had never seen Jane looking as stylish and clearly London was already having an influence on her. The style of the dress was emphasised by a subtle pattern formed from several shades of green; and Jake decided it was absolutely right for looking round the jewellers and, assuming they found a ring they both liked, for whatever followed. Jane kissed Jake and said, 'This is a really important day in our life. I have never felt so excited before but, just at the moment, I could do with a cup of coffee.'

Jake agreed, and while they were waiting for their coffee, Jane said she had looked in the windows of several jewellers and there was an amazing choice of engagement rings. Jake asked if she knew what kind of ring she wanted. She nodded and said, 'I have always liked simple rings with just one diamond. They always look so stylish and somehow embody the whole idea of deciding to spend the rest of your life with one special person. However, looking at the jewellers on the way to this café, I saw one or two that included a small ring of different precious stones around the diamond, and I have to say they looked wonderful. So, we must take our time and look at all the various options and see if we can agree on the right symbol for our love.'

Jake had listened carefully to Jane's ideas about her engagement ring and then said, 'You are right, and I think we will both know what is right for us when we see it.'

When they had finished their coffee, they began looking in the windows of Hatton Garden's remarkable jewellers. After nearly an hour, during which they discussed many of the rings they saw, Jane said, 'For some reason I want to go into the jewellers just across the road. They had an exceptional choice of rings and there were at least two that looked right to me.'

The shop assistant who came to help them was clearly very experienced and listened carefully as Jane explained what they were looking for. She brought out three trays of rings and picked four rings out which she said may be the kind of ring they wanted. One had just one large, beautifully cut diamond, and the other three had a similar diamond surrounded by smaller coloured jewels. On one ring these were blue, on another they were ruby coloured and the third had small green stones around the diamond. Jane and Jake stared at the rings and then they both reached out to pick up the ring on which the diamond was surrounded by sapphires. Jake put it onto Jane's finger and they both stared at it with broad smiles on their faces. The shop assistant said, 'That looks amazing. It is so obviously exactly right for you. I can see from both your faces that this is the engagement ring for you.'

Jane moved her hand around, put it near her face and then folded her arms so the ring was right in front of her. She looked at Jake and said, 'This is it. This is our engagement ring.'

Jake just said to the shop assistant, 'We will take it and thank you so much for helping us find such an amazing ring.'

The shop assistant asked if Jane was going to wear the ring straight away or whether they planned some romantic moment when Jake could put it on her finger? Jane immediately said that they would take the ring in its box, and she would wait for Jake to find the right moment to ask her to marry him.

Jake used his credit card to pay for the ring and the shop assistant put the ring in a beautiful box and gave it to Jake. They walked out of the shop holding hands and feeling that life was amazing. Jake and Jane found themselves wandering through Bloomsbury and on into Regent's Park. They found the Boathouse Café overlooking the Boating Lake and decided to get lunch. They both decided on the tuna salad, which was delicious, and sat looking at people boating on the lake. Suddenly Jane said, 'We should take a boat out this afternoon. It looks idyllic out on the water; and you can give me my engagement ring. I cannot imagine finding a more beautiful place for us to remember where we became engaged.'

Jake was not sure about taking a boat out, but Jane seemed very sure about this idea. She said that she would steer if Jake was happy to do the rowing. Jake had rowed a few times before and settled into the boat with Jane sat facing him holding the small tiller which she looked entirely confident using. Jake quite quickly managed to get the two oars coordinated and they made good progress across the boating lake. Then Jake suddenly noticed that Jane was sitting with her legs fairly wide apart because the wooden block, which supported his feet while he was rowing, was right in front of her. As her dress had a very short skirt, Jake had an uninterrupted view of her white, lacy knickers which were very revealing. It was almost as if Jane was showing him, as she steered them to where she wanted to get engaged, what they would enjoy together when they were married.

Jake's mind was racing with a multitude of confused thoughts when Jane asked him to stop rowing while she steered the boat alongside a small island. It came to rest under a large tree and Jane suggested that Jake should rest the oars. They tied the boat to a root of the tree that had become exposed as the bank had been eroded by the lake, and Jane came and sat next to Jake and leant against him in way which let him see most of both her breasts. His mind immediately began to wonder if this was another subconsciously determined chance for him to see the advantages of being married to Jane. As his mind struggled to understand what message Jane was giving him, she said, 'Jake, I think you had something to ask me.'

Jake put his arm round her, took the box containing their engagement ring out of his pocket, opened it and pulled her gently towards him as he said, 'Jane, my lovely Jane, I love you and I want us to be married, So, Jane, will you marry me?'

Jane's whole face broke into a gorgeous smile as she said, 'Yes Jake, I would love to marry you.'

Jake then put the engagement ring on her finger, and she pulled him into a passionate kiss. When they eventually parted, they sat with their arms around each other for some time, both feeling totally happy. After what was probably no more than a quarter of an hour, Jake suggested they should take the boat back to the boat house and decide how they should celebrate this great day in their lives.

Jane agreed and returned to her seat opposite Jake. Once he had sorted out the oars and started rowing, he looked at Jane who was sat with her legs even further apart. Jake was sure he could now see every detail of her vagina through her lacy knickers. They had become almost transparent; and Jake guessed they had become damp due to Jane's sense of excitement at getting engaged. When he looked at her face, she was smiling broadly but seemed to be concentrating on steering the boat back to the boat house; and as far as he could tell, was totally unaware of the significant and beautiful image she was providing for her fiancé.

Chapter 11

Jake and Jane managed to return the boat to the Boathouse and decided to walk back to Jake's apartment because as Jane said, 'It will let us see some interesting parts of London.'

As they were walking down Regent Street and enjoying the shop windows, Jake suddenly remembered that Linda was staying with him, and he had not mentioned this to Jane. At that moment they were looking at a display in the window of ladies' clothes shop; Jake turned towards Jane and said, 'Something in this window display has reminded me that Linda James turned up at my apartment last night. She needed to use the second bedroom as she is working in London on Saturday and Sunday evening. I meant to tell you, but I had just not thought about it until now.'

Jane stared at him and then smiled and said, 'Okay, this may give me a chance to meet Linda.'

When they arrived at Jake's apartment, Linda was sat in the kitchen with a cup of tea and a sandwich. She was clearly surprised to see Jane and mumbled, 'Sorry, I was just getting ready for this evening's performance. I didn't know you both were coming back just now.'

Jake smiled and introduced Jane and Linda to each other. Jane said, 'I've heard a lot about you and your group. Do you often perform in London?'

Linda replied, 'No, most of our performances are in and around Birmingham but since we met Ruby James, she has started asking us to perform at her London clubs.'

This reminded Jane that she had arranged to meet Ruby James at her club that evening. She explained to Jake that she needed to get to the club early, and in fact she really needed to go quite soon. Jake said that he would get changed and he would be quick. Linda said that she also needed to get to the club and offered to get Jane a cup of tea. Jane thanked her and said that she would wait until they got to the club for something to drink and then added, 'Don't let me delay you getting ready and then we can all walk to the club together.'

Linda asked Jane if she would be staying the night and Jane explained that she had her own apartment provided by the bank she worked for; and in any case you are already using the spare room in Jake's apartment. Linda was clearly surprised by Jane's answer, but Jane did not explain her views about sex and marriage.

While the two women were talking, Jake got changed into the suit he liked wearing in the evenings. When he came back into the kitchen, he found Linda looking at Jane's engagement ring. She was obviously impressed and was saying how beautiful it was. Then seeing Jake, she added that her group's last performance at the club was after midnight, so she would be quite late getting back to the apartment but was happy to let herself in, and she would probably sleep in late on Sunday.

Jake, Jane and Linda walked to the club where they found Ruby James who invited Jane to her office. Jake said he would find a table and get some drinks. Once Ruby and Jane had left them, Linda said to Jake that she was early as the rest of her group had not arrived, so she would have a drink with him while she waited. Jake found a table that gave him a clear view of the stage where *The Good Time Girls* would be performing later that evening and asked the waiter for three glasses of wine. Linda sat very close to Jake and leaned towards him as they took their first drink. She said, 'Jane is obviously a very clever woman, she is lucky to be marrying you.'

She had now crossed her legs in a way that made her skirt slide off her thighs which were now pressed now against Jake's leg. She leaned closer towards him and asked, 'Are you looking forward to seeing me perform this evening? I will be singing and dancing for you, as a way of saying thank you for letting me use your apartment. It would be difficult for me to perform in London without your help and I am very grateful.'

Linda continued to flirt with Jake until Jane returned carry a small folder of papers. She was clearly surprised to see Linda so obviously flirting with Jake and pulled the remaining chair close to Jake, put the folder down on the table surprisingly hard and sat down as she said, 'Well, Linda, thank you for entertaining Jake while I was away but now, I guess you have work to do.'

Linda laughed and said that she thought the rest of the group had now arrived so she would join them. She added, 'I hope you both enjoy our performances this evening. I may well not get back to the apartment until well after midnight. So, Jake, I will see you tomorrow when I eventually wake up.'

To change the subject, Jake asked Jane if her meeting with Ruby James had gone well. Jane nodded and said, 'Yes, she gave me a copy of all the financial information she had shown her own bank . This gives me enough information to understand the financial state of her nightclub business as well as preliminary estimates of the likely cost of bringing Ruby's nightclubs up to date.'

Jake asked, 'So, what do you need to do now?'

'My first task is to work out the best deal my bank can offer; but I will start thinking about that tomorrow morning. Then on

Monday, I can talk with my bank manager and check exactly what we can offer Ruby. When that is sorted out, I will arrange another meeting with Ruby to tell her what the bank can offer her.'

Jake said, 'You really do sound like a bank manager. It's very impressive listening to you talk about your work.'

'Thank you. I am taking this seriously because the bank may well get a new customer as a result of all this, and I hope the manager will be pleased with my initiative.'

Jake nodded as he said, 'So he should be. You are impressive as well as beautiful.'

They were both happy chatting about the changes in their lives right through dinner. As they finished eating, they noticed that the club was filling up, so they decided to take advantage of the small dance area while there was still some room on it. They had both enjoyed three dances when Ruby came onto the stage to announce that *The Good Time Girls* were going to start their first performance of the evening. Jake had a good view of the group as they came onto the stage and felt that Linda was looking straight at him. She looked even more glamourous that Jake remembered, and he was sure that the costume she was wearing was more revealing than he remembered when he had seen her perform before. The group began with a number that allowed the four girls to dance very suggestively. This ensured that they had the full attention of everyone in the club. Jake concentrated on watching Linda and somehow, he felt that she was doing particularly suggestive dance moves just for him. They continued in the same style for some twenty minutes or so and then finished with a number that enabled the girls to concentrate on their sexiest style of dancing.

As they finished their first performance, Jane said to Jake,

'You really like this group, don't you?'

Jake laughed and nodded. Then he looked at Jane who was staring at him with a puzzled look on her face. She continued, 'They are good. The words of their songs are interesting, and the music are good, but I don't know why they feel the need to be quite so explicitly sexy.'

Jake smiled as he said, 'That is one of their main attractions. It helps ensure that they have the full attention of their audience.'

'Well, they certainly had your full attention.'

Very carefully Jake said, 'Yes, I like them; but now what do you want to do?'

'This is a good nightclub. Let's enjoy it for a while and then I should get back to my apartment. I want to be wide awake tomorrow morning so that I can understand all the financial information that Ruby James has given me, and then think about what our bank can do to help her finance the up-dating her nightclubs.'

Jake and Jane stayed at the nightclub till just after midnight. *The Good Time Girls* performed again just before they left, and Jane felt this performance was even sexier than their earlier one. They certainly had Jake's full attention, but Jane decided not to comment on this as they agreed it was time to leave. They both went back to Jane's apartment which Jake thought was comfortable but much smaller and less stylish than his. Jane made them both a cup of coffee and they relaxed on her settee as they drank them. Jake kissed Jane several times and then she said, 'This is lovely, but I do need to get a reasonable night's sleep so that I can work on Ruby James' financial information in the morning. So, my love, it's time to say good-night and I must let you go.'

Jake travelled back to his apartment wondering if Linda

would have returned yet. She was not there when he arrived, so, he decided to go to bed. Next morning Jake got up reasonably early and decided that Linda probably needed to sleep in as her group would have finished their last performance at the nightclub very late. He had just finished his breakfast and got dressed when she came into the kitchen. She was wearing a short, slightly transparent night-dress and immediately apologised to Jake saying that she had not brought a dressing gown. Jake smiled and said, 'That's fine; you look good. Would you like a cup of coffee?'

She accepted the coffee and then asked if she could have a piece of toast and marmalade. Jake said he would get this, and Linda sat down at the table in the kitchen and watched him get her breakfast. Jake brought the toast and marmalade and two cups of coffee over to the table and sat down next to Linda. Her flimsy night-dress meant that Jake had an almost clear view of her body. As Linda concentrated on her breakfast, Jake found himself deciding that every part of her body was exceptionally attractive. This thought filled his mind and as he subconsciously checked that she had what he could only regard as a perfect body, he became increasingly aroused.

Seeing Jake's obvious interest in her, Linda finished her toast and marmalade, and then slowly turned towards Jake in a way that revealed the most intimate parts of her body. She could sense the effect she was having on him as she asked him what he planned to do for the rest of the day. He smiled as he said, 'Well Jane is busy this morning with some work she needs to get done but we haven't made any plans for the rest of the day.'

'So, we should find something to do for the rest of the morning. What would you like us to do together?'

Jake really wanted Linda to stay where she was so that he

could keep on enjoying her amazing body; so, he said, 'I'm very interested in the words of your group's songs. Even though you look amazing while you are performing, I often find myself really listening to the songs and in my view many of them have interesting messages. I think you said before that you write them yourselves and I wondered which ones are your favourites.'

Linda was clearly pleased by Jake's compliment and said, 'I guess my favourite is always the one I am working on at the time. It happens that I am working on a new song at the moment. I'll go and get the current version of it, and you can tell me what you think of it.'

Linda came back into the kitchen a few minutes later still wearing just her night-dress. She was carrying a notebook which she put on the table in front of Jake. Then she opened it and said, 'These are the words of the song I am writing at the moment. I was inspired to write this while I was watching a play on television about young girl who escaped from a war zone in the Middle East and travelled across Europe to England. She was trying to influence people in this country to campaign for the war to be stopped. I was really impressed by her energy and how she thought so much about other people.'

Jake read the words of the song several times; and then said, 'This is really good. In fact, it's inspiring. It will connect to young people everywhere. We all need to think about how we sort out the messy, unequal world that previous generations have left us in. No one else is going to do that. It's up to us.'

Jake then paused and looked hard at Linda before he continued, 'You have very real talent. You should take up writing seriously. You could have a real influence on our generation.'

Linda leant across to Jake and pulled him into a long kiss. As they parted, she said, 'That is the best thing anyone has ever said to me. No-one has ever reacted to my writing with such a clear understanding of what I am trying to do. I love you, Jake.'

As Jake moved back towards Linda to kiss her again, his phone rang. It was Jane to say that she was struggling to work out the true value of Ruby James' nightclub business and it was likely to take her all day to decide whether the bank should offer her a loan and if so on what terms. She added, 'So, Jake, I'm really sorry but I need to work on this today.'

They agreed to meet on Tuesday evening after work and Jake wished her good luck with understanding Ruby James' business. As he put the phone down, Linda asked if he had a problem and when he explained that Jane would be busy all day, she said, 'This is fate at work.'

She was sat very close to Jake and put both her arms round his neck as she added, 'We should explore our relationship. I think you find me attractive, and I want you.'

She slipped the straps of her night-dress off her shoulders and let it fall down to her waist as she kissed Jake again. He was clearly excited by having this beautiful, virtually naked woman in his arms. As they parted, Linda stood up, letting her night-dress to fall to the floor and she then led Jake into her bedroom. She pushed him onto the bed and lay down beside him and pulled him on top of her. Linda then unfastened Jake's trousers and pushed them and his underpants down his legs. She then pulled Jake into a long kiss and reached down to caress his penis. As it hardened, she slid herself onto it and began moving rhythmically. Jake became more and more excited and as he reached a climax, Linda faked her own climax and pulled Jake into a long and passionate kiss.

'We must do this again. Let's just rest for a moment and then try again. It was wonderful. I do love you, Jake.'

Linda carefully pulled off all of Jake's clothes and threw them onto the bedroom chair. Now they were both totally naked. She then kissed Jake and slowly pushed him onto his back and moved so she was on top of him. She then sat up and slid herself onto his penis and slowly caressed it. As he became more excited, she moved faster and faster until he reach another massive climax. Linda lay down on top of Jake and kissed him again and again. His mind was a whirling muddle. This was amazing. He had never experienced anything so satisfying; but what was he doing? He was engaged to Jane. Having sex with Linda was the most exciting thing he had ever done. He had never seen anyone who looked so beautiful and who made him feel so complete.

Linda and Jake slowly relaxed and lay side by side totally naked. After several minutes, she turned towards Jake and said, 'We must do this again but just now, I think we need some lunch. Last night I noticed a small restaurant that looked really interesting; and it's just a few minutes' walk from here. What do you think?'

Jake agreed that sounded like a good idea and less than an hour later they were sat in the restaurant ordering lunch. Jake had ordered a good bottle of wine and a plate of nibbles that they found were surprisingly varied and very tasty. Their main courses were equally satisfying, and this all helped them relax and enjoy sitting together in what they agreed was a very stylish restaurant. Linda was wearing a summer dress that had a very revealing top. She made a point of leaning towards Jake so he could see most of her breasts, and she pushed her leg between his as she asked Jake what he wanted to do this afternoon. He smiled and said, 'I have to admit that my mind is filled by what we were doing this morning, so, I haven't thought about this afternoon.'

'So, are you saying you want to do the same again this

afternoon. I think we could do even better. We can take our time and enjoy every aspect of sex. Let's skip dessert and go back to the apartment.'

Jake did not know at all what to say and just smiled. Linda took his silence as agreement and suggested they ask the waiter for the bill. Jake added a generous tip and paid for their lunch. Once they were outside, Linda took his hand and led the way back to the apartment. As Jake unlocked the front door, Linda said, 'Let's try your bedroom this time.'

She led Jake into his bedroom and kicked off her shoes, let her dress drop to the floor, and stepped out of her panties. Then standing naked in front of Jake, she helped him undress and led him over to the bed where she lay down and guided him on top of her. They kissed for several minutes as Jake caressed her breasts and then slid his hand into her vagina. Linda responded by stroking Jake's penis and then pulling him into her. They both enjoyed the most satisfying sex that either of them had ever experienced.

They stayed in this position for a long time, occasionally kissing but mainly just enjoying feeling totally happy. Eventually Linda said that she had to get to the nightclub by six o'clock so that the group could get ready for their first performance. Jake said he would come with her, and Linda smiled broadly as she said, 'I hoped you would come to the nightclub and watch us perform, because I want you to know that I am singing and dancing just for you.'

Jake laughed, 'I'll bear that in mind.'

In fact, Jake felt the evening dragged on. He totally enjoyed watching Linda perform as it made him think about everything they had been doing that day; but between their performances, Jake found himself thinking about his design for the new

Swindon University. He was happy with the overall concept he had agreed with Sir Andrew, but he needed to be working on the detailed design. This thought made him think about the design of the science building. He was proud of the idea that it reflected the emergence and development of humanity on Earth. Could he continue this theme in the rest of the university? The buildings based on Salisbury Cathedral and The Houses of Parliament did not culminate in a modern element. Whereas Sydney Opera House provided the inspiration for the science building's beautiful roof. Could he design a modern version of Salisbury Cathedral's spire and the Big Ben tower? He needed to be working on these ideas, but he was sat in a nightclub waiting for the beautiful Linda to finish her work. This made him think about Jane. They were engaged to be married for the rest of their lives. What was he doing having sex with Linda? These questions churning around in his head stopped Jake thinking about his design for Swindon University, and probably contributed to him drinking too much.

Some ten minutes after *The Good Time Girls* had finished their last performance, which was greeted by warm applause from all the club's customers, Linda joined Jake and suggested they went back to his apartment. As they walked through the almost empty streets, Linda asked Jake what he thought of their performances that evening. She added that Harry Masters, the guitarist and effective leader of their group, had said that he thought that the performance just after midnight was their best ever.

Jake smiled as he said, 'It was certainly the best I have ever seen you perform. You looked beautiful and I thought the words of the last two numbers you sang were really interesting.'

Linda thanked him and said that she had written the lyrics

for both of their last two numbers. Jake was impressed and said so. Then he added, 'You really should think about doing some writing. Maybe a book for people of our age. Your songs contain really important messages for our generation, and it makes sense for you to publish them. Maybe you could do a book that includes the songs you have written and links them to characters that could be quite like us. I don't know what kind of story you might devise but you would think of something interesting; I know you would.'

Linda looked hard at Jake and asked, 'Are you serious? Do you really think I could write a book based on the lyrics I have written?'

Jake assured her that he was being absolutely serious, and he was sure that she had the talent to be a successful author. Linda said, 'That is the most amazingly beautiful thing anyone has ever said to me. You are the best thing that has ever happened to me. Let's get back to your apartment, so I can show you how grateful I am.'

It then seemed totally natural, when they reached the apartment, for Linda to lead Jake into his bedroom, slip out of her clothes, help him to get undressed and pull them both onto the bed. She pulled Jake on top of her and said, 'I do love you, Jake. Let's make tonight a night to remember.'

Jake's mind was totally focused on this beautiful, naked woman pulling him into sex. The amount he had drunk almost certainly helped him continue their sexual intercourse for an amazing length of time. When he eventually came, he began kissing Linda again and again. 'You are amazingly beautiful. This is pure heaven.'

They eventually fell asleep in each other's arms. It was gone eight o'clock next morning before they woke, and Jake immediately realised that he was going to be late getting to Sir Andrew Zain's office. He should have been working on the detailed design for the new Swindon University campus; and he did not want Sir Andrew to have any doubts about his commitment to his work. Turning up at the office late was not a good idea. So, Jake had a quick wash, got dressed and as he left, he said to Linda, 'Last night was wonderful but I need to show Sir Andrew Zain that I am fully committed to working with him. I will not be back until this evening. So, see you then.'

Linda was shocked by Jake treating her in this off-hand manner. She had thought that he felt the same about her as she did about him. That was the impression she had got from last night's wonderful sex. Was she deceiving herself? Was he just having sex with her because she was available? She needed time to think and decided to go back to Birmingham. Linda wrote a short note saying she needed to go home as the group had to practice some new numbers that afternoon and put it on the kitchen table where Jake would see it when he got home.

Chapter 12

When Jake arrived at the office on Monday morning, just after nine o'clock, Sir Andrew Zain's secretary told him that Sir Andrew wanted to see him. Sir Andrew seemed excited as he told Jake that he had just been contacted by the Vice-Chancellor of Swindon University. Sir Andrew continued, 'He has been approached by a large international manufacturing company. They have developed a highly sophisticated system of manufactured building components which they want to use to construct the new university campus. Their main business is manufacturing cars, but they see construction as a huge potential market for the future; and the Vice-Chancellor wants to work with them. My impression is that he hopes this will mean that the university is built quickly, generates a lot of publicity and gives him a basis for setting up a new department of architecture, engineering and construction management.'

Jake asked, 'Does this mean that the buildings we have designed to form the new campus will be manufactured in a factory and we will not be using traditional methods of construction?'

Sir Andrew smiled, 'My understanding is that the manufacturing company is able to produce components that can mimic any architectural style or form of construction. They achieve this by using computer-based technology to, in effect, print out the external walls and roofs. So, we can be as creative as we like; and the Vice-Chancellor seems to have persuaded the company developing the new technology that the university campus is an ideal project to demonstrate what is possible.'

Jake asked, 'Does this mean we can keep all the different styles in our design, even though they will not be constructed by craftsmen on site?'

Sir Andrew nodded as he said, 'That is my understanding. Anyway, we have a meeting tomorrow with the Vice-Chancellor and people from the manufacturing company. We need to think about the implications of using modern technology and decide what information we need.'

Jake and Sir Andrew spent the rest of the day working on their design to ensure they had enough information to show the manufacturing company the variety of buildings and styles of architecture they planned to include in the university campus. That evening, back at his apartment, Jake continued working on the drawings and finding images on the internet that illustrated the style of buildings that formed the design for the new campus. He did not notice Linda's note telling him why she needed to get back to Birmingham until late that evening; and when he did read it, Jake realised that he had not given her any thought since he had left for work that morning; and now felt reasonably pleased that she would not be interrupting his work.

Next day Jake and Sir Andrew went to the Vice-Chancellor's office and were shown into a meeting room. The Vice-Chancellor was already there with the university's Buildings Officer and four representatives of the manufacturing company that hoped to launch a new approach to building construction. The Vice-Chancellor chaired the meeting and began by asking everyone to introduce themselves. Once this was done, the Vice-Chancellor asked Sir Andrew to describe his design for the new campus. Sir Andrew began by saying that the design was in fact the work of

Jake Brown and he was cooperating with him, so, it made more sense for Jake to describe the design.

Jake used his computer to show everyone at the meeting images of the overall design and the individual buildings and then he showed them images of existing buildings that illustrated the various styles of architecture they intended using. When he had finished his presentation, the senior representative of the manufacturing company asked when the design would be complete and how long it would take to get all the various formal permissions from the local authorities.

Jake replied, 'Well, we need good information about the technology that will be used to construct the campus before we can finalise the design. When we understand that, we can work out how long it will take to produce the information needed by your company.'

This led the company's senior representative to ask the woman who had been introduced as the head of their marketing team to describe their ideas for the new technology and how it related to the work of architects and building contractors. The woman, who was called Molly Jenkins, used her computer to help describe a system of construction based on a steel frame that supported panels which formed complete buildings. The panels could mimic the look of any form of traditional or modern construction and incorporated sophisticated electricity, water and drainage systems.

Jake and Sir Andrew listened carefully to Molly Jenkins' description of the new technology. When she finished her description, Sir Andrew said, 'This sounds very much like an up-dated version of the systems developed by groups of local authorities in the nineteen sixties. They made good use of the technology that existed back then but the main problem I had with them was that they limited the quality of architecture I could produce. So, I avoided using those old systems. How much more flexible is the approach you are planning?'

The most senior of the manufacturing company's representatives replied, 'You are absolutely right in seeing some similarities between our ideas and the systems used by local authorities in the sixties and seventies. I also agree that one of their main weaknesses was the way they limited the architecture. That is where our approach represents a big step forward and that is why we want to work with you on the university campus. Your design is an example of the very best architecture and I believe we can manufacture it to a standard that you will be very happy with. That is what we are to discuss this morning.'

Jake looked at Sir Andrew and could see that he was thinking about the implications of their design being prefabricated in factories and then assembled on site; so, he decided that he should respond, 'I know that the local authorities' system was used to construct at least two new universities. I am pretty sure they are Bath and York. I have visited these universities and my main criticism from an architectural point of view is that the external walls are divided into panels, and they all have flat roofs. Our design for the buildings that form the new campus in Swindon have traditional brick or stone walls and most of the buildings have pitched roofs. Will this be possible if the buildings are formed from panels supported on a steel frame? Won't the joints between the panels break up the visual appearance of the external walls and for that matter, the roof as well?'

Molly Jenkins nodded at this question and then said, 'That is probably the most important issue that we have had to deal with in developing our ideas for the new system. We hope to get the computer systems that print the external surface of the wall and roof panels to form joints that do not interrupt the pattern of brick walls or stone walls or traditional roofs. The idea is that they will form matching shaped edges to adjacent panels that follow the pattern of the brickwork or stonework or roof tiles and fit together rather like a jig-saw puzzle. Then the joints can be sealed in a way that matches those in the wall or roof. In other words, they will blend in with the rest of the wall or roof, and our hope is that you will not be able to see where there are joints between the panels. We are aiming to make it look just like traditionally construction.'

Sir Andrew said, 'That is fascinating because as Jake suggested, the main weakness of those old local authority systems was the way they were divided into panels. We will need to see your ideas in a full-size mock-up. Is that possible?'

The senior representative immediately said, 'This is exactly what we intend to do next. I suggest that you let us have a copy of your design and we will assemble a mock-up of the various types of external walls and roofs that you have included. These will include joints between adjacent panels so you can see if our ideas work well enough for your architecture.'

The Vice-Chancellor interrupted at this point to say, 'We have not yet decided that this is the approach we will use but if it works for all of you, and the price is acceptable, then I think we will decide to have the campus manufactured. So, we would certainly like Sir Andrew and Jake to work with the manufacturing company over the next week or so and then we should meet again and make a decision about the way forward.'

Everyone decided that this signalled the end of the meeting and the senior representative from the manufacturing company arranged for Sir Andrew and Jake to come to their factory early on the following Tuesday. He said that they needed that time to produce examples of their panels and get them set up, and then, once Sir Andrew and Jake had looked at them, he hoped they would spend the rest of the day working together to ensure they had all the key design details. This was agreed, and Jake gave the senior representative copies of the design details he had already produced. He also agreed to concentrate on completing as much of the detail design as he could before the meeting.

As Jake and Sir Andrew travelled back to London, Jake remembered that he had arranged to meet Jane that evening. She came to his apartment just after six o'clock and seemed very happy as she told Jake that her bank had agreed, just that afternoon, to offer Ruby James a loan to finance the re-development of her nightclubs. Jake asked if Ruby had accepted the money and Jane said they were meeting later that week to discuss all the details. Jake then said, 'I have some interesting news as well about the new university campus; but let's find somewhere to have dinner and I can tell you all about it.'

Jake needed to change into more casual clothes and while he was doing this, he could hear Jane obviously looking round the apartment. This was explained when Jane asked him how long Linda had stayed with him. He told her that Linda had used the apartment for two nights while her group was performing at the nightclub. Jane looked hard at Jake as asked, 'Do you enjoy having her to stay with you?'

Jake managed a thin smile as he said, 'She needs somewhere to stay when she is working in London. Staying at a hotel in central London is too expensive for her and I have the spare room; and it's interesting to talk with her about how her career is developing.'

'So, she's not your girlfriend?'

Without hesitating, Jake said, 'No; I'm engaged to marry

you and I love you. Linda is just a friend, and it so happens that I can help her career develop by giving her somewhere to stay when she is working in London. That's it.'

Jane looked at Jake for several moments and then just said, 'That's fine. Let's get some dinner.'

As they walked to the restaurant where they had decided to have dinner, Jake's mind was wrestling with issues raised by the fact that he had just lied to his fiancée. Should he have got engaged? What were his feelings for Linda? How was he going to deal with having two women in his life? Once they were in the restaurant, and had decided what to order, Jake cleared his mind and began telling Jane about the company that might manufacture the buildings which would form the new university campus. When he had shown Jane the latest design, she said, 'All the buildings do look very traditional. Can that be achieved if they are built from components manufactured in a factory?'

Jake then explained that he and Sir Andrew Zain were going to the manufacturing company's factory the following week to see for themselves what was possible. Jane then asked if she could have another look at the images of Jake's design for the university campus. As she studied them, she said, 'This is very impressive. One thing that slightly surprises me is that there no reference in any of the buildings to Swindon's past role in building the railways. I would have thought that is a proud part of the town's past; and that should be reflected in some way in Swindon University.'

'What did you have in mind?'

'I don't know exactly what you could include but I would have thought that the university authorities would want some reference to the town's history.'

Jake could see the logic in Jane's thinking and said, 'I don't think we could include a railway track; but maybe we could have a railway engine mounted on a plinth that describes Swindon's role in the industry. It would make a spectacular addition to the main entrance to the campus. Is that the kind of thing you were suggesting?'

Jane smiled as she nodded and said that she liked the sound of Jake's idea. Jake got out a notebook and began sketching his current design for the main entrance to the campus, but it now included a railway engine on a large plinth. It was the first thing visitors to the university would see when they turned into the campus. Jake was increasingly excited by this idea and said to Jane, 'This is a really great idea. It gives the university a distinctive identity; but it is based on the town's past. Is there some way we could add a similar reference to its future?'

Jane asked, 'What is its future? What do you think of now when you think of Swindon?'

Jake agreed that was an important question; and then added, 'We must show this idea to the Vice-Chancellor and see if he has any ideas about what would provide an up to date symbol of the town. Then maybe we can add an appropriate image on a second plinth. This would give the university a really distinctive entrance that tells students about the town's history and its ambitions.'

Jake and Jane had an enjoyable evening chatting about their work; and just after ten o'clock Jane said she would like to go back to her apartment, so she was ready for work next day. As she explained, she was finding her new job challenging . Then she added, 'If it's okay with you, Jake, I need to concentrate on my work for the rest of the week, so, would it be all right if we don't meet until Saturday.' Jake said that he knew what Jane meant and he also needed to concentrate on his work and spending Saturday together sounded fine. Jane was happy to go back to her apartment on her own. As she said, 'I feel safe on the tube at this time of night.'

As soon as Jake was back in his apartment, he began working on his sketch of the main entrance to the university campus. He used the internet to look at images associated with modern technology. He gradually designed a plinth for a statue that hinted at computers, mobile phones, television screens and the chips and wires they depend on. Then he added a microscope and finally a telescope to represent science. It was gone midnight before he had a sketch that he felt was interesting enough to show to Sir Andrew Zain. Jake fell asleep as soon as he got into bed; and he woke up late the next morning.

After a hurried breakfast, Jake was late getting to the office where Sir Andrew Zain's secretary said that Sir Andrew wanted to see him. Jake immediately apologised for being late and said that he had been working on an idea for the main entrance to the university until very late last evening. Sir Andrew looked interested as he asked if he could see Jake's idea.

Jake found his sketches of the two plinths and explained that they represented Swindon's past and future. Sir Andrew looked at the sketches for what seemed to Jake to be a long time. Then he smiled and said, 'I very much like this idea. I'm sure the university will be able to get a railway engine from the local museum and we should invite an established sculptor to develop your ideas for a plinth that represents the future into a real work of art.'

Jake then said, 'A thought that kept coming into my mind as I was working on the two plinths is that our design is much more related to the railway engine than it is to the images of modern technology.'

Sir Andrew stared at him and was obviously thinking about

175

what Jake had just said. Eventually, he nodded and said, 'That is true. Nevertheless it is an impressive design; but if you feel the need to bring it more up to date, I suggest you work on any ideas you have, and I will also think about what we might change, and then we can meet at four o'clock this afternoon and see what we both think is the right style for the university.'

Jake then spent much of the morning thinking about the design of the new construction related department which was influenced by Salisbury Cathedral and included a tall spire . He played with the idea of turning the whole building into a spire which started at ground level and soared up skywards. He included narrow bands of windows at each floor level and found that having seven floors seemed to work best. He then tried to fit all the internal spaces needed by the department into these seven floors and the spire was not nearly big enough. So, he tried making it much bigger which made it look more like a pyramid than a spire. Now it accommodated all the internal spaces but looked very different from the rest of their design for the campus.

Maybe this was a good thing. Maybe they should review the other buildings, keeping the image of the pyramid in mind. Was the pyramid too dramatic an image for Swindon? As these thoughts filled Jake mind, he tried to think how he could modify the building that would house the university's administrators. It was inspired by the Big Ben tower that was part of the Westminster Houses of Parliament. It was hard to see how this could be changed into a modern looking building. Maybe it should be another pyramid. Jake did not like this idea, so, he began to try to sketch a modern looking tower block. He began by drawing a circular tower with a domed roof but decided this looked too ordinary. So, he sloped the sides of the tower outwards starting from the fourth floor. This provided a visual link to the pyramid and by playing with several different angles of slope and starting the slope at the third floor and then the fifth floor, Jake managed to decide which of the towers looked the best. Then he added a large main entrance to the building which included a large clock based on those in the Big Ben tower.

Jake felt that his design for the science faculty building was already sufficiently modern; so, he began to think about the smaller buildings which were based on the style that is traditional in the Cotswolds. Could he keep these as they were to provide a historical contrast to the three modern buildings? Or should he introduce some modern elements into this part of the design? Jake was excited by this idea and decided to grab a quick lunch and then explore various modern designs that might look right for the smaller buildings.

Jake used the internet to look at recent prize-winning designs and was delighted to see that these included two of Sir Andrew Zain's best designs. These led him to a major change in the design of the smaller buildings. He gave them a very modern look based on white concrete external walls, large panes of glass to provide elegant windows and a mixture of gently sloping and flat roofs. He added curved balconies to nearly fifty percent of the buildings which would give the users an uninterrupted view of the central nature reserve which formed most of the university campus. Then he added spiral external staircases to five of the buildings to give them a very distinctive appearance. Finally, he added small towers to seven of the buildings to create an interesting skyline for anyone looking at the complex from a distance. Four of these were topped with a small spire and the other three were clearly influenced by the Big Ben tower. He kept the individual buildings fairly small and arranged them at various angles to each other. As he worked on this, Jake kept thinking of the overall impression

177

formed by the main streets in small rural towns. He tried various patterns for the overall layout and then created a new three-dimensional image on his computer. This showed the whole design which brought together the three major buildings and the 'streets' of smaller buildings that linked them together into a genuinely impressive campus. He looked at this new image from every angle and changed the detailed layout several times to create a design which he knew was the best he had ever created.

At that moment Sir Andrew came into Jake's office to remind him that they were meeting to discuss the design of the university campus. Sir Andrew added, 'I must admit that I have been thinking about the new entrance rather than our whole design, but let's discuss your ideas. Jake used his computer to show Sir Andrew images of his new design. Sir Andrew sat down and stared at the computer. It was obviously impressed, but as he continued staring at the design, Jake began to worry that Sir Andrew didn't like his new ideas. After several minutes, during which Sir Andrew stared at Jake's new design from every possible angle, he turned towards Jake and said, 'This is the most amazing design I have seen for a very long time. It is creative, interesting, beautiful and by any standards, this is truly great architecture. It is amazing how you have steadily changed and improved separate elements of the design until it all suddenly comes together in this truly great creation. You are in danger of becoming a great architect.'

Jake just sat in his chair and stared at Sir Andrew. Could he believe what he was hearing? Sir Andrew smiled broadly at the effect he was having and shook Jake's hand and said, 'This design will win major architectural prizes and establish your reputation. I can only congratulate you on a work of real genius.'

Jake just said, 'Thank you. I have never been so pleased by

anything anyone has ever said to me before.'

Sir Andrew was clearly excited as he said, 'We will enjoy working together. I know this is just the first of many examples of great architecture that will emerge from our cooperation. Now I must talk with the Vice-Chancellor to prepare him for tomorrow's meeting. I need to build up his sense of excitement and expectation. Then when he sees your design, I hope he will be blown away.'

At the meeting next day, the Vice-Chancellor began by saying that he had been looking at examples of the world's best modern architecture and was ready to see what Sir Andrew and Jake had to show him. Sir Andrew replied, 'I will leave Jake to show you his new design.'

Jake then used his computer to show the Vice-Chancellor what he was sure was the most impressive view of his new design for the campus. The Vice-Chancellor stared at the image and began nodding and smiling broadly. Jake then worked through more images of his design, explaining what each showed before moving on to the next image. When he had finished, Sir Andrew asked, 'What do you think? Was I right in describing this as an amazing piece of modern architecture?'

The Vice-Chancellor looked at Jake and then Sir Andrew and said, 'You are right, this is amazing. It will make a serious contribution to establishing Swindon University as a significant establishment. We must discuss this design with the manufacturing company. I think it will be easier for them to manufacture and build than the Cotswold style design you showed me before. We should go ahead with developing this new design. I assume you will make the whole complex sustainable so that we can publicise the fact that the new Swindon University does not in any way contribute to global warming.'

Jake assured him that he had carried the ideas they had used in designing the science block on into all the buildings so, it was highly likely that Swindon would have the most sustainable university campus in the world. The Vice-Chancellor was clearly delighted. This was very evident as he said, 'Your design provides everything and more than I could have hoped for, but we need to get a robust estimate of the cost so that we can ensure that the university can afford it. Also, we need to make sure that the manufactured technology is robust and will provide suitable buildings for our long-term future. Given that, what needs to happen next?'

Jake was the first to reply. 'Obviously we need to tell the manufacturing company about this new design so that they can make a mock-up for us to look at next Tuesday.'

Sir Andrew agreed and added, 'That is probably the right time to think about the various design options. I am sure that seeing mock-ups of the company's technology will help us to decide how we move forward with the design.'

The Vice-Chancellor said that sounded sensible and he was already looking forward to seeing mock-ups of the various possible walls and roofs. As he explained, 'It will be good to hear what the manufacturing company think as well as listening to your opinions. Then we can make a final decision and concentrate on moving the project forward. This is all very exciting for me.'

The following Tuesday, Jake and Sir Andrew travelled by train to the manufacturing company's factory which was just north of Birmingham. Sir Andrew asked Jake what he had been doing over the weekend and Jake said, 'I spent most of it with my fiancée. We went to the theatre to see a play she had heard about from colleagues at the bank where she works. It was very interesting, and it gave me an opportunity to have a close look at one of London's best theatres. On Sunday we took a trip along the Thames to Greenwich. I have to say that the National Maritime Museum is housed in an amazing building and the museum is really interesting. We both enjoyed the day and are starting to understand why London is seen as such a great city.'

Sir Andrew smiled as he said, 'Now we must concentrate on creating an equally important piece of architecture for the Swindon University campus.'

When they arrived at the manufacturing company's factory, they were met by Molly Jenkins who explained that the mock-ups of the various walls and roofs were set up inside the factory. She added that the Vice-Chancellor had already arrived, so, she led Sir Andrew and Jake into an area at one end of the factory. Here they could see sections of the various walls and roofs they were considering as part of their design for the campus buildings. The Vice-Chancellor was already discussing these with the senior representative of the company who they had met at Sir Andrew's office. He reminded them that he was called Robert Sutton and invited Sir Andrew and Jake to examine the walls and roofs.

They were both impressed by all the finishes and by how robust they seemed to be when they pushed and pulled each of the mock-ups. Robert Sutton explained that the panels which formed the walls and roofs were attached to the steel frame by joints that allowed the walls and roof to remain stable even when the frame moved due to heavy loads or unusual heat or cold. He took the visitors round to look at the back of the mock-up of the brick external wall and pushed one of the columns that formed part of the supporting frame. The column moved slightly but the wall did not move. He then pushed the wall, but no matter how hard he pushed, it did not move.

Robert Sutton then said, 'My understanding is that you are thinking of having all the external walls made of concrete. As it happens, when we developed this system of construction, concrete was the first type of external wall we included in the system. Over the years, we have devised several different finishes to the concrete, and I can show you samples of the current range.'

Robert Sutton then led the visitors to the far end of the factory where he showed them eight concrete panels, each of which was a different colour or texture. Jake was clearly excited by this and almost immediately picked a panel of white concrete that had a texture which made it look as if it was sparkling. He turned to Sir Andrew and the Vice-Chancellor as he said, 'This is exactly the finish I had in mind when I was designing my latest ideas for the campus. It's the kind of finish used in many of the buildings that are now seen as the world's greatest modern architecture.'

He then turned to Robert Sutton and asked how the concrete walls were made. He added, 'In the mock-up you showed us, I could not see any joints in the walls.'

Robert Sutton smiled and explained, 'We erect the frame and then where we are providing concrete walls, we attach steel reinforcing mesh. Once this is all in place, we put steel formwork both sides of the mesh. The formwork on the outside is lined with plastic sheet decorated with whatever pattern we want on the external walls. Then we pump the concrete into the formwork where it is reinforced by the mesh. I have to say that this is one of the most innovative parts of our system and in the early days we had to do a lot of development on pumping concrete to get the appearance of the walls exactly how we wanted it. Anyway, once the concrete is pumped into place and has set and hardened, which usually takes seven days, we remove the formwork and peel the plastic sheet off the external surface. I have to say that this all works very reliably. Something that I am particularly proud of is that the formwork and the plastic sheet that forms the external finish is reusable. We clean the plastic sheet after it is stripped off the walls and then feed it into the machines that make new sheets for us. So, it is a very sustainable form of construction; there is no waste. All the material we use either forms part of the finished building or is reused in constructing future projects.'

The Vice-Chancellor said, 'That is an important message for us to include in our publicity about the new campus.'

Sir Andrew agreed and then added, 'I am happy with Jake's choice of finish. The sparkling white concrete will look good; and I recognise that it is a feature in much of the world's greatest architecture. I must also say that I am impressed with this system of construction, and I particularly like the way that the concrete external walls are not divided up by a mass of joints.'

Robert Sutton sensed that this was the time to invite the visitors to have lunch in his private dining room. They all agreed and were taken to small, stylishly furnished room above the factory floor where they enjoyed a good lunch and some very fine red wine. As they came to the end of the meal, during which they discussed the campus design and the system of construction, Sir Andrew asked, 'I think we have decided to go with Jake's latest design using the system of construction we have been shown this morning, including sparkling, white concrete for the external walls. Does everyone agree?'

The Vice-Chancellor nodded and then said, 'I am very happy to go ahead on that basis provided we can afford it. When will we get a good estimate of the likely cost of constructing the whole campus?'

Sir Andrew answered, 'We need our quantity surveyors to talk with Robert Sutton's people and come up with a new estimate. I will get them to start on this straight away and hope to have a figure for you as soon as possible.'

The Vice-Chancellor thanked him and added, 'We now seem to have a firm basis on which to move forward. This has been a very important meeting and I thank you all; but now I need to get back to Swindon.'

This clearly signalled the end of the lunch and Robert Sutton said that he would get his secretary to order a taxi to take them all to the railway station. On the train back to London, Sir Andrew and Jake both felt happy with the day and chatted about the system of construction they had decided to use for the university campus. They agreed that it complimented the uncompromisingly modern style of Jake's design and was exactly right for a new university. They talked about the details of the design and Jake made sketches of any new ideas they agreed. Jake said this would give the firm's draughtsmen a good basis to produce the working drawings. Sir Andrew agreed and asked Jake to spend the rest of the week making sure that the draughtsmen had everything they needed. Sir Andrew then surprised Jake by telling him that next week he hoped they could start working together on the first design ideas for the new town that was being planned by a group of local authorities based between Nottingham and Leicester. He added, 'This is one of the most exciting challenges that I have ever had; and I think that together we will create something amazing.'

Chapter 13

Jake and Jane had arranged to meet on Friday evening so they could plan what they would do over the weekend. Jane came to Jake's apartment, and they decided to get dinner at a restaurant in Soho that they thought looked good. Luckily the restaurant was not full, and a waiter showed them to a small table in a quiet corner. They both felt comfortable, and they had much to talk about. Jane was clearly excited by the varied experience that working at the bank in the City of London was giving her. As she explained, she was dealing with a surprising variety of individuals and companies. Jake was particularly impressed by her description of the meeting she had with a self-made multi-millionaire. This was a woman who had set up three restaurants specialising in African cuisine. They were all successful, and she now wanted to develop an entirely new business that would produce her most popular meals on a large scale and sell them through super-markets across the country.

Jake was happy to let Jane talk about her work as he enjoyed the red wine they had ordered. Eventually Jane asked him what he had been doing at work that week and Jake described his new design for the Swindon University campus. Jane listened carefully and was clearly impressed by the images of his design that Jake had on his mobile phone. This led to them talking about modern architecture and then deciding to spend at least part of the weekend looking at some of the best examples in London.

On Saturday morning they took the tube train to Broadgate.

Jake said he thought it had been designed by Arup Associates in the nineteen eighties. They were both impressed by the sheer quality of the buildings and the variety of public open spaces that had been created between them. Jake took photographs of the design details of many of the buildings and open spaces. As he said, 'This really is very high-quality architecture. You can see that in the detailed design of the junctions between different materials. Look at the way the concrete cladding emphasises the windows and doors. I must match this quality in the details of the university campus. Also, the way the buildings shape distinct pedestrian areas in which each of the external spaces is different and interesting. I must keep these ideas in mind as we start to think about the new town that Sir Andrew wants to start work on. If we could create this quality and variety across a whole town, it could well change the way people think about urban areas.'

Jane looked hard at Jake as she said, 'That is a very ambitious objective. If you could make a whole town as interesting and beautiful as this development, it would be amazing.'

'I need to sit down and think. Let's get some lunch in one of these restaurants. I must get some ideas down on paper.'

Jane picked a small restaurant and as soon as the waiter had showed them to a table, Jake took out a notebook and began sketching. Jane ordered their lunch and then watched Jake as he worked furiously on a series of sketches. Then, as the waiter brought them a plate of nibbles and two glasses of wine, he stopped sketching and looked at Jane and said, 'I'm sorry, but I feel really excited about the idea of designing a completely modern town. It will be a real challenge because it must be sustainable both environmentally and economically; and it has to be world-class architecture.'

'You can do it. I wouldn't claim to know very much about architecture, but I know that Sir Andrew Zain is one of the best architects in the world and he obviously respects your talent. I can see from the way you are concentrating on these sketches, that you are excited by the challenge you are about to start. I think the next few months could well establish your own reputation as a great architect. This is a very significant time for you Jake. I am so pleased that we are together.'

Jake stopped sketching and looked at Jane. Then sitting back in his chair, he said, 'We should be together more. Talking with you is really good for me. It helps me think clearly. When are we going to get married? It should be very soon.'

Jane looked surprised and then smiled broadly as she took Jake's hand and said, 'I agree. Let's get married. I guess we should talk with our families first but as soon as it can all be arranged, feels right to me.'

They sat holding hands and they both looked happy. Eventually, Jake said, 'We must tell our families. I think we should go home next weekend and tell them what we have decided. Then we can settle on a date. Where do you want to get married?'

'I have always thought that I would get married in the village church. It's very pretty and it's just down the road from home. We could have the reception in the garden of the village pub. They sometimes put up a marquee for special events and I have been to some of these, and they were very good.'

Jake didn't say anything and was obviously thinking hard. Jane asked if he was happy with her ideas for their wedding. Jake nodded and then said, 'As far as I can remember, I have only ever been to three weddings. The point is they were all civil ceremonies. All three were in really interesting old buildings. The formal ceremony felt similar to what I understand a church wedding is like. The guests were sat either side of an aisle. The bride's family and friends one side and the groom's the other. The beginning of the ceremony was signalled by music being played. I think in two of these marriages, the music was provided by a small group of musicians and in the other one, recorded music was played over a loud-speaker system. Anyway, when the music began, everyone stood up and the bride walked down the aisle on her father's arm to where the registrar was sat, and the groom and his best man were waiting. Then the civil ceremony was conducted by the registrar and the bride and groom walked back down the aisle as everyone applauded. Then there were the formal photographs and after quite a long time during which everyone congratulated the bride and groom and took lots more photographs, we all went into another part of the building where tables were set out for a formal meal. This all worked very well, the food and drinks were good, and the speeches were not too long. After the meal, we all went into yet another part of the building where there was a bar, where people could get a drink and chat, and a dance floor with a group playing a variety of dance tunes. I remember part way through the evening, after several drinks and few dances, that I said to my mother this is the kind of wedding I would like.'

Jake paused and looked at Jane who was clearly surprised by his obvious enthusiasm for a civil ceremony. She asked, 'Are you saying that you don't want to get married in a church?'

'I guess that would work as well. Since you ask, I am not attracted by religions. They seem to me to be organizations that have been set up to manage and control people. I know many people do good in the name of religion; but equally many people do bad things. There are lots of cases on the news of children being abused in what claim to be religious organizations set up to look after them when they have, for whatever reason, lost their parents. Many religions treat women as inferior to men. When for example will we have a female pope?'

'So, are you saying you do not believe in God?'

'That is a different question; and to be honest, I don't know. It's not something I think about very much mainly because I don't have any very clear views about God.'

Jane was clearly trying to work out the implications of what Jake was saying. Then looking very hard at Jake, she asked, 'So, are you saying you will, or you would rather not get married in my local church?'

'If it's important to you, that's what we will do. I don't mind. So, if it's important to you, then that's fine with me. But you don't go to church regularly. In fact, I don't remember you ever saying that you had been to church. So, why is it important?'

'I guess I have always just assumed that I would get married in the village church. It feels right. It's what people in my family do. My parents were married there and everyone I know from the village has got married in the church. It's just what we do.'

Jake smiled broadly as he said, 'That makes sense. We shouldn't break with your traditions. Presumably we need to talk with the vicar, and then we will need to get all the arrangements set up. How long do you think that will take?'

Jane squeezed Jake's hand as she said, 'I think it will probably all take several months if we are going to get everything right. Why don't we go home tomorrow and tell our families that we are going to get married? I can phone Mum and ask her if she can talk with the vicar about arranging the wedding service and the landlord of the pub about the reception. We should both go home and tell our parents face to face. Then we can all start thinking about everything we need to do.'

Jake sat back with a broad smile on his face just as the waiter brought the main courses that Jane had ordered. They both had a large piece of fish in an interesting looking sauce with a few new potatoes. Jake said, 'This looks good.'

Then as they started eating, he said, 'We could go home this afternoon and talk with our parents this evening. Then I could come over to you in time for the morning service at the church on Sunday. It would be good to get the feel of the place and see the vicar in action.'

Jane laughed and then agreed that this was a good plan, but she would need to go back to her apartment to get the things she would need over-night. This reminded Jake that he also would need a few things, so they agreed to meet at Paddington station and travel to Cirencester where they could tell Jake's parents their news and Jake could get his car. Then they could drive to Jane's home and tell her parents they were getting married.

This all worked surprisingly smoothly. This was no doubt helped by Jake and Jane both feeling very happy about the idea of getting married sometime in the next few months. Jake's parents almost certainly sensed the young couple's obvious confidence and excitement and seemed delighted by their son's news. They both agreed that it made sense for the wedding to take place in Jane's local church and the reception to be in the village. So, Jake and Jane set off to discuss their plans with her parents feeling that life was good.

Jane's parent's reaction to the news that she was planning to get married surprised Jake. They congratulated him in a very formal manner and said that they had spoken to the vicar and the local publican and the dates that suited them the best were the middle Saturday in December of the last Saturday in January.

After some discussion, Jane said that she thought the end of January was better as it gave her more time to make sure that everything was just perfect. Jake agreed and Jane's father said they could check this with the vicar and the pub landlord on Sunday.

Jake sensed that as far as Jane's parents were concerned, that was the end of the discussion and they expected him to leave. So, he said that he would come back just before the service in the church started on Sunday. Then Jane walked with him back to his car and said, 'I think this was all a bit of a surprise for my parents, but they will come round to the idea of having a married daughter. So, I will see you tomorrow.'

Jake went back to Cirencester feeling that there was something Jane and her parents were not telling him. There certainly seemed to be something odd about their reaction to the news that their daughter was going to get married. He decided that he would ask Jane about it. When he got home, his parents were very excited and eager to talk about his wedding plans. Then his mother asked if it would be all right if they came to the church with Jake on Sunday. He agreed that was a nice idea and added, 'It will be good for you to meet Jane's parents. I have to say that they did not seem as excited about our wedding as you obviously are. It will be interesting to see what you think of their reaction to getting me as a son-in-law.'

They all laughed, and Jake's father said he would be sure to ask Jane's parents what they thought about their daughter getting married. Next day Jake and his parents drove to the church separately so that he could spend the afternoon with Jane. When they arrived, Jane and her parents were waiting outside the church, and once they were all introduced, they all went into the church. Jake was impressed by the interior. It was smaller than he had expected but he thought that was good as it gave the church a very comfortable feeling. Once they were all sat down, Jake concentrated on looking at the church interior, he decided that there were some interesting details in the stonework on the columns and around the windows. Also, the stained-glass windows were beautiful, especially in the windows where the sun was shining through. He looked at Jane and decided that this was the ideal place for them to get married.

When the service ended and the vicar had spoken to most of the congregation as they left the church, he invited Jake and Jane to come into the vestry. He explained that he had agreed the date for their wedding with Jane's parents and then he carefully explained in some detail what would happen during the wedding service. Once he was sure that they understood what they were each expected to do during the ceremony, the vicar said that he looked forward to seeing them in church on the Sundays leading up to their wedding. He then added, 'I really hope this wedding all goes ahead as we have discussed.'

Jake thought that this was a slightly odd thing to say but he just thanked the vicar and said that he was very much looking forward to what he felt was the most significant day of his life. Jane just thanked him, and then they found their parents waiting outside the church enjoying the sunshine. Jane's father said, 'We have decided to have lunch at the pub where the wedding reception will be held. This will give you a chance to see what the pub provides and have chat with the landlord about the arrangements.'

As they walked to the pub, Jake said to Jane, 'I thought it was bit odd for the vicar to say that he hoped the wedding would go ahead. Have there been cases in the village where weddings have not gone ahead?'

Jane looked embarrassed and her cheeks were suddenly very red as she gripped Jake's hand unusually hard. He asked, 'What is the matter?'

'Maybe I should have told you, but I have been in this situation before. Three years ago, I was engaged to someone else, and we got to just this point in arranging to get married; but over the next few days I realised that I was making a mistake. He had pressured me into getting engaged, and he was not the right person for me to marry; so, I called it off. But this is very different. I know for certain that I want to marry you and maybe that previous experience, helps me to be certain that we are right together.'

Memories of his many previous girlfriends flashed through Jake's mind as he said, 'So that is why your parents and indeed the vicar reacted in what I thought was a somewhat odd way. They were remembering that you have been here before.'

Jane stopped and pulled Jake into a kiss. Then she said, 'That is all behind me. I guess I am relieved that you know but Jake, I love you and I don't have any doubts that getting married is exactly right for us.'

Jake looked at her and then very carefully said, 'We all have a past, and it does make us stronger and better able to make good decisions. So, we are ready to move forward together; and thank you for telling me.'

Lunch in the public house was very enjoyable as Jake and Jane's parents talked about their own weddings, and how much they had enjoyed the day. This led to them advising the young couple to make sure they concentrated on everything that happened during their wedding day. As Jake's mother said, 'It all seemed to go along so fast. There was getting to the wedding, the actual ceremony and then the lunch afterwards with the formal speeches and lots of talking and laughing. Everyone seemed so happy. Then we set off for our honeymoon in London which was all wonderful; and now here we are with Jane and Jake setting off on the same road. It all seems so right.'

Everyone agreed and it was nearly four o'clock before Jake's father suggested that it was time they went home. He settled the bill for lunch and said, 'There will be lots of expenses for us all in ensuring that this wedding is a great occasion; and I am very happy to make the first contribution.'

Jake and Jane said they wanted to take a walk around the village and then they had to get back to London for next week's work. As they walked in the afternoon sunshine, they agreed that the lunch had been a real success and their parents had all got on with each other amazingly well. They agreed that Jane would get ready to go back to London, then they could drive to Cirencester where Jake could pick up whatever he needed, and they would get the train to London.

Next day Jake walked into Sir Andrew Zain's office feeling very happy with life and looking forward to starting work on the design of a new town. When he arrived, the receptionist told Jake that he was to join Sir Andrew in the small drawing office. When he got there, Jake found Sir Andrew looking at an ordinance survey map of an area between Nottingham and Leicester. Sir Andrew immediately said that all the information the government had given him about their ideas for the town was set out in the file on the desk and the map included the area where they wanted the new town to be located. He suggested that Jake should read the main pages in the file. He added, 'There is inevitably a lot of detail but the main features of the town that the government want are set out on the first couple of pages in each section.'

Jake read the summary pages and then looked hard at Sir

Andrew before saying, 'This is very ambitious. They want a town that is sustainable environmentally, economically and socially. It must have first rate health and education facilities, an effective police force alongside real pressure on everyone to behave lawfully. They want first rate residential areas which must provide good places to live for everyone and be close to a rich variety of good shopping facilities. Then they want excellent facilities that enable people to take part in a wide variety of sports. They want several good theatres and cinemas, nightclubs and so on and so on. It's an amazing ambition; and as far as I can understand they have already worked out how this can all be financed. It certainly sets a challenge for us to produce an overall design.'

Sir Andrew smiled broadly and nodded his agreement. Then he said, 'You have got the overall idea and the organization set up to achieve all this, which is the organization that has commissioned us to produce an overall design, have produced very detailed descriptions of all the buildings and infrastructure. This gives us sufficient information to work on a very detailed design. This is what I want us to start on today.'

Sir Andrew then showed Jake a detailed map of the area where the town was to be situated. He let Jake look at it for several minutes and then said, 'You will have noticed that there are good main roads close to the site and a railway line running across the western side of the site. This starts to give us a structure for the transport systems. There is also an obvious source of water for the town in the River Soar. We will need to take water out, use it, get it back to an uncontaminated state and return it to the river. We will need to include sustainable sources of electricity capable of providing all the power needed by the town. It's good that the organizers of this project are already in contact with firms and organizations capable of providing the water and electricity. So, our first job is to work on the overall layout of the town and its major facilities. I suggest we think about the town centre and which buildings this needs to include. Then when we have decided exactly where this should be sited, we can start arranging the other facilities and areas around the centre, letting the structure of the landscape dictate where things should go, so that we gradually build up the complete town.'

Sir Andrew had already decided where the town centre should go, and he showed Jake a sketch of his idea. This showed the town centre sited it in an area that was slightly higher than most of the surrounding area. Jake could see that this would help make the centre stand out and he began to think of creating a distinctive architectural statement that would give the town a real sense of identity. He quickly sketched a series of impressive buildings sited on a small hill. Sir Andrew immediately said, 'That is exactly the kind of thing I had in mind. You need to look at the descriptions we have of the buildings that will form the centre and fit them into your design. Then we will see how well this all works.'

Jake spent the rest of the day working out exactly which buildings would form the centre and fitting them into more detailed designs. By four o'clock he had a sketch of the main town square which was mainly surrounded by shops and offices but dominated by the town hall in the middle of one side and a theatre in the middle of the opposite side. He then added the town's railway station and next to it a bus depot that were both accessed from the street that ran behind the buildings that formed one side of the town centre. He decided that he should now show the design to Sir Andrew. He was clearly impressed with the overall image that Jake had created and said that they provided a good basis for the heart of the new town. He then showed Jake the sketches he had been working on which showed an arrangement of separate residential areas each supported by small shops, offices, medical surgeries and other facilities that people needed near their homes. Between these areas he had added large open areas that each included a mixture of sporting facilities.

Sir Andrew explained that he liked the idea of a distinctive town centre because it would help give the town a sense of identity and, to emphasise this, he wanted his design for the rest of the town to provide a lower key, but nevertheless interesting and varied context for the centre. Jake could understand what he was aiming to create and said, 'I have to say that this is all coming together in a very exciting way. I think we have a really good design for the overall structure of the town. Obviously, there is a mass of work to do in designing all the individual buildings, but this overall structure gives us a robust basis for moving forward. It has been an amazing day and I am certain that we have made a huge step forward in designing the new town. It really is all very exciting.'

Sir Andrew laughed and said that Jake had expressed exactly what he was thinking. The next few weeks were amongst the most memorable that Jake had ever experienced. He and Sir Andrew concentrated on developing their design for the new town. This involved many meetings with the local authorities that were cooperating to create the town, companies who were considering setting up new businesses in the town and companies that were developing the most interesting sustainable technologies. In parallel to all of this, he and Jane were discussing all the details of their wedding and honeymoon. Jake was clearly very excited by the thought of being on honeymoon with Jane and this sense of excitement seemed to carry over into his work in designing the new town with Sir Andrew. Their meetings with companies producing leading edge sustainable technology were producing answers that would enable the town to not only be sustainable but go further and have a positive impact on environmental sustainability. Reasonably predictably, they decided to make electricity the only type of power used in the town. In general, this was produced using solar panels and wind turbines, but they went further towards true sustainability by deciding to get the carbon levels in the town's atmosphere back to the levels that existed before the first industrial revolution. This included planting many trees in the open spaces between the separate housing areas . However, more importantly, they adopted highly innovative technology which captured carbon from the atmosphere and fed it deep underground where it did not add to global warming. One unexpected bonus from this technology was that it enabled Jake and Sir Andrew to use technology capable of capturing heat from deep under-ground which could be used to generate electricity when the wind and solar technologies were not able to produce sufficient to meet the town's needs. As Jake said to Sir Andrew as they were returning to the office after one particularly interesting meeting, 'We really are designing a future that will allow humanity to survive on this planet.'

Sir Andrew looked very thoughtful and then said, 'That is exactly how we must publicise the new town. Its demonstrating to the world how we can all have a sustainable and fulfilling life. We need to discuss this with the local authorities. It will give them the kind of publicity I think they are searching for.'

As soon as they reached Sir Andrew's office, he phoned the chairman of the committee set up to oversee the development of the new town and discussed the idea that the new town provided a vision of a positive future for mankind. The chairman was obviously excited by this idea. He thanked Sir Andrew for telling him about his thoughts and said that he needed to talk with some of his contacts in the media and he would get back to Sir Andrew when he had decided how to promote this important and very exciting idea.

Sir Andrew explained this to Jake and said that he felt they had finished work for the day, and he hoped the chairman would get back to him next day. As Jake walked back to his apartment, he phoned Jane and explained that he had finished work early and suggested they met for dinner. She immediately agreed and once they were settled into a restaurant that they both liked, Jake began to tell her about his idea that the new town represented a future that will help humanity to survive on this planet. Jane said that several of her major clients at the bank had similar ideas about their own businesses. She then used her mobile phone to look up some of the publicity material these clients had produced. It described various aspects of an ideal future in terms that Jake felt expressed what he had in mind for the new town. He made a note of website addresses of the most interesting descriptions and told Jane that this was likely to be very helpful in publicising their design.

Jake and Jane then discussed his ideas about the future and after some twenty minutes or so, Jake said, 'This is really exciting. It's giving me a new vision of the architectural style we should use for buildings in the new town. We really could be producing the future. It's incredible. Jane you are a real inspiration. I am so pleased that we are getting married.'

Jane smiled and the said, 'I do think we have the basis for a really happy marriage. We both have significant contributions to make to every aspect of our life together. We will be able to give our children a rich understanding of life. Between us we understand and have experience of art, finance, business, creativity, sport and so much more. We are so lucky.'

Jake stared at Jane and then said, 'Having children is not something I have thought about, but you are right, the whole point of marriage is to have children. I do hope we have a boy and girl. That would be so good.'

Jane leant towards Jake and kissed him. As she moved back into her seat, she smiled and told him that he was a wonderful man and having a family with him would make her life complete. Jake smiled broadly and then very carefully said, 'I will keep that in mind as I work on the design for the new town. It needs to be a place where I would be happy for my son and daughter to live. This really will help me think about exactly what the town should provide. It gives me a real focus for the whole design and all the individual areas and the kind of things that need to be in the town. I can think about kind of experiences we would want our son and daughter to have as they live in and explore the town.'

This focus became increasingly important in directing Jake and Sir Andrew's ideas for the town. They gave a lot of attention to the open spaces between the individual housing areas so that they provided a variety of natural environments. Sir Andrew contacted groups and organizations dedicated to saving Britain's most endangered wild animals. They helped him design individual areas to provide ideal habitats for the kind of animals they were committed to saving. This led Jake to suggest that the town should include a small zoo so that people could see some of the most beautiful animals in the world. As he said, 'I am always amazed whenever I see a tiger. They are beautiful and we must do whatever we can to ensure they survive and flourish. There are good zoos and game parks in the UK, but we can add another one.'

Jake also ensured that all the areas of housing had good access to primary schools and that the town included several well-equipped secondary schools and a university. As he said to Sir Andrew, 'Finding staff for the schools and university will bring intelligent, well-educated people to the town. This in turn makes it more attractive for the leading-edge industries we want to attract. I see the town becoming a centre for creativity and innovation supported by excellent public services. We just need to be ambitious in everything we include in the town. The hospital should be a first-class teaching hospital doing research into serious medical conditions. Local surgeries need to be well equipped to attract good general practitioners. The town should demonstrate how business, industry and public services can work together to give people a really satisfying life.'

Sir Andrew looked hard at Jake as he said to him, 'You are becoming an outstanding visionary as well as a good architect. Let's get on with turning your vision into reality.'

Chapter 14

The local authorities organizing the construction of the new town that Sir Andrew Zain and Jake Brown had designed decided the time had come to make a formal announcement about their plans. They asked Sir Andrew and Jake to work with their publicity departments and produce a description of the town in a form suitable for television. When this was ready, the leaders of the two authorities made their formal announcement and sent the description to all the main national television companies. This aroused massive interest in all the media and Sir Andrew and Jake were interviewed by the BBC and several commercial television companies.

The reaction to the idea of a totally sustainable town was widely welcomed and seemed to be popular with the public. Many people up and down the country began asking their local authorities why they were not doing more to make their own town or city more sustainable. Also, Sir Andrew and Jake were approached by companies producing building materials in a sustainable manner. One of the first of these produced what they called green concrete. Their approach captured all the carbon dioxide produced during the calcination process which traditionally results in more than half of the emissions involved in cement-making. The company injected this back into the cement which made it stronger than normal concrete. They stored the remaining carbon dioxide under-ground. The other fifty per-cent of the carbon dioxide resulting from the production of traditional concrete comes from the production of the energy needed to provide the heat needed in the calcination process. The company maintained its green credentials by using electricity produced by solar panels and wind turbines.

Jake described this process during one of his interviews on television and as a result a stream of yet more companies contacting him and Sir Andrew. They all claimed to produce various building materials sustainably. As they discussed the claims made by these companies Jake and Sir Andrew realised that they needed expert advice on the credibility of what they were being told. As they wondered exactly how they should move forward, the Vice-Chancellor of Swindon University contacted them to say that he now had all the formal permissions and finance needed to start work on constructing the new university campus. They agreed to meet next day to discuss the next steps; and then on the spur of the moment, Sir Andrew asked the Vice-Chancellor if he could help them evaluate the claims made by the companies claiming to produce construction materials using sustainable technologies. The Vice-Chancellor said he would discuss this with some of his staff and give him an answer at their meeting next day.

In fact, the Vice-Chancellor brought three members of his academic staff to the meeting. They were researching various technologies that took carbon dioxide and methane out of the atmosphere and used it to create fuel that could be used to produce electricity in a totally sustainable manner. They were interested in Sir Andrew's list of companies claiming to produce building materials sustainably. As they looked at the various claims made by these companies the three scientists became increasingly excited. They used the internet to check several of the claims and they seemed to reach firm conclusion about which of the firms looked as if they were worth talking to. The youngest of the three academic staff was a woman who seemed to play a leading part in these discussions, she looked at Sir Andrew, Jake and the Vice-Chancellor and then said, 'It seems that there is a lot of very interesting and effective work being done by several of these companies. I assume the idea is to use construction materials produced using sustainable methods to build the new university campus. As far as we can see from all these advertisements, we think this is a real possibility; and more to the point, we think this is something that the university should do.'

Sir Andrew reminded the Vice-Chancellor that they were planning to use components manufactured in a factory to assemble the university buildings. The Vice-Chancellor nodded and then said, 'I think we should discuss this with the manufacturing company. If we can get them to use sustainable materials, we may be making real progress in bringing the construction industry into this century.'

The member of the university staff who looked as if he was the oldest of the three added, 'Some of the materials being advertised as sustainable are still in a fairly early stage of development, but the university could well help speed up this process. There is substantial government funding for research in this area. As you know, we already have the funding for two major research projects that aim to ensure that some of the more interesting of these sustainable materials are properly tested and developed. I think it could well help our work if we could link it to a modern approach to manufacturing buildings in factories.'

The Vice-Chancellor asked how quickly it would be possible to know if it is possible to link sustainable materials to manufacturing technologies and use the results in constructing the new campus. The woman, who was called Mary Dobson, said, 'It looks from their advertising material that several companies are already producing fully developed, sustainable construction materials. I suggest we work with Sir Andrew Zain and Jake Brown and the manufacturing company they are already talking with. That way we can see if all the materials they need are available is a sustainable form; or if their design can be changed to use the materials that are available. I would hope that this process could be completed during the next month. Then we will know for sure what is possible.'

The Vice-Chancellor looked round the room and then, clearly coming to a decision, he said, 'That is what I want you to do. Manufacturing the buildings that form the new campus in factories using completely sustainable materials is something I know the Prime Minister will support. So, if we need extra funds to make all this possible, I am sure that he will find them for us.'

Sir Andrew smiled as he said, 'This is obviously something we will be very happy to be a part of but what exactly do we need to do?'

The Vice-Chancellor immediately said, 'I suggest this meeting continues with Sir Andrew and Jake Brown and our three scientists working out the answer to that important question. I am happy to leave you to that and I look forward to you letting me know the outcome.'

With that he left the meeting saying that he would be in his office when they had worked out a plan of action to ensure that the new campus was manufactured and assembled as quickly as possible and is fully sustainable. The people left in the office were all clearly wondering what to do next, so, Jake suggested that the university staff came to the office in Swindon the next day. He explained, 'The technicians are working on the detailed drawings and specification for the construction of the new campus, and they will be able to tell you exactly what is needed.'

This was agreed and Jake phoned John Brentford, the partner in the architectural practice who was responsible the project and explained what was happening. It was agreed that that the technicians and the university staff should work together to identify suitable companies to provide all the materials needed. Then we can introduce them to the manufacturing company. As this plan was agreed, Sir Andrew had a phone call from a company who constructed small nuclear plants that generated electricity. As he talked to them, he became increasingly excited and when he finished, he looked round the room and said, 'This really is the future. The company who contacted me can produce an entirely safe and sustainable way of using nuclear energy to produce all the electricity the university will ever need. They have considerable government support which almost certainly means that the cost will fit within the overall budget. I think we need to give this very serious consideration, so, I am meeting representatives of the company here in my office tomorrow. I suggest that Jake and maybe one of the university staff also comes to the meeting.'

Mary Dobson immediately said that she had done some work on using nuclear technology in this way and would be happy to come to the meeting. This was agreed and next day, Sir Andrew, Jake and Mary Dobson met three representatives of a major and well-established manufacturing company. The representatives explained that the government had approached them to work on developing small nuclear power plants because they trusted the quality of their products. As their senior representative explained, 'We had no previous experience of nuclear energy but, with the government's help, we have assembled a team of experienced nuclear engineers. These are all people who have been working on the idea of using nuclear power to generate electricity on a small scale for several years; and, as luck would have it, they had reached the point where they just needed the knowledge and experience of our engineers to produce a prototype unit. The first unit has been working for the last three months and we are now ready to go into production and the new university campus is exactly the kind of development which should include one of our units.'

This was discussed for over two hours during which the nuclear power company showed the other people at the meeting detailed test data which certainly seemed to show that the nuclear units were safe and produced electricity reliably and at a surprisingly low cost. It was agreed that the idea of using a small nuclear plant was sufficiently interesting to discuss it with the Vice-Chancellor. At this point Mary Dobson interrupted to say that if they were going to put the idea of including a nuclear power plant in the new campus to the Vice-Chancellor, they would have to explain why they were planning to include solar and wind electricity generation in the design as well as nuclear. As she said, 'It sounds over the top. Most of the time the university will be supplying electricity to the national grid, and it is very unlikely that it would ever need to take any from the grid. You need to think this through before talking with the Vice-Chancellor.'

Sir Andrew looked at her and then said, 'That sounds very sensible and Miss Dobson, I would be interested to know your feelings on the matter. Should we include a nuclear plant in the scheme or is a bad idea?'

Mary Dobson nodded and then replied, 'The idea of having a nuclear power plant in Swindon will inevitably result in local opposition. People will protest. There will be marches and sit-ins on the site; but this will all give the university publicity, so, I am not sure what view the Vice-Chancellor will take. My view is that we should go ahead with the nuclear plant but that means we don't need the solar panels and wind turbines because my understanding is that nuclear plants need to keep running. They are not easy to switch on and off at short notice.'

The senior representative from the nuclear power company agreed and added, 'I can't see the point of having solar panels and wind turbines as well as our plant. The obvious back-up for the rare occasions when our plant is not working, which we hope happens very rarely, is the national grid. Most of the time, we would be contributing to the grid, so it is the obvious back-up.'

Jake was frowning hard as he interrupted by saying, 'The future has to be sustainable sources of energy; and solar and wind are the obvious answers. I can see the benefits of nuclear power, but it comes with real risks. I think we should put two schemes to the Vice-Chancellor. One based on providing electricity by including a nuclear power plant and one based on our current design which is based on the power coming from solar and wind. We need the capital and running costs of both schemes and some judgement about how secure the energy supply would be from the two alternatives.'

Everyone looked at Jake and then Sir Andrew said, 'I agree. It will give us all a clearer picture of the decision we need to make; and it doesn't rule out including all these forms of power generation in the final design, but what Jake has just suggested will give everyone, including the Vice-Chancellor, a chance to think clearly about the choices.'

This was agreed and the meeting quickly decided on what needed to be done so they were ready to discuss the choices with the Vice-Chancellor. When the meeting ended, Sir Andrew said to Jake, 'You were very impressive in that meeting. We could have gone on discussing all the options for hours, but you cut through all the difficult choices to give us a way forward. Now we need to get to work; and another thought that occurred to me is that this is all very relevant to our thinking about the new town which we need to concentrate on as soon as we have made all the design decisions on the university campus. In fact, I suggest that you take the lead in providing all the design information needed to take the two options to the Vice-Chancellor. Ask me anything you need advice on but think of it as your project. I will concentrate on the new town.'

The immediate task for Jake was designing a building to accommodate the nuclear power plant. Essentially it needed a large box with sophisticated insulation, but this was very different to all the other buildings that made up the new campus. After trying several different designs, Jake settled on a simple box shaped building clad in copper and surrounded by trees. His idea was to make the building in effect disappear as the copper weathered and turned green, he hoped it would blend in with the trees. He then positioned it close to the lake where it was remote from all the other buildings. He hoped this would ensure that the nuclear plant was hardly noticed and so would not be too controversial.

Jake was so absorbed in his work that he only saw Jane once or twice a week. She seemed to understand that he was at a crucial stage of his career and seemed happy to give him the time to concentrate on his work. When they did meet, she encouraged him to talk about his designs, but she did get him to discuss their wedding plans and to agree who they would invite to the ceremony. In addition to their relatives and Jane's friends from her village and the bank, the list included most of Jake's colleagues from the Swindon practice and the key players in the Cirencester cricket team. He also included Sir Andrew Zain and his wife. When he suggested this, Jane agreed that it was a nice idea and asked Jake what the great architect had said when he told him that he was getting married. This made Jake realise that he had not told Sir Andrew that he was about to get married. In fact, he did not discuss any personal aspects of his life with him. They just talked about designs. He laughed to himself and then explained to Jane that he had just realised that Sir Andrew did not know that they were going to get married. She told him that her manager at the bank knew and was happy for her to take whatever time off she needed. Jane then added, 'That means that we can go on honeymoon which is something we haven't discussed. Do you have any ideas about where we should go?'

Jake said, 'It would be good to go somewhere warm. They we can relax on a beach and have a complete break from work. It will be great. Have you had any thoughts?'

Jane smiled and said, 'I do like your idea. I have been thinking about similar possibilities and have been looking at Egypt which has good weather at that time of year. There is a great hotel at Sham El Sheikh which is on the Red Sea. It has beautiful swimming pools and easy access to the beach.'

Jake got increasingly excited as he looked at the description of the hotel. It had three swimming pools, all overlooking the ocean, that each provided guests with a wide choice of swimming and sunbathing possibilities. It also had three restaurants, which between them served a variety of cuisines throughout the day and were all highly rated by various international experts. They agreed that this was exactly what they wanted and so they decided to use the internet to book ten days at the hotel. The hotel's website allowed them to choose a suite overlooking the white sandy beach which looked particularly beautiful from the bedroom window.

Jane laughed and kissed him. Then she said, 'This is all wonderful. I still have many things to do to make sure our wedding is just as perfect, but it is all going well, I do love you, Jake.'

As she pulled him into a long kiss, Jake thought that life was perfect, and it was getting even better all the time. The honeymoon would be wonderful. Sleeping with Jane; having sex with her; spending all day in their swimming costumes by the pool or in the ocean; it was going to be perfect. Then he remembered that he had to tell Sir Andrew that he was getting married and would need some time off to go on honeymoon. Jane immediately realised that something had changed, and she asked Jake if he had a problem. He said, 'We have just booked our honeymoon hotel and I haven't told Sir Andrew that we are getting married.'

Then he laughed and added, 'I'm sure he will be fine; but I must tell him.'

Next day Jake told Sir Andrew about his wedding and honeymoon plans. Sir Andrew seemed delighted and immediately agreed that Jake could have all the time he needed for a honeymoon in Sham El Sheikh. He added, 'Egypt is a fascinating country. There are so many ancient monuments there that really are world class. You must at least go and see the pyramids. You will, of course have seen many pictures of them, but being there is totally different. They have a presence that astonishes every architect who is lucky enough to get the chance to walk around them. I should add that Egypt has many other examples of ancient architecture that are amongst the finest that exist anywhere. I particularly like the Valley of the Kings which is one of the most amazing places I have ever visited. It is a really good choice of a place to go for your honeymoon. It will be memorable for many reasons.'

Then he added, 'I would really like to meet the woman you are marrying. Maybe you could both come to dinner with my wife and myself. Find out what dates suit you and your fiancée over the next week or so.'

This was all arranged, and on the agreed evening Jake and Jane met and then took a taxi to Sir Andrew's house which overlooked Hyde Park. Sir Andrew's wife, Gill, was younger than him and was clearly pleased to welcome the young couple. Dinner was set out on a small dining table with just four chairs around it. They were soon discussing the idea of creating a new town, which was the project taking up most of Sir Andrew's time. Jane was clearly very interested in this idea and asked a series of questions before saying, 'One reason I am so interested in this is that several of the bank's main customers are venture capitalists who might well be interested in funding this kind of development.'

Sir Andrew asked several questions to make sure he understood what Jane was suggesting and then said, 'The local authorities who are taking the lead in this project have some government funding, but my impression is that beyond that they are hoping that the companies planning to set up businesses in the new town will provide the rest of the money. I don't think they have firm assurances that this will all work. Your idea is not something that I have heard them discuss but it's certainly something I would like to suggest to them. I will need a clear understanding of what is possible. Could this be discussed with some of the companies you have in mind?'

Jane said that the firms she was thinking of normally dealt

with the managers at the bank, so she would need to talk with her immediate manager. Sir Andrew seemed excited by the idea of helping the local authorities to get their hands on a new source of finance. This was evident when he suggested that he should come to the branch where Jane worked to discuss the funding options with the manager. Jane agreed to set up the meeting and Sir Andrew said he would wait until after the meeting to mention it to the people from the two local authorities that he was working with. This all served to make the evening very enjoyable and probably helped ensure that Sir Andrew and his wife said they would be happy to come to the wedding.

Sir Andrew had arranged for a taxi to take Jake and Jane back to their apartments and as they settled into the back seat, they both agreed that it had been a very enjoyable evening and Jane added, 'It might turn out to be very significant for my career. If the bank can link one of the major financial organizations that we have as customers with the new town, I could get the credit for taking an important initiative.'

Jake smiled as he said, 'So, the new town might be important for both our careers.'

This indeed turned out to be the case but in ways that neither Jake nor Jane could have anticipated.

Chapter 15

Estimates of the cost of constructing and then running the new Swindon University campus with electricity provided by solar panels and wind turbines and the alternative of including a small nuclear power plant was prepared surprisingly quickly. Then a meeting was arranged for Sir Andrew, Jake and Mary Dobson with the university Vice-Chancellor to discuss the two schemes. The Vice-Chancellor listened to Sir Andrew's description and asked several questions to make sure he understood the financial implications of the two options. Then he said, 'The economics of the two schemes don't really help very much. The nuclear power plant is more expensive but provides a more reliable source of electricity. This means that if we just use solar and wind generation, we are likely to need more electricity from the national grid to make up for times when the sun and the wind fail. That means that within about five years, the costs pretty much balance and then the nuclear option gives us lower running costs. However, I am left with two questions. First, what will be the reaction to having a nuclear plant on the campus; and second, did you consider the technologies that Mary Dobson and her colleagues are researching? My understanding is that they are researching technologies that take carbon dioxide and methane out of the atmosphere to create fuel that enables electricity to be produced in a totally sustainable manner. That could be a better long-term approach than either of those you have described.'

Mary Dobson said, 'In the long-term that may well be the

case, but at present the commercial development of the technology is at an early stage. There is a company in America that claims to be planning to use this approach to supply electricity for a new shopping complex in Chicago but I'm not sure of the timescale. So, I do think that the two options we are considering represent what is currently available as alternatives to using electricity produced from fuels that damage the environment.'

The Vice-Chancellor persisted, 'Are you telling me that the technology you are researching is still at a theoretical stage?'

Mary Dobson seemed to be uncomfortable at the way the discussion was going but very firmly said, 'The science is well established but to date there is no example of the technology being put into practice on a commercial scale. Just to be clear, I don't think there is a commercially viable way of applying the science I am researching to the generation of electricity. So, it seems to me and my colleagues that, at present, the two options we are here to discuss are the best approaches for the university campus.'

The Vice-Chancellor was clearly thinking hard and after a few moments silence, he changed the discussion by saying, 'I will be surprised if the idea of using a nuclear plant does not provoke a great deal of opposition. I wonder if there is any research that shows nuclear power to be very safe? It would be useful to know that before we make a final decision. The nuclear option is more reliable but the solar and wind option is initially cheaper, even allowing for the need to use power from the national grid when the sun and the wind let us down. I can see from your figures that nuclear is likely be less expensive in the long run, mainly because for most of the time we would be supplying power to the national grid. Let's meet again, next week, and in the meantime find out what studies have been done on the safety of the nuclear generators. Also, Mary, I would like you to find out for certain what the American company working on generating electricity from carbon dioxide and methane could offer us. That really could be the sustainable way forward and it would be foolish for us to miss this opportunity to be at the forefront of what is, without doubt, a major step forward for mankind.'

Sir Andrew added, 'We will help you approach the American company because I like the idea of linking our architecture to the leading edge of sustainable technology. This is obviously more important for Jake and Mary and their generation. So, I think they should be talking to the Americans, but I do feel a responsibility for helping to correct the mistakes of the past which are so damaging for Earth's environment.'

This surprised Jake because he had not heard Sir Andrew talk about environmental issues in that way before. So, he added, 'I agree; in many ways this is the most promising way forward and I suggest that we contact the American company and maybe we should go and see exactly what they can provide.'

Mary said, 'I would certainly be happy to visit the American company. I have their contact details and can try to set up a suitable meeting. I suggest that I go with Jake and work out if there is any possibility that they can provide a practical source of electricity for the new campus.'

The Vice-Chancellor looked at Sir Andrew and then said, 'Go ahead and have the meeting with the American company and then we can decide once and for all on the best way forward. Also, I want to know if there is any information about the risks and safety of nuclear power generation that will help us to make the right decision.'

Mary said that she would look into what the American company are able to provide. She added, 'We have exchanged some of our research results with a team at Chicago University who are doing similar research to us. They may well have some links with the company offering to produce a plant to supply electricity for a new shopping complex.'

Sir Andrew said, 'I will ask the company that manufactures the nuclear plants what information they have about the safety of their approach.'

This was all agreed and the Vice-Chancellor said they should meet again as soon as Jake and Mary had all the key information. Mary suggested that Jake should come to her office, and they could organize their visit to the USA. As they walked from the Administrative Building to the near-by building where Mary did her research, Jake really looked at her for the first time. He decided that she was an unusually attractive woman, and he felt an odd sense of excitement at the prospect of going to America with her.

Mary managed to telephone the leader of the research into the use of carbon dioxide and methane at Chicago University. He confirmed that his research team had been working with the company that was planning to use these ideas to supply electricity for a new shopping complex . He also agreed that she could visit the university and discuss their research interests and added that he could introduce her to the company planning to put their ideas into practice.

The visit to Chicago was all arranged surprisingly quickly and Jake and Mary were booked on a plane to fly to the USA just three days later. Jake had spent most of the three days ensuring that he had a good description of the university campus and working out exactly what questions he needed to get answered.

During this time, he had seen Jane just once. They had dinner together and Jake had explained why he needed to go to Chicago while Jane was more interested in talking about the detailed arrangements for their wedding. When he got back to his apartment after his dinner with Jane, Jake realised that he had not mentioned that he would be going with Mary Dobson. He couldn't decide if this had just not cropped up in their conversation or if he had deliberately kept it secret.

Jake and Mary met at Heathrow and checked in together. Mary was wearing a smart suit which had a surprisingly short skirt. Jake struggled to get the thought out of his mind that Mary was a very attractive woman. Once they were on the plane, Mary took her jacket off and settled into the window seat. She was wearing a very revealing shirt that gave Jake a disturbingly clear view of her breasts. They talked almost non-stop all the way to Chicago and Jake discovered that she was not only a very attractive woman, but she also had a distinguished academic career. She explained that she had taken the research job at Swindon University was because it allowed her to pursue her own research interests. She also mentioned that she had been offered a job at Oxford University but that would have meant working for other researchers on their ideas and interests.

They were met at Chicago airport by the leader of the research team at Chicago University that Mary had been corresponding with. He took them to a hotel in the centre of Chicago, ensured they checked in and then he said that he would pick them up at eight thirty next morning. Jake and Mary decided to take a walk around the main shopping area of Chicago to get some exercise before having dinner. Once they were in the street, Mary took Jake's hand and smiled as she said, 'I don't want to lose you in this crowded street.'

They were both fascinated by their first experience of a major American city and Mary insisted on looking round a big departmental store which seemed to Jake to be very similar to those in England. Then they found a small restaurant which was next to a night club. Mary immediately said, 'Let's eat here and then if we feel good, we can see what the night club has to offer.'

A waiter showed them to a table where they could sit side by side on big wooden bench. They had both given the waiter their overcoats and Jake was now very aware that Mary was wearing a very revealing lacy top and an extremely short skirt. They both quickly ordered their dinner and Mary then turned towards Jake and said, 'We should check exactly what we need to discuss with the company claiming to be able to generate electricity from carbon dioxide and methane.'

Jake found it difficult to think clearly as his mind was dominated by Mary's breasts and thighs. She was very beautiful and the way she leant forward and turned towards him seemed to suggest that she was very available. He did manage to say, 'I think you will be taking the lead as you need to be clear that the company's technology is soundly based; but given that, I need to find out exactly what kind of construction would be needed to include a plant that generates electricity from carbon dioxide and methane.'

Mary agreed and added, 'This is very exciting for me. This is a subject I have been working on for almost two years and now there may be a real opportunity to put the results into practice. We have generated electricity in the laboratory but for the company to operate on a commercial scale, they must have solved several problems about reliability that we think are bound to be very difficult.'

The portions of the starters and main courses they had

ordered were surprisingly large. They were well presented and very tasty but neither Jake nor Mary were able to finish any of the dishes. They both decided that they could not manage a dessert and Mary said, 'I guess we will have to get used to American style food but now I want to see what the night club is like. A few dances will help us digest this amazing meal.'

Jake laughed and agreed. The night club was very stylish but surprisingly dark. Jake and Mary choose a table which overlooked the dance floor and gave them a good view of the stage where a group of jazz musicians were playing a slow number. Mary immediately said that she wanted to dance, and they joined the crowded dance floor. Mary pulled Jake into a close hold and moved her body suggestively in a way that made Jake think about sex. She murmured, 'This feels so good. You do move well. It feels right.'

The evening continued in this way with Jake increasingly feeling that Mary wanted to seduce him. Back at their table, they ordered drinks that sounded interesting, and Mary said, 'This is a really good night club. We are lucky to have found it on our first night together. It's great to be here with you Jake. You are an amazingly attractive man.'

At that moment the waiter brought their drinks which were more ordinary than the descriptions had suggested, but Jake was pleased to suggest that they drink to a successful meeting with the company. The evening continued in much this way with Mary becoming ever more explicitly sexy. As they drank more, Jake found his thoughts dominated by this very attractive and apparently very available woman. Their dances became more explicitly sexy and several times Jake felt that he was close to ejaculating. Mary was encouraging him to caress her breasts every time they danced and then as they sat back at their table, she guided Jake's hand onto her thighs. After an explicitly sexy dance, Mary pulled Jake into a long kiss and said, 'I think we are ready for bed.'

Back at the hotel, she led Jake into her room and before he really realised what he was doing, they were in bed together having sex. It was totally satisfying and when they had both reached a climax, Jake settled back on the bed, and looked at Mary. He could see that her face and indeed every part body were amazingly beautiful. Next morning Jake was woken by Mary sliding on top of him and pushing herself onto him. The she began slowly moving back and forth as Jake caressed her breasts. They again both reached a climax together and Jake said, 'I never knew sex could be so exciting. You are wonderful, beautiful and so good at making love. I'm in danger of falling hopelessly in love with you.'

Mary smiled, 'That is my aim. You are the most amazing man I have ever met, and we are so good together; but now we have an important meeting to deal with.'

The meetings with the university researchers and the company planning to construct a plant that generates electricity from carbon dioxide and methane took up most of the day. During Jake's meeting with the engineers who were designing the new plant, they were joined by one of the partners from the firm of architects who were designing the shopping complex that would be supplied by the electricity generated by the ground-breaking plant. He seemed to be very interested in the design for Swindon University's new campus and several times checked that Jake was working with Sir Andrew Zain. After spending over an hour looking at all aspects of the design and asking a lot of questions, he said to Jake, 'This is very impressive. I would like to continue this discussion in our office tomorrow if that is possible.'

The construction firm's engineers said that Jake would have all the information he needed to include their plant in his design, so, the architect invited Jake to come to his office the next day. Jake felt excited by being taken seriously by an American architectural practice, so, when he met Mary that evening, he said that he had a lot to talk about. Mary was also clearly excited by the research she had been discussing and explained to Jake that she now had several new ideas for taking her own work forward in an interesting direction. As she said, 'The American researchers work with industry much more as a matter of routine than we do in England. Their view is that this cooperation provides benefits to the academics and the industrialists. It's certainly something I need to think about when we get home. Having said that, they certainly took me seriously and I have another meeting with the research team leader tomorrow morning.'

Jake said how pleased he was that Mary's day had gone well and added, 'I am sure the company hope that I can give them useful contacts that might well lead to them being asked to construct their plants in the UK. They were certainly very helpful in giving me all the information I need to include one of their plants in the design for the new university campus. More interestingly, I have a meeting tomorrow with the architects who are designing the shopping complex which will use electricity from the plant you have been discussing. I met one of the partners from the architectural practice and he wants to see me tomorrow.'

They quickly agreed to have a quick dinner and then they both wanted to spend some time checking the notes of their meetings to make sure they had everything they needed or if there were any unanswered questions. As a result, they both spent the night in their own hotel rooms and met very briefly over breakfast as Mary needed to get to the university early. Jake decided that she looked excited and very beautiful as she set off for the university. This made him think that he had missed the chance to spend the night with her. Then he thought about Jane and began to wonder what he was thinking.

These thoughts were still churning around in his mind as he made his way to the architect's office. Once inside the building, he could see that it overlooked Lake Michigan. He was shown into the office of the partner he had met the previous day. This had spectacular views out across the lake. The partner could see that Jake was impressed by the view from his office and he said that he was sure this was one of the most attractive places to work in the whole of Chicago. He then reminded Jake that he was called Adam Jefferies and showed him to an armchair that gave Jake spectacular views of the lake. Jake said, 'This is amazing. I agree that this is a really beautiful office.'

Adam Jefferies smiled and said that he was pleased that Jake liked Chicago. Then he added that he wanted to have another look at the design for the Swindon University campus. He asked a series of detailed questions about the design and was very interested in Jake's thinking about the overall layout and many of the detailed design decisions. Jake enjoyed talking about his design to a man who was clearly interested in his approach to design. Then Adam Jefferies smiled and sat back as he said, 'Jake, I guess you may be wondering why I am so interested in your work. We are looking to recruit a new architect capable of taking this practice forward. Your approach of first ensuring you have a clear description of the spaces needed in whatever building or buildings you are designing; and only then thinking about the design is unusual and obviously very effective. I am in no doubt that you have the kind of distinctive talent that we are looking for. I realise that this is not something you would have expected, but what are your immediate thoughts?'

Jake sat back in his chair clearly very surprised. Then very slowly he said, 'This is not anything I have thought about. Working with Sir Andrew Zain is very satisfying, and my career is growing rapidly and in the right direction. This is an amazing country, but I don't really know enough about it to know where to start thinking about your amazing offer.'

Adam Jefferies laughed and said, 'I fully understand your reaction. I have a formal statement of what we are offering you in this file. It's what we have prepared for whoever we decide to try to bring into the practice. I suggest that we find you somewhere to sit so that you can read and then think about our detailed offer. Then we can talk again.'

This was quickly arranged, and Jake found himself sat in an office overlooking the lake with the file which set out exactly what he was being offered on the desk in front of him. He slowly opened it and began reading. It was obviously intended to provide the basis for a formal contract of employment, and it clearly set out the terms and conditions that would apply to whoever they invited to join the practice. The main points were that Jake would be working for the practice for a year and then if Jake and the partners agreed he would become a partner in the practice. Initially he would be earning rather more than twice what he was currently earning and if he did become a partner, his annual income would more than double again. The document gave Jake a general description of the practice, the people it employed and its annual balance sheet.

Jake read the file carefully and then stared out of the window at the lake. This was another world for him. He needed time to think and maybe discuss all of this with Sir Andrew Zain and the Swindon practice which still employed him and which, he was sure, had plans to make him a partner. He spent some time re-reading the file and decided that he needed time to think.

Jake asked the secretary who was working in the space outside the office he was in if she could tell Adam Jefferies that he was ready to talk. She immediately said that she would take him to Adam's office as she knew he was keen to talk with Jake. Adam Jefferies welcomed him back to his office and asked if he had made any decisions. Jake smiled briefly before replying, 'This is a very generous offer that anyone would want to take very seriously. I need to think about what is right for me because I am at a key stage in my career and working with Sir Andrew Zain has already taught me a lot; but I am sure I still have much to learn and working in this practice would take my career even further forward So, I would like a few days to think about what you have offered me so I can be certain that I am making the right decision. I would like to have a copy of the information in the file, which I will of course keep to myself, and I will make a firm decision by this time next week.'

Adam Jefferies looked slightly surprised by Jake's statement but said, 'I think that is very sensible and if there is anything else you need to know, contact my secretary and she will ensure you get our reply as quickly as possible. I look forward to working with you and, in due course, welcoming you into the practice as a partner. Now, what are you doing for lunch?'

Jake explained that he did not have any plans for lunch and Adam Jefferies offered to show him the staff restaurant. He added, 'We provide a simple lunch, but it will give you a chance to meet some of the people you will be working with when you join us.'

The restaurant area was surprisingly large and operated on a self-service basis. Adam Jefferies guided Jake through the area where the food was laid out and they both helped themselves to an interesting looking lunch and then joined a table where six people were already seated. Adam Jefferies introduced Jake to each of them and explained that he was a British architect who may well be coming to work with them. The conversation turned to American sport which Jake admitted that he did noy know a great deal about. A young woman sat opposite him said, 'When you come to Chicago, you will be able to see some of the best baseball and American football.'

Then Jake found himself trying to explain why a cricket test match took five days to complete. This amused everyone around the table who quite simply could not understand why people would actually go to watch a game that took five days and often ended as a draw because it was not completed, even after the full five days. The conversation then turned to the new shopping complex the practice was designing and the possibility of it using electricity generated from carbon dioxide and methane. Jake found himself describing his design for the university campus which was considering using this same form of energy. The lunch seemed to pass very quickly in this manner and Adam Jefferies said that it was time to get back to work. He took Jake to lift which went down to main entrance and exit and said, 'Jake, I am very much looking forward to welcoming you into the practice. I can see from our entertaining lunch that you will fit into our practice very well. Please, let me know as soon as you have made a decision; and if there is anything else you need to know, let my secretary know and we will get back to you with our best answer.'

Jake spent most of the afternoon walking round the edge of the lake looking at Chicago's architecture. He was not keen on all the high-rise buildings, which may have been why, when he saw a bookshop, and went in and found two books about the architecture of the city. He was pleased to find many interesting low-rise buildings in districts of Chicago away from the centre. He bought the one which looked most interesting and then found a small café where he sat and studied the book for over an hour. As a result, Jake got back to the hotel at almost the same time as Mary Dobson. They went up to her bedroom as Jake began telling her about his surprising day when she suddenly interrupted him by saying, 'I am struggling to believe what you are telling me because the university have offered me a job. We could both be working here in Chicago. This is fate at work.'

Jake was obviously astonished by Mary's news and gave her his full attention as she explained that the university would employ her in a role that allowed her to continue her research. She would be required to hold one or two seminars each week with students doing master's degrees. These would begin by her describing some aspect of her research and then the students could comment or ask questions. Mary added, 'The attraction of this is that the discussions with master's students will almost certainly raise interesting ideas that help my research. I have done a few seminars like this at Swindon but here in Chicago, I would be paid a much higher salary and be working in significantly better laboratories and have better technical support in pursuing my research ideas. So, it would be fantastic if you were also working here in Chicago.'

Then she pulled Jake into a long kiss and said, 'This is fate. We are meant to be together.'

Jake was not at all sure what to say, so, he suggested they went out and found somewhere where they could have dinner and discuss what they both should do. Mary clearly had a different idea as she gently pushed Jake onto her bed and lay down on top of him pulling him into a long, passionate kiss. Then she began unfastening his trousers and unfastening her dress. Jake helped get them both totally naked and Mary moved so she was right on top of Jake and pushed his penis right into her vagina. By moving gently at first and gradually pushing him further and further inside herself, Mary ensured that they both totally enjoyed their sex for over twenty minutes. They both came together and as Mary rolled back onto the bed, she murmured, 'That was the most amazing experience of my life. We are made for each other, my darling Jake.'

Jake turned towards her and kissed her. Then as he looked at her, he decided that he had never seen anyone who looked as beautiful as Mary did at that moment. He kissed her again and then moved so that he was on top of her as his penis gently hardened. He said, 'We can do that again.'

As she smiled, he slid back into her and began gently moving back and forth. Gradually his penis got harder, and they were both totally absorbed in their completely satisfying sex. When they both came again, Jake managed to say, 'You are so beautiful in every way. This is amazing.'

They lay side by side on the bed, both feeling totally happy, until Jake suddenly said, 'I feel hungry. I noticed that the hotel brings meals to the rooms and the menu looks interesting.'

Mary agreed and they both decided what to order. The food was ordinary, but they were hungry, and their minds were filled with thoughts about what they had just been doing. Jake's mind was suddenly dominated with the question that he was planning to get married, so what was he doing here with another woman? Mary seemed to sense a change in Jake's demeanour, and asked, 'Do you have a problem? You seem to have changed. Suddenly you seem to be different.'

Without thinking, Jake blurted out, 'I am engaged to be married. We are planning our wedding for early next year. Yet here I am with you; and it all felt so right.'

Mary sat up and pulled the sheet up round her breasts. She stared at Jake and then got off the bed saying, 'You have just ruined one of the most beautiful experiences I have ever had. I can't believe you. You are a total a fraud.'

She picked up Jake's clothes and threw them at him as she shouted, 'Get out of here. I don't ever want to see you again.'

Chapter 16

Jake spent a confused night in his hotel bedroom following the disastrous ending of his evening with Mary. He washed and dressed early, still try to work out why he had told her he was getting married. Everything had been going so beautifully up to that point and then he had so stupidly ruined their relationship.

Their flight back to the UK was scheduled for that morning and he was still sat wondering what to do about Mary, when he got a call from the hotel reception telling him that the taxi had arrived to take him to the airport. He tried to contact Mary but there was no response when he knocked on her door. There was no sign of her when he got to the reception area, and then the receptionist told him that she had already checked out and taken an earlier taxi to the airport.

There was no sign of Mary at the airport and when Jake got onto the plane, the seat next to him was empty. He slept for most of the journey back to London and it was only when he was waiting for his luggage that he saw Mary. She was standing with her back towards him on the opposite side of the luggage collection area. He walked over to her and said, 'I missed you on the plane. Can we talk.'

Mary glanced at him and walked away without saying anything. As Jake stood staring at her as she walked to the other side of the luggage area, the luggage began to arrive. Mary collected her case and walked out through the exit, totally ignoring Jake. His luggage came through irritatingly late and when he did get out into the general area of the airport terminal, there was no sign of Mary. Jake spent some time looking round for her and tried to phone her but got no response. Eventually Jake caught a train into central London and during the journey, phoned Jane to tell her that he was back in London. After some discussion during which Jake said that he was feeling very tired, as it had already been a long day, they agreed to meet the following evening.

Jake walked from the station to his apartment still thinking about Mary and how attractive she was and what a mess he had made of their relationship. Consequently, he had very mixed feelings when he reached his apartment to find Linda James in the kitchen drinking a glass of wine. She immediately stood up and said, 'Jake, I'm so pleased to see you. I have been trying to contact you for the last two or three hours.'

'What are you doing here? It must be ages since I last saw you.'

Linda smiled at Jake's question and then said, 'The Good Time Girls are working in London for most of this week. We have been in Manchester and Liverpool for quite a long time, and then we also did a few performances in Scotland. So, it must be almost two months since we were last in London but this week we are working here. So, I used the key you gave me to let myself in. I hope that is all right?'

Jake laughed and then said, 'It's always good to see you; and you are looking great. I must try to come and see your group perform. Where are you working this week?'

Linda told him and then had to tell him the address of the nightclub because he had never heard of it. She added, 'My understanding is that it is a very smart club just off Park Lane. That means that many of the customers are wealthy businessmen staying in Park Lane hotels.'

Jake said that he was already looking forward to seeing the club and The Good Time Girls. Then he laughed and added, 'I will do my best to look business-like when I come to see the group.'

Then he remembered that he had arranged to meet Jane, so, he said, 'I am going out tomorrow evening, and I have just got back from America so I need to sleep but I will try to get to see you the day after tomorrow.'

Linda smiled and said that she was already looking forward to Jake coming to the club as she always did her best performances when Jake was in the audience. Jake laughed and said that he needed to get to bed. Linda looked at him in a strangely intense manner and said, 'I will come with you. I don't need to be at the club until eight-thirty. Come on.'

Jake was totally startled by Linda's suggestion and could not work out what to say. Before he had really given any thought to how he should respond, they were both naked on Jake's bed. Linda was caressing Jake's penis as she slid herself on top of him and pulled him into a long kiss. Then she pushed herself onto him and began slow, rhythmic sex that lasted for more than twenty minutes. Jake was totally captivated by having this very beautiful woman satisfying every aspect of his sexual feelings. Eventually they both came almost at the same moment; and then Linda slowly moved so they were lying side by side holding each other's hands.

They lay like this for over half an hour until Linda said that she really ought to get ready for that evening's performance. She smiled and said, 'I will be thinking of you when I am doing my most sexy movements in our dances.'

Jake was feeling very tired and just said that he needed to

sleep, and he would see her again in the morning. Jake woke early next morning to find Linda asleep next to him. She looked even more beautiful than she had the evening before. Jake just lay quietly staring at this amazing woman and wondering where she fitted into his life. After nearly an hour, during which time Jake could not reach any convincing conclusions about his relationship with Linda, he suddenly remembered that he should be in the office discussing everything he had learnt in America with Sir Andrew Zain.

Jake's meeting with Sir Andrew was surprisingly short as they quickly decided they could keep the essential design of the building to house the plant generating electricity the same as the one they had agreed for a nuclear plant. The building was a slightly different size and needed a different form of insulation, but they agreed that a copper box surrounded by trees looked right irrespective of what was inside it. Jake spent most of the day working out all the details so that late that afternoon, he gave the quantity surveyors all the information they needed to calculate the cost. This included contact details for the American firm who would be supplying the technology that converted carbon dioxide and methane into electricity. Jake checked that they had everything they needed and then he walked home feeling happy with life. As he reached his apartment, Linda was just leaving to go to a rehearsal by The Good Time Girls at the nightclub they would be performing at that evening. Jake then remembered that he was meeting Jane.

Over dinner Jane described all the arrangements she had made for their wedding and said, 'It is going to be a beautiful day. I get excited every time I think about it. I know that planning our wedding is distracting me from my work but none of the managers have complained yet.'

Jake asked what he should be doing, and Jane looked thoughtful and then said, 'I will set out the schedule for the day and we can check that it all suits you. That way you will know exactly what you need to be doing.'

'That is a good plan. We are very busy at work designing both the university campus and the new town. I cannot remember having more to do at work than I have just now; but it's all interesting and exciting. I guess I am lucky to be involved in these major projects.'

Jane smiled as she said, 'It just shows how talented an architect you are.'

Jake laughed, 'I must make time to study your design for our wedding.'

Jake felt very happy as he travelled with Jane on the underground railway to where Jane had an apartment. She invited him in when they arrived and then made them both a cup of coffee and snuggled close to Jake on the settee in her living room. They kissed and cuddled for nearly an hour as they talked about Jane's plan for their wedding day. Eventually, she said that Jake should go back to his apartment so that she could finalise the schedule for their wedding day and send it to him.

Jake got the schedule next morning just as he got to Sir Andrew Zain's office. It was impressively detailed and as Jake read through it, he began to envisage the day. This made him think about his own situation. Why was he having sex with Mary and Linda while Jane was concentrating on planning their wedding so well? Was he ready to get married? Jane was beautiful, intelligent, had a successful career in the bank and clearly wanted to marry him; but was he ready to make that commitment?

The more Jake looked at Jane's schedule for their wedding

day, the more concerned he felt. Jane had obviously thought about every detail of the day and decided what she wanted to happen. It was impressive, but Jake could not envisage how anyone could think like this. He began to wonder if Jane planned her whole life like this, and if so, was this something he could live with? The more he thought about this, the more examples he thought he had noticed in Jane's behaviour. She always arranged a precise time for when they would meet and then, as far as Jake could remember, she turned up on time. She always liked to know exactly what they would be doing whenever they met.

The schedule for their wedding day carried these examples of her behaviour to another level but was this how Jake felt that he wanted to live? As he thought about this, Sir Andrew came in and said that his design for the new town had reached a stage where he would be interested to have Jake's comments. He gave Jake a pile of sheets of paper on which he had been sketching his ideas and he also transferred the current version of his overall design onto Jake's computer. As he left, Sir Andrew said, 'The local authorities, that are leading this whole enterprise, want the town to be sustainable and the people who live there to have beautiful streets, squares and parks to walk through; and, of course, they will need to have good places to live, work and play.'

Jake spent some time just looking at the design that Sir Andrew had produced. It essentially provided an overall layout for the town plus a few ideas on the general style of the buildings and public spaces. Jake was intrigued by the approach that Sir Andrew had taken to the shopping areas. These were clustered around narrow streets that were intended to be only for pedestrians. These were formed by a mixture of small shops and entrances to larger stores that were mainly located behind the smaller shops. The bigger stores, as well as their entrances from the narrow pedestrian streets, had entrances on the opposite side of the store which were right next to a large multi-storey car park.

Jake began sketching detailed designs for fronts of the shops facing the pedestrian streets and a very different style for the fronts of the stores facing the car park. He was aiming to make the pedestrian streets a modern interpretation of the narrow medieval style streets in cities like York and Winchester. In stark contrast, the fronts of the stores facing the car park were ultra-modern and provided a whole new approach to the look and style of shops and stores. Jake developed these ideas into three dimensional images of the two facades of the shopping areas. As soon as he was happy with these, he took them to show to Sir Andrew Zain.

Once he had understood Jake's overall idea and looked carefully at the three-dimensional images, Sir Andrew turned to Jake and said, 'This is real genius. You are building on the best architecture from across the centuries and creating an entirely new style. I think you should look at all the other areas of the town. These include the residential areas, there are several small factory areas, then there are office areas, provision for local government, the police, fire service and of course the hospital and doctors' surgeries. We also have a theatre and three cinemas as well as all the sports facilities. We need your thinking on all these buildings and the open areas that help define the character of the town. I think you should go ahead and develop your ideas for all the different facilities that make up the town.'

Jake's head was now buzzing with ideas and Sir Andrew seemed to sense this as he added, 'I suggest you go and get your immediate ideas down on paper. I will come to your office tomorrow afternoon to see how you are getting on.'

Jake thanked him for supporting his work in this way and

promised to develop his ideas as quickly as he could. Back in his office, Jake studied the overall layout of the town that Sir Andrew had designed and decided to work on the three main squares that defined the centre of the town. These were surrounded by major buildings that defined what were intended to be attractive open spaces. Jake found himself thinking about Trafalgar Square in London which beautifully combines major buildings and interesting places for people to relax.

The square that Jake began working on included the town's theatre, a cinema and a small museum and art gallery. He tried to develop a design style that combined the ideas he had used for the two very distinctive facades of the shopping areas. This did not seem to work, and Jake decided that what he was producing looked messy. As his mind wandered through several different compromises, he found himself thinking about his wedding. This led him to look at the schedule for the day that Jane had given him and as he read through it, he suddenly realised that he had not decide who he wanted as his best man. He naturally thought about the people he had played cricket with. Although he had not known him for very long, Ben Stanley stood out as the kind of person he thought he wanted. He's well organized, he looks good, and Jake thought that he would do it.

Almost without any further thought, Jake phoned Ben Stanley and they agreed to meet that weekend to discuss the possibility of Ben being Jake's best man. Jake then phoned his mother to check that it would be okay for him to be at home on Friday and Saturday evenings. His mother readily agreed and said that she was looking forward to hearing all about his wedding plans. Jake was about to get back to thinking about the new town, when he decided that he should tell Jane that he would be in Cirencester that weekend. He left a message on her phone and added that he would phone her when he had finished work that day.

He went back to working on his design for the square in front of the town's theatre. Jake knew it was looking good, but it needed a distinctive centre to make it complete. Still thinking about Trafalgar Square, Jake defined the centre of the square with an ornamental fountain and four large statues. He linked the statues to the theatre by basing each of them on a character from one of Shakespeare's plays. He spent some time just looking at the images of the square on his computer before he decided the design was complete. Jake next turned his attention to the square that included the local authority's offices. He envisaged the authority's buildings around three sides of the square leaving the fourth side open. In this way the square seemed to continue out into the countryside. Jake smiled as he thought that this might help ensure that the local government had a broad outlook on life. He reflected this thought by giving the square a mixture of urban and rural features. These included grass areas, flower beds, trees and winding paths lined with seats which led to a dramatic centre. This was centred on a small pyramid shaped structure that was both interesting and attractive and it could also be used as a stage by musicians and other entertainers. Jake hoped, that in addition to encouraging the local government to look beyond their own narrow interests, this mixture would encourage people to connect with their local authority.

As Jake walked back to his apartment that evening, he phoned Jane and she immediately told him that she had arranged to go home that weekend so they could meet. They agreed that it made sense to talk after Jake had met Ben Stanley and found out if he was happy to be the best man. As he finished the phone call, Jake remembered that he had said he would go to the nightclub where The Good Time Girls were performing. When he reached his apartment, Linda was having an early dinner and smiled broadly as he came in and said she was looking forward to performing for Jake that evening.

Jake felt oddly out of place in the nightclub. Most of the other customers were older than him and almost all of them were more smartly dressed. Also, he was the only person he could see that was on their own. He had decided to sit at the bar and had just ordered his third cocktail when the compare announced The Good Time Girls. The curtain drew back as the four musicians who played the music the girls danced began to play a lively number. Jake remembered it from a previous performance he had watched and then remembered it had led to one of Linda's sexiest performances. Then the three girls danced onto the stage. This provoked an immediate burst of applause which obviously encouraged the girls to launch into one of their most explicit dance routines. Linda looked amazing and Jake's mind was filled with a very explicit memory of having sex with her. He took a long drink of the cocktail which the barman had just put in front of him. It seemed to be very alcoholic, and Jake felt that Linda looked as if she was reaching a sexual climax as she moved ever more explicitly. The Good Time Girl's opening performance was warmly applauded by everyone in the nightclub.

The group continued with a variety of numbers, but Jake's mind was totally focused on Linda. He felt she was miming sexual intercourse and looking straight at him. Jake was increasingly aroused as he sat at the bar imagining they were having sex together. The group's final number made him feel ever more excited as Linda danced just for him. As the group finished their performance to enthusiastic applause from all parts of the nightclub, Jake rushed to the toilet, found an empty cubicle and checked the state of his penis. It was still just under control, so he sat down on the toilet and relaxed.

Jake sat there for some time with his mind racing with thoughts about Linda, his marriage to Jane and having sex with Mary and Linda. What did he want? He was meeting Ben Stanley tomorrow to talk about him being Jake's best man at his wedding to Jane. Yet here he was having just managed to avoid ejaculating in his trousers as he watched Linda dancing. He began to think about the schedule that Jane had prepared for their wedding day. She was so well organized and surely, he needed to move on to a more mature stage of his life. Not having sex with Jane until after they were married was the 'proper' thing to do. His career was going well. Sir Andrew Zain seemed to be treating him as a real colleague. His designs were good. Now he had to get the rest of his life into order. Not have sex with every attractive woman he met. He needed to get married and be faithful to Jane.

Jake went back to his apartment and then remembered that Linda would come back when she finished her performances at the nightclub and join him in bed. He sat down at the kitchen table and wrote a note telling Linda that he needed to concentrate on getting married and she should use the spare bedroom. He put this in the entrance hall where was bound to see it. Then Jake went to bed and fell asleep almost immediately.

Next morning, Linda was still in the spare room when Jake left for the office. He mentioned to Sir Andrew that he was going home to Cirencester that evening as he was meeting the man who he hoped would be his best man. Sir Andrew said, 'That sounds like an important meeting. I hope it goes well. Why don't you go home early and call into the practice in Swindon who are doing the working drawings for the new university campus. You can check that they are getting our design right. In fact, that would be very useful.'

So, Jake phoned John Brentford, the partner in the Swindon practice that he worked with, to check that it was convenient for him to come to the office that afternoon. This was agreed and Jake had a useful meeting with John Brentford and the practice's head draughtsman during which they discussed several aspects of the design he had created with Sir Andrew Zain. Jake felt that there were several minor changes that needed to be made so that the details in the working drawings properly reflected their design. He explained the changes that were needed, and John Brentford said that he would work on these over the weekend and meet again on Monday to check that the working drawings were right. Jake phoned Sir Andrew Zain, and this was agreed.

The discussion of the details continued for some and as a result, Jake just had time to get home, change into more comfortable clothes and get to the pub where he had agreed to meet Ben Stanley on time. Ben was already there and looked very pleased to see Jake. He said, 'I have arranged for some of the members of the cricket club to join us later but first we should discuss your wedding.'

'So, you are happy to be my best man?'

'I feel very proud of being asked by you to play that role in your marriage ceremony.'

Jake then showed Ben the schedule that Jane had prepared for what she expected to happen on their wedding day. He was obviously impressed and said, 'This is obviously a very well-organized woman that you are marrying. She seems to have mapped out what you and I will need to do on the day. I don't see any problems with any of that. I have been a best man twice before, so I do recognise what I need to do. That leaves us to plan the Stag Night. Do you have any ideas about what you would like to do?'

This led them into a lively discussion of what they might do on the evening before the wedding. Eventually Ben smiled as he said, 'I think we have more than enough ideas to be going on with. Over the next few weeks, we can settle on a clear plan but now, I wondered if you could up-date me on the new campus for Swindon University. I know you mentioned my firm to the Vice-Chancellor, and he has contacted us. We had a brief discussion of the role we might play but it would be very helpful to know exactly where you have got to with the design.'

Jake showed Ben the latest images of the new campus that he had on his mobile phone. Then he explained that he had been working of the detailed design that afternoon at the architectural practice's Swindon office. They discussed the general nature of the design details for several minutes and then Jake asked what role Jake expected to be playing in the construction of the campus. Ben smiled broadly and then explained, 'The construction firm I work for is changing into a construction management practice. I am taking the lead in organizing this change. We still employ the craftsmen, but their work is now mainly concerned with repairs and alterations to existing buildings. Our focus now is almost entirely on large new construction projects. Obviously, the campus is very attractive to us.'

Jake seemed startled by what Ben was telling him about what he had always regarded as a small local builder. He asked, 'What exactly do you mean by construction management?'

Ben explained that his firm planned the construction activities and then organized the appointment of appropriate construction firms to carry out the actual construction. He added, 'We manage all the financial actions as the work is carried out, so the client has a clear view of the costs involved. My firm has employed two quantity surveyors to ensure that this is all carried out in a professional manner.'

Jake was clearly impressed and said that he was looking forward to working with Ben on the university campus. Ben smiled and agreed they would make a great team. He then said that most of the guys he had invited to join them have arrived, so, they should begin what he thought of as the first practice at Jake's Stag Night.

Ben had booked a room at the pub, and he led Jake to where the other guests were assembling. There was a noisy burst of applause when Jake entered the room, which made him smile. Ben then announced that everyone could get whatever drinks they wanted from the bar and added, 'As you know, we are going to sort out the money after we have had our first celebration of Jake's wedding. Now let's begin the party.'

Jake really enjoyed chatting with so many of the people he had played cricket with over the last few seasons. Henry Roberts, the club chairman, was already thinking about the next season and told Jake that they hoped he would be able to play for them. Jake had to admit that he really did not know what he would be doing that far ahead but he really did hope that he would be able to play for Cirencester. As the evening progressed and they all had more to drink, the conversations became louder and livelier. They were discussing Jake's marriage plans and this led to the older men present thinking about their own marriages and giving Jake a variety of wise, sensible and silly advice on how to deal with his wife. Just before midnight, Ben Stanley announced that Jake needed to go home now, and everyone wished him well with his forthcoming marriage and said they looked forward to coming to the wedding.

Ben said that he would walk home with Jake and as they strolled through the dimly lit streets of Cirencester, Jake said, 'I really enjoyed that. It was a very simple evening, but I feel good about life, and I hope that I can play for the club next season. The most interesting thing about tonight was that I was given useful and surprisingly thoughtful advice about being married. I am so pleased that you will be my best man and I am already looking forward to my real stag do. I am suddenly very happy that I am going to marry Jane. I know it is the right thing to do. Thank you, Ben.'

Chapter 17

The months leading up to Jake and Jane's wedding seemed to pass surprisingly quickly. Jake was busy ensuring that the all the design details for the Swindon University campus were as good as he could get them and checking that the manufacturing company could produce them. He was also working with Sir Andrew Zain on the design for the new town situated between Nottingham and Leicester. They spent a lot of time making sure that the whole town was genuinely sustainable; and a key part of this was incorporating a large plant that converted carbon dioxide and methane into electricity. This not only supplied all the electricity the town needed but in almost all circumstances contributed power to the national grid.

Jane was equally busy as she was clearly making a success of working in the City of London. The two of them met regularly to have dinner, go to the theatre and occasionally to a nightclub. Jake enjoyed dancing with Jane and was looking forward to all the benefits of being married to her.

Linda had disappeared from Jake's life. He had found the note that he wrote telling her to use the spare bedroom in the kitchen, all screwed up and next to it Linda had left the key for his apartment that he had given her. He never heard from her again and felt surprisingly happy with that outcome to their relationship. Neither did he ever meet Mary Dobson again. He had several meetings at Swindon University that she might well have been involved in, but she chose not to be at any of them.

As a result of these changes in his relationships with other women, Jake was increasingly keen to get married. Jane seemed to sense this and was happy to give Jake every encouragement by subtly changing the way she dressed so that she looked more explicitly sexy; and when they danced together moving in ever more suggestive ways. She also frequently mentioned their honeymoon in Sham El Sheikh and how much she was looking forward to it.

Their wedding went exactly as Jane had planned it. She looked amazing in a long white wedding gown and had three bridesmaids dressed in green and white. Jake had decided to wear a dark, formal suit enlivened by a bright yellow and green tie he had bought at Lord's Cricket Ground when he was there watching England play Australia. Their wedding service was in the village church which was filled by their relatives, friends and colleagues. Jake had invited all the key members of the Cirencester cricket team, the partners and colleagues he had worked with from the Swindon architectural practice and Sir Andrew Zain and his wife. Similarly, Jane invited colleagues from both the Swindon and the City of London branches of the bank she worked at. As all these people were also coming to the reception, the landlord of the village pub had arranged for a substantial marque to be erected on the pub lawn. Even though it was a bright sunny day, everyone was pleased, given it was the middle of winter, that there were effective lights and heaters in the big marque.

The food was good and there was plenty to drink, so the atmosphere was relaxed and happy as the speeches began. Jane's father spoke briefly to say how happy he and his wife were to see their daughter looking so beautiful and marrying such an impressive young man. This was warmly applauded and then Jake stood up to thank him and continued, 'As well as thanking

Jane's parents for today, which I do hope you have all enjoyed, I am glad of this opportunity to thank them for all they have done to help Jane be so lovely and exciting. She is a real credit to them in every way. I must also thank my own parents for all their support over the years. Any success I am now enjoying is built on their love and care for me. They have showed me how to make the most of whatever talents I happen to have, and I know that without them I would never have such a happy and exciting life to look forward to with my beautiful wife. I must also thank Jane's bridesmaids who all look amazing and have made sure that our wedding went exactly as we planned it.'

Jake paused at this point and looked at Jane. Then he bent down and kissed her before continuing, 'Jane is not only beautiful and loving, but she works at ensuring that all her relationships work out well. Jane, you are everything I could ever have wanted in a wife, and I am really looking forward to us spending the rest of our lives together. I love you.'

Jane leant forward and took Jake's hand; and as he paused, she said, 'I love you. '

Jake kissed her and then looked at all guests before finishing his speech by saying, 'I must thank all of you for helping make our wedding such a great success and finally, I must thank Ben, my best man, for ensuring that I have been in the right place at the right time throughout today. He has been a real support for me, and I am looking forward to his speech. So, ladies and gentlemen, the best man.'

Jake then sat down to warm and long applause. As this ended, Ben stood up and asked everyone to drink a toast to the bride and groom. Then he made a short speech that mainly consisted of doubtful jokes which were greeted with sustained laughter and applause. He finished by proposing a toast to the bride and groom and wishing Jake and Jane a long and happy life together.

The only joke that Jake remembered was about when Ben started work and his manager, who was very interested in cricket, had three trays on his desk labelled: In, Out and LBW. Ben said that he eventually asked his manager why he had a tray called Leg Before Wicket on his desk. The manager laughed and said that LBW stood for Let the Buggers Wait.

When the time came for the newly married couple to leave, both Jake and Jane felt very happy with the whole day. The wedding ceremony and the reception had gone even better than they had hoped, and everyone seemed very happy with the day. They had a taxi to take them to a large hotel situated in the countryside near Heathrow. They planned to spend one night there and next morning, fly to Sham El Sheikh.

Jake could not remember ever feeling so happy as he sat in the back of the taxi with his wife. Jane looked equally happy as they held hands and talked about the day. They had arranged for everything they needed for the honeymoon to be in their room at the hotel and for Jane's parents to collect Jane's wedding gown and anything else they would not need in Sham El Sheikh. When they arrived at the hotel, the manager was waiting to greet them and show them to their room. He checked that they had everything they needed and suggested that they might like to use the hotel's room service to order anything they needed to eat or drink. He added that the hotel had a fine dining room but, in his experience, newly married couples welcomed the chance to spend time together on their wedding day.

Jake and Jane quickly agreed to take his advice and Jane took off her wedding dress and carefully hung it in the wardrobe. Then she turned to Jake and with a big smile on her face, she asked,

'What would you like to do now?'

Jake had just hung his suit in the wardrobe and turned to look at Jane. She was stood wearing just a bra and small, lacy pants. Jake slowly unbuttoned his shirt and took it off and then took Jane in his arms and kissed her for several minutes. She responded enthusiastically and asked, 'What do husbands and wives do on their wedding day?'

Jake unfastened her bra and then slid her pants down so that they fell on the floor. He then led his wife over to the bed and lifted her onto it. Then he pulled off his vest and underpants; and totally naked, he lay down beside her. Jane smiled and told him that she had taken sensible precautions, so there was no risk that they would create a child. Then she guided his hand onto her vagina, began caressing his penis and pulled him into a long kiss. Their first experience of sex together was everything they could have wished for. As they both came, almost together, Jane murmured, 'I had no idea that being married would be so wonderful. When can we do that again?'

In fact, they both fell asleep in each other's arms and did not wake until almost midnight. They had sex again and then slept until the hotel receptionist phoned the room to tell them it was seven thirty. They had a taxi coming at nine o'clock to take them to Heathrow in time to catch their flight to Sham El Sheikh, so Jake asked the receptionist to send their breakfast to the room. In this way they just managed to be ready when the taxi arrived and set off for their honeymoon.

The hotel in Sham El Sheikh was everything the website had promised, and their room included a small balcony overlooking the beach and the sea beyond. It was all perfect. Jake could not remember being so happy with life. They unpacked and put all their clothes away and Jane said she needed to go to the bathroom. When she came out, she was naked and pulled Jake into a long kiss. Then, as she walked over to the bed and lay down, she said, 'We have time before dinner to remember we are married now.'

Their honeymoon continued in this happy way and included memorable visits to Cairo, including the Egyptian Museum where Jake thought that Tutankhamun's mask was amazingly beautiful. The most memorable visit they made during their honeymoon was when they visited the Pyramids. They walked around these great monuments for over an hour. Jake was captivated by the size of these man-made mountains that he felt quite overwhelmed by the idea that they were thousands of years old. He wondered if anything that he ever designed could possibly last for anything like as long. Equally memorable was their visit to the Valley of the Kings. This began with a tour of Luxor and Karnak, continued with a short trip on a steamer along the Nile and then a guided tour of the valley. Jake was fascinated by Tutankhamun's tomb because it had survived for so many centuries and their guide had to insist that it was time to move on as there was still much to see.

They both loved the hotel and beach and spent most days sunbathing next to one or other of the hotel's three swimming pools. Jake enjoyed swimming in the sea because, by using his snorkel, he could see the beauty of the Red Sea coral and the fish swimming around it. Jane was happier staying on the beach, but after listening to Jake's enthusiastic descriptions of what he had seen, she agreed to a trip in a glass bottomed boat. Jake knew that this gave her only a superficial look at the coral, but she was very happy to see what Jake had been talking about so much from the safety of the boat.

They stayed up late on Saturday night because there was a

formal dance at the hotel which was very stylish and really good fun. As a result, they were late in going down for breakfast on Sunday morning. The hotel provided copies of the British newspapers for their guests to read, and Jake noticed that the front cover of the colour supplement in one of the papers showed pictures of three of Sir Andrew Zain's most famous designs. He took the colour supplement to their table and found the article about Sir Andrew. It began: "This is a tribute to one of Britain's greatest architects, Sir Andrew Zain, who was tragically killed in a road accident on Friday."

Jake just stared at this in disbelief. Jane asked, 'What is the matter?'

Jake looked at her with tears running down his face, as he mumbled, 'This is saying that Sir Andrew is dead. He was killed in a road accident on Friday.'

'That's terrible. What does it mean for you? You are working with him, and we are planning to live in the apartment he provides for you. What are you going to do?'

Jake just looked at Jane and clearly did not know what to say. Eventually Jane asked if there was anyone that he could phone to find out what happened. Jake began to look through his phone and trying to decide if he knew anyone who might have more information about Sir Andrew.

Meanwhile Jane had fetched the full newspaper and the report on Sir Andrew's sudden death. She then told Jake that Sir Andrew had been driving on the M1 motorway and it looked as if he had started to overtake a lorry at the same moment as the lorry had pulled out to overtake the vehicle in front it. As a result, Sir Andrew had accelerated straight into the back of the lorry and he and his wife were killed instantly.

Jake did not have private phone numbers for anyone in Sir

Andrew's practice and could not think of who else to contact. Jane asked him if he had any idea how this would affect his work and his use of the apartment in Mayfair. He shook his head as he said, 'It's all too much of a shock to think about what it might mean. I'm pretty sure that Sir Andrew did not have any children so I have no idea who might inherit everything he and his wife owned. I don't know what this will mean for his architectural practice because, although he had two partners, the practice was very much based on his reputation. Luckily, I am employed by the practice in Swindon, so there is no direct effect on my employment, but I have no idea what it will mean for the projects that I was working on with Sir Andrew, nor for my free use of the apartment.'

Jane asked if Jake felt they should go back to London early. Jake slowly shook his head and looked at Jane. Then he said, 'We are on our honeymoon, and we are going back to the UK on Wednesday. We should stick with that. Maybe by then all the people affected by Sir Andrew going in this way will have had time to think about the implications. We will still have use of the apartment, so that will be okay for the immediate future. Now, we should try to concentrate on enjoying our last few days.'

Jane agreed that this was the best thing to do but the last few days of their honeymoon were, inevitably, often spoilt by Jake thinking about possible implications for his work and how long they might be able to live in the apartment. Jane realised this and was always willing to discuss any worries that Jake expressed but mainly she did her best to make Jake as happy as she could. As a result, they both felt happier when Wednesday came, and they travelled back to London. When they reached the apartment, everything seemed normal. Jake looked through his post and there was nothing from Sir Andrew's practice or the Swindon practice. He felt relieved about that and managed to concentrate on helping Jane settled into the apartment. She had brought all her possessions to the apartment the afternoon before they got married and spent the night at home with her parents. Now she had to sort out where all her clothes and other things should go. The spare room was a great help in providing extra storage space, but they struggled to find sensible places for all their kitchen tools and equipment much of which was duplicated.

It was almost eight o'clock before they agreed it was time to get something to eat. They worked together to prepare a simple meal of cold meat, potatoes and baked beans. Jake opened a bottle of wine and as they sat down for their first meal as a married couple in their own home, he said, 'I feel happier with our life together than I ever have before. Everything suddenly seems right. I know that sorting out the implications of Sir Andrew's death will throw up unexpected issues, but we can deal with life together. Jane, I do love you.'

Jane was clearly moved by this short statement of Jake's love and reached across the table to hold his hand as she said, 'We can face anything that life throws up, as long as we are together. I have never been happier, and I know we have a wonderful life to look forward.'

They had both decided to go back to work on Thursday, so as not to use up more of their annual holidays than they needed to. As Jake walked to Sir Andrew Zain's office, he wondered what he would be faced with. He could never have anticipated what happened. This began with the Office Manager greeting him as he reached the office, 'I'm so pleased to see you back. We need your help in deciding how we deal with the practice now that Sir Andrew is not here. We have several important projects that depended on Sir Andrew's amazing design skills which neither of the remaining partners can match. Our only hope is that you can rise to the challenge of completing his work and maybe give some of our major clients the confidence to continue to employ us as their architects.'

Jake agreed to look at the projects that the Office Manager was talking about and then discuss the best way forward for each of them. They decided that the best place to do this was Sir Andrew's office. The Office Manager had obviously made some preparations for this work as there were several piles of drawings and files on the desk. He began, 'The most urgent project is the new town you have already been working on. The local authorities want a meeting early next week to discuss progress and agree a timetable for the project.'

Jake had some idea of the progress they had made on their design but was surprised when he started to look through the pile of drawings by how much work Sir Andrew had done on the design. After looking through all the drawings and reading the brief that Sir Andrew had agreed with the local authorities, Jake said, 'The sketch plan is almost complete. We could easily have enough information to get a first estimate of the cost by early next week. Then it's just a case of how long the quantity surveyors will need. Can I leave you to sort that out and tell the local authorities when we will be ready to talk with them?'

The Office Manager agreed and then asked Jake to look at the information about the university campus . Jake started looking at the pile of information and then said, 'Of course this project belongs to the practice in Swindon. Sir Andrew made a great contribution to the design, but I don't know what formal arrangement is in place between the two architectural firms.'

The Office Manager nodded as he said, 'There isn't any formal agreement. It's much the same with your situation. As you know the Swindon practice have continued to pay your salary and we have been paying your expenses and of course providing the apartment. This will all need to be sorted out, but my main aim now is to make sure our clients are happy to continue working with us.'

Jake looked at the other piles of information about the projects that Sir Andrew had been working on and then said, 'I have not been working on any of these projects; so, what do you want me to do?'

The Office Manager said, 'There are design decisions to be made on each of them and it would be helpful if you could look at them and decide what we should be doing.'

Jake agreed and then the Office Manager added, 'The remaining two partners in the practice are meeting tomorrow to discuss how they should take the practice forward and they would like you to join them.'

Jake was clearly puzzled by this, and the Office Manager added, 'They want to discuss the possibility of you being involved in the practice on a long-term basis, but I must leave them to tell you what they have in mind.'

Jake agreed to come to the meeting and to look at the other projects that Sir Andrew had been working on. The Office Manager thanked him and added, 'You could play an important part in ensuring this practice has a real future.'

The Office Manager then said that he other matters to attend to and left Jake in Sir Andrew Zain's office. As he began looking through the projects that Sir Andrew had been working on, his phone rang. It was John Brentford, the partner in the Swindon practice that Jake had always worked with. He congratulated Jake on his wedding and hoped that his honeymoon had gone well and then said that the partners needed to discuss the firm's relationship with Sir Andrew Zain's practice but before they did that, they wanted to talk with Jake. It was agreed that Jake should come to the partner's regular meeting on Monday morning.

Jake sat, looking around Sir Andrew's office as he wondered why both sets of partners wanted to talk with him. After failing to reach any very convincing answers, Jake concentrated on looking through the piles of design information that the Office Manager had prepared for him. These were fascinating; Sir Andrew had been working on five very interesting designs. Jake was particularly captivated by the sketch design for a new theatre in Glasgow. He could see what Sir Andrew had in mind but felt that there were several changes needed in order to make the theatre work properly. He spent the rest of the morning working on his new ideas and looking through the information in the files relating to the theatre that the Office Manager had left with him. This helped Jake feel more settled. By the end of the morning Jake was sure that he had a good design and when the Office Manager came into the office to ask him what he was doing for lunch, Jake suddenly realised that he was very hungry.

The Office Manager suggested they go to the restaurant just across the road. Jake ordered a pizza that sounded good and decided to have a glass of cider. The Office Manager ordered the same and then turned to Jake to say, 'I have been wondering how you see your own future developing. The news about Sir Andrew was terrible; but he did insist on driving himself, although I am not at all sure that his eyesight was good enough for long journeys. Not that I would say that to most people; but I hope we will become colleagues. That is what the partners want to discuss with you tomorrow. Do you have any thoughts about what you want to do going forward?'

Jake shook his head and then replied, 'Well, Robert, I have

the meeting tomorrow with the two partners, and I have been asked to go to the partner's meeting at the Swindon practice on Monday morning. I guess that I should be thinking about what I want. Do you have any advice?'

Robert Scott smiled as he said, 'You are a talented architect. Sir Andrew treated you quite differently to anyone else who has ever worked with the practice. He clearly recognised that you have real talent and was happy to treat you as a colleague. I know his two partners understand this and respect his judgement. I am not saying that they see you as a replacement for Sir Andrew, but they need someone of outstanding talent to ensure the practice's future. I suggest you listen to what they have to say; and then think about it. Also, of course your practice in Swindon may have similar ideas and want to discuss them with you on Monday. So, my advice would be to listen to what both firms have in mind before you make any decisions.'

Jake kept this advice in mind over the next few days as the partners in both firms invited him to join them as a partner. He had discussed the offer from Sir Andrew Zain's partners with Jane over most of the weekend; and told her about the advice he had been given by the Office Manager. She agreed that was good advice and suggested that he should wait until he had met the Swindon partners on Monday before beginning to make any decisions. She also looked through the information the Office Manager had given Jake. It gave her a broad description of the practice, its financial situation, the projects it was currently working on and the terms and conditions that would define Jake's relationship with the firm and the other partners. As she handed the information back to Jake, she said, 'This is a major opportunity. The firm is very solidly based and have an impressive list of clients. To be offered the chance of becoming

257

a partner is a huge achievement by you. I agree that you need to wait until you have talked with the partners in the Swindon practice; but this is a real opportunity to take your career forward in a spectacular way.'

Jake had these comments in mind as he arrived at the Swindon office just as the partners were beginning their meeting. He was offered a cup of coffee and asked to wait until they had dealt with their routine business. After less than thirty minutes, Jake was invited to join the three partners. The senior partner, Henry Masterton, welcomed him and invited him to sit down. Then he came straight to the point, 'Jake, we have been thinking about the future of this practice and we are all getting closer to the time when we would like to retire. The work you have been doing over the last few months and your ability to work effectively with one of Britain's greatest architects has left us in no doubt that you are the right person to take the practice forward in the long term. So, we have decided to invite you to become a partner and we have set out the terms and conditions of this offer for you to consider. Do you have any immediate questions?'

Jake immediately said that he was very flattered to have such an offer. Then he decided to continue by being very open with the three partners, 'I feel that I must tell you that I have been invited by Sir Andrew Zain's two partners to join them, not as a replacement for Sir Andrew, but as someone they think will maintain the firm's reputation. I have not made any decision, but I think it is only right that I tell you what is happening.'

The three partners were clearly surprised, and John Brentford asked Jake if he knew which of the two opportunities he preferred. Jake smiled, 'It's too soon to make any decision but I need to study exactly what I am being offered and discuss the two options with my wife. I think it sensible to say that I will make a firm decision by the end of the week.'

Henry Masterton said, 'I am not surprised, given the sudden, tragic death of Sir Andrew Zain, that the firm want you to join them. We are certain that you are the right person to take this firm forward and, of course, you have a good understanding of how we work.'

John Brentford suddenly interrupted by saying, 'Is there any chance that Jake could accept both offers? Would the two firms fit together in any way? Is that worth exploring? It seems to me that, as Jake looks at the two opportunities he has, he might think about us working together. I suspect we have certain strengths and advantages that maybe compliment those of Sir Andrew Zain's practice. One reason for saying that is the way the firms have worked together, through Jake, on the Swindon University campus. I have seen both practices benefitting from each other's strengths. What do you all think?'

Henry Masterton and Bill Connelly both looked totally surprised. After a long pause during which everyone was clearly thinking hard, Henry Masterton asked, 'Jake do you have any immediate comment on John's amazing suggestion?'

'My immediate comment is that I need time to think; but it had occurred to me that the two practices do have different strengths; so, the issue is whether they fit together. It's an amazing idea. Let me think about it. I won't mention it to anyone in the London practice but suddenly it seems to give me a clear way forward; but I do need some time to think.'

As Jake was leaving the Swindon office, John Brentford invited him into his office. Then he said, 'Jake, I hope you accept our offer. I am in no doubt that you are the right person to take the major design responsibilities of this firm forward. Perhaps I should explain. Most successful architectural practices have partners with a mix of talents. I am the leading designer in this practice which is why it was right for you to work with me over your training. It was always clear that you are an exceptional designer. But my partners each play different roles. Henry Masterton mainly deals with our clients and potential clients, and then Bill Connelly deals with the financial and contractual aspects of our projects and indeed of the firm as whole. I think it is obvious that Sir Andrew Zain was the main design talent in his practice, and I would guess that the other two partners play similar roles to those that Henry and Bill play in this practice. So, they need an outstanding designer, and you are an obvious choice.'

Jake was clearly listening very carefully to what John Brentford was telling him. These were matters that he had not ever thought about. He then asked, 'Henry Masterton and Bill Connelly do designs, and you manage complete projects. So, what do you mean by describing different roles?'

'You are right. We all handle complete projects but the way we decide who tackles each project is based on the distinctive knowledge and skills we each have. So, any project that provides a major design opportunity is given to me to handle. Projects that, for example, are likely to throw up tricky planning regulation issues are handled by Bill Connelly; and new clients, and indeed difficult clients, are always dealt with by Henry Masterton.'

Jake thanked John Brentford for explaining these practical issues and promised to make a firm decision by the end of next week. He the continued, 'Whatever I decide, I want to thank you for all the help and support you have given me since I joined the firm. I do really hope that we continue to work together.'

It was almost lunch time and Jake decided to walk around Swindon Old Town and think. He had a quick lunch in a small café and then wandered down into the main town and on to the railway station. As Jake travelled back to London on the train, he looked through the information about the Swindon practice and how he would relate to it if he accepted the offer of a partnership. In many ways the information looked very similar to that which Sir Andrew Zain's Office Manager had given him on Friday describing their practice and his possible future relationship with it.

Jake hoped that Jane would be able to help him understand the financial implications of joining either of the two practices as a partner. It was obvious that the work undertaken by the two practices was different. Sir Andrew's firm undertook large projects that in one way or another were regarded as being important by the clients. The Swindon practice was much more involved in smaller projects that were, of course, important to the clients but usually not of great significance to the local community that lived or worked near the new or altered building.

Jake got back to the apartment just as Jane arrived home from work. Jake told her what had happened at his meeting in Swindon, and she said, 'We need to look at both opportunities very carefully and decide what is best for us both. I will get dinner and I suggest that we both need to look through all the information the two practices have given you and then discuss what we should do.'

Jake agreed, 'Thank you. It's good to have your help in thinking clearly about our future. This is a big moment in our lives, and we have time to make sure we do the right thing.'

Chapter 18

Jane had become very certain that the best option for Jake was to accept the offer from Sir Andrew Zain's two remaining partners. As she said, 'The firm has a great reputation, it is based in London which is where I am working so there will be no complications for us, and they need you to replace Sir Andrew. Whereas in contrast the Swindon practice already has a partner responsible for design so you would be competing with John Brentford for the most interesting design projects.'

Jake agreed that all made sense, but then said, 'I feel a sense of loyalty to the Swindon practice. They always treated me well and the training I got from John Brentford played a big part in developing my ability as an architect. That is why the idea of linking the two practices is attractive. Do you have any ideas about that?'

'I can see the attraction of not having to make a choice, but I do think trying to become a partner and build links between two very different practices will throw up all kinds of problems. The two practices are about the same size and their financial performance is surprisingly similar; but Sir Andrew's practice deals with relatively big and usually important projects, while the Swindon practice deals with a much more mundane range of work. This is bound to lead to different attitudes and methods in the two practices; and I can see you being caught in the middle. I think you should become a partner in Sir Andrew Zain's practice and agree to stay in touch with the Swindon practice and where it makes sense get them to work together. My guess is that over time, a new pattern of cooperating will emerge if indeed that is a good idea. In other words, you will be an informal link between the two firms.'

Jake was clearly thinking hard, so Jane sat and waited for him to respond. After several minutes, Jake said, 'That makes good sense to me. It's good to be able to discuss the options with you. You look at the whole picture. I guess that comes from your work in the bank.

Jane nodded in agreement and said, 'I have learnt a lot in the last few months. Many of our customers come into the bank to discuss the various situations and opportunities they have; and I enjoy discussing their values and priorities so I can give them relevant advice.'

Next day Jake continued looking through the projects that Sir Andrew Zain had been working on. Then, just before lunchtime, the Office Manager told him that the funeral for Sir Andrew and his wife would take place on Wednesday. He added, 'It will be a small ceremony as Sir Andrew and his wife did not have any children and neither of them had any brothers or sisters. In other words, they really didn't have any family. I have always thought that is why this practice was so important to Sir Andrew. I think he saw us, in a way, as his family.'

Jake asked if he would be able to attend the funeral and the Office Manager said that would be appropriate. He continued, 'On the assumption that you become a partner, you will have a lot to thank Sir Andrew for.'

Jake nodded in agreement and then the Office Manager said, 'You will not know yet but the solicitor dealing with Sir Andrew's will has contacted us and apparently it leaves his share of the practice to the remaining partners and that will include you if you become a partner. More than that, he has left his house to the practice, and the will says, that if he had identified someone to take over his role in the practice before he dies, that they should be given his house. Sir Andrew also owned the block of apartments where you are living at present, and these also come to the practice. So, you would have a third share of that property as well.'

Jake looked amazed and just about managed to ask, 'Are you saying that as well as the financial arrangements set out in the documents you gave me last week, I would own the house overlooking Hyde Park and a share of the apartment block.'

'Yes; you would own the house but when you die it would revert to the practice and be passed to whoever replaced you as the lead designer. I know this is all difficult to take on board but, as I explained, neither Sir Andrew nor his wife had any close relatives, so, the practice was his whole life, and clearly, he wants it to continue to be a success.'

Jake sat in total silence as he tried to come to terms with what the Office Manager seemed to be telling him. The house must be worth many millions of pounds and even a third share of the apartments would worth an enormous sum. He would, for all practical purposes, be a multi-millionaire and a partner in one of the best architectural practices in the country if not in the world. The Office Manager said, 'I can see this is a surprise to you. I must admit that I was surprised by the generosity of his will until I thought about Sir Andrew's lack of a family and how important this practice was to every aspect of his life. He just wants it to continue as his real legacy; and its very lucky that he found you before his tragic death.'

That evening when Jake told Jane that if he became a partner in Sir Andrew Zain's practice, he would inherit his house for as long as he lived, and own a third of the apartment block because it was shared equally by all the partners. This would include him if he agreed to join the practice. She just stared at him and asked him to repeat what he had just said to make sure she understood exactly what they would gain from Jake becoming a partner. The she said, 'That settles it. You must become a partner in the practice. Owning those properties in London would mean that we suddenly have at least ten million pounds worth of assets. We would be rich for the rest of our lives. This is an amazing opportunity. We must take it.'

Jake could not think of any reason to disagree. He would be working on more significant projects, and they would be very rich. There was no way that the Swindon practice could get anywhere near matching this. Then making a clear decision, he said to Jane, 'I will tell both practices what we have decided but I think I should wait until after Sir Andrew's funeral.'

Sir Andrew Zain's funeral service was held in a small chapel that he attended most Sundays. The ceremony was short and essentially very simple. The only parts that Jake remembered were Sir Andrew's two partners in the architectural practice speaking about how much they had learnt from Sir Andrew and that it had been a privilege to work with him. Then the President of the Royal Institution of British Architects described his work and concluded by describing him as one of the greatest architects of all time. Sir Andrew's body was taken to be cremated and the service ended. Jake spoke briefly to the two partners, and they said that the office would get back to work next day.

As he was leaving, the President of the Royal Institution of British Architects introduced himself and then said, 'I understand that you are likely to join Sir Andrew's practice as a partner. I have seen reports of some of your work and I can understand why

Sir Andrew was keen to work with you. I would like to see you involved in the Institution's work in the future. I realise that you will have a lot to deal with over the next few months but if I may, I will get my secretary to contact you later in the year and arrange for us to have lunch together.'

Jake thanked him and then decided to go for a walk in Hyde Park and think about his own future. Was he certain that he and Jane had made the best decision? He thought about what the President of the RIBA had said at Sir Andrew's funeral. Jake particularly thought about his description of Sir Andrew as one of the greatest architects of all time; and now he, Jake Brown, was being asked to replace this great architect in his practice. He would be living in Sir Andrew's house, working in his office and dealing with all his clients. Jake found a small café in the park and bought a sandwich and a cup of coffee. Then he sat outside thinking about how he should relate to the other two partners in the practice. After nearly an hour, Jake suddenly decided that he could deal with the various challenges he now faced; and the sensible way forward to make sure that he enjoyed taking over from one of the greatest architects of all time.

Next day he told the two partners that he wanted to accept their offer. They were pleased and explained that the firm's solicitors would take a few days to draw up all the necessary contracts and agreements, but he could start work in Sir Andrew's office straight away. Jake then phoned John Brentford and told him that he was leaving the Swindon practice and John Brentford said, 'I'm not really surprised. I think in your situation, I would have made the same decision. We will make the move as straight forward as possible and, I hope it goes without saying, that if you want the two practices to cooperate with each other on anything, just let us know.'

John Brentford then wished Jake every success and ended the phone call. The Office Manager then reminded Jake that next day there was a meeting with the local authorities organizing the design and construction of the new town. He said that Jake should go to the meeting and that Carl Jefferson, the partner who normally deals with the practice's clients, would accompany him. The he added, 'The senior partner in the quantity surveying practice that has been preparing the cost estimates will also be there.'

Jake asked the Office Manager. Robert Scott, if he knew what the quantity surveyors thought the new town was likely to cost. The Office Manager said that he had not seen any cost estimate, but he would see if he could find out. Jake thanked him and said, 'I must look through the design information we have given the clients and make sure that I am happy with it all. Also, if you can get me a copy of the quantity surveyor's estimate that will be very helpful.'

Jake then concentrated on making sure that he understood the design until Robert Scott brought him a copy of the cost estimate. It was a surprisingly detailed document that reflected the fact that the construction would begin with the town's basic infrastructure and then be developed area by area over the following four years. This meant that the cost was likely to be spread over at least the next six years. As he read through the detailed cost estimate, Jake could visualise the town growing surprisingly quickly and becoming the amazing town that he and Sir Andrew had designed. There was still a lot of detail to complete but they had settled on the broad picture and the general style and quality of the various districts of the town. He could see that this was all reflected in the cost estimate; and Jake began to feel reasonably confident about the next day's meeting.

In fact, the meeting with the local authority representatives was very challenging for Jake as right at the start, he was asked to describe the design. He had not really prepared for this; but, maybe as a result, everyone at the meeting listened very attentively to his description. When he finished, the local authority representatives thanked him for such an interesting and detailed description of the new town and then asked the quantity surveyor to take them through the likely costs. Henry Maxwell, the senior partner in the quantity surveying practice listed the main assumptions that he had made and then asked the local authority representatives to look at the summary of the resulting cost estimates. He explained the assumptions he had made about the sequence in which the various elements and districts of the town would be constructed and how long each would take. Then based on those assumptions, he had calculated the likely annual expenditure for each year.

Then the man who had been introduced as the representative of the organization that was going to provide the finance for the new town asked several questions about the annual cost estimates and then he said, 'This is all heading in the right direction. I like the main shopping area and I must say that I think you have taken the right approach in creating the look and feel of traditional pedestrian streets and public squares but still using modern architecture in the design of the buildings. I do think that the various squares are an important feature of the town, and we must make sure that they are very attractive. Also, I very much like the residential areas you have included in your design. These will give people very attractive places to live. Indeed, I have a son who is likely to get married over the next year or so, and I might well decide to get him a house in the new town. So those are all real strengths; but there are a few things I would like you to have another look at. My thinking is that we should have more features that will attract visitors to the town. As a start, I would like to see a bigger theatre that would attract the top entertainers and in that same area, we should have several nightclubs. Then, we need a major sports stadium. I am in discussion with three leading football clubs that need a modern stadium. This could also host major athletics meetings in the Summer and big concerts by some of our top pop-groups. In fact, I would like to see more sports facilities in the town. A top-class golf course, a high-quality tennis club and maybe a few other sports facilities. My aim is to give the town a real identity so that people want to visit it. Of course, that means we will need to include several hotels. So, Jake, you have made a good start but now let's up our game and make the town the top place to visit in the Midlands.'

Carl Jefferson immediately replied, 'This is very exciting, and we will certainly come back with a revised design aimed at creating a truly significant new town.'

At the same time Jake was remembering that when they had gone to dinner at Sir Andrew's house, Jane had suggested that her bank had several financial companies as customers who might well be interested in funding the new town. He was sure that Jane had not been asked to help. So, the local authorities must have found the finance company without Jane's help. He made a mental note to ask her if she had been involved at all.

Various ideas were discussed over the next hour and Jake concentrated on making notes and sketching his immediate ideas. Then the representative of the financial organization said, 'I can see that Jake has taken our ambitious plans on board; so, I suggest we meet again in three weeks to look at what I hope will be the design and cost estimate for the future capital of the Midlands.'

Everyone smiled at this challenging ambition and the

meeting broke up. Then the representative of the financial organization invited Jake and Carl Jefferson to join him for lunch. He had a large chauffeur driven car that took them to a small restaurant on the edge of Leicester. The man from the financial organization reminded them that he was called Martin James, and then said how sorry he had been to hear of Sir Andrew Zain's sudden death; but he was now confident that Jake was a remarkable replacement for him and was entirely happy for the firm to continue to develop the design. Jake realised that this was an important vote of confidence in him, and this certainly helped ensure that he enjoyed the lunch. It was also helpful to listen to Martin James as he explained that he wanted the town to be sustainable and of really good quality as one of his reasons for financing the town was so that he could select which parts of it he would own; and he intended these to provide a source of income for the long term.

As they came to the end of their lunch, Martin James asked Carl Jefferson to ensure that he was given regular reports on how the plans for the new town were developing. Then he got his chauffeur to take Jake and Carl Jefferson to the railway station. On the way back to London Jake and Carl mapped out a broad schedule for the work needed to get the design to the point where construction could start. It looked as if this would take at least six months because they would need detailed designs for whole districts of the town so that the basic services, including roads, drainage, water and electricity supply could be planned taking account of the likely needs of the people using the buildings. Carl said that he would set up a team to work with Jake so that he had the resources needed to complete all the design work in accordance with this ambitious timetable.

Jake then asked what he should be doing about the university campus and indeed the other projects that Sir Andrew had been working on. Carl looked long and hard at Jake and then said, 'As you know the university campus is not our project. The practice you used to work for in Swindon are the architects for that project, so it is for them to sort out what needs to be done. I know that you and Sir Andrew played a large part in producing the design but that was a strangely informal arrangement; and if you want to remain involved, you will need to talk to the partners in your previous practice. As far as the other projects that Sir Andrew was working on, my understanding is that Robert Scott, the Office Manager, has given you up to date information about the actions that are needed. I am happy for you to decided what you work on which projects are the most urgent.' He paused at this point and then added, 'That is all part of being a partner.'

This left Jake deep in thought. He was suddenly beginning to realise what he had taken on. He was responsible, with the other two partners, for ensuring that the practice did the work that their clients needed, efficiently and on time. He also needed to think about how far he wanted to be involved in completing the design and then supervising the construction of the Swindon University campus. Carl Jefferson smiled and said, 'I sense that you are beginning to understand what it means to be a partner in a major architectural practice. I can just about remember the same point in my own career, and it is challenging. Let me say, that I will always be happy to discuss any issues you are not certain about. Also, I know that Roger Grenville will be able to help you make decisions. We three need to work together and our weekly partners' meetings provide the opportunity to discuss any tricky decisions we happen to be facing. So, beginning at the meeting on Monday morning, we will be happy to discuss anything you are not sure about.'

When they got back to London, Carl Jefferson said that he was going home and suggested that Jake did the same. As he walked back to the house, which he still thought of as Sir Andrew's house, he could not stop thinking about the Swindon University campus. How far did he want to be involved in this important project? To a significant extent, it was his design. Certainly, Sir Andrew had played the leading role, but they had worked together; and it just seemed wrong for the Swindon practice to get the credit for their design. On the other hand, he would be very busy working on the design of the new town and there were the other projects that Sir Andrew had been involved in at the time of his tragic accident.

Jake decided to talk to John Brentford. He realised that the Swindon practice would want to get the credit for the design because the university had employed them to design the campus . Nevertheless, Jake felt a real sense of pride in the design that he and Sir Andrew had produced, but at the time he was working with Sir Andrew, he had still been employed by the Swindon practice; so, in a sense they had played an important part in creating the design. On the other hand, he had decided to leave the Swindon practice . As Jake struggled to work out what he should say to John Brentford, he, almost instinctively, phoned him. John Brentford answered his call immediately and said, 'Hello Jake, it's good to hear from you. I've just been speaking to the Vice-Chancellor at Swindon University. He wants to discuss your design for the new campus next week. There are a few changes he wants but generally he seems ready to go ahead with the project. I need to discuss with you how far you will be able to be involved.'

Jake laughed and said, 'This is amazing. I was just thinking about the design and how it should be taken forward. I understand that your practice owns the project and I have now left the practice, but I do think it is a very good design and I want to make sure that it goes ahead as I and Sir Andrew Zain envisaged.'

John Brentford said, 'That is exactly what I want to talk to you about. Is there some way that our two practices could cooperate on taking the design forward?'

'That is exactly what I would like to do. Can I ask my partner, Roger Grenville, to think about some formal arrangement and then talk to you, or one of your partners, about what is the best arrangement?'

John Brentford agreed and added, 'It's right that you should get the credit for the design but obviously we want to keep the project in our practice. So, get Roger Grenville to phone me and I'm sure we can work something out. It's a big, important project and we want to ensure the integrity of your design.'

Jake suddenly felt very confident and asked, 'When does the Vice-Chancellor want to meet?'

John Brentford checked when Jake was available in the following week and then said that he would let Jake know when the meeting was arranged. Next morning Jake found Roger Grenville and explained to him that the Swindon practice wanted him to continue to be involved in the Swindon University campus design and that he had agreed to go to a meeting with the Vice-Chancellor. The he asked Roger if he would sort out the formal arrangements needed so that he could work on a project that belonged to the other practice. Roger immediately agreed and said, 'This was a not uncommon situation with Sir Andrew. He was frequently involved in important projects that really were the responsibility of other practices. We usually managed to agree on arrangements that ensured we were not out of pocket and Sir Andrew got the appropriate credit for his contribution to the

273

design.'

Jake said that those were the issues he was concerned about, and he would be very grateful if Roger could agree how the practice would get paid for his work and that he got the credit for his role in creating the design. Roger said that he would let Jake know when he had sorted this out with the Swindon practice. Then he added, 'I suggest that you assume for the moment that it will all be okay. In other words, you should do whatever is needed to take the design forward. I know that Sir Andrew was very pleased with the design, and he mentioned several times how big a part you had played in creating it. This will be good for our practice, and it could well be an important step in establishing your reputation. We need to do everything we can to get people to recognise that you are the right successor to Sir Andrew Zain.'

Jake thanked Roger and said that he would concentrate on deciding what needed to be done on the projects that Sir Andrew had been working on. The he added, 'I feel very comfortable knowing you will sort out the contractual arrangements with our clients.'

When Jake went home that evening, he found Jane in the kitchen. She kissed him and said, 'I am beginning to work out how everything in the kitchen works. I think Sir Andrew Zain probably did very little cooking because the cooker and so on are very old-fashioned. They work, but I am used to more modern equipment. Maybe we can have the kitchen updated. Anyway, I have something to tell you about the company providing the finance for the new town. You may remember that I did say that maybe I could find a suitable company to provide the finance. Then you mentioned last evening that the local authorities were working with a financial company headed by Martin James. I was a bit disappointed, and maybe because of that, I looked at what my bank knows about his company. It seems to be somewhat controversial. He has been investing in various developments around the world for several years. He seems to have an unlimited supply of finance; but it is not at all clear exactly where it all comes from. What is known, is that the source is somewhere in Russia. My manager at the bank let me see a confidential report from the bank's directors warning the managers in the city branch about Martin James' activities. Apparently, our government suspects that the money comes from the Russian government, and this means that Russia is secretly getting ownership of significant property around the world. No one has worked out why they are doing this, but the obvious worry is that they might somehow use their ownership of key parts of the new town to try and influence government policy. Maybe you should get the local authorities to talk to my manager.'

Jake just stared at her and clearly had no idea how to respond. Eventually, he just said, 'This is a lot to take in. Martin James seemed to be a straight-forward kind of a man when he took me and Carl Jefferson to lunch. We didn't discuss the source of his money, but he certainly had ambitious ideas for the new town. He did mention that he expected to own parts of the town; but this didn't sound suspicious. I think he just said he wanted the income. What do you think I should do?'

Jane said, 'Well as I suggested, you probably should get someone from the local authorities to talk to my manager.'

Jake said he would talk to Carl Jefferson before deciding what he should do. Jane gave Jake the name and phone number of the manager in the bank that she had asked about Martin James. Next day Carl phoned the bank manager and then contacted the local authorities involved in developing the new town.

On the Monday of the next week, Jane came home late and explained to Jake that her manager had been contacted by the Treasurer from one of the local authorities involved in the new town. She said, 'This led to one of the most exciting days at work that I can ever remember. It began when an official from central government came to the bank and insisted on seeing the bank manager. Then I was called into the meeting with my manager and told not to discuss Martin James' involvement in the new town with anyone. He then told us that several national governments are concerned about his financial company. It is virtually certain that the Russian government provides his finance, but no-one knows for sure why they are funding developments in other countries. He showed us a list of properties that Martin James' company already owns in Europe and the USA. As far as the central government official knew, Martin James does not own any property in Britain. That means the new town is his first target in the UK. Anyway, the plan is to go ahead with the new town as currently planned but when he has made some significant financial contributions to the project, the government will insist that he reveals the source of his money.'

Jake listened in amazement and then asked, 'Presumably this is all secret; but what happens to the new town if Martin James just walks away from the project when the government get inquisitive?'

Jane explained that the government had told the key people from the local authorities what was happening and agreed that if Martin James did withdraw as a result of their enquiries, then the government would fill the gap until a new source of funding could be found. Jake slowly shook his head and eventually asked, 'What does all this mean for my involvement in the project?'

'You should just carry on as normal and make sure not discuss this with anyone.'

'What about my partners. They should know about the government's concerns.'

Jane looked at him unusually carefully and then said, 'Jake, it is up to you. I was asked not to discuss this with anyone apart from you; but if you now discuss what is happening with your partners, that increases the risk that Martin James will realise that he is under suspicion.'

Jake laughed in an odd way and just said, 'I must sleep on all this. I am not used to being in the world of inter-government relationships. My first instinct is that I should tell my two partners. They are far more experienced than I am, and they may well have a view about what we should do. Also, if they were in a similar situation, I hope they would tell me. I don't think that partners should have secrets from each other. As I said, I need to think; but I will tell you if I do decide to discuss all this with Carl Jefferson or Roger Grenville.'

Jane kissed Jake and then holding him very close said, 'I found today oddly exciting and for some reason I now feel like going to bed early with my partner. If that's okay with you, I suggest we have dinner and then we can take some time to explore the nature of our partnership.'

Chapter 19

The meeting with the university Vice-Chancellor to discuss the next stages of the construction of the new campus began with a real surprise for Jake. This was because Ben Stanley was at the meeting. The Vice-Chancellor explained that to help him think about the construction stages of the project, he had employed Ben Stanley as a construction manager. He added, 'Ben Stanley has helped me decide the sequence in which the buildings should be constructed to fit in with my plans for re-organizing and expanding the university.'

Ben Stanley then took over and began by saying that he intended using a construction management approach to the construction. He continued, 'Just to be clear, this means that I will plan the construction activities, and then employ the appropriate construction firms to carry out the work. Now in working with the Vice-Chancellor, it has become apparent that it will be more convenient if we make a few changes to the design. The aim is to match the sequence in which the various buildings are constructed with the sequence which is most convenient for the university departments to move into their new accommodation. Also, we have given each department a final opportunity to check that the design gives them everything they need. This gave rise to a few more changes, mainly to the internal layout of the spaces but in one or two cases the department needed some additional internal spaces. All the necessary changes are set out in this file. We have several copies of it; so, whoever needs to know about the changes can take a copy away with them.'

The Vice-Chancellor thanked Ben Stanley and then invited Jake Brown, John Brentford and Henry Maxwell, the partner in the quantity surveying practice involved in the project, to have an initial look at the file to see if there were any immediate questions or comments. Jake opened his copy of the file and could see that the main changes were to the sequence of the various academic departments in the rows of buildings between the three outstanding buildings in his design. He could not see any problems with this except it would mean that he would have to alter quite a few of his drawings. John Brentford obviously reached the same conclusion because he said, 'I don't see any problems with these changes, but it does mean re-doing some of our drawings.'

Henry Maxwell nodded and then said, 'I don't think that the design changes will alter our estimate very much, but we will need to see the revised drawings before I can be certain. Then we will do a revised estimate of the likely cost.'

The Vice-Chancellor looked pleased and said, 'That all sounds fine; so, please go ahead with the changes and assume that the project will go ahead as planned. It would be helpful if you could remind me of the likely timetable and the sequence in which the buildings will be constructed.'

Ben Stanley immediately said, 'It's probably best if I remind you of the sequence we have planned for the construction. We will begin with the administration building. You will remember that it is close to the main entrance to the campus and is broadly based on the Westminster Houses of Parliament. At the same time a separate team will start constructing the row of buildings between the administration building and the building in the south-east corner of the site. This is based on Salisbury Cathedral and will house the architecture and construction engineering and management departments. As the teams constructing the administration building finish their stage of the construction, they will move to the architecture and construction engineering and management building. As they finish that they will then move on to the third major building. This is in the south-west corner of the campus and will house the science department in that amazing design based on Sydney Opera House. Meanwhile the teams constructing the row of buildings between the three major buildings will work along the rows constructing the various buildings for departments and students in the sequence set out in the drawings.'

The Vice-Chancellor thanked Ben Stanley for such a clear description of the plan for constructing the new campus. As the discussion developed, Jake became increasingly impressed by the way Ben Stanley took the lead in concentrating everyone attention on the key decisions. As a result, Jake made sure that he was sat next to Ben Stanley when they all went for lunch. As they chatted, Jake realised that he had not been playing any sport since he had been working in London. He resolved to find out where he and Jane could play badminton. Ben Stanley agreed that this was a good idea. He said that he played squash several times a week even in the cricket season because he could get a lot of good exercise in a reasonably short time. Jake said that he might try that if he couldn't find a good badminton club.

When Jake got home that evening, Jane was busy getting dinner. She asked him about the meeting, and he said, 'It went well. There are few final changes to the design. This is so the university will get the accommodation for the various departments in the most convenient order. In many ways the most interesting thing about the meeting was that Ben Stanley was there. You may remember he joined Cirencester cricket team last season. Anyway, the firm he works have been appointed as construction managers for the university campus; and he is taking the lead in that. He was very impressive at the meeting. and we had lunch afterwards. He asked me what sport I am playing, and it made me think that perhaps we could look for a badminton club.'

Jane immediately said that was a good idea and she had heard some of her colleagues at the bank talking about badminton. She agreed to find out where these clubs were based, and Jake said that he would ask around his office to see if any of the staff played badminton. As a result, Jake and Jane were invited to come to three different badminton clubs. They decided to try the one that played nearest their house. Jake had been told about it by Rose Nelson, who was in the administration team at the architectural practice. She said she would be at the club on Wednesday evening, as that was the main club night, and she would be happy to introduce him and his wife to the club chairman.

When Jake and Jane got to the badminton club, Rose was already there and seemed very pleased to welcome them and introduce them to the club chairman. He checked that they had played before and then invited them to play as a couple against him and Rose. They all enjoyed a close, keenly contested game, which the chairman and Rose narrowly won. As they played, Jake became increasingly aware of just how attractive Rose was. She was wearing very short shorts and rather revealing top and she was a good badminton player, comfortably covering the net and consistently hitting the shuttle into parts of the court that challenged Jake and Jane to return it.

When they finished that first game, the chairman told Jake and Jane that he would be very happy for them to join the club. He explained that club nights were Monday and Wednesday and because they were more than half-way through the season, they could pay a nominal subscription to join the club. Jake thanked him and said, 'I'm sure we will enjoy playing at this club and Jane and I will come to club nights as often as we can. The chairman said that he looked forward to seeing them regularly, and then explained how the club nights were organized so that throughout the evening all the members had several chances to pick who they played with. As a result, Jake and Jane played several more games as a pair but also played with other people. Towards the end of the evening Jake found that he was partnering Rose in a game that Jane was not involved in. Jake could not help thinking that Rose was a good badminton player and an unusually attractive young woman. This second thought was forced into his mind by the unusual way that Rose gave Jake the shuttle when it was his turn to serve. She seemed to be deliberately giving him a very clear view of her breasts while she smiled invitingly at him as she did so.

As they came of the court, Rose asked Jake if he was planning to have a secretary or would he just rely on the administration department to organize his meetings and paperwork and so on. She explained that the other two partners both had their own secretary, but Sir Andrew Zain never did. She added, 'There is quite a lot of speculation in the office about this and who you might select to be your secretary. It goes without saying that I would love to play that role for you.'

This was not something that Jake had thought about and neither Carl Jefferson nor Roger Grenville had mentioned the possibility of him having a secretary. So somewhat hesitantly he said, 'I like the idea of having someone to deal with my day-to-day administration. I have been asking the Office Manager whenever I needed something doing inside the practice. I must talk to the other partners about this; and I will keep your kind offer in mind.'

Next day Carl Jefferson and Roger Grenville both told Jake that if he felt that he needed a secretary, he should sort it out with the Office Manager. He immediately agreed that it was a good idea and explained that Sir Andrew not having a secretary tended to create more work for the admin people to deal with. He then said that there were several suitable people who already worked for the practice, and he would pick two or three for Jake to interview. Jake asked if these would include Rose Nelson. The Office Manager was obviously surprised and asked why Jake had mentioned her. Jake explained that it had been Rose who had mentioned the possibility of him having a secretary. The Office Manager looked thoughtful and then said, 'Rose Nelson is certainly a very capable young woman. She has not been working in the practice for very long; but yes, I will include her on the list of interviewees.'

On Friday evening Jake and Jane decided they both wanted to go to the badminton club again. They had enjoyed it and felt that playing some active sport was good for them. They arrived early and had finished their first game, in which they played together and just managed to win, when Rose Nelson arrived. She immediately said how pleased she was to see them at the club again and that she hoped this meant they had decided to join the club. Jake and Jane looked at each other and then Jane said, 'We do think that this club will suit us well. Its reasonably near our house and it's the right standard for us. So far, we have had good, competitive matches.'

Rose smiled and said, 'I'm so pleased to hear that. I like playing here; and I hope I will soon have a closer working relationship with Jake.'

Seeing Jane looking puzzled, Rose added, 'I'm being interviewed for the job of being his secretary next week.'

Jane was clearly surprised, and Jake quickly explained that this was something the Office Manager had organized but he hoped this arrangement would help him deal with all the paperwork and admin work.'

Rose said, 'That is exactly what I want to be doing. It is very interesting working in an architectural practice, seeing the designs develop and working with all the different clients as they decide what they need in their new buildings. I really enjoy it and I'm looking forward to the interview next week.'

Jake smiled and said, 'That's good but now we need to play badminton. Jane and I have just managed to win our first game this evening. Why don't you find a partner Rose, and we will play you?'

The evening continued in this way, and both Jake and Jane enjoyed playing badminton and felt it was good for them. As they walked home, Jane asked if Jake intended to appoint Rose as his secretary. He said, 'I think she would do a good job, but I need to wait until I have interviewed all three candidates that the Office Manager has selected before making any decision.'

Jane smiled and said, 'She certainly appears to be the right kind of person to help you deal with all the admin involved in being a partner in a major architectural practice. I hope that will gives us more time together. Playing badminton together was good. We should find more things we can do together. They are what I love most.'

Over the weekend they tried several things that they could

do together including playing squash, visiting The National Gallery, walking in Regents Park and going to the theatre. They finished Sunday evening by having dinner in a small, stylish restaurant and agreed that this was a good way to finish a very enjoyable weekend. Jake certainly felt refreshed when he walked into the office on Monday morning. The morning post included a copy of the quantity surveyor's estimate for the Swindon University campus. It was higher than their previous estimate which reflected the changes and additions that Jake had been asked to make. It looked sensible to Jake, and he phoned the Vice-Chancellor to ask him if he planned to go ahead with the development now that he had seen the new estimate. The Vice-Chancellor said he was happy with the new estimate, and he was happy that the latest design included the plant that generated electricity from carbon dioxide and methane. He then added, 'It makes economic sense for the university to generate some electricity but the earlier idea of including a nuclear power plant was too controversial. I have already had staff telling me that their students are already planning protests if we include a nuclear plant; and I am sure that it would make it more difficult for us to attract good staff and students. The carbon dioxide and methane option is a much better option and I am sure it will prove to be an important feature of the new campus. So, now I am ready to go ahead as quickly as possible.'

Jake suggested that the next step was to ask Ben Stanley to agree the contracts with the manufacturing company and the necessary site-based contractors; and so long as they fitted within the quantity surveyor's estimate, to instruct them to begin the work. The Vice-Chancellor agreed and thanked Jake for all his help in reaching this key stage of the project. He added, 'I know you have now left the Swindon practice and I'm sure they can deal with the next stages of the project; but you will always be welcome to come and see how we are getting on with turning your design into full three-dimensional reality.'

Jake told Robert Scott, the Office Manager, what the Vice-Chancellor wanted done and asked him to make all the necessary arrangements. As a result, preliminary construction work started on the new campus just two weeks later and the manufacturing company began making the components that would form the super-structure of the university buildings. Meanwhile Jake turned his attention to the new town in the Midlands and to the interviews to select a secretary.

During the interviews, the Office Manager asked a series of questions to test each of the candidate's understanding of how the practice worked, while Jake was interested to hear about their other interests. As a result, the Office Manager decided that Rose and one of the other candidates would be a good secretary for Jake and he should decide which of them he wanted. With very little thought, Jake decided to give the job to Rose. The Office Manager smiled at this decision and said, 'I'm not at all surprised, the two of you get on very well together. I hope this appointment works out well; but if you have any problems, let me know.'

Rose was obviously delighted when they told her that she would be Jake's secretary and asked if she would be starting right away. The Office Manager agreed that made good sense and told Rose that she would be using the office next to Jake's office. Jake added that she could have the rest of the day to move into her new office and he would see her first thing next morning. In many ways having his own secretary was a big change for Jake, but his immediate challenge was to make progress on the design for the new town. He spent much of the day making sure he had all the latest design information that he or Sir Andrew Zain had produced. It provided a broad overall picture of the town and more detailed designs for some of the buildings . Then he realised that he did not have any obvious way of checking that the design included everything that the local authorities wanted in the town. He began looking through the formal brief which was not very precise in listing exactly what buildings and public spaces should be included. He then remembered that this had been discussed at the last meeting with the local authorities that he had attended with Sir Andrew. He found the minutes of that meeting and they mentioned that the subject had been raised but then referred to other documents.

Jake walked into Rose's office, where she was sorting out a filing cabinet. He said, 'I need your help with the new town. I cannot find a complete list of all the buildings and public spaces the local authorities want included in the town. Could you go through the files and produce a list of everything they have told us they want?'

Rose looked pleased to have what sounded like an important job to do and immediately said that she would start work on it. In fact, Rose spent the next two days going through everything she could find about the new town, and she contacted the local authority officials who were involved in the project. As a result, on Thursday afternoon, she came into Jake's office and gave him a detailed list of the buildings and public spaces the local authorities wanted in their new town. She was able to tell Jake that the local authority officials responsible for the town had agreed the list and she was sure it was complete. Jake looked at the list and then thanked Rose and added, 'I think having you as my secretary is going to be a great help for me. Well done; this is an excellent start.'

The list helped Jake to identify several things they had not included in the design for the new town. These included public toilets, tennis courts, a water treatment plant, an old people's home and two nursery schools. He spent some time deciding where each of these should be included in the overall design and then started working on detailed designs for each of these facilities. He was able to work reasonably quickly because he and Sir Andrew Zain had agreed the overall style they would use for the town. He spent some time over the weekend working on the designs for the old people's home and the nursery schools. So, as he walked into work on Monday morning, he was looking forward to the week because he felt that he was making good progress.

As he got to his office, Rose Nelson, his secretary came in and obviously wanted to say something to Jake but was hesitating. He asked her what she wanted and speaking slowly and carefully, she said, 'I've been thinking about all the information I read about the new town when I was preparing the list of the buildings and public spaces the local authorities wanted in their new town. There were reports of several public statements about it being a fully sustainable town in the papers that I read, but I couldn't see how this is reflected in the list I produced. That is apart from the system for generating electricity from carbon dioxide and methane; but there is so much more that could be done. I would expect there to be green spaces throughout the town. Maybe tree lined paths that run from the residential areas into the centre of town so that people feel they are walking or cycling through the woods to the town centre. Then there is the whole business of how water is used and re-used; and how waste is dealt with. I have read about cities where waste is used to produce fertiliser; and water is re-used for various purposes. Also, it would reduce the use of cars if there was cheap, efficient public transport. I read about a city where people planning to use the local buses and trains, put details of their planned journey into their mobile phones and this information is used to ensure that buses and trains run where and when they are needed. Sorry to go on, but my point is that I could not see that our design takes very much account of sustainability.'

Jake stared at Rose and then very slowly said, 'That is true. I have been working on the design in my normal way and that does not really take very much account of sustainability. I know that at least some of the people at the local authorities have sustainability as an aim but we have not really discussed what that means. You seem to know a lot about it; is this something you have studied?'

Rose nodded as she replied, 'I did start a degree course in Sociology that focused on sustainability at the London South Bank University but for various reasons, I dropped out and started full time work here.'

Jake was surprised to hear this and was not at all sure how to respond. After an embarrassingly long silence, Jake said, 'I didn't know that, but I guess it's good that you can now use what you did learn. It would help me if you made a note of your various ideas for making the town sustainable. Is that something you can do for me?'

Rose was clearly surprised but immediately said, 'I would like to do that. It may take a couple of days to get all my ideas sorted out, but I can give you a note of what seems to be the best current thinking.'

Jake then looked again at his design for the new town and realised that he needed to think about Rose's comments. He began adding green corridors that linked the green areas next to the residential areas to the town centre. These provided footpaths and cycle tracks surrounded by trees. Then he used the internet to read current thinking on sustainable water use and treatment. This made him realise that the treatment plant already included in the design was based on outdated thinking in which water was just used once and then made fit to feed into a river or the sea. He would need to talk to some engineers to work out the best answer for the new town. Jake spent much of the next few days searching the internet for ideas about sustainable development and the more he read, the more certain he became that he needed to talk with the local authorities. This view was reinforced when he read Rose's notes about sustainable development, so, he asked Rose to organize a meeting with the local authorities as soon as possible. Then, without thinking, he suggested that she should come to the meeting. She was obviously surprised, but immediately agreed and thanked Jake for taking her that seriously.

When he heard about the meeting, Carl Jefferson said that he wanted to come to the meeting. So, Jake, Rose and Carl Jefferson travelled by train to Nottingham. During the journey, they discussed the design of the new town, and Rose said, 'One thing that occurred to me as I was making the list of buildings and so on that are needed in the town is that it may be a good idea to include a technical college. This would train young people for specific jobs in the town. This could include various crafts, administrative and management jobs, as well as preparing people to work professionally. This would keep the various businesses in the town supplied with properly prepared young workers.'

Carl Jefferson immediately agreed and added that he was surprised that a college was not already included on the list of facilities. He added, 'I presume that there are primary and secondary schools.'

Jake confirmed that the design included three primary schools and a secondary school that had a sixth form. He added, 'There are nurseries as well to provide care and basic training so that mothers can work if they choose to.'

Then he added, 'I guess the local authorities have not included any higher-level education because there are good universities in Leicester and Nottingham and of course, lots of other universities around the country.'

Rose looked at the two men and then said, 'It was thinking about my own experience at university that made me think that the town should have a college that trains people for specific careers. My course at university was good but I could never see it leading to any specific job. It was interesting learning about the damage we are doing to the planet, but it tended to generalise about possible solutions. That's why I left and joined the architectural practice. I have never regrated that decision; and I have to say that being involved in creating a new town, even in a small way, is very exciting.'

Jake and Carl Jefferson were clearly impressed by what Rose had just said, and Carl suggested that Rose should get involved in the discussion at the meeting when she felt she had something relevant to say. Jake thought that this was an interesting endorsement of his decision to make Rose his secretary. He also thought that she very much looked the part of an efficient secretary in the way she dressed and behaved. This reminded him of their first meetings, when he had seen her looking very sexy. Obviously, this had been to try to make sure that she was offered the job as his secretary. Maybe now that he had some power and influence, attractive women who seemed to be coming on to him, were really looking for some favour and not suggesting they should have sex. Jake smiled as he thought that he would have to get used to this new possibility when he met sexy women.

When the trio from the architectural practice got to the meeting, they were met by representatives of the local authorities involved and Martin James, the man who was providing much of the finance needed for the project. It started with Jake being invited to explain the stage reached in producing the overall design. He was ready for this and illustrated his description of the overall design by showing a series of images of the important buildings and public spaces. As he finished Carl Jefferson suggested that the town should have a technical college and asked Rose to describe her thoughts about what it should provide. Rose smiled and very clearly and confidently repeated the ideas they had discussed during the train journey. Surprisingly, the local authority representatives immediately agreed and said they were surprised that this had not been included in the design. The most senior explained, 'We envisage a town that is as self-sufficient as is technically possible. That includes educating and training young people to do all the work needed to enable the town to be sustainable and efficient, while giving the people who live there every opportunity to live a satisfying and enjoyably life.'

The meeting continued in this business-like way, and, after less than an hour, the senior representative of the local authorities said, 'This all sounds as if it is exactly what we want; and now we can agree that this is the overall design for the town and move on to the next stage. Perhaps Carl, you could describe what we need to do next.'

Carl said, 'The next stage is to get a new estimate of the likely cost. This is just to check that the finances are available. Then we need to produce detailed drawings and a specification for the whole town. Obviously, this is a big undertaking, and we will need to decide the best sequence for the construction so that we can produce the detailed design information in the right order. Then construction can begin.'

Jake had a sudden idea at this point and said, 'I have been involved in a large project in Swindon. This is constructing a new university campus and the construction is being handled very efficiently by a firm of construction managers. I could get their representative to talk to you about the service they can provide if you wish.'

The senior local authority representative said, 'That is an interesting idea. Maybe you could arrange for the construction manager to contact me, and we can meet and discuss the service he could provide. It had occurred to me that this is by far the biggest construction project any of us have ever been involved with, so, it makes sense to bring in experienced professionals.'

Martin James had sat listening carefully to the discussion. He now said, 'I feel very happy with the way this whole project is developing; and Jake Brown clearly provides an excellent replacement for Sir Andrew Zain. I know Sir Andrew developed the initial ideas, but they are being taken forward in a very professional manner. I am very happy to be involved in this important development. It promises to provide a living model of how we humans should live on this planet.'

Jake and Carl Jefferson made rapid progress following this successful meeting, and as a result, the quantity surveyors were able to produce a revised estimate of the likely overall costs early the following week. This appeared to be reasonable, so Jake and Carl Jefferson, decided to send it, together with the most up to date design information, to the local authorities and Martin James.

Jake realised that he now needed to wait for a response to

the design and estimate. So, he asked Rose to bring him the up to date information on the other projects that Sir Andrew Zain had been working on at the time he was killed in the road accident. As Jake looked through these, he realised that his two partners had taken over the most urgent of these other projects leaving him to concentrate on the new town.

While he was trying to decide what to do, Jake phoned the Swindon architectural practice where he had previously worked and who were responsible for the university campus project. He spoke to John Brentford who told him that construction work was just starting but there was nothing of any great interest to look at as the contractors were concentrating on the underground services and the road layout. John Brentford added that he was entirely happy for Jake to visit the site and that he would let Jake know when the construction of the first buildings reached an interesting stage. This left Jake with nothing urgent to work on, so he went back to looking at the information about the projects that Sir Andrew Zain had been working on that his partners had not yet taken over. The one that captured Jake's attention was extending and updating a bank in the City of London. He smiled at the thought that Jane might well have some ideas that could be used in producing the design.

He spent some time studying the brief from the client and then checked with the Office Manager to find out who was working on the design and which office they were in. He then found the architect, Jason Williams, and explained that he was interested in the design for the city bank that he was working on. Jason was clearly surprised but seemed to be pleased to discuss his design ideas with Jake.

After looking at Jason Williams' design for the city bank for some time, Jake said, 'You have produced an interesting, classical style city bank. I agree that we should keep the classical exterior. It fits in with the rest of the street architecture; but inside we could think about a more modern, relaxed style aimed at making the customers feel more comfortable. The public spaces and meeting rooms could be more open and casual.'

Then he began sketching and after Jake had produced several possible designs, Jason Williams said, 'I have been looking on the inter-net, and the latest banks from around the world are more like you are suggesting. Can we work out how these ideas might fit into the existing building?'

Jake agreed and suggested that the proposed extension could be used to help change the internal character of the bank. Jason Williams was clearly getting excited by the freedom that Jake's suggestions gave him to be more creative. The two of them worked for much of the rest of the day and created the basis for a completely different interior. As they reached the end of the working day, Jake said, 'I think we have made some significant progress. My wife works in a city bank, and I will see what she thinks of our ideas this evening.; and thank you for letting me help with your design.'

That evening Jake began to explain to Jane what he envisaged for the city bank, but she interrupted to say, 'You have reminded me that we had a request today from a branch of the government intelligence agency for any information we had about Martin James' financial company. I remembered that you had told me that he was providing at least some of the finance for the new town you are working on. I didn't mention it because I thought it was best to discuss this with you first. Should I tell the intelligence agency that he is involved in financing the new town in the Midlands?'

Jake asked if Jane knew why the authorities were interested

in Martin James. She said that her understanding was that the intelligence agency is concerned about Russian finance and that is where they think that most of Martin James' funds come from. Jake asked why that might be a problem. Jane smiled and said, 'Russia is not an ally. Everything about them is treated with suspicion. I don't know how the government would react to the new town being funded by Russian money but clearly it would be a matter of concern.'

They discussed this for some time and then agreed that Jane should report the fact that Martin James was funding the new town. As Jake said, 'If you don't report it and the bank realises that I am involved in a project funded by Martin James, you could well be in trouble for not reporting it.'

Jane thanked him and then said that she would like to see Jake's ideas for the up-dated city bank. After looking carefully at Jake's sketches of the public spaces in the bank, Jane said, 'I can see what you are doing. I think I agree that a modern bank should feel more informal and welcoming to its customers. I do think that in the past, banks tried to make their customers feel overawed and respectful when they came in. Times have changed and of course most banking is done online nowadays; so, people don't come into the bank as much as they used to; but when they do, we should make them feel welcome and comfortable. I like your design ideas. I think you have got it about right.'

Over the next couple of days, Jake worked with Jason Williams to produce a complete re-design of the bank's public spaces. On the second evening Jane told Jake that she had done some investigating to find out why the intelligence agency was concerned about Russian finance. She continued, 'The government is concerned that Russian money is being used to buy up influence in British politics. Apparently, they did not know about Martin James' involvement in the new town but now they are concerned that it may be a plot to create a base which brings together a group of powerful Russians. Several of the companies planning to set up a branch in the town, depend on Russian funding. I don't know what the implications of all this will be for the new town but obviously it's best that you know about the government's interest in the project.'

Jake had no idea what the possible implications might be for his work on designing the new town. So, he asked Jane if she thought that central government would want to get involved. She thought for a few seconds and then said, 'I would have thought that is quite likely. I can't think that would be happy to have a Russian enclave in this country; but then they do believe in free markets; so, if Martin James has the money, maybe they will just let him get on with it. I don't know what is most likely to happen.'

Jake had no idea what actions he should take so, he just said that he would have to discuss the Russian involvement with his partners. Next morning Jake asked Carl Jefferson and Roger Grenville to join him, and he told them about Martin James' connections to Russia. After some discussion, they agreed that it was not really their problem, but they should tell the local authorities what they had learnt about the source of the finance for their project to construct a new town. Carl Jefferson agreed to tell both local authorities.

Two days later Carl Jefferson came into Jake's office and told him that he had just had a message from the local authorities responsible for the new town project and they had instructed him to put everything on hold. They would not give him any explanation but as Carl said to Jake, 'it is very likely that central government has decided there is a problem with having a town in the UK funded by Russia.'

Chapter 20

When the three partners of Jake's architectural practice met for their regular Monday morning meeting, Roger Granville began by saying, 'The new town is by far the biggest project that we are working on and having everything put on hold may create financial problems for the practice.'

Jake asked him to explain what he meant in more detail. Roger Granville said, 'Well the arrangement we have with the local authorities is that as we work on the design, they pay us a regular sum each month. Every so often, I meet the local authority treasurers. This is usually every few months to check how the fees we are due relate to the payments they are making. This usually produced some additional money for us, but broadly the payments covered our work. Now that has all stopped, we are short of almost thirty percent of our monthly income.'

Carl Jefferson said, 'In the past we could always rely on Sir Andrew to get enough new commissions from the various organizations that he was linked to. This meant that our finances were very stable, and the practice always had enough work to keep all our employees busy. So, now we are in a new situation.'

Carl Jefferson then said, 'I have been thinking about this and it seems to me that we need to build Jake's reputation. We need to get him some good publicity and then use it to persuade clients to give us new projects.'

Roger Granville agreed and asked Jake if he could think of anything he was working on that might be newsworthy. Jake replied slowly, 'Well, I think the design for the new town has some interesting features; and the university campus in Swindon includes some very distinctive buildings that I designed with Sir Andrew Zain. I don't know how we might get publicity for them, but maybe we could link my work on these designs to Sir Andrew in some way.'

Carl Jefferson immediately said, 'We could tell the media that Jake Brown has clearly emerged as an outstanding successor to Sir Andrew Zain and send them the best images of the designs that Jake mentioned as evidence of the quality of his work. This could work. Jake, you need to get us about a dozen outstanding images of your designs; and meanwhile Roger and I will use all our contacts in the media to build some interest. I think this could work well. Let's get on with it.'

As a result, Jake was invited to do interviews by both the BBC and ITV. These were both broadcast as part of the Thursday evening news and they aroused comments in most of the national newspapers over the following weekend. Jake was then asked by the BBC to help put together a programme about the new town. This was supported by the local authorities who were persuaded by the idea that this might help get central government to let them continue with the project. In the programme, Jake was invited to describe his ideas for the main buildings in the town and the public open spaces that they defined. Then a woman from one of the local authorities explained the benefits this would all provide for the people who decided to live and work in the town.

The programme led to more aggressive articles in national newspapers, and it was increasingly clear that central government felt under pressure to provide the finance needed to enable the local authorities to go ahead with the new town. This was added to by an influential statement from Martin James. It was published in a leading national newspaper. The heart of it read, 'I know people are concerned about Russian money being used to finance the new town, but I have to tell you that my money comes from many sources. Some is from Russia, but this is usually less than twenty percent in any year. I have investors based in the USA, China, the European Union, the Middle East and Australia. This is invested in major companies worldwide, very few of which have any connection to Russia, and it is the income from those investments that I plan to use to finance the new town. The new town is an important initiative by the UK which will demonstrate that it is at the leading edge of developing and using sustainable technologies. I want it to go ahead with the creation of a highly significant development, and I urge the key decision makers to look to the future and in doing so, add to Britain's reputation as a leading country.'

The direct consequence was that Carl Jefferson was contacted by the local authorities responsible for the new town early in the next week, and told the project was going ahead because they had been promised significant funding by central government. They also arranged a meeting at the end of the week to plan the next stages of the project. Jake and Carl Jefferson went to the meeting and were surprised to find that the people present included academics from Leicester and Nottingham Universities who were researching sustainable technologies. The senior local government representative explained that they had asked both the local universities if they could help ensure that the new town was as sustainable as is currently possible. There was also a woman from a local construction management company who had been invited to advise the local authorities on the best approach to ensuring the new town was constructed as quickly and efficiently as possible.

It became very clear, as the meeting got underway, that the local authorities were under considerable pressure from central government and local politicians to make rapid progress, and to ensure that the town would be a model of sustainability. The researchers from the two universities were fascinated by Jake's designs for the various buildings and began suggesting materials that would create the appearance that Jake was aiming to achieve, and at the same time be at the leading edge of sustainable forms of construction. These included a material which promised to provide a cheap alternative to concrete but is significantly less polluting to manufacture and is stronger. Other suggestions were based on recycled plastic, wool insulation, recycled timber, and smart glass which retains heat in Winter but keeps it out in Summer. Jake became increasingly interested in these ideas and agreed to work with the academics in ensuring that his design made full use of the new materials. The local authority representatives seemed pleased and asked the woman from the construction management company to work with the team to ensure that the materials they decided to use would be available at a reasonable price when they were needed to construct the new town.

The meeting then turned to the road layout and agreed that Jake's design was reasonably efficient. The researchers from the universities said that having the footpaths that led from the areas of housing to the town centre lined with trees were an excellent idea. As one of them said, 'These will make very attractive walks and help persuade people to walk about the town rather than use their cars.'

This led the meeting to agree that they should do everything they could to persuade residents and indeed visitors to use electric cars. The three service stations in the town would provide charging points but not sell petrol or diesel fuel. All the public transport systems would use electric vehicles and the local businesses would be given financial incentives to use electric lorries and vans.

The meeting continued in this way for nearly an hour, and then the senior representative from the local authorities said, 'I am now confident that our aim of creating the most sustainable town on Earth is in good hands. I suggest that the architects, construction managers and the university researchers work together to complete the design and agree a plan for the construction to begin and be completed as quickly as is sustainably possible.'

Carl Jefferson immediately said that he agreed with this exciting plan and his practice would do everything needed to ensure that construction could begin as soon as possible. This seemed to bring the meeting to a conclusion and the local authority representative, who was hosting the meeting, invited everyone to have lunch in the hotel across the road from the council offices.

Jake found himself walking to the hotel with the woman from the construction management company. She reminded him that her name was Susan Rafferty, and said she was looking forward to working with Jake to ensure the construction was undertaken efficiently. She added, 'I suggest we arrange to meet regularly over the next few weeks to ensure that your design details fit in with my plans for the construction. Obviously, I am not suggesting changing the look of your design, but there are often details in the design of some buildings that make the construction more difficult than it needs to be. I find it much more sensible to sort these issues out in the design stages rather than waiting until construction is underway.'

Jake agreed this was a good idea and they arranged for her to come to Jake's office on the following Monday so that they could work through the design together. Jake told Carl Jefferson about this arrangement while they were travelling back to London after a surprisingly good lunch. Carl advised him to make sure that he concentrated on ensuring that his design was not compromised by the construction manager trying to make it easy to construct. He explained, 'In the past, I often saw Sir Andrew Zain having heated arguments with contractors about the details of his designs. He was always adamant that it was up to the contractors to work out how to create exactly the appearance he wanted. As he said, the building will be here for decades, and we have a responsibility to future generations to make it as attractive and interesting as possible. If that means taking a bit longer or spending a bit more money now, it is worth it for the benefit of many future generations.'

Jake smiled and said that he would keep that advice in mind as he worked with Susan Rafferty. When Jake and Carl Jefferson reached London, they agreed there was little point in going to the office. When Jake got back to his house, Jane was already there. She looked hard at Jake and said, 'You look as if you have had another busy day. Let's have a comfortable evening in, and we can chat about what we have been doing this week.'

Jake immediately agreed and said that Jane was right, it had in fact been a very busy week. As they chatted, Jane mentioned that Martin James' companies were doing badly on the financial markets. She explained, 'The companies in which he has an interest have lost almost twenty percent of their value over this week. There is a lot of talk about the government refusing to allow him to invest in the new town that you are designing. This has made people suspicious about the source of his money, and many of them are deciding that investing in his companies is not a reasonable risk. It will be interesting to see how he reacts.'

Jake replied, 'The local authorities who are responsible for the new town told us that central government are now funding the development, and so Martin James is no longer involved in any way.'

Jane nodded and then said, 'My understanding, from the discussions at the bank, is that people are expecting some reaction from Martin James to the government's decision not to allow him to finance the new town. I have no idea what he may do, but our senior managers are clearly concerned because he has many investments in the City of London, so, he could cause trouble.'

Jake shook his head as he said, 'I don't pretend to understand any of that, and from my point of view, the new town project is going ahead. Indeed, I have a meeting on Monday with the construction manager that the local authorities have appointed to plan the construction. We are meeting to agree how we work together to make sure that my design information helps the town to be completed quickly and efficiently.'

Jane agreed that was good news but added, 'You should keep in mind that many of the companies that were planning to buy the shops and office blocks in the town do depend, to some extent, on finance from companies in which Martin James has an interest. The local authorities may be able to find other companies willing to set up new businesses in the town, but this could create some uncertainty for the whole project.'

In fact, the effect was to push Jake into a series of meetings with companies considering opening a shop or setting up a new office in the town. It became increasingly obvious to him that the local authorities were using him to sell the idea of setting a new business in the town. He was asked to suggest new designs for the front entrances and the internal layouts of many of the shops. The companies considering buying an office block in the new town seemed to be even more demanding as they searched for ways of making their business more efficient and more profitable. This all interfered with Susan Rafferty's plans for the construction. After several difficult discussions with the local authorities, it was agreed that construction could start on the roads and public spaces and the housing areas. However, the shopping areas and the office blocks would have to be put on hold until the local authorities knew exactly who was going to buy them.

Jake had difficulty in dealing with these meetings because felt he felt that he was involved too much in administrative issues rather than doing what he understood and enjoyed, which was designing. As he said to Jane one evening, after a day spent entirely in three meetings with companies the local authorities hoped to attract to the town, 'It takes time to get into the right frame of mind to develop my design, and I keep being interrupted by having to talk to different companies who want different kinds of spaces for their offices and shops. I'm afraid my design is falling apart because I am finding it difficult to keep my original image in mind. I'm distracted by the various companies I am being forced to spend time with. That makes it difficult for me to make good design decisions. I can't just call up my original image at short notice. I need time to envisage the whole town and where the individual parts fit in. Constantly being asked to change them is destroying the integrity of my design; and I really don't like to see that happening.'

Jane said, 'That is interesting. It made me think about the way I deal with our different customers. I have a notebook in which I have a separate page for each of the main customers I deal with, and immediately after dealing with any one of them, I make a note of anything that seems relevant to their way of thinking or doing business. Then, before I next meet them, I have a quick look at my notebook and that helps me tune in to their way of thinking.'

Jake was obviously impressed by what Jane had just said, as he replied, 'What I need to recall is the image, or rather the series of images that help me make my design decisions. They are somewhere in my head, but I do rely on my memory to call them up; and despite my best efforts, I am sure that quite often the images I think of are different from those that inspired my original design. In the past, I had time to concentrate on whatever it was that inspired my design, but with all the meetings with potential shop and office owners, I just don't seem to be remembering my original inspiration.'

'I think I understand the difference in the kind of work we do. It's interesting for me to hear you talk about how you create your original designs. I guess the real issue for you is working out how you can cope with your new responsibilities as a partner in an important architectural practice and keep hold of your creative genius?'

Jake laughed, 'It's very kind of you to use that description of my work; but what you suggest is true. I love designing. It's what I think I am good at. Running an office, dealing with the administration and so on, just gets in the way. John Brentford dealt with all that on my projects in the Swindon practice. So, I guess I need to get Carl Jefferson and Roger Grenville to do the same in my new practice.'

Jane nodded as she said, 'That's the challenge. Let's have a weekend away somewhere and get your mind clearly focused on what you think is likely to be the best arrangement for letting you concentrate on your design work.'

They decided to drive down to Bournemouth on Friday evening and stay in their favourite hotel. Over the weekend, Jake and Jane spent a lot of time walking on the beach and enjoying various restaurants and cafes. Jane was happy to talk about Jake's approach to design and clearly found his ideas interesting. She helped him find a series of images on the internet that he felt were close to those he had in his mind as he designed the campus for Swindon University and the new town in the Midlands. He stored these on his computer and agreed that they were likely to help him focus his design ideas. Jane also suggested that when he was using any one of the images, he should search the internet for other linked images as they may very well help him develop his design ideas. As Jane had expected most of the images were of great architecture and a few were of great paintings that she knew Jake admired, but she was intrigued by Jake including images of tigers and cats. Jake explained that he thought that these were very beautiful animals and they helped him concentrate on doing everything he could to make sure his designs are beautiful.

They both enjoyed the weekend and Jake felt he had a clearer picture of how he should combine his work as a designer with playing a full role as a partner in a major architectural practice. The immediate effect was that he was happy to be back at work on Monday morning; and felt fully involved in the partner's regular Monday morning meeting. Carl Jefferson was able to report that the publicity generated by the television and newspaper reports about Jake's design for the new town had resulted in the practice being approached by several potential clients who were thinking about new developments. In particular, he wanted Jake to meet representatives of a new enterprise that

307

hoped to re-develop an area dominated by old blocks of flats on the edge of the City of London. The representatives wanted to come into the office that afternoon.

In fact, three people, two men and a woman, came to the office just after lunch time. They explained that hoped to redevelop the whole area to create a new public square surrounded by shops and several high-quality restaurants and cafes, all of which have between six and eight floors of apartments above them. In principle the local authority is willing to approve this development but obviously this depends on the design being acceptable to them . The woman then added, 'We want the whole development to provide attractive, modern architecture. That is why we would like Jake Brown to design it for us.'

Jake thanked them for this compliment and then asked if there any similar developments that they particularly admired. He explained, 'Obviously I want to create something that you will be proud of and knowing something about your taste in architecture will help me.'

The man who seemed to be taking the lead in the discussion replied, 'There are several new shopping centres in London that we admire. These include two Westfields, one near White City and one in Stratford. We like the Bullring in Birmingham but probably our favourite is Bluewater in Kent. However, these are primarily shopping centres and we want to create a new, high quality residential centre that also includes restaurants and cafes as well as shops.'

Jake thanked him and said it would be helpful knowing the standard of architecture they wanted. The leading man gently shook his head as he said, 'We hope that by coming to you, we will get something even better than these existing centres.'

They all smiled at this, and Jake said, 'I will do my best to meet your challenge.'

The meeting continued by discussing the basis for the group's budget and the timescale they hoped to work to. Jake made careful notes and, as the discussion was clearly coming to an end, said, 'I am already thinking of possible ideas for the design and, as far as I can judge, the money and timescale seem to be realistic. I will work on some preliminary design ideas, and we could meet again next week to discuss my ideas.'

This was agreed and when the three people had left, Jake felt very happy with the challenge they had given him. He looked at the various shopping centres they had mentioned on the internet and decided to sketch his immediate ideas and then, next day, to go to the Bluewater centre in Kent. He spent most of the next morning wandering around the shops and when he felt hungry, he picked an attractive looking restaurant to get lunch. It was all very impressive, and Jake realised that he would have to design something quite spectacular to match the best modern shopping centres. He had the added problems of creating a public open space and providing several hundred apartments.

Jake spent the rest of the week trying various design ideas but none of his ideas matched what he had seen in Kent. No matter what he tried, the apartments dominated the shops and the public open space. Late on Friday, he began sketching a shopping centre arranged around a square that included a fountain and a small lake and places for people to sit. Then around this centre, Jake designed blocks of apartments that were ten stories high. These were surrounded by natural looking areas of grass, shrubs and trees. These areas included footpaths that linked the apartments to the shops. He added large under-ground car parks under the central square and each of the apartment blocks.

Finally, he added the roads that essentially linked the existing roads around the site to the underground car parks.

He went home late feeling that he now had the basis for his design. When he showed his ideas to Jane, she spent some time asking questions and looking at Jake's sketches. Then she said, 'This is really amazing. It will be a great place to live, and I would certainly want to visit the shops and restaurants there . It is your best work yet.'

Jake said that he needed to do more work on the designs for the individual buildings; and Jane said that she could find some work to do about the house. They had dinner first and then Jake spent more than four hours working on the individual buildings. Eventually he agreed to go to bed but most of the weekend was dominated by Jake developing and improving his design. Jane was happy to see him working so creatively and found things to do so that he could concentrate on developing all his ideas.

When his two partners saw how much progress he had made with the design, Carl Jefferson immediately said, 'This design looks extremely good. We should get the quantity surveyors to check that it is within the client's budget.'

Roger Grenville said that he would arrange this and checked that he had Jake's design on his computer. Roger received the estimate on Wednesday morning and then explained to Jake that the design was over budget and the quantity surveyors had suggested that they should consider doing away with the underground carparking and replace it with three separate buildings that provided carparking. Jake's immediate reaction was that these would be dull buildings and almost certainly spoil the look of the whole development. Then he added, 'I think we need to show my design to the clients and then discuss with them how we move forward.'

The meeting took place on Friday and the same three people who had been at the briefing meeting came to the architectural practice's office. They were all clearly excited by the design as Jake showed them his original design. Then Carl Jefferson said, 'We have an estimate of the likely cost and unfortunately it is higher than the budget you set.'

Roger Grenville then showed the clients the quantity surveyor's detailed estimate. He began by showing them the likely cost of each element of the development and finished by admitting that providing everything in Jake's design took them over the budget. The man who seemed to be in overall charge of the development asked what they could do to reduce the cost . Jake realised that everyone was looking at him, so he said, 'One option is to put the car-parking in separate buildings that are above ground. That way we avoid the costs of creating under-ground carparks. I have looked at that, and in my view, it spoils the look of the overall development. It's cheaper but it really does not look as good.'

The man who had asked the question then suggested that they should think about the sequence in which the separate buildings were constructed. He explained, 'As individual buildings are completed, we aim to sell them. I think we need to get a detailed valuation of each of the buildings in Jake's design as he has described it for us; and then work out the likely cash-flow. It may be financially viable because I do think that these buildings are probably more valuable than we had assumed when we calculated our budget. I suggest you go ahead with the design, and we will work out the sequence in which we want the individual buildings to be constructed. This may mean that the whole project takes longer than we had assumed but I think that we must keep the design that Jake Brown has shown us. It is

311

brilliant and will give us a new and very attractive area of London.'

Jake was obviously pleased with this decision as he said, 'I am keen to develop my design to the stage where we can start on the working drawings and so begin construction as soon as possible.'

Everyone at the meeting seemed happy with the point they had reached and agreed that Jake should get on with completing the design. It was obvious to Jane, as soon as Jake got home, that the meeting must have gone well. He was much more relaxed than he had been over the weekend and almost immediately asked her what she wanted to do that evening. In fact, Jane had already started getting their dinner, so she said, 'Let's have a comfortable evening watching something on television; and then we can go to bed early.'

Chapter 21

Nearly two years had passed since Jake had finished his design for a new commercial centre on the edge of the City of London when Jane gave birth to their first child. It was a boy and the decided to call him Andrew. The major projects that Jake had designed were all complete, or at least very nearly complete. The university campus, the new town and the new commercial centre were all widely regarded as great architecture, and within the profession of architecture, Jake was seen as one of the world's leading architects. He could pick and choose which projects he worked on and his architectural practice, which was now called Jake Brown and Associates, was financially very successful. There was considerable pressure on the government to give Jake a knighthood from the media and senior people in the construction industry.

Jane and Andrew had come home from the maternity hospital and Jane had left Jake holding their new baby while she sorted out his cot. Jake looked at his son and decided that he was beautiful and that he seemed to be happy to be at home. Life was good; he had a beautiful wife and son, they had an amazing home in the centre of a great city, and he totally enjoyed his work. Jane came into the room and said that she was going to feed Andrew and then put him in his cot. Jake asked how he could help, and Jane said, 'I feel really thirsty and could do with a cup of tea; and if we have anything to eat in, I fancy something sweet.'

Jake made the tea and felt pleased that he had bought Jane's favourite cake. As he brought the tea and cake into the lounge, Jane was breast feeding Andrew. Jake put the tray down and sat down and just watched this truly beautiful scene. After several minutes, he said, 'This is just the most perfect time of my life. We are so lucky to have everything that anyone could ever want. Bringing up Andrew is going to be wonderful. I must take a photograph of you and our son. It's such a memorable moment, I want to be reminded of exactly how you both look.'

Jake in fact took several photographs and as he looked through them, he said, 'These are the most wonderful images I have ever seen. You and Andrew are truly inspirational. I should design something as a monument to this perfect day.'

Jane laughed and said, 'I think you will have many opportunities to see this scene. Our son is a very hungry boy. I am feeding him almost every three hours. It doesn't leave me much time to do anything else; but I guess in a while, he will settle into a more reasonable pattern.'

In fact, Jane did have to spend much of her time feeding Andrew for most of the next two months. This meant that Jake had to do a great deal of work in running the house. Inevitably this meant that his two partners, Carl Jefferson and Roger Grenville seemed to be making unreasonable demands on his time. They were dealing with a steady stream of potential clients and needed Jake to play a full part in dealing with them. It was one afternoon when Jake had a series of phone calls in quick succession that Jane realised that he was under unreasonable pressure. That evening she said, 'I can see that you are very busy with me and Andrew, the house and your architectural practice to deal with, I suggest we get some help in running the house. Then we can both concentrate on what is most important to us.'

Jake looked at her and almost immediately said, 'That is the obvious answer to our situation. Why didn't I think of that?'

'I guess you were too busy. I have been looking on the internet and there are several agencies that can provide people to do the housework and cooking. That would let us concentrate on doing the important things like looking after Andrew and designing great architecture.'

Jake immediately kissed his wife and said, 'I do love you. You are beautiful and very sensible. Show me the agency you think may be best for us.'

The next day a woman who looked as if she was in her mid-thirties arrived to take over the running of the house. She told Jake and Jane that she liked to be called Mary and if they decided it would help, she would be happy to move into one of the spare bedrooms. It was agreed that they should see how they felt about that after Mary had been looking after the house for a week or so. She seemed happy with this suggestion and asked Jane to show her around the house and tell her what she needed to do.

Mary was a very energetic woman and over the next few days, she had the house looking immaculate and Jane feeling much more relaxed and able to concentrate on looking after Andrew. The change was, if anything, more beneficial for Jake, who could concentrate on his designs and spending any spare time with his wife and son. Two weeks after she had first arrived at their house, Jake and Jane agreed to invite Mary to move into the largest of their spare bedrooms.

Jake's son, Andrew, seemed to grow up fast and when, just after his second birthday, his sister was born, he was clearly excited as he ran about shouting, 'I have a sister called Eve. I now have a sister and we call her Eve.'

This was not the only major event in Jake's life at that time. He went to the partner's regular Monday morning meeting a few weeks after Eve was born and sensed that his two partners had something important to discuss. They worked through all the usual routine matters unusually quickly and then Carl Jefferson said, 'Jake, we have something important to tell you. We have both decided it is time for us to retire. You are clearly very capable of running the practice successfully and there are things both of us want to do and places we each want to visit before we get too old. So, we suggest that, over the next three months, we work out how you want to run the practice and find the right people to take over our responsibilities. You may want one or maybe two of them to become partners but that will be your decision. Do you have any questions?'

Jake looked hard at his two partners and then very slowly said, 'I am sure you realise that this is a great surprise for me; and I need a few days to think about all the implications. You say that we need to find the right people to take over your roles in the practice. Do you have anyone in mind?'

Roger Grenville said, 'We do have some ideas about the best people in the practice to take over our various responsibilities. We have been ensuring that they have the right skills for some time now but as Carl said, it must be your decision.'

Carl Jefferson added, 'We will arrange for you to talk informally to the two people we have in mind. We have not told them of our plans as it is now for you to decide how you deal with them.'

Jake said, 'It would be very helpful for me if, before I meet the people you have in mind, you both set down a broad description of your own view of the responsibilities you currently have in the practice.'

Both Carl Jefferson and Roger Grenville looked slightly surprised by this, but then Carl said, 'I think that is a very good idea. It will give you a clear picture of why you need capable, senior people to help run the practice.'

Jake smiled and said, 'Let me say that I am surprised by your decision, but I can see the advantages from your own points of view. I have to say that I will always be grateful for the way you have helped me fit into the practice. I could not have had the success that is reflected in all the good publicity my designs get in the media without your advice and support. You will always be welcome here if you ever want to visit us after you have retired; and indeed, I am sure that there will be times when I need to discuss things with you. Anyway, this is obviously going to be a very important few weeks as we sort out the future of the practice.'

This brought the meeting to an end and Jake walked slowly back to his office looking around the various rooms and spaces he passed in an entirely new light. He was clearly going to be the senior partner and he could choose who he brought into the partnership. He needed to think very carefully. As he realised this, he decided that he needed to discuss the mornings events with Jane and he wanted to do that, face to face. So, he decided to walk home.

Jane was surprised to see him so early, but she quickly realised that Jake had something important to say. Both their children were asleep, so they sat down in the lounge and Jake told her about the decision made by his two partners. She immediately said, 'I am not totally surprised. Things you have mentioned over the last few months made me think that you have been emerging as the senior partner. I guess Carl and Richard recognise that this is the right time for a generation change in the running of the practice and from what you have just said, it sounds as if they want to help make sure that the change is made smoothly and successfully.'

Jake smiled broadly at his wife as he said, 'That is exactly why I have come home early. I want to discuss all the implications with you and plan the next few months.'

Jane leant across to Jake and kissed him. Then she said, 'I am so lucky to have you as my husband; and now we have our two lovely children, I do feel that life is wonderful. Let's think about our future together and how it will be shaped by you becoming the senior partner in a major architectural practice. It would help me focus on the possibilities if I looked at the partnership's financial situation. Could you get me the annual accounts for the last two or three years and a statement of what it owns?'

Jake said he would ask the Office Manager to give him this information. Jane then asked what the Office Manager did. Jake was not sure, so, he said he would find out. Next day, Jake went to the Office Manager's office and explained that he wanted to understand the partnership's financial situation. That afternoon the Office Manager brought Jake a complete picture of the practice's finances and then said, 'I have just heard that the other two partners have decided to retire leaving you as the sole remaining partner. I did wonder if you wanted to discuss what actions we need to take in this new situation.'

Jake invited the Office Manager, who was called Robert Scott, to sit down. Jake then asked him to describe his own job as it is, and as he would like to see it develop in the future. Robert Scott looked hard at Jake and then clearly making an important decision, said, 'I joined this practice a year after I graduated with a first-class degree in psychology. I had spent the year travelling right around the world and growing up. I have always admired great architecture, and during my gap-year I saw some amazing buildings. So, working in what is arguably the best architectural practice in the country was very attractive. I have been given more responsibilities over the time I have been here, and I like the title of Office Manager; but the fact is that Carl Jefferson and Roger Grenville manage the office and relationships with clients. They give me jobs that they don't want to do, and I have been thinking of looking for a new job somewhere else; but if you want to work in a different way and give me real responsibility, I will be very happy to work with you.'

Jake realised this was an important moment in his career; and so, he said very slowly, 'Robert, I suggest we discuss how the practice is run over the next few weeks and make some decisions.'

Robert Scott looked pleased at this proposal and then said, 'Something I would like us to think about is how we raise the quality of architects the practice employs. In my view, we have relied too much on Sir Andrew Zain's great ability and not invested in recruiting and developing talented young architects. It was very fortunate that Sir Andrew found you before his untimely death, but I think you should make sure that the practice becomes a pool of real talent. I do think that you should have a hard look at the architects in the practice and decide if you think they are good enough to create a truly great architectural practice that does not over rely solely on your undoubted talent.'

Jake nodded as he agreed, 'That is an important statement. I like the idea of helping talented designers realise their potential. There were several very good designers on my course at university but nearly all of them drifted into safe, dull jobs. We have a lot to think about; so, I suggest we meet regularly to develop our ideas about the future of the practice.'

During the time leading up to Carl Jefferson and Roger

Grenville's retirement, Jake and Robert Scott met regularly, had dinner with their wives at each other's homes, and decided that Robert should become a partner in the practice. He would take responsibility for all the legal and administrative matters, and very importantly continue to foster their relationships with local authorities and financial institutions that provided links with potential clients. This would mean that Jake could concentrate on designing their most important projects; and finding and developing talented young architects. They both felt happy and confident about these arrangements, and this helped ensure that Carl and Roger were given a memorable retirement party. All the staff, their wives and husbands and several regular clients of the practice all assembled after work at a hotel close to the office. The evening began with champagne and nibbles and Jake presenting Carl and Roger with gifts that they had chosen to commemorate their retirement. Carl had chosen an old and very ornate table lamp and Roger had decided he wanted a beautifully crafted model of Saint Paul's Cathedral to remind him of his happy days at the practice. As he said in his thank-you speech, he passed the cathedral every day on his way to work. After the five-course dinner, Jake made a speech in which he thanked Carl and Roger for the efficient way they had run the practice and helped him to develop as an architect. As Jake and Jane walked home after the dinner, Jake thought about the fact that he was now the senior partner in a major architectural practice. His actions and decisions would affect the careers and lives of all the staff and his new partner, Robert Scott. Suddenly he turned to Jane and said, 'Would you consider looking after the practice's financial affairs? Robert is good at all the admin and so on, but I don't think he has your understanding of finance.'

Jake stopped and looked hard at Jake before she said, very

quietly, 'I would like that. I could see from the accounts you showed me that it is in a good position financially, but you need someone to make sure that situation continues. Let's think about this for a day or two and then we should talk with Robert. I did manage to talk with him this evening and he seems to me to be a good man with the best interests of the practice in mind in everything he does; but he is not trained in finance in the way that I am. I should add that Mary is good at looking after the children. So, I do feel able to spend some time working with your practice.'

As a result, Jake, Jane and Robert met to discuss how they would work together. At this meeting Robert raised an interesting issue. This was that the practice employed several experienced architects who were given projects to work on in a random way. As Robert explained, 'Whichever one of them happens to have the least work is given the next project that we get. So, they may be designing a block of flats one week and then working on a new theatre the next week. This seems inefficient to me; so, I wondered if we should get these experienced designers to specialise in one specific kind of building. That way they would know the rules and regulations that apply, the way the design of that kind of building was developing worldwide, and the most important clients. My idea is that that this would save us a lot of time at the start of projects and probably mean that clients were given much better information about current developments and so on.'

Jake said that he could see the sense in that and agreed it would help him at the start of projects to have an internal expert in the specific kind of building. When he got home that evening, he told Jane about the idea of developing specialists within the practice. She seemed impressed by this idea, and then asked,

'Why don't you have a meeting of the staff where you could discuss this idea and maybe get people to volunteer to specialise in this way?'

Jake and Robert liked this idea, and the meeting was arranged. There was wide agreement that having specialists would provide real benefits. Also, the most experienced architects very quickly began to suggest the kind of building they would like to specialise in. As a result, the meeting agreed to create specialists in residential buildings, offices, manufacturing, health care, transport facilities, shops, education, entertainment and restaurants. The meeting also agreed to provide a budget to help each of the specialists build their knowledge and reputation in their chosen specialism.

The practice quickly settled into the new arrangements which attracted a surprising amount of interest in the architectural press. Journalists were interested in how Jake intended to take the practice forward and this led to several universities that had architectural departments, inviting him to talk to their students. Over the following months this led to the practice being invited to design several new buildings for various universities and Jake spending time with final year students discussing their design ideas. He mentioned to Robert Scott that he had met three remarkably talented architects in the final year of their university courses. They agreed to tell each of them that they would like to discuss the possibility of them being employed by the practice. All three said that they already had the promise of employment with other architectural practices but would like to come and discuss their future with Jake Brown.

This was all arranged, and Jake and Robert spent a whole afternoon in discussions with the three young architects. During the discussions, Jake explained that, if they decided to join the practice, their first year would be divided into three periods of four months during each of which they would work with one of the senior architects who specialised in a particular category of buildings. Jake added that they would be given a choice as to which specialists they wanted to work with. This seemed to be an attractive proposition for the young architects and all three agreed to join the practice.

In an odd way, Jake and Robert seemed to take this as an endorsement of their plans and they began organizing the new arrangements over the next few weeks. There were several unexpected consequences but by far the most significant was that as the senior architects developed their individual specialisms, they began to attract new commissions from clients wanting the type of building they were becoming experts in. Robert was particularly excited as he realised that this was happening. As he said to Jake just after they were invited to design a new residential area in Bristol, 'This approach gives potential clients the confidence to talk to us about their ideas. They realise that we have real expertise in whatever it is they want to achieve, and we can help them ensure their new development takes account of the latest thinking.'

Jane was able to add further encouragement by reporting to Jake and Robert that the firm was now achieving a much healthier level of profits than it had ever achieved before. She said to them, 'We are attracting bigger projects and we are dealing with most of them more quickly that in the past. I guess under the old way of organizing the practice, each new project involved an initial learning process but now we already have this essential knowledge in-house.'

The next year continued in this same very successful manner which led Jake, Jane and Robert to discuss how they should reward their staff. It was Jane who mentioned that, when she was in the bank, she had worked with a company that gave the staff a share of the profits each year. Then she added that as far as she could remember, the firm gave each person an extra share for each year they had worked for the firm. So, someone who had been with the firm for ten years would be given ten times as much as someone in their first year. Jake and Robert thought about this for several minutes and then both agreed that sounded like a very good scheme. They discussed the details several times over the next week and then called a meeting of all the staff and described the new bonus scheme they would like to introduce. There was some discussion to clarify exactly how the scheme would work; and then clearly the staff were very happy to have the extra payments. One of the senior architects said, 'I think I am speaking for us all when I say that we are very happy to be working for this excellent practice and we want to say thank you to Jake, Jane and Robert for letting us share the profits in the way they describe.'

This was followed by a round of applause, and it was clear that everyone was indeed happy with the new arrangement. This was reflected in subtle changes to way everyone worked so that at the end of the first financial year in which the profit-sharing scheme was in operation, the partnership made the largest profit it had ever achieved. Jane was at home when she realised that this had happened, and that evening when she told Jake this good news. He smiled and then said, 'I feel we have achieved a lot in building on the practice's undoubted success that Sir Andrew Zain left for us. Now we have a more efficient organization, and I think we have maintained the quality of our designs. My clear impression is that all the staff feel proud to be part of the practice. When I think back to how far I have developed since my early days in the practice in Swindon, I feel good about life; and you, my lovely Jane, are the central part of that.'

At that moment, Andrew came into the room and said, 'Mary

says it is time for me to go to bed. So, can Mummy come and read me a story?'

As Jane smiled and took Andrew's hand, she said, 'Let's go upstairs and we can discuss what you want to do tomorrow. Daddy will be home so we could play some more cricket in the park. Eve seemed to like that the last time we played, and you are a very good bowler.'

As Jake watched his wife and son, walk hand in hand up the stairs, he thought it was true that the practice was a real success but his family, Jane, Andrew and Eve, were his real achievement. Life was good; and he had a real and happy family. He sat enjoying this thought for ten minutes or so, and then decided to go and say good night to his son.

Jane was just finishing the chapter she was reading to Andrew when Jake came in. Andrew sat up and said, 'Daddy, can we play some more cricket tomorrow. I like batting; it is good fun, but bowling is better. The bowler decides what happens more than the batsman, who just has to try and understand what the bowler is doing. I want to be a bowler.'

Jake smiled and agreed that they could go to the park and Andrew could practice his bowling. Then Jane said it was time for Andrew to get some sleep. Jake and Jane looked in at Eve who was already fast asleep and looked beautiful. Then they walked downstairs hand in hand, and as they reached the hall, Jake looked at Jane and said, 'Our life together feels complete. I think we will look back at these last couple of years as the start of the best time of our life.'

Jane kissed Jake as she agreed, and then added, 'You are already recognised as a great designer of buildings and now you are well on the way to being an amazing designer of family life. I do love you.'